NINJA BASE[redacted]

Kyum[redacted]

STORY & ART BY

SHUNSHIN MAEDA

[redacted]

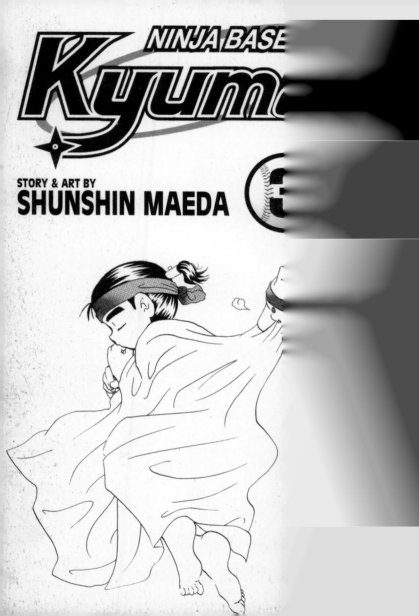

HOW TO READ MANGA!

Hello there! My name is **Kyuma,** and this is my very own book - **Ninja Baseball Kyuma**! It is a comic book originally created in my home country of **Japan,** where comics are called **manga.**

A manga book is read from **right-to-left,** which is **backwards** from the normal books you know. This means that you will find the first page where you expect to find the last page! It also means that each page begins in the top right corner.

If you have never read a manga book before, here is a helpful guide to get you started!

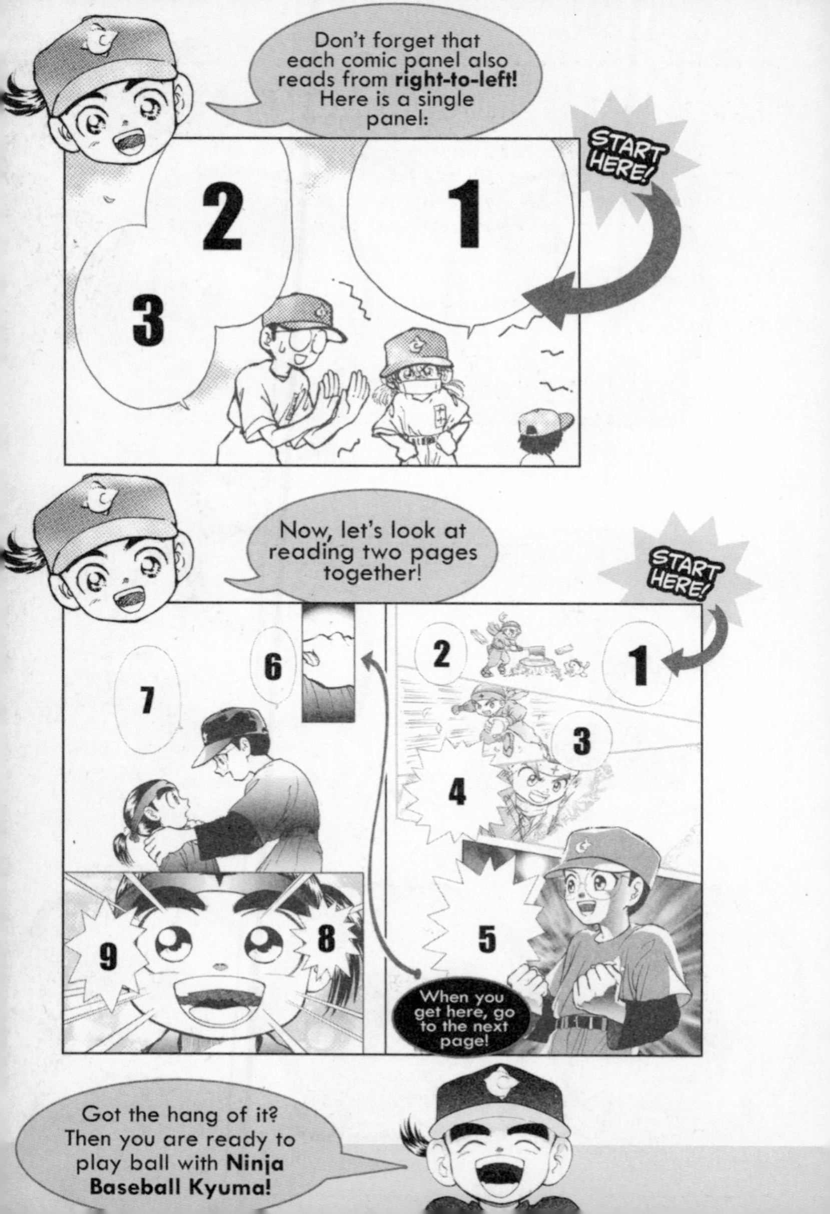
Don't forget that each comic panel also reads from **right-to-left!** Here is a single panel:
START HERE!
1
2
3
Now, let's look at reading two pages together!
START HERE!
1
2
3
4
5
When you get here, go to the next page!
6
7
8
9
Got the hang of it? Then you are ready to play ball with **Ninja Baseball Kyuma!**

NINJA BASEBALL
Kyuma!

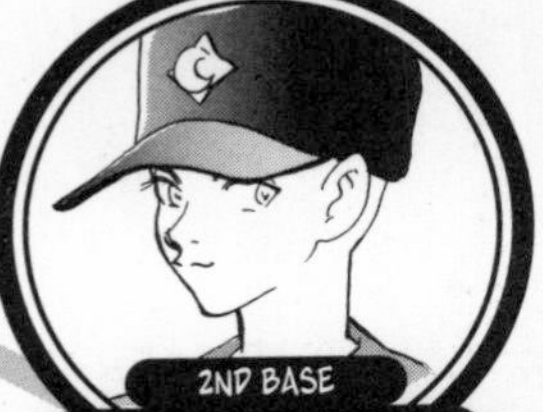

2ND BASE

MICHI

Assistant Captain, always cool and calm.

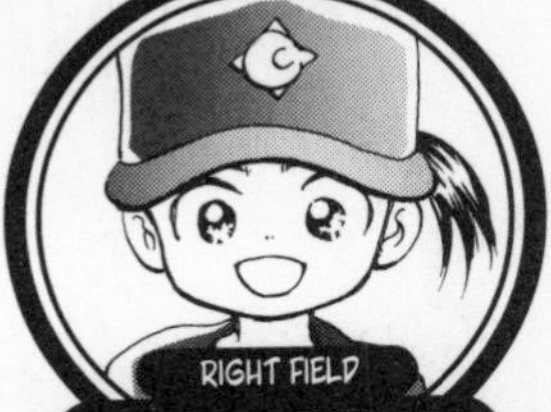

RIGHT FIELD

KYUMA

A ninja who has been living in the mountains since birth.

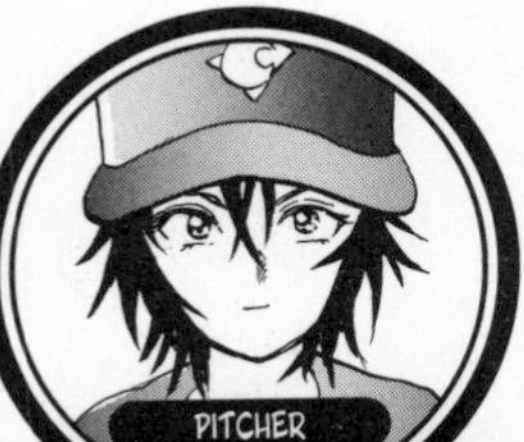

PITCHER

LUO

The slightly timid Ace.

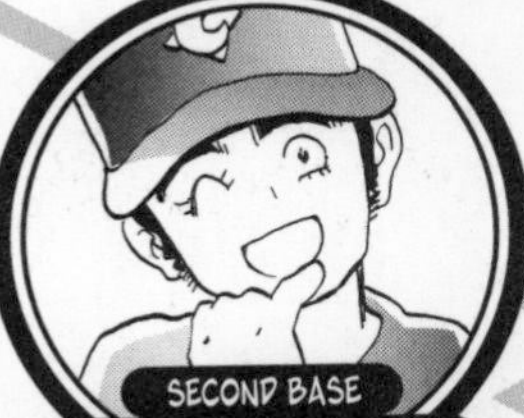

SECOND BASE

KUNOSUKE

Moves in strange, flexible ways.

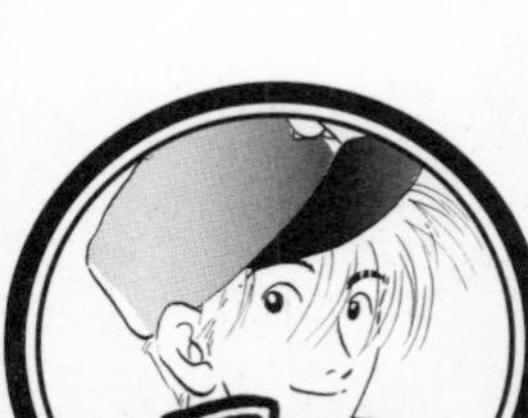

COACH

TAMORI

A funny coach, always cheerful.

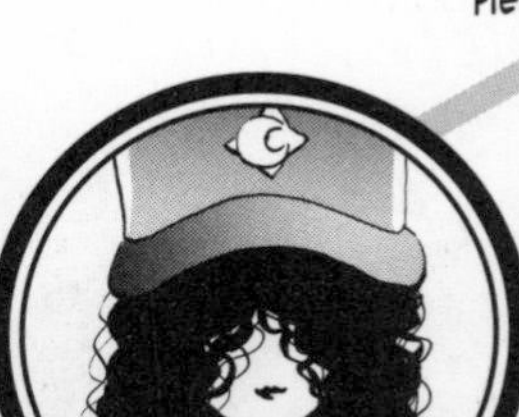

BENCH

YOHKO

100% accurate with her divinations.

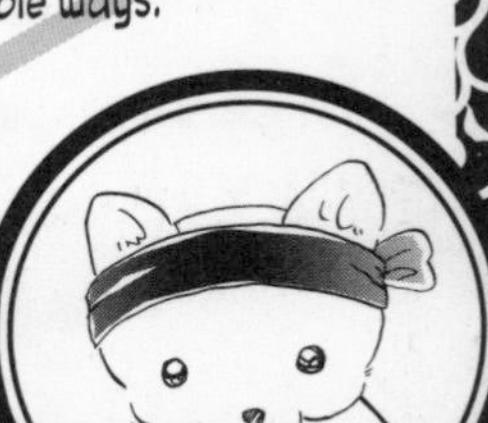

BENCH

INUI

A ninja dog, Kyuma's best friend.

MOONSTAR BASEBALL TEAM ROSTER

LEFT FIELD
NANA

A strong-willed girl.

CENTER FIELD
IWATA

Has a large build, but is quite quick on his feet.

THIRD BASE
TETSU

Full of energy, keeps team morale up.

SHORTSTOP
LINKI

A kind-hearted boy who loves plants and animals.

STORY SO FAR

With some help from Kyuma, the Moonstar little league team quickly made its way past the second round of the Platinum Bat Cup! Their third game has them up against The Toya Owls, the team that won their game against Kido's team...!

CATCHER
KAORU

The Captain of the team, very responsible.

CONTENTS

PITCH 15
A REASON TO CHEAT

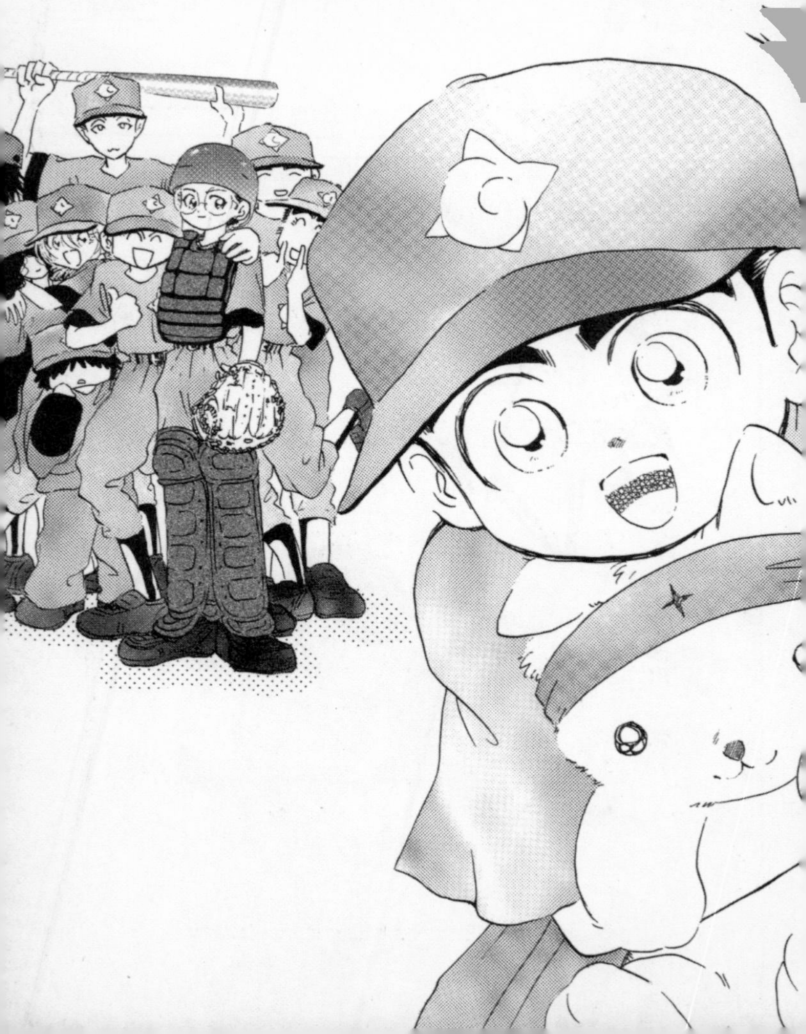

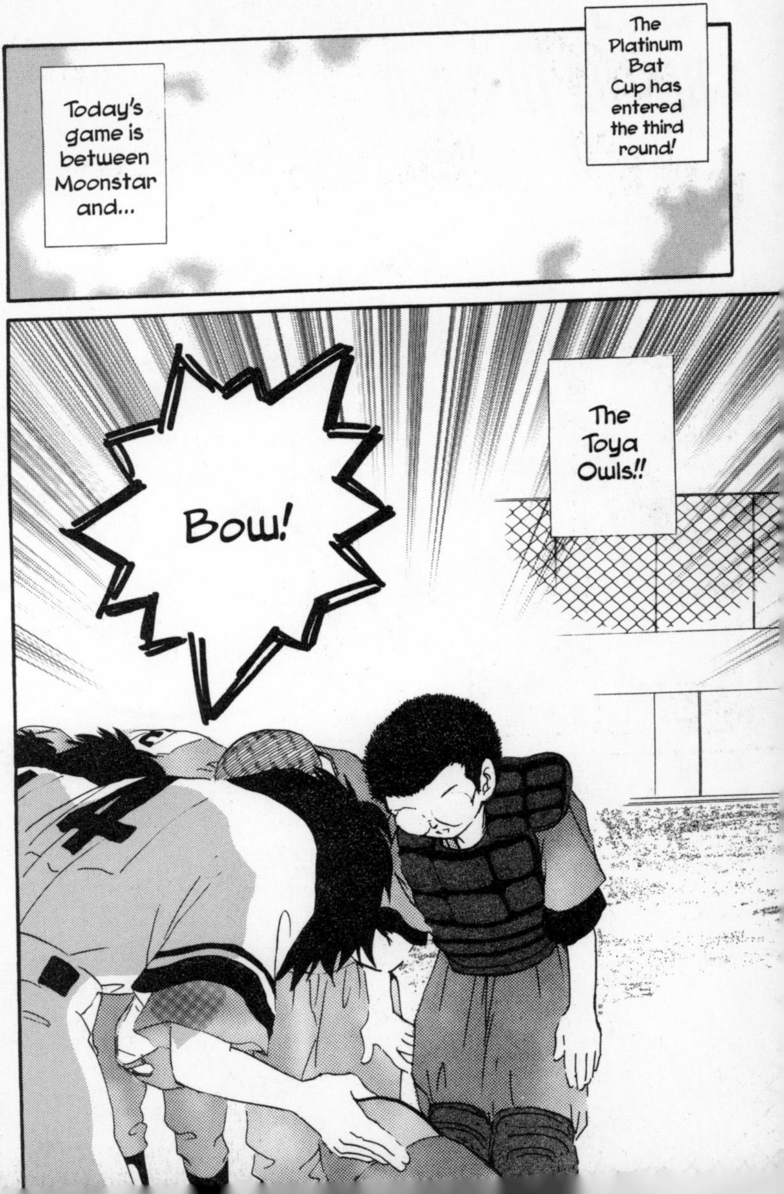
The Platinum Bat Cup has entered the third round!
Today's game is between Moonstar and...
The Toya Owls!!
Bow!

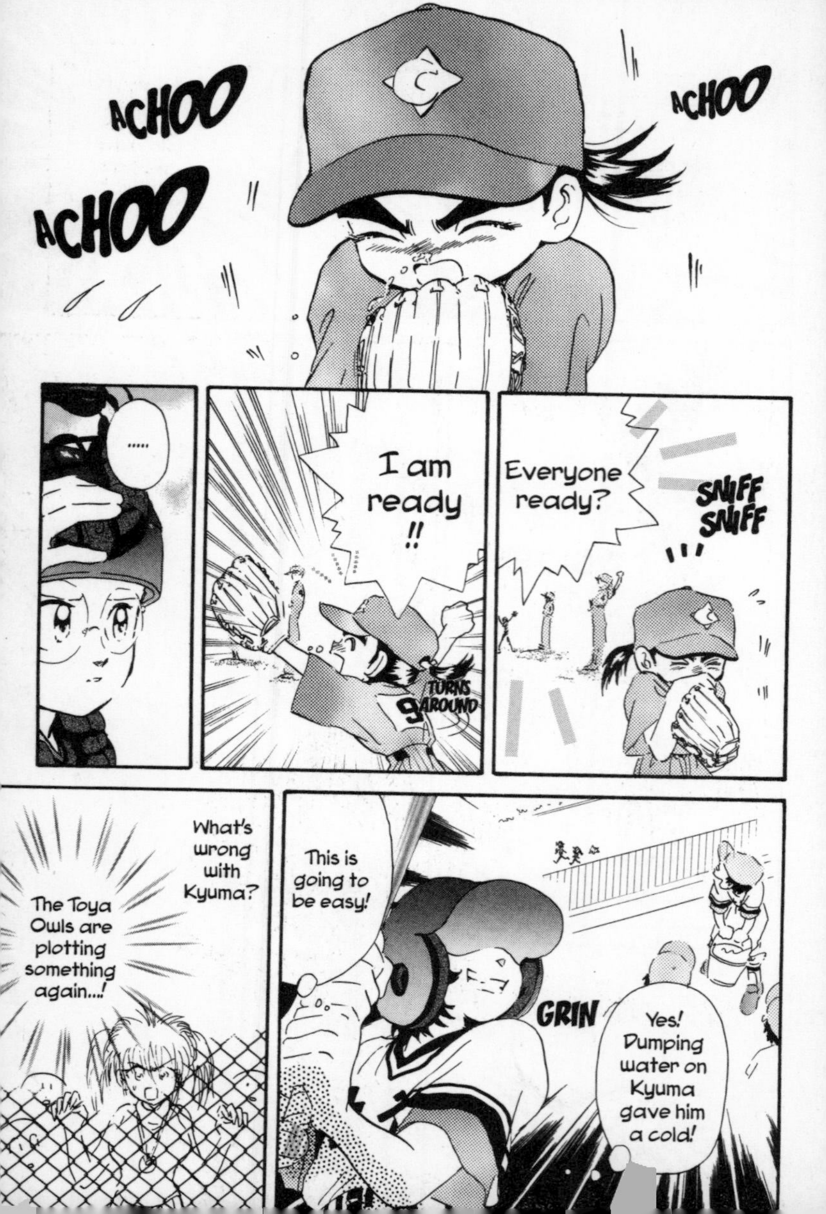
ACHOO
ACHOO
ACHOO
Everyone ready?
SNIFF SNIFF
I am ready !!
TURNS AROUND
.....
This is going to be easy!
GRIN
Yes! Dumping water on Kyuma gave him a cold!
What's wrong with Kyuma?
The Toya Owls are plotting something again...!

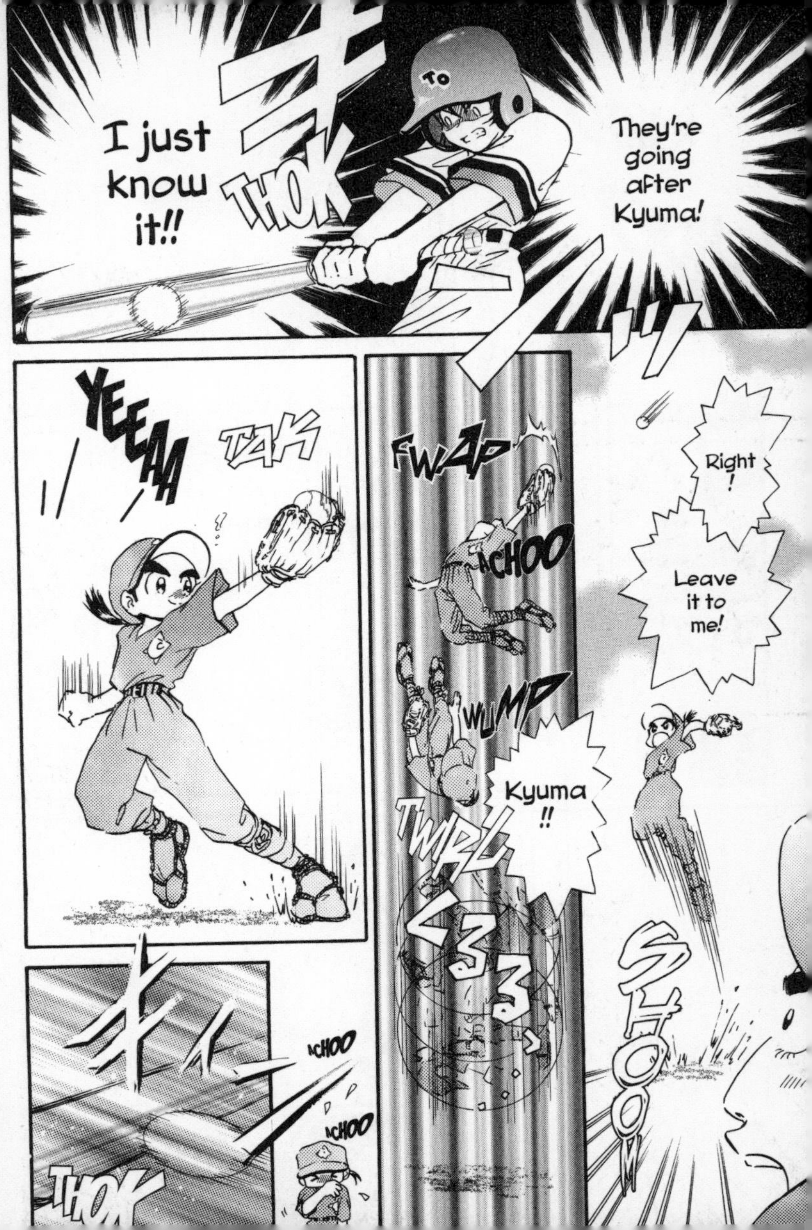
They're going after Kyuma!
THOK
I just know it!!
Right!
Leave it to me!
SHOOM
FWAP
ACHOO
WUMP
Kyuma!!
TWIRL
YEEAAA
TAK
ACHOO
ACHOO
THOK

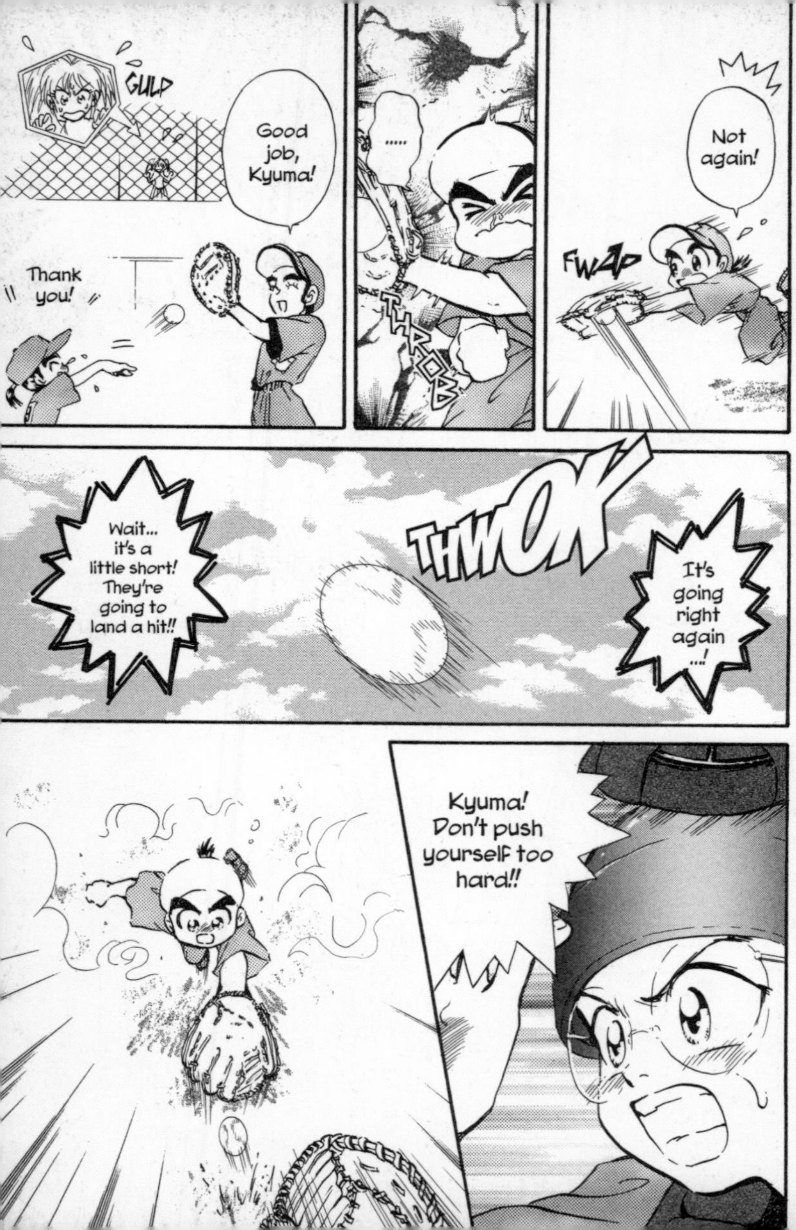

Not again!
FWAP
.....
THROB
Good job, Kyuma!
GULP
Thank you!
It's going right again...!
THWOK
Wait... it's a little short! They're going to land a hit!!
Kyuma! Don't push yourself too hard!!

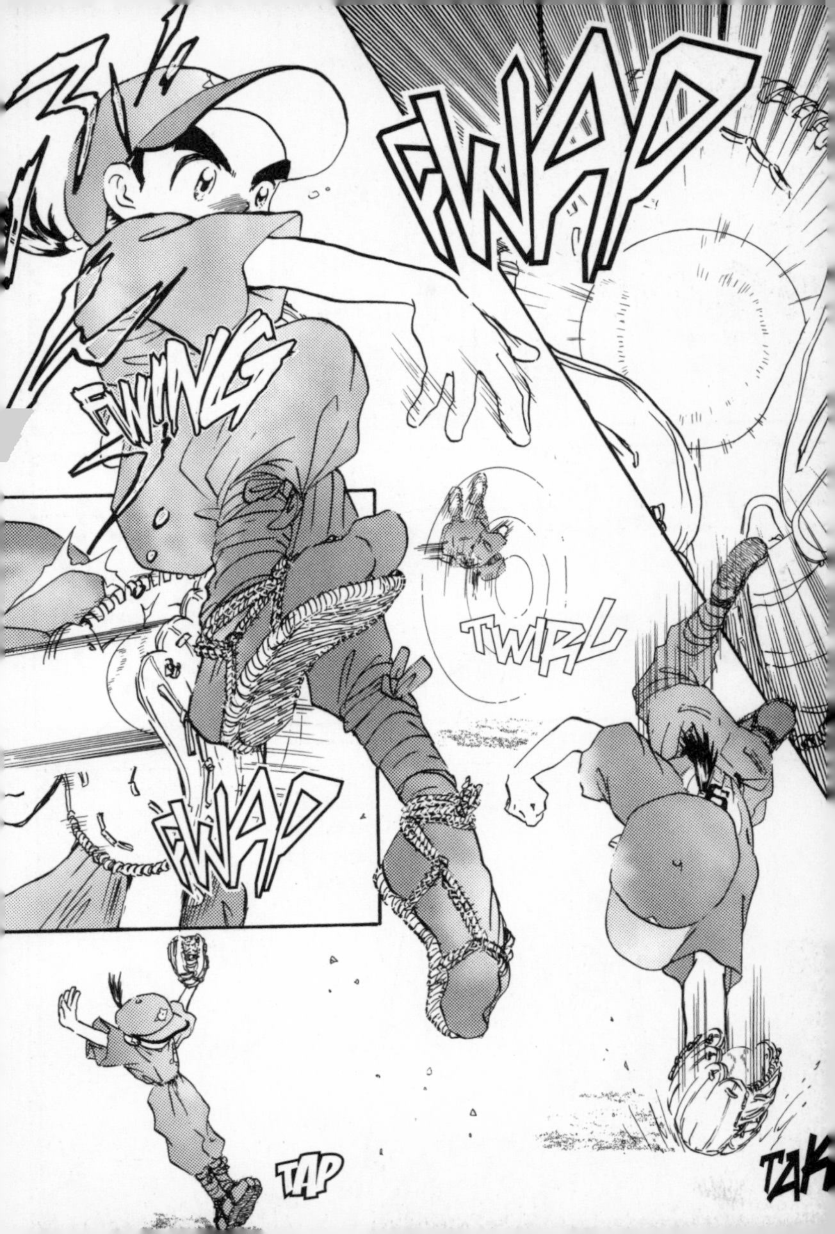
FWAP
FWING
TWIRL
FWAP
TAK
TAP

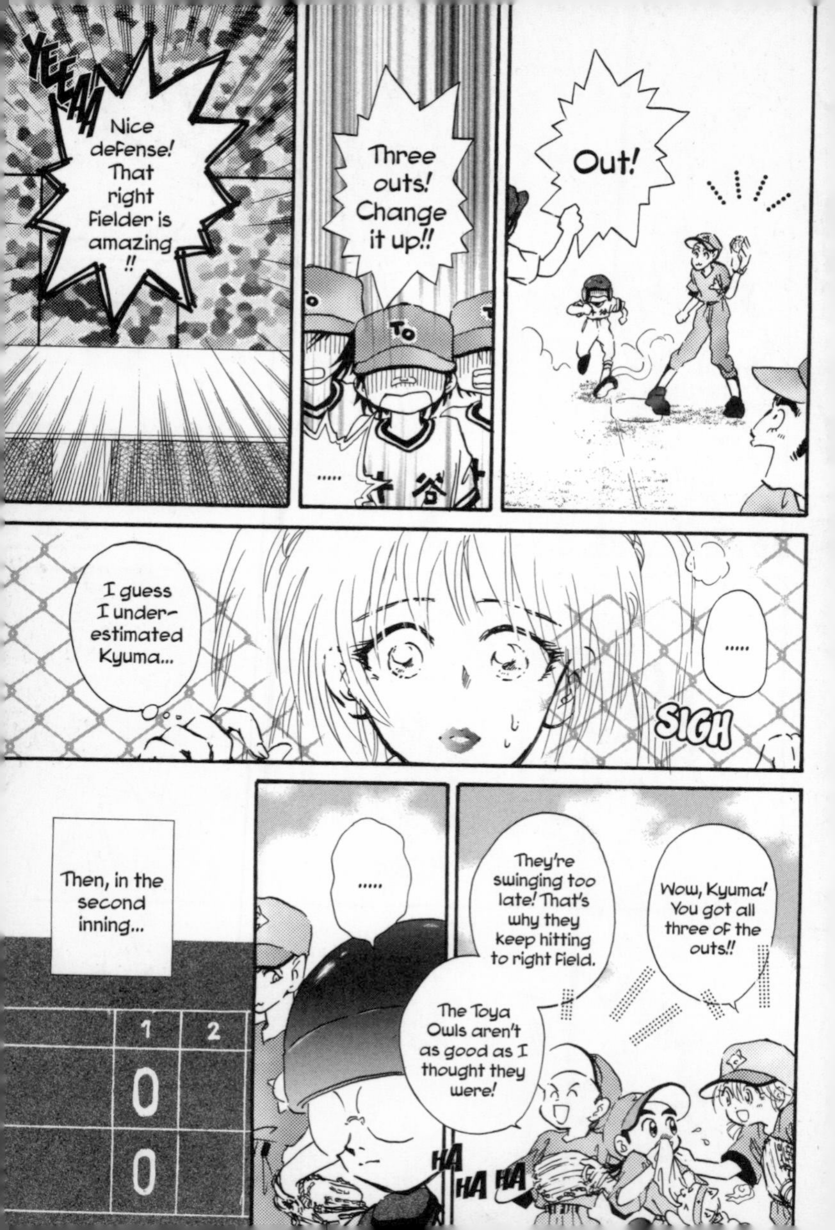

Out!
.....
Three outs! Change it up!!
.....
YEEAH
Nice defense! That right fielder is amazing!!
.....
SIGH
I guess I under-estimated Kyuma...
Wow, Kyuma! You got all three of the outs!!
They're swinging too late! That's why they keep hitting to right field.
The Toya Owls aren't as good as I thought they were!
HA HA HA HA
.....
Then, in the second inning...
1 2
0
0

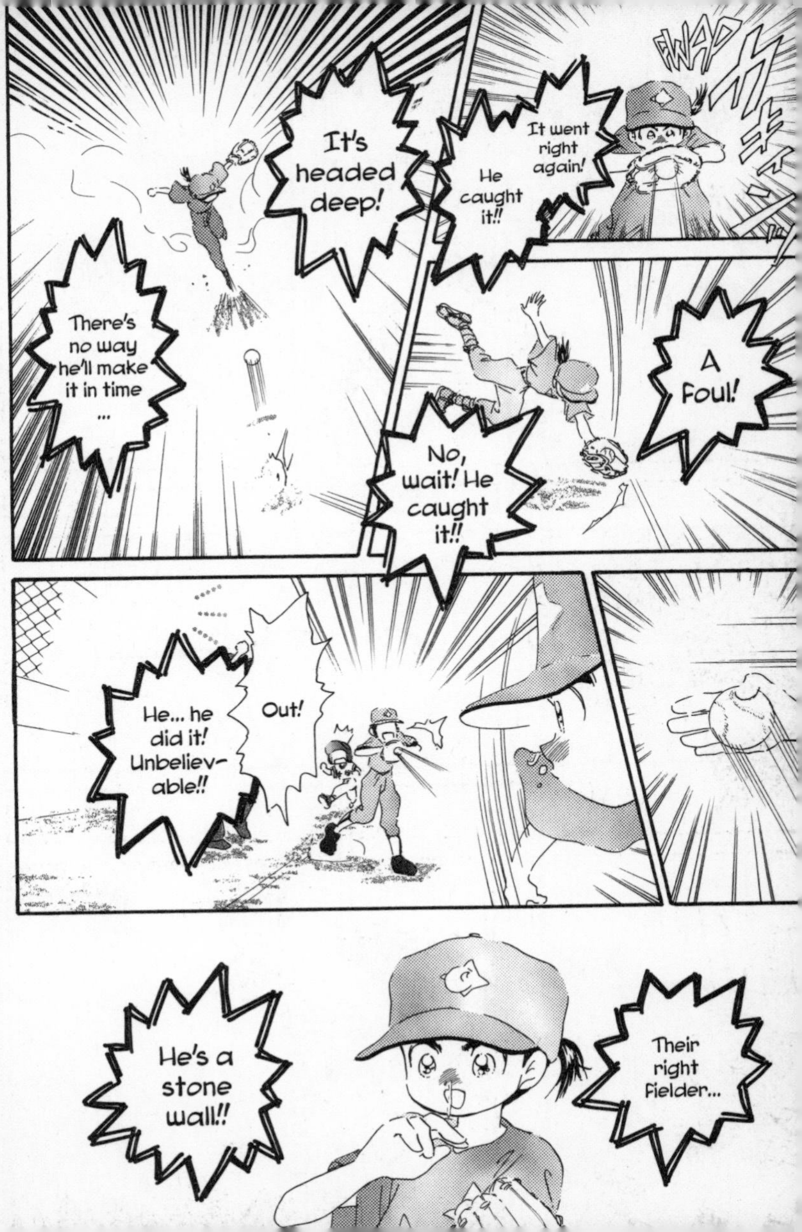
FWAP
It went right again!
He caught it!!
A foul!
No, wait! He caught it!!
It's headed deep!
There's no way he'll make it in time ...
Out!
He... he did it! Unbelievable!!
Their right fielder...
He's a stone wall!!

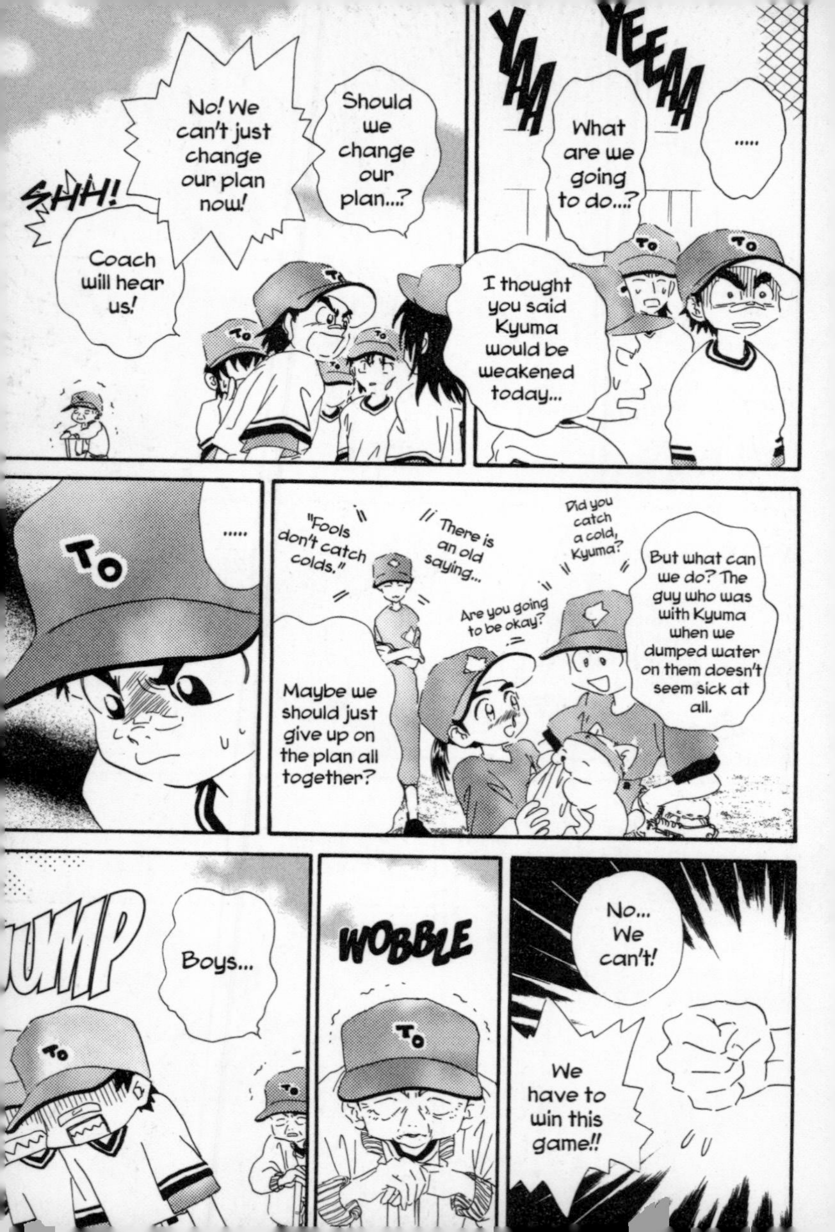
.....
YEEEAAA
YAAA
What are we going to do...?
I thought you said Kyuma would be weakened today...
Should we change our plan...?
No! We can't just change our plan now!
SHH!
Coach will hear us!
Did you catch a cold, Kyuma?
But what can we do? The guy who was with Kyuma when we dumped water on them doesn't seem sick at all.
There is an old saying...
"Fools don't catch colds."
Are you going to be okay?
Maybe we should just give up on the plan all together?
.....
No... We can't!
We have to win this game!!
WOBBLE
Boys...
UMP

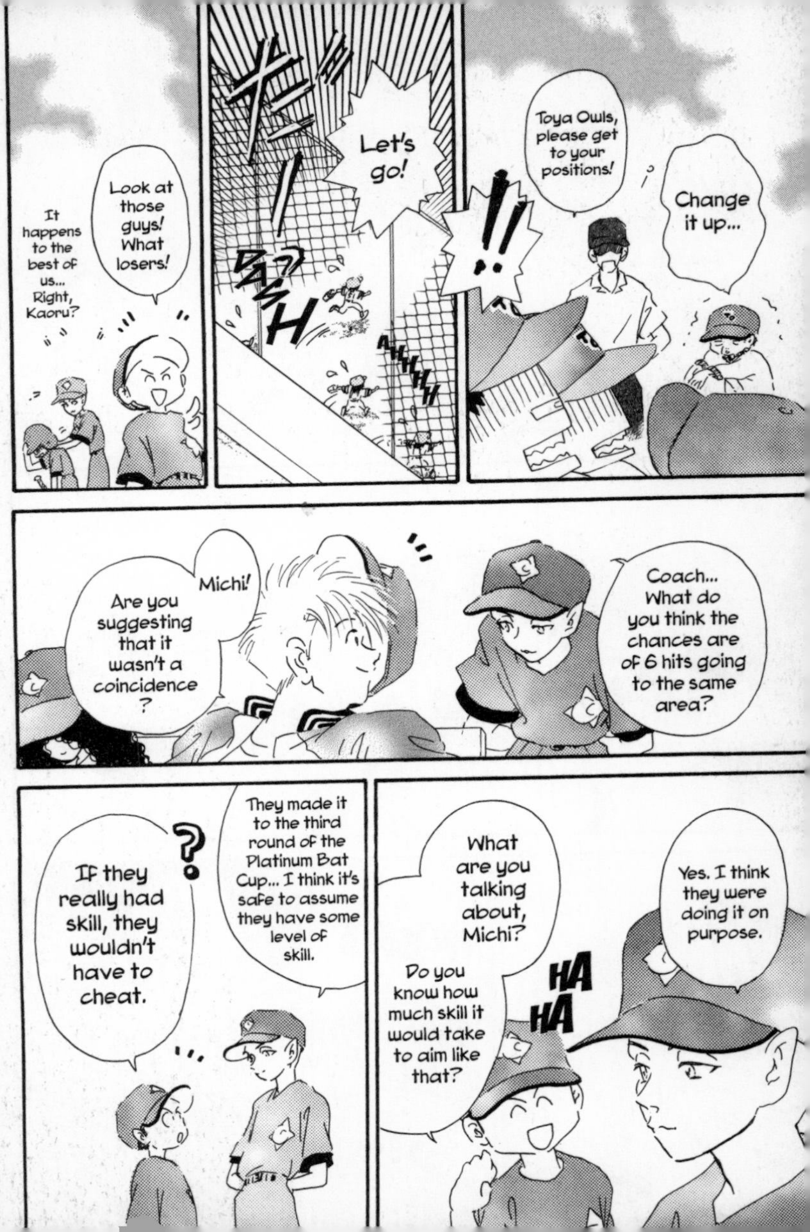
Toya Owls, please get to your positions!
Change it up...
!!
Let's go!
DASH
AHHHHH
Look at those guys! What losers!
It happens to the best of us... Right, Kaoru?
Coach... What do you think the chances are of 6 hits going to the same area?
Michi! Are you suggesting that it wasn't a coincidence?
Yes. I think they were doing it on purpose.
What are you talking about, Michi?
HA HA
Do you know how much skill it would take to aim like that?
They made it to the third round of the Platinum Bat Cup... I think it's safe to assume they have some level of skill.
?
If they really had skill, they wouldn't have to cheat.

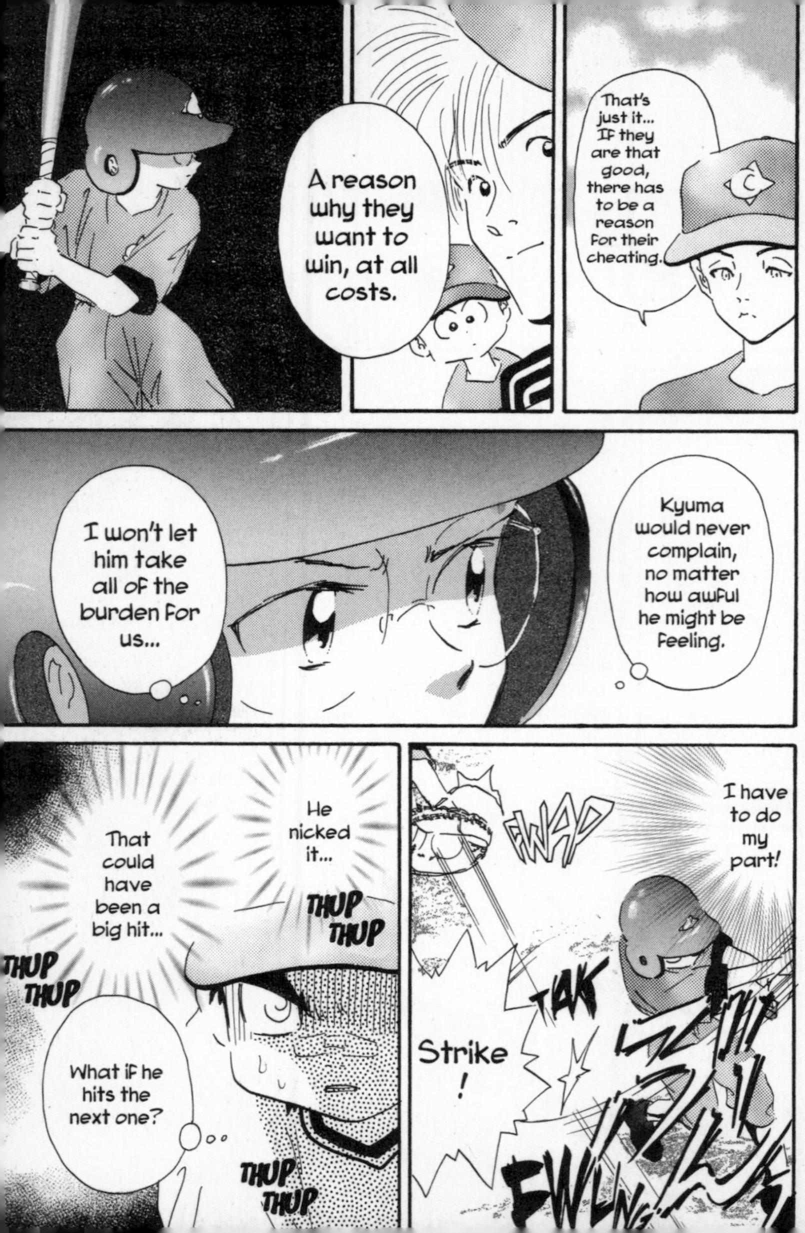
That's just it... If they are that good, there has to be a reason for their cheating.
A reason why they want to win, at all costs.
Kyuma would never complain, no matter how awful he might be feeling.
I won't let him take all of the burden for us...
I have to do my part!
FWAP
TWAK
Strike!
FWUNG
He nicked it...
THUP THUP
That could have been a big hit...
THUP THUP
What if he hits the next one?
THUP THUP

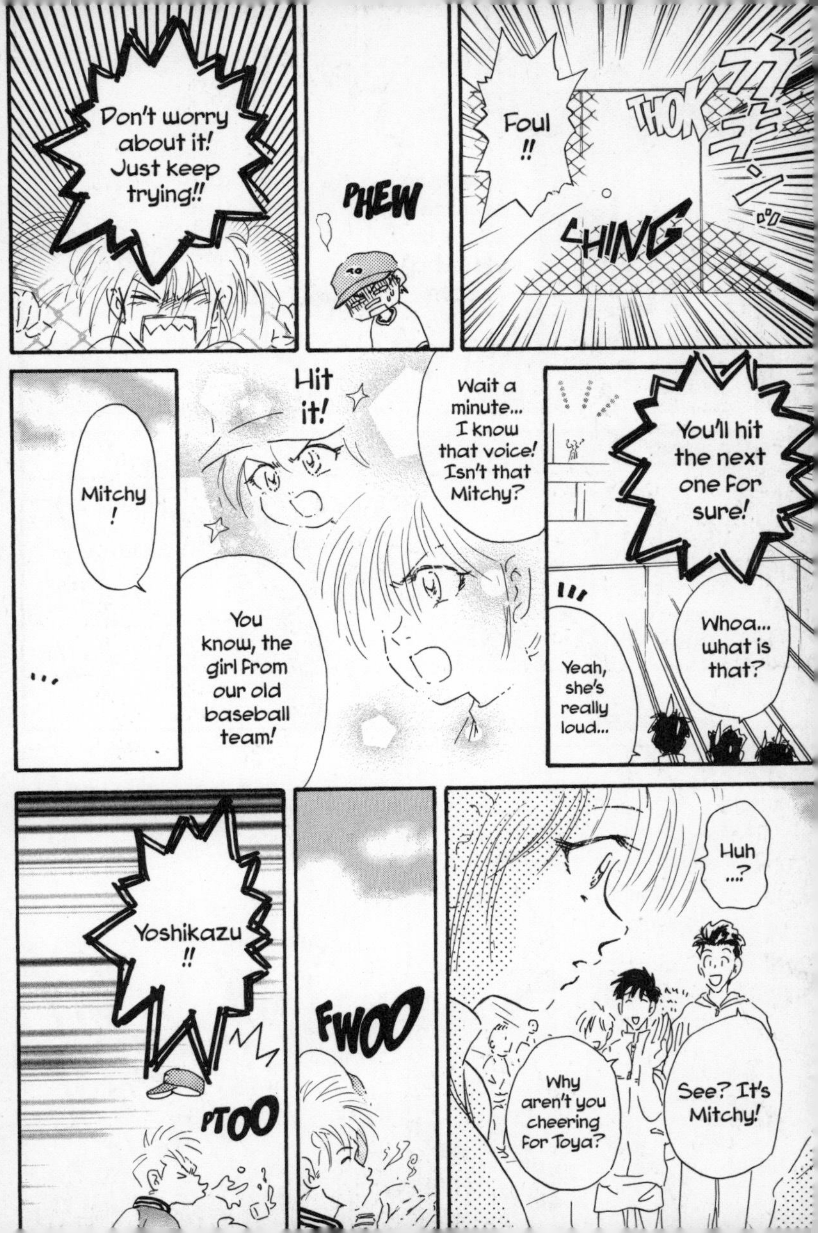
Foul!!
THOK
CHING
PHEW
Don't worry about it! Just keep trying!!
You'll hit the next one for sure!
Whoa... what is that?
Yeah, she's really loud...
Wait a minute... I know that voice! Isn't that Mitchy?
Hit it!
You know, the girl from our old baseball team!
Mitchy!
...
Huh...?
See? It's Mitchy!
Why aren't you cheering for Toya?
FWOO
Yoshikazu!!
PTOO

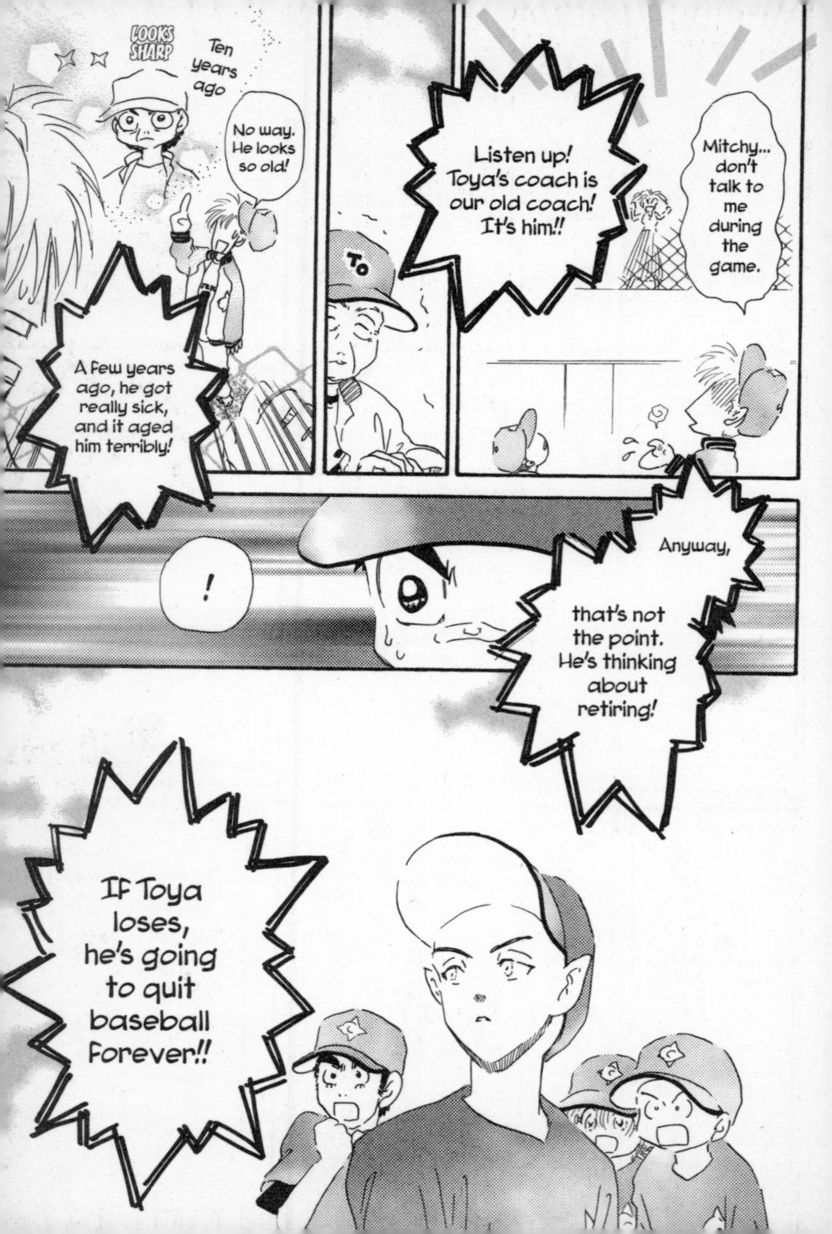
Listen up! Toya's coach is our old coach! It's him!!
Mitchy... don't talk to me during the game.
No way. He looks so old!
Ten years ago
LOOKS SHARP
A few years ago, he got really sick, and it aged him terribly!
Anyway,
that's not the point. He's thinking about retiring!
!
If Toya loses, he's going to quit baseball forever!!

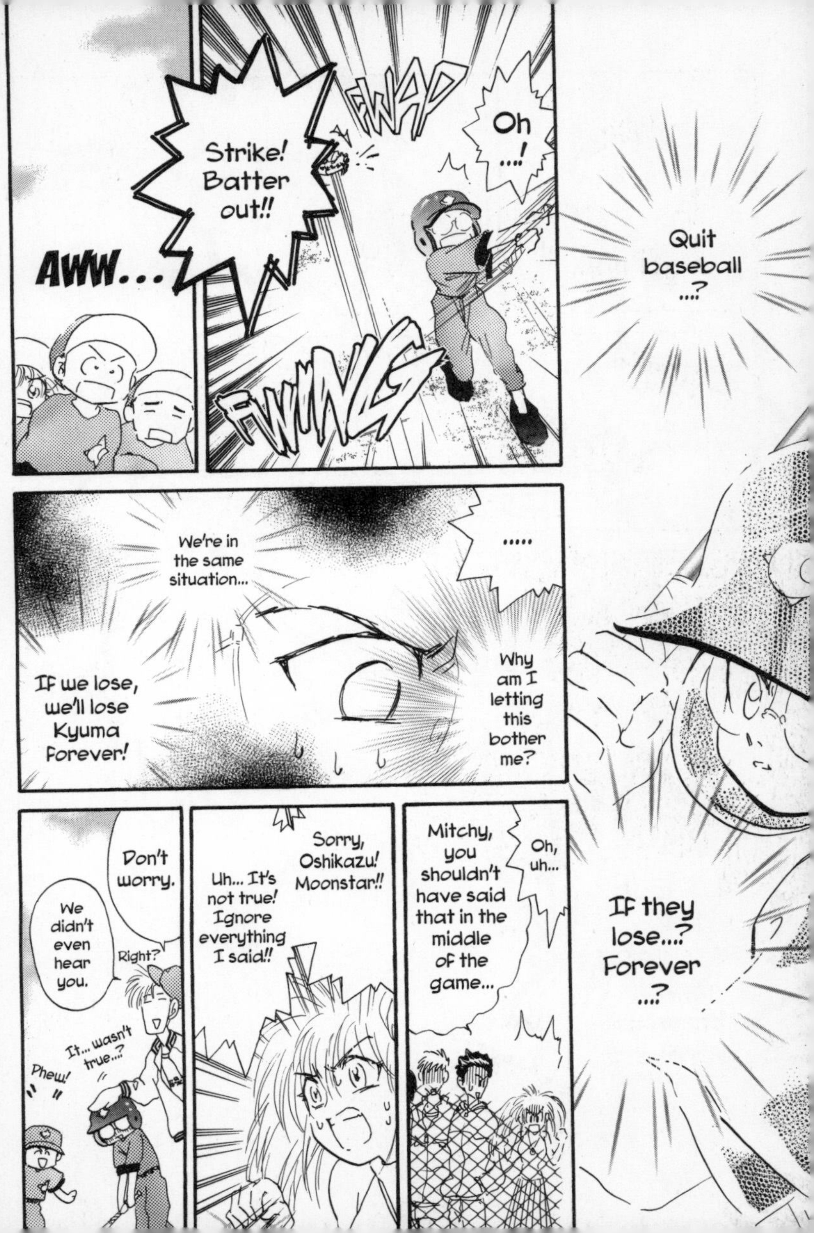
Quit baseball ...?
If they lose...? Forever ...?
Oh ...!
FWAP
Strike! Batter out!!
FWING
AWW...
.....
Why am I letting this bother me?
We're in the same situation...
If we lose, we'll lose Kyuma forever!
Oh, uh...
Mitchy, you shouldn't have said that in the middle of the game...
Sorry, Oshikazu! Moonstar!!
Uh... It's not true! Ignore everything I said!!
Don't worry.
We didn't even hear you.
Right?
It... wasn't true...?
Phew!

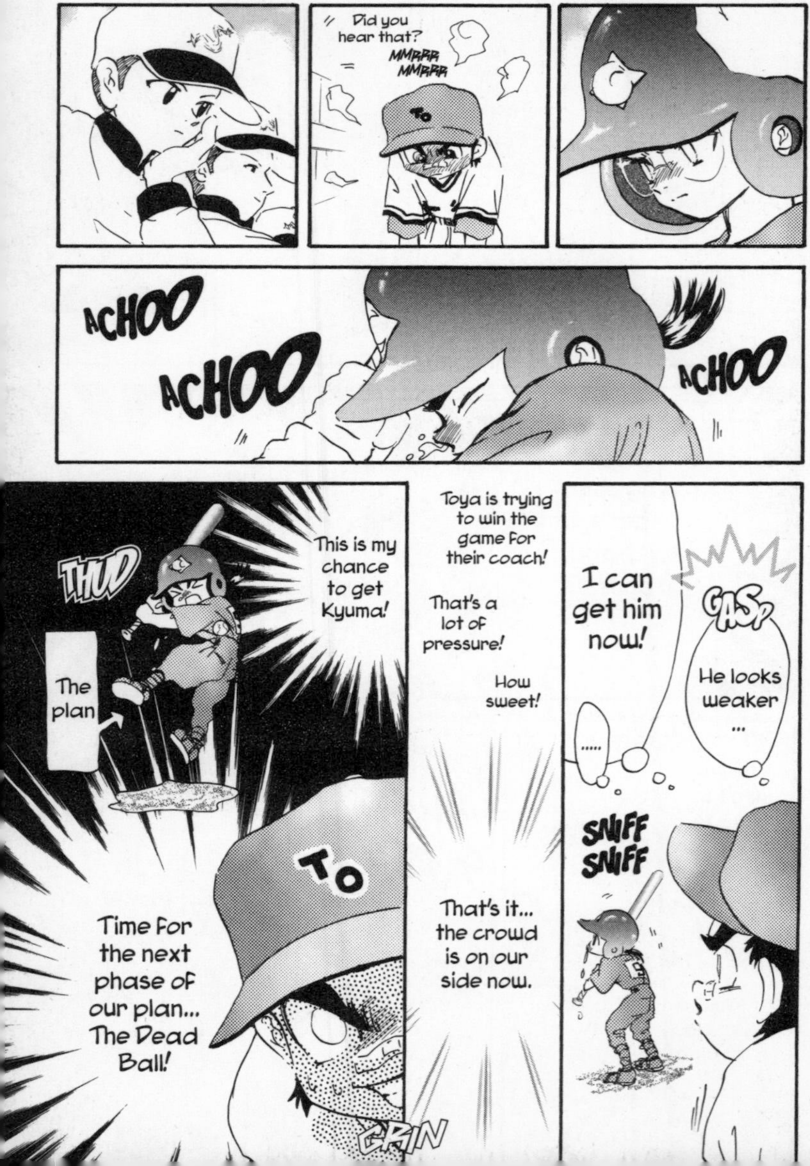
Did you hear that?
MMRRR MMRRR
ACHOO
ACHOO
ACHOO
GASP
I can get him now!
He looks weaker ...
......
SNIFF SNIFF
Toya is trying to win the game for their coach!
That's a lot of pressure!
How sweet!
That's it... the crowd is on our side now.
This is my chance to get Kyuma!
THUD
The plan
Time for the next phase of our plan... The Dead Ball!
GRIN

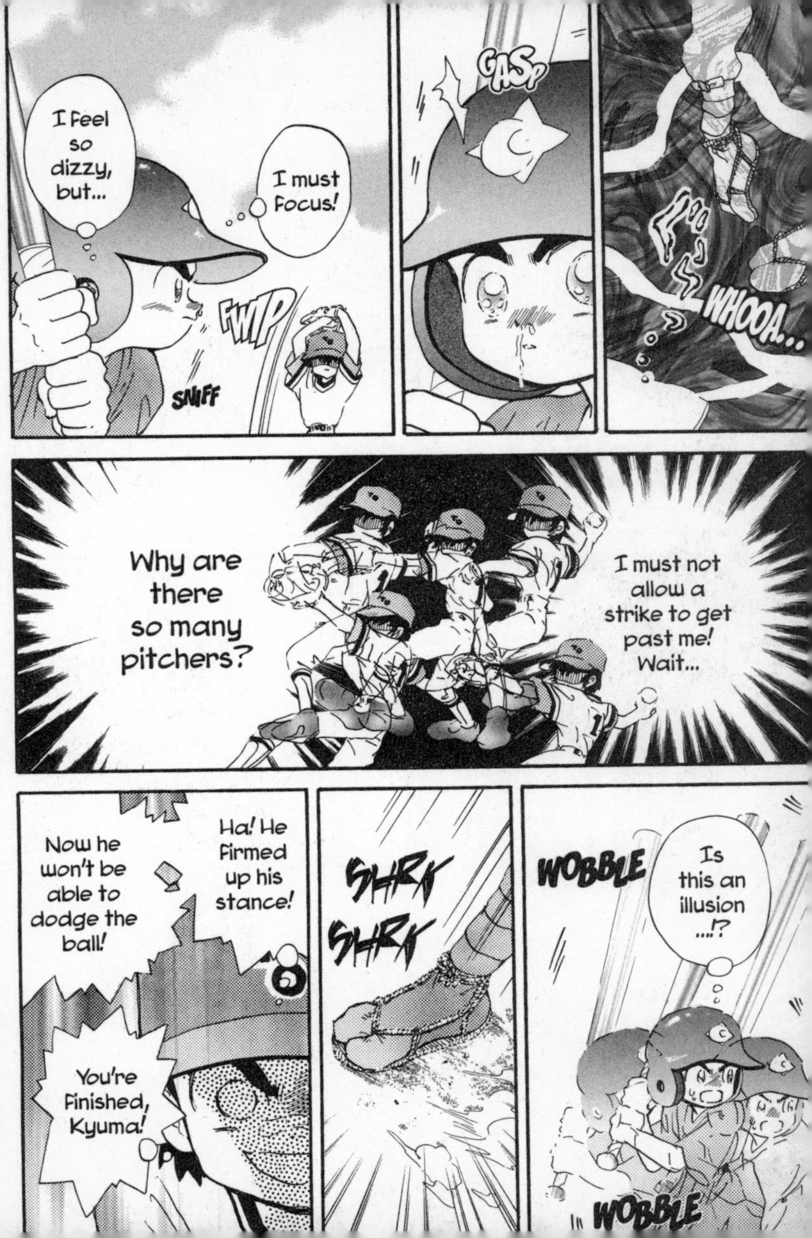
WHOOA...
GASP
I feel so dizzy, but...
I must Focus!
FWIP
SNIFF
I must not allow a strike to get past me! Wait...
Why are there so many pitchers?
WOBBLE
Is this an illusion ...!?
WOBBLE
SHRK
SHRK
Ha! He firmed up his stance!
Now he won't be able to dodge the ball!
You're Finished, Kyuma!

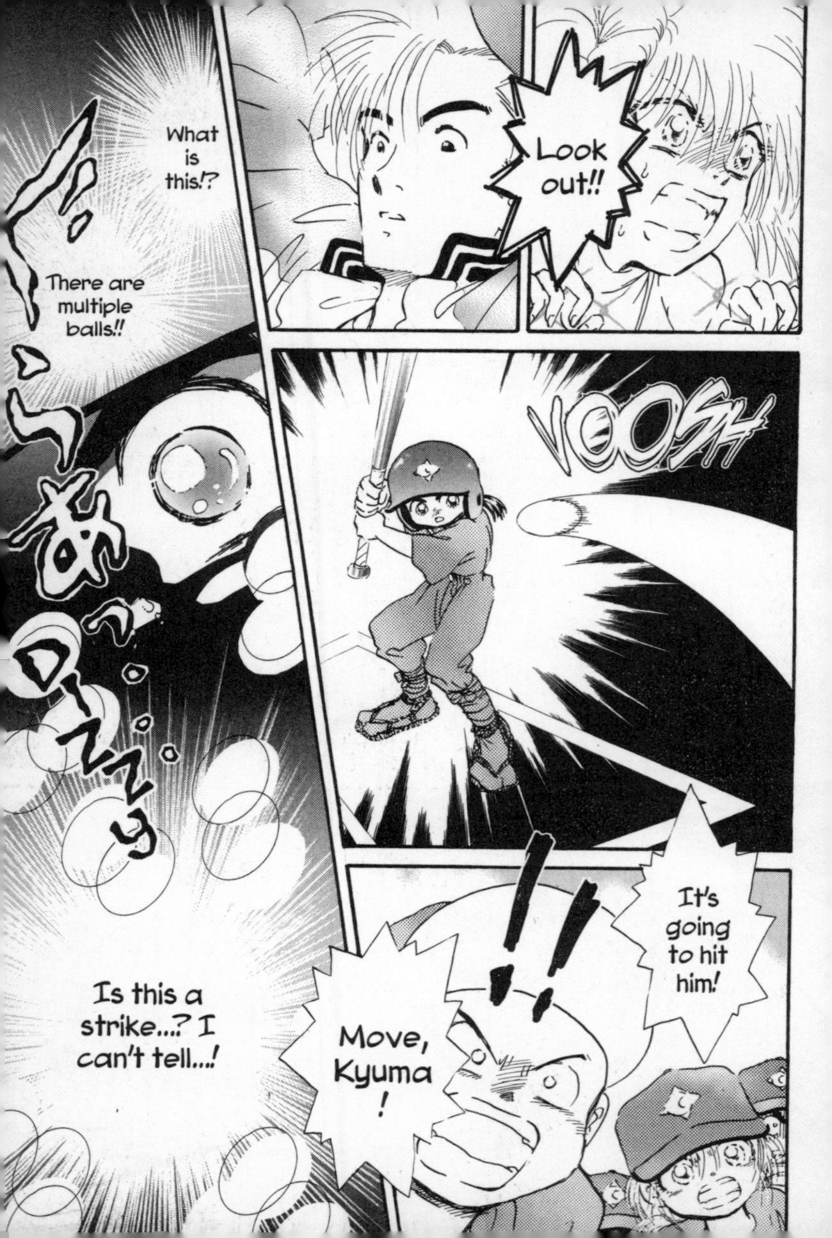

Look out!!
VOOSH
It's going to hit him!
Move, Kyuma!
What is this!?
There are multiple balls!!
Is this a strike...? I can't tell...!

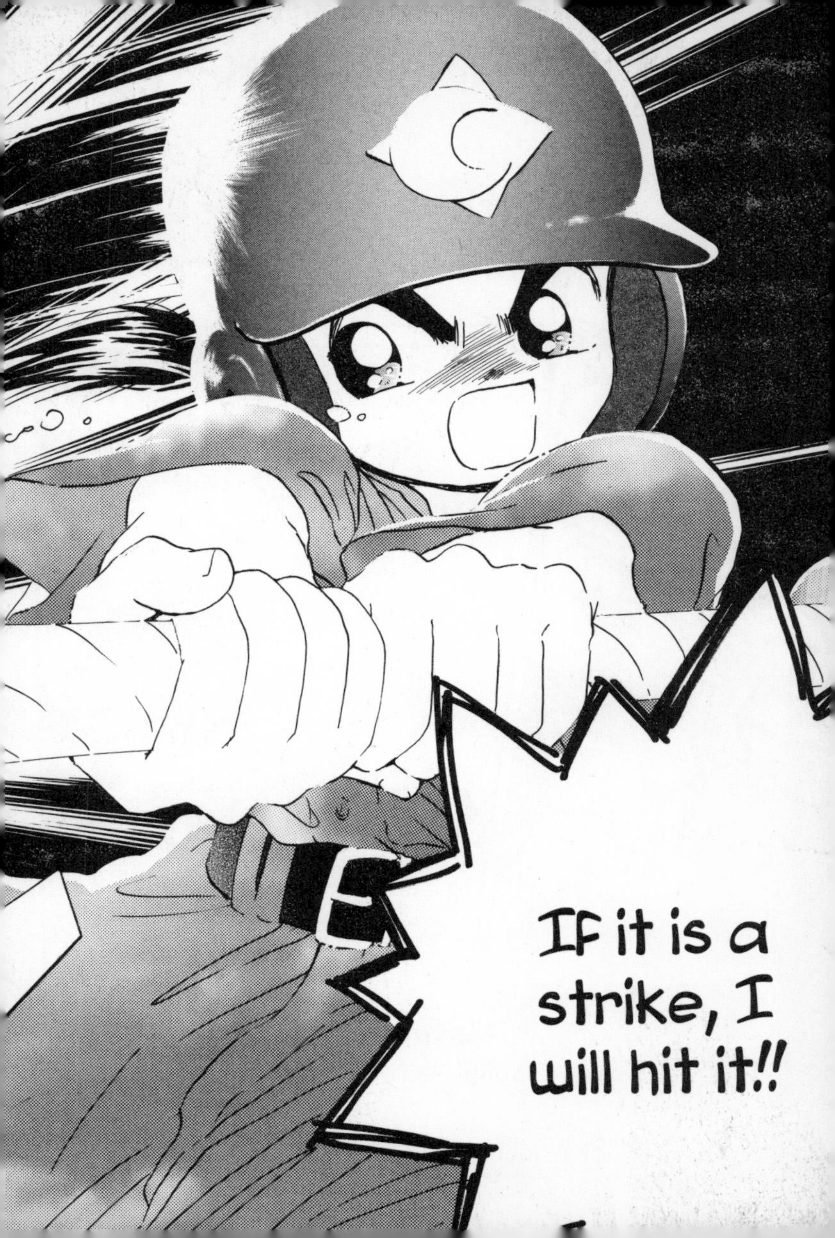
If it is a strike, I will hit it!!

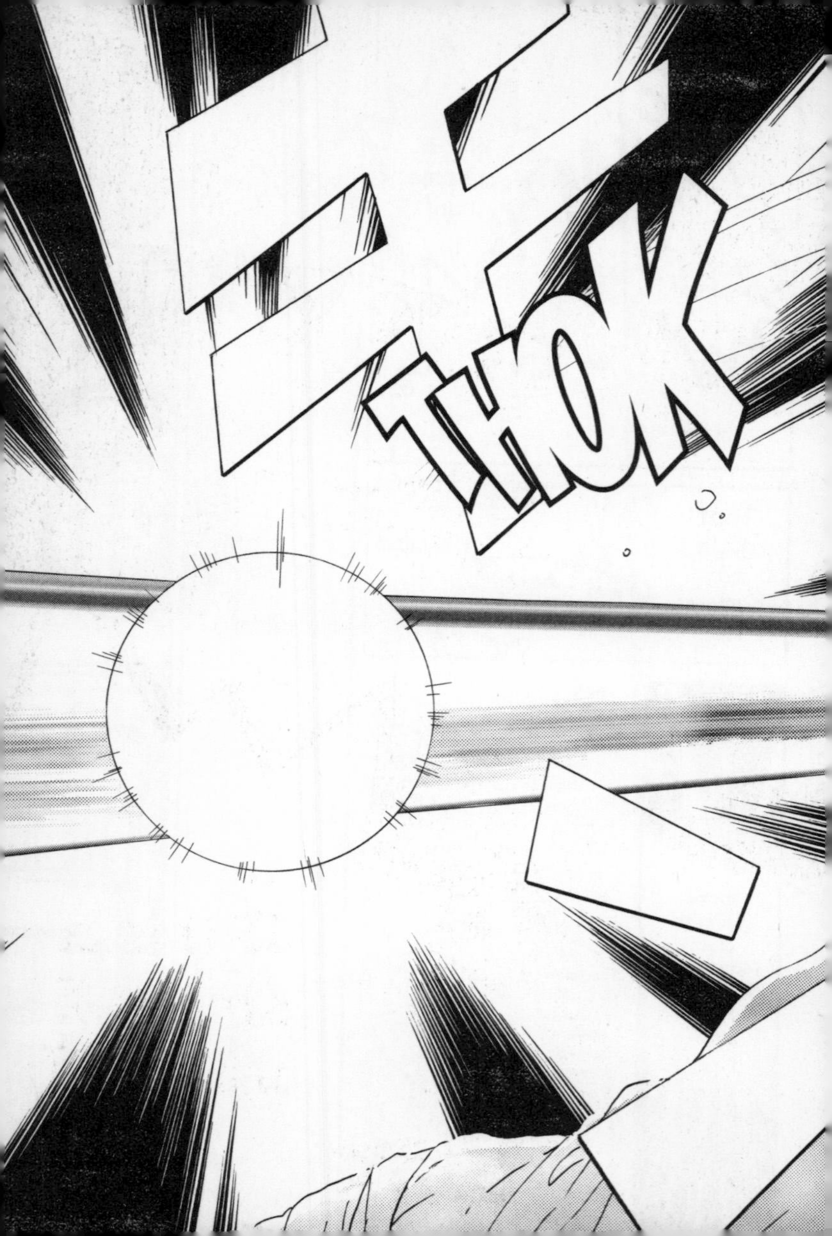
THOK

RUSTLE
Whoa, a home run!
YEEAAA
Way to go, Kyuma!
Kyuma ...
GRRR
That guy's not human !!
We might lose our coach!
They could never under-stand!
They don't know what it's like to have to win for someone!
You're going to lose, Moonstar! We're going to crush you!!

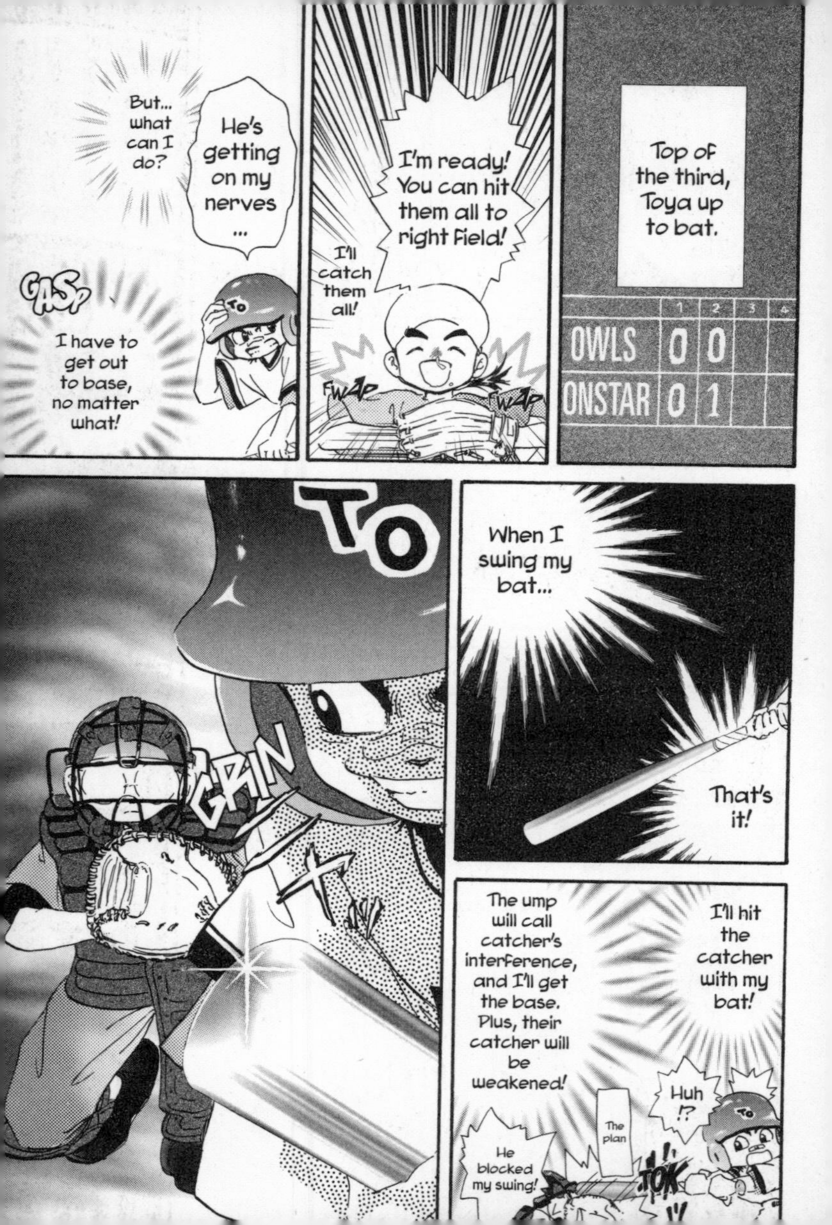
Top of the third, Toya up to bat.
1 2 3 4
OWLS 0 0
ONSTAR 0 1
I'm ready! You can hit them all to right field!
I'll catch them all!
FWAP
FWAP
He's getting on my nerves ...
But... what can I do?
GASP
I have to get out to base, no matter what!
When I swing my bat...
That's it!
I'll hit the catcher with my bat!
The ump will call catcher's interference, and I'll get the base. Plus, their catcher will be weakened!
Huh !?
The plan
He blocked my swing!
TOK
TO
GRIN

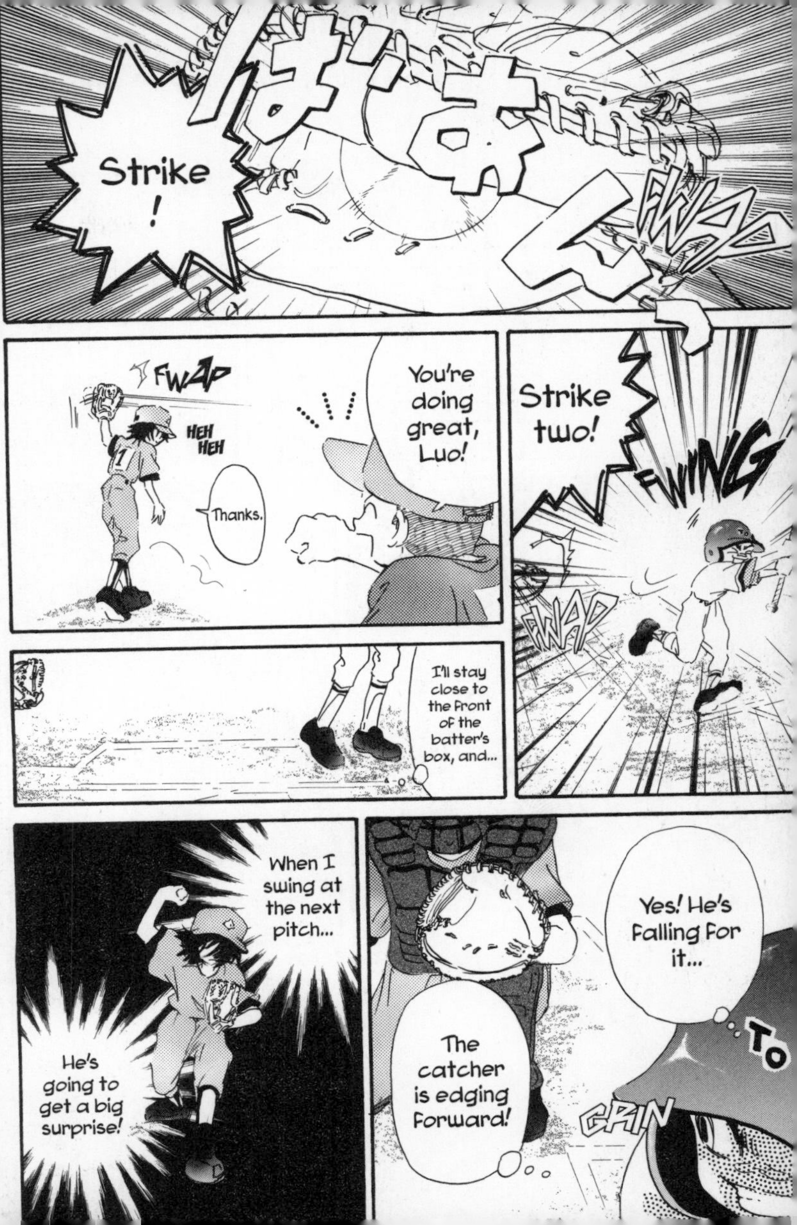
FWAP
Strike!
Strike two!
FWING
FWAP
You're doing great, Luo!
FWAP
HEH HEH
Thanks.
I'll stay close to the front of the batter's box, and...
Yes! He's falling for it...
TO
The catcher is edging forward!
GRIN
When I swing at the next pitch...
He's going to get a big surprise!

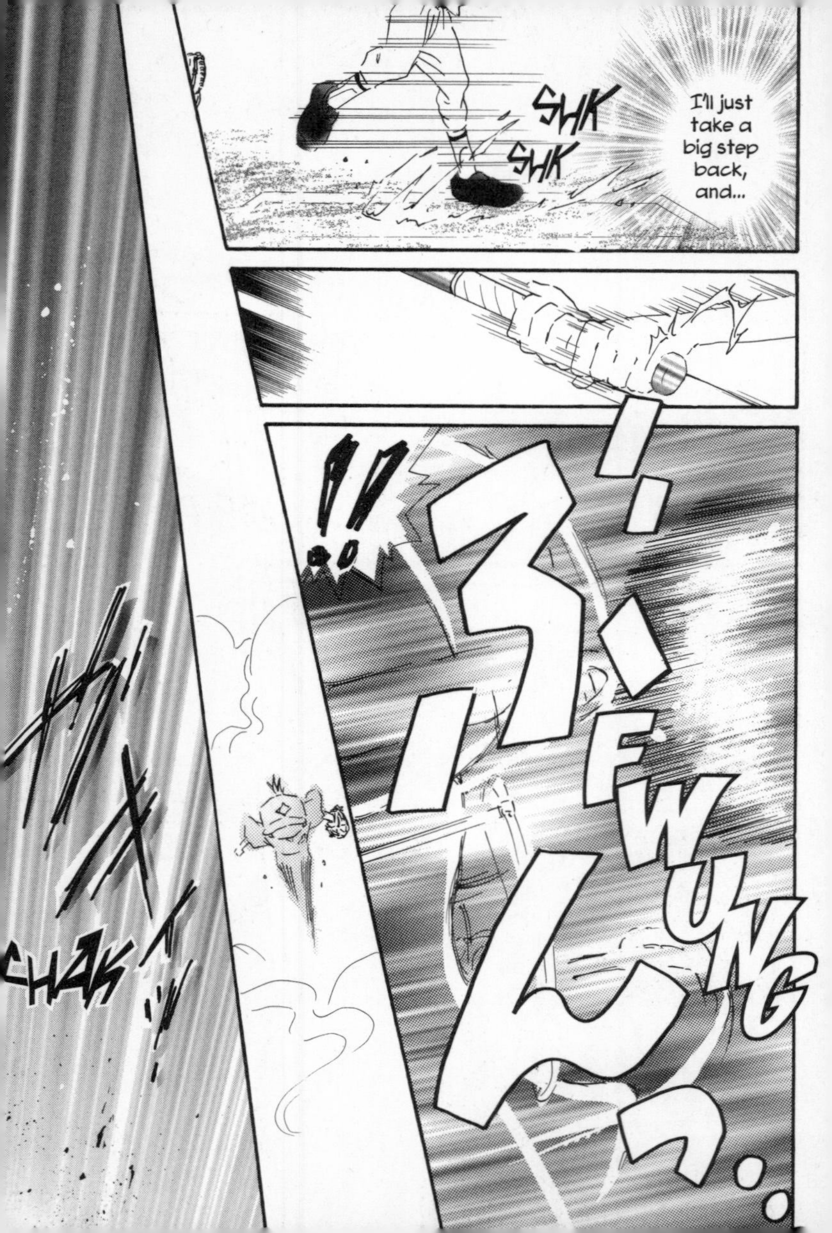

I'll just take a big step back, and...
SHK
SHK
!!
FWUNG
CHAK

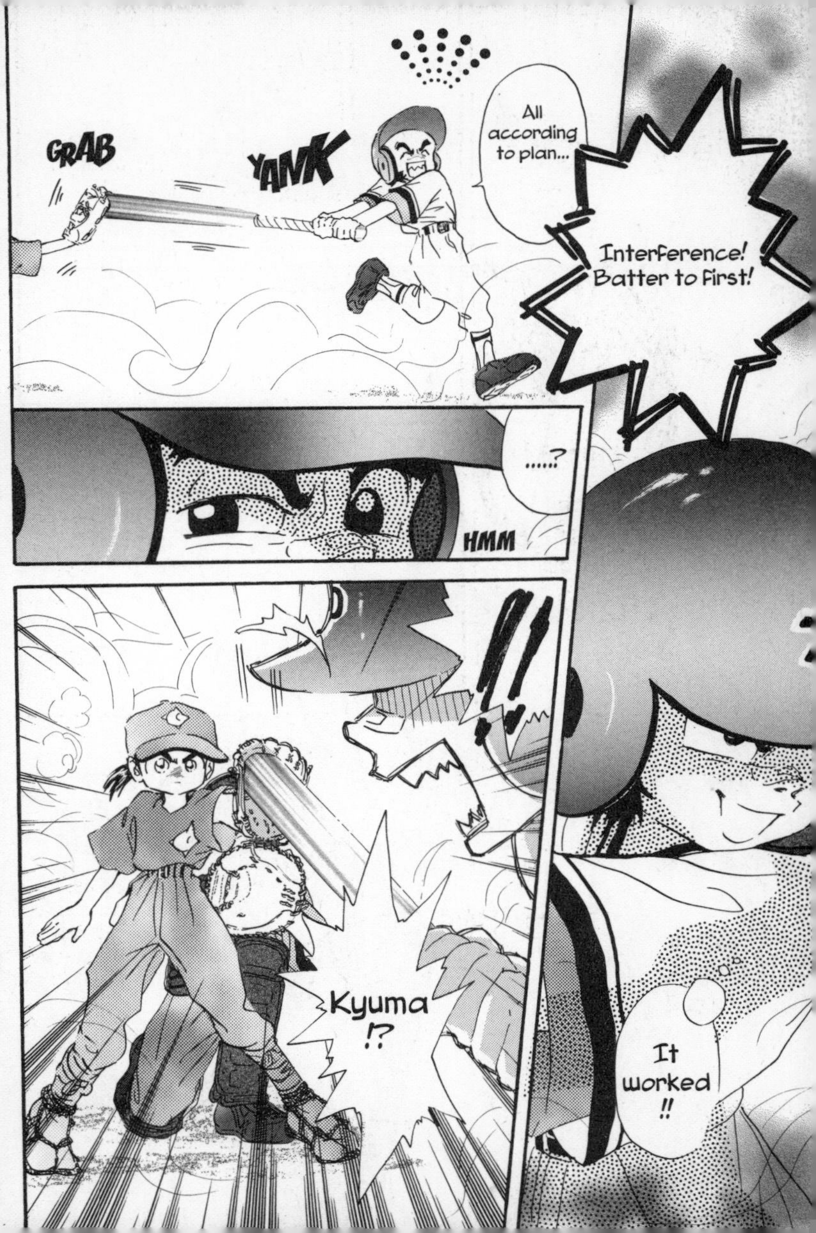
Interference! Batter to first!
It worked !!
All according to plan...
YANK
GRAB
.....?
HMM
Kyuma !?

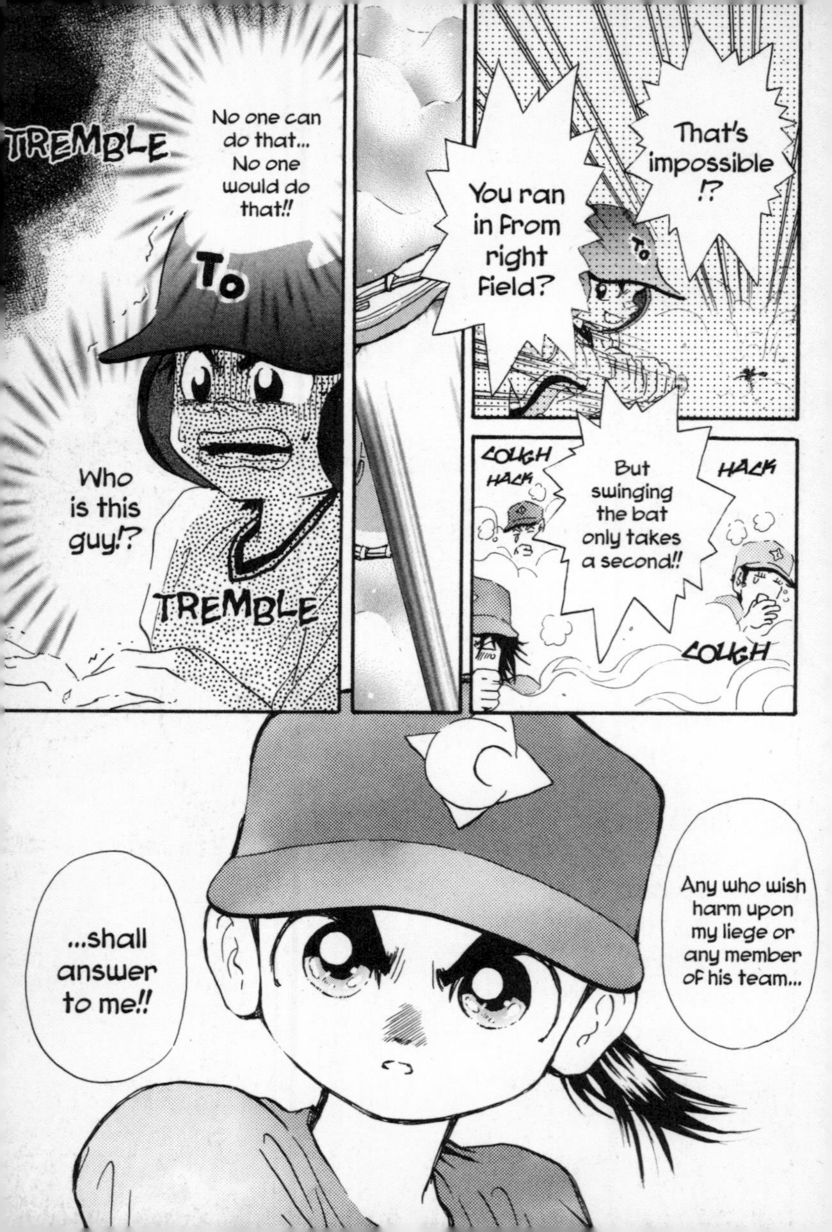
That's impossible!?
You ran in from right field?
HACK
But swinging the bat only takes a second!!
COUGH
HACK
COUGH
No one can do that... No one would do that!!
TREMBLE
Who is this guy!?
TREMBLE
Any who wish harm upon my liege or any member of his team...
...shall answer to me!!

My name is Kyuma Hattori... and these people are under my protection!
Though it may mean my life, I will not allow any harm to come to them! You and your people have been warned!!

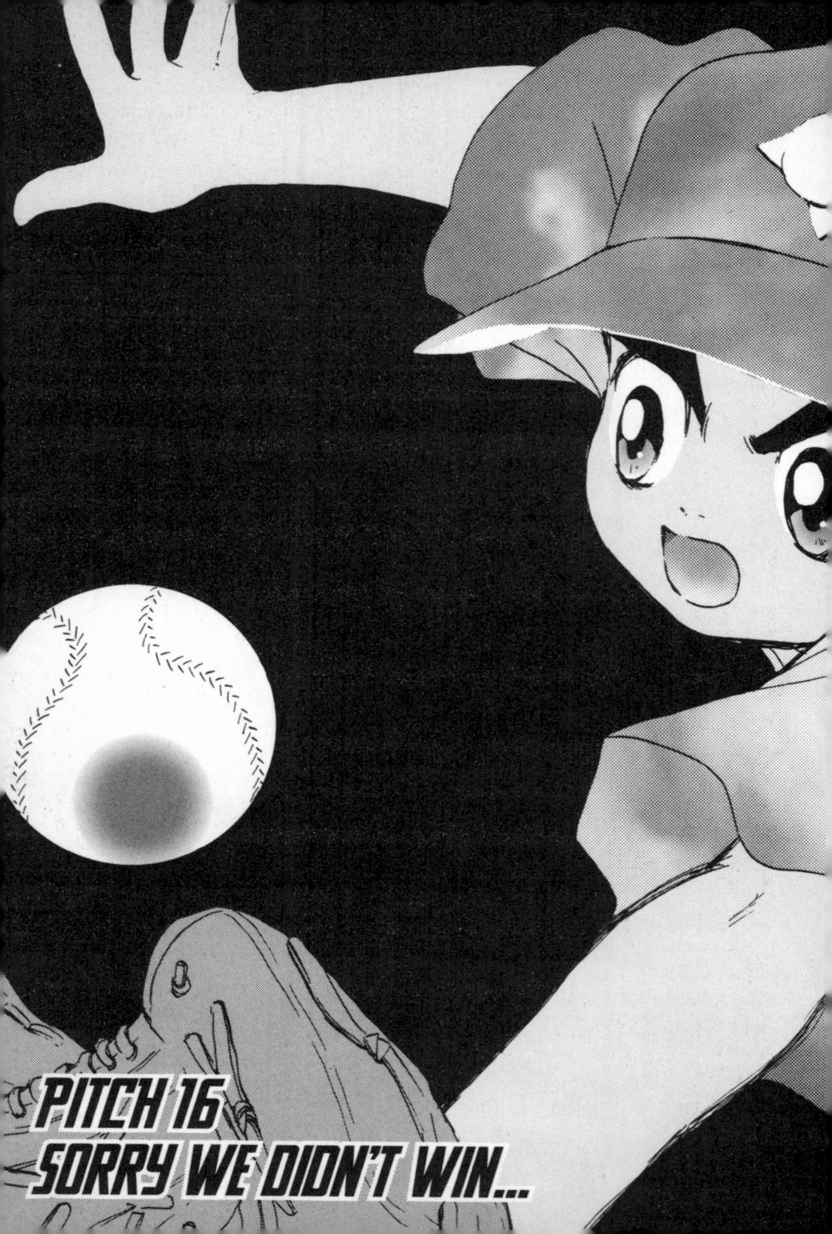
PITCH 16
SORRY WE DIDN'T WIN...

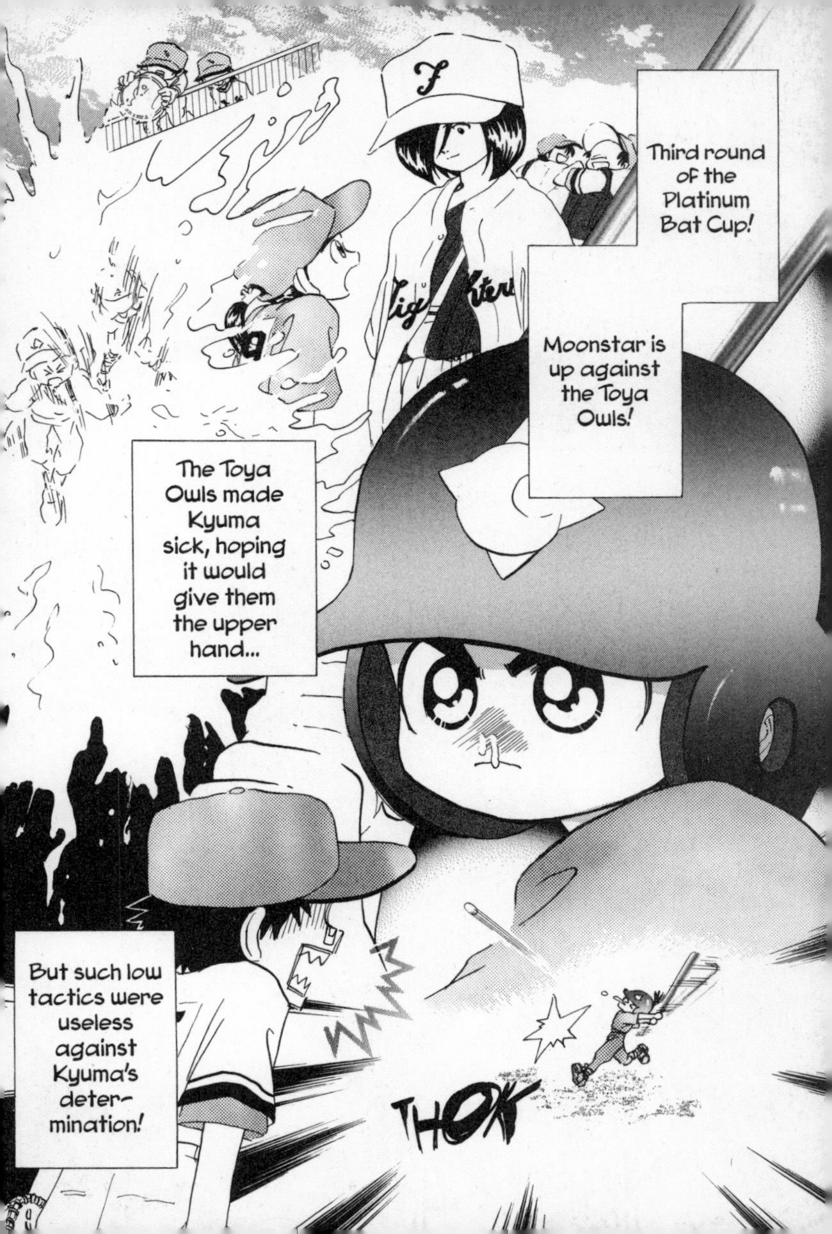
Third round of the Platinum Bat Cup!
Moonstar is up against the Toya Owls!
The Toya Owls made Kyuma sick, hoping it would give them the upper hand...
But such low tactics were useless against Kyuma's deter-mination!
THOK

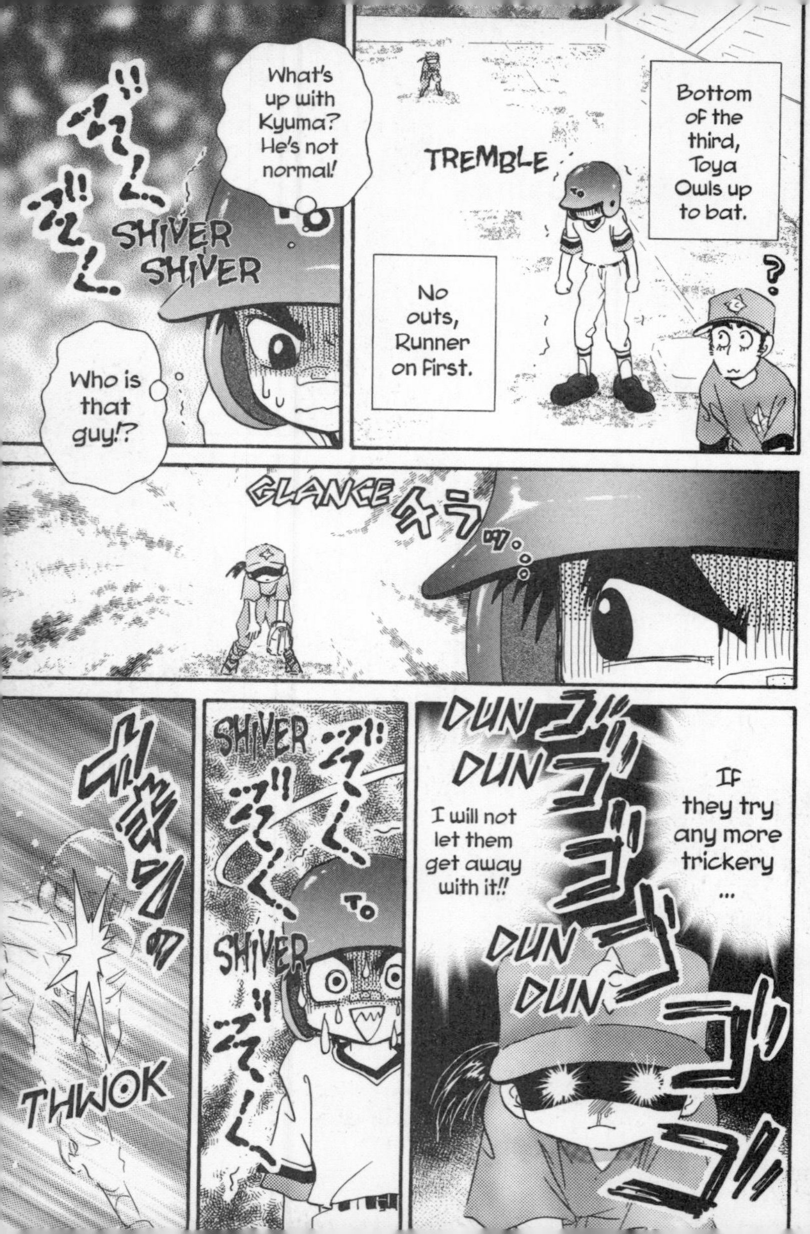

Bottom of the third, Toya Owls up to bat.
TREMBLE
?
No outs, Runner on first.
What's up with Kyuma? He's not normal!
SHIVER SHIVER
Who is that guy!?
GLANCE
If they try any more trickery ...
DUN DUN
I will not let them get away with it!!
DUN DUN
SHIVER
SHIVER
THWOK

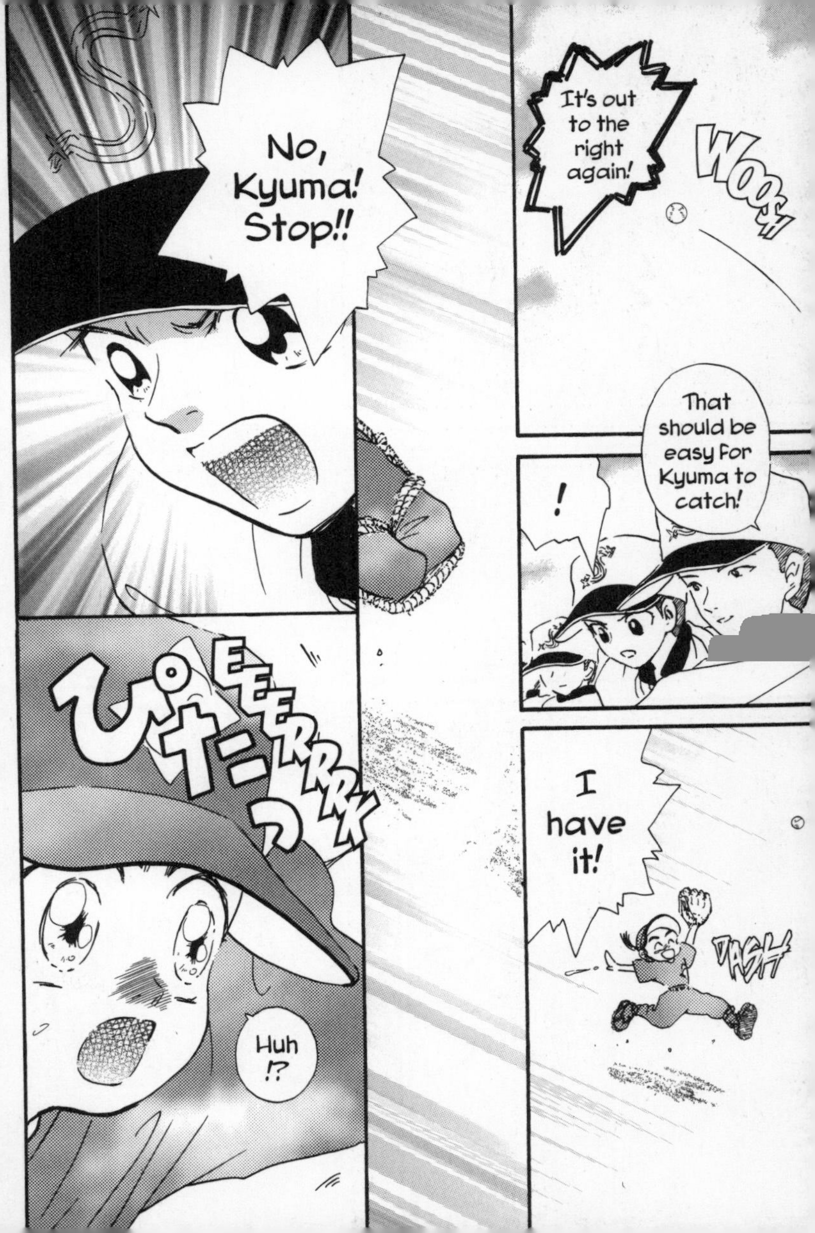
It's out to the right again!
WOOSH
That should be easy for Kyuma to catch!
!
I have it!
DASH
No, Kyuma! Stop!!
ぴたーっ
EEEERRRRK
Huh!?

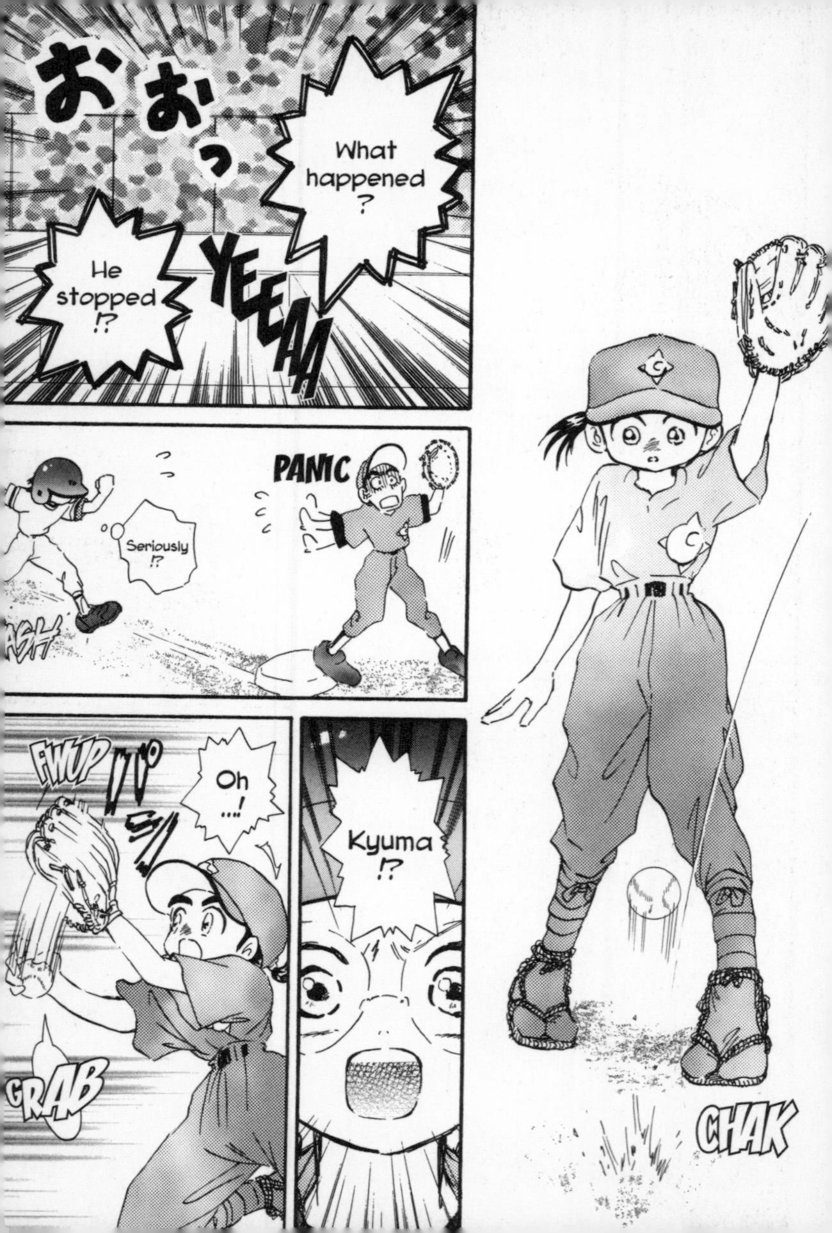

CHAK
What happened?
おおっ
YEEAAA
He stopped!?
PANIC
Seriously!?
Kyuma!?
Oh ...!
FWUP
GRAB

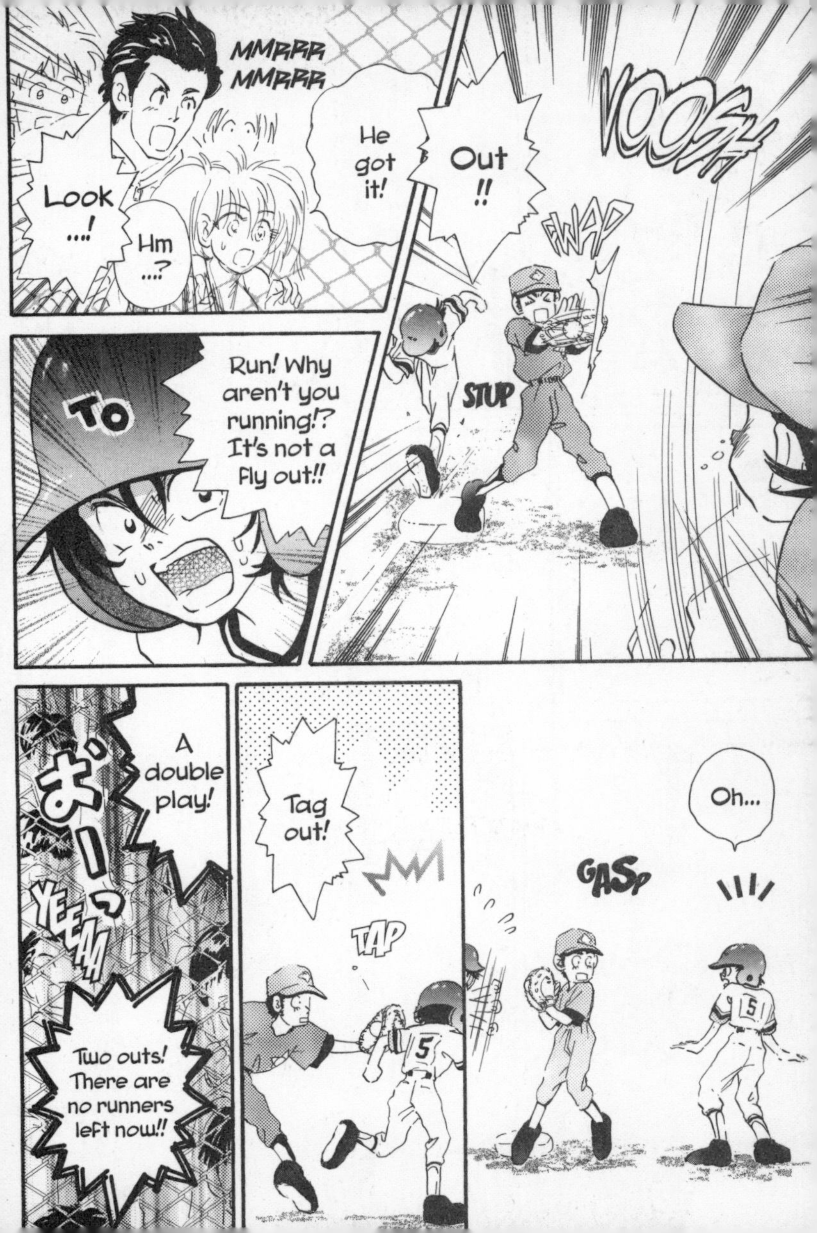
VOOSH
Out !!
SWAP
STUP
He got it!
MMRRR
MMRRR
Look ...!
Hm ...?
TO
Run! Why aren't you running!? It's not a fly out!!
Oh...
GASP
Tag out!
TAP
A double play!
お゛ーっ
YEEAA
Two outs! There are no runners left now!!

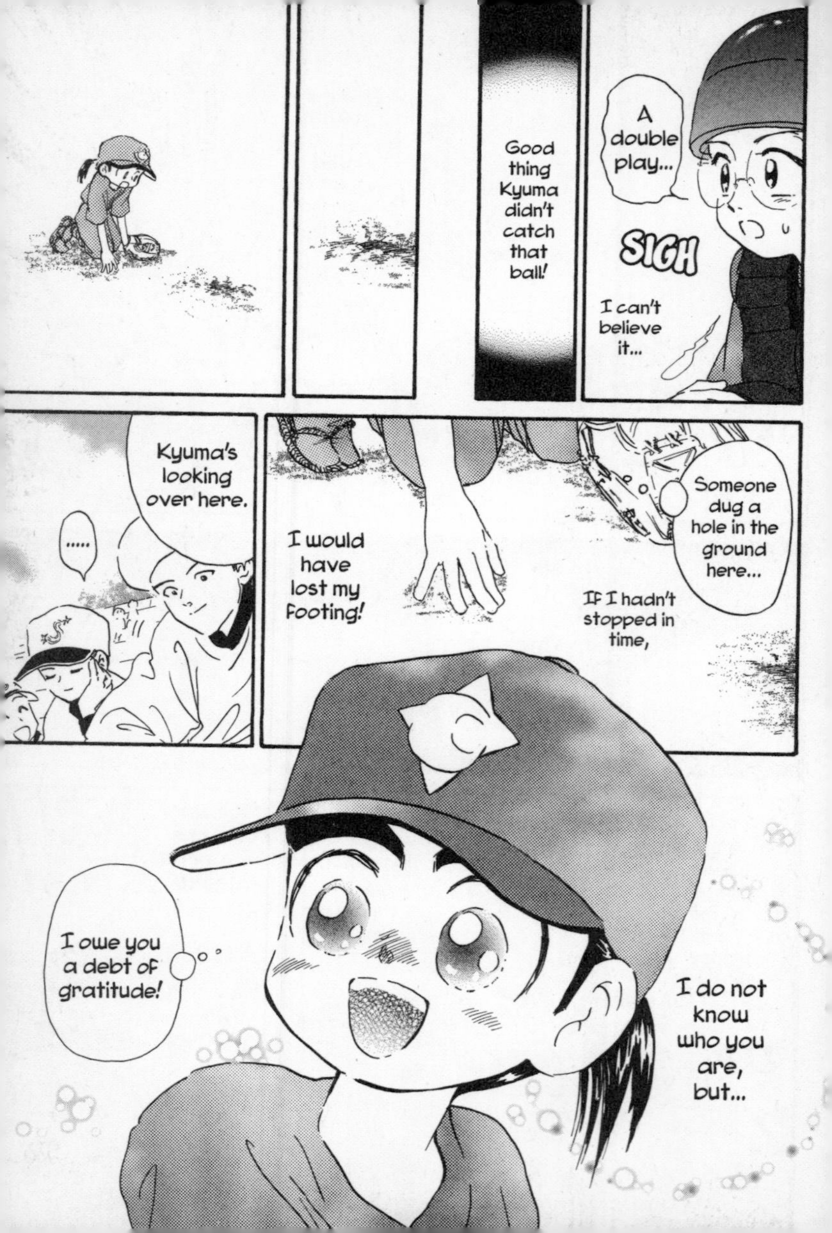
A double play...
SIGH
I can't believe it...
Good thing Kyuma didn't catch that ball!
Someone dug a hole in the ground here...
If I hadn't stopped in time,
I would have lost my footing!
Kyuma's looking over here.
.....
I do not know who you are, but...
I owe you a debt of gratitude!

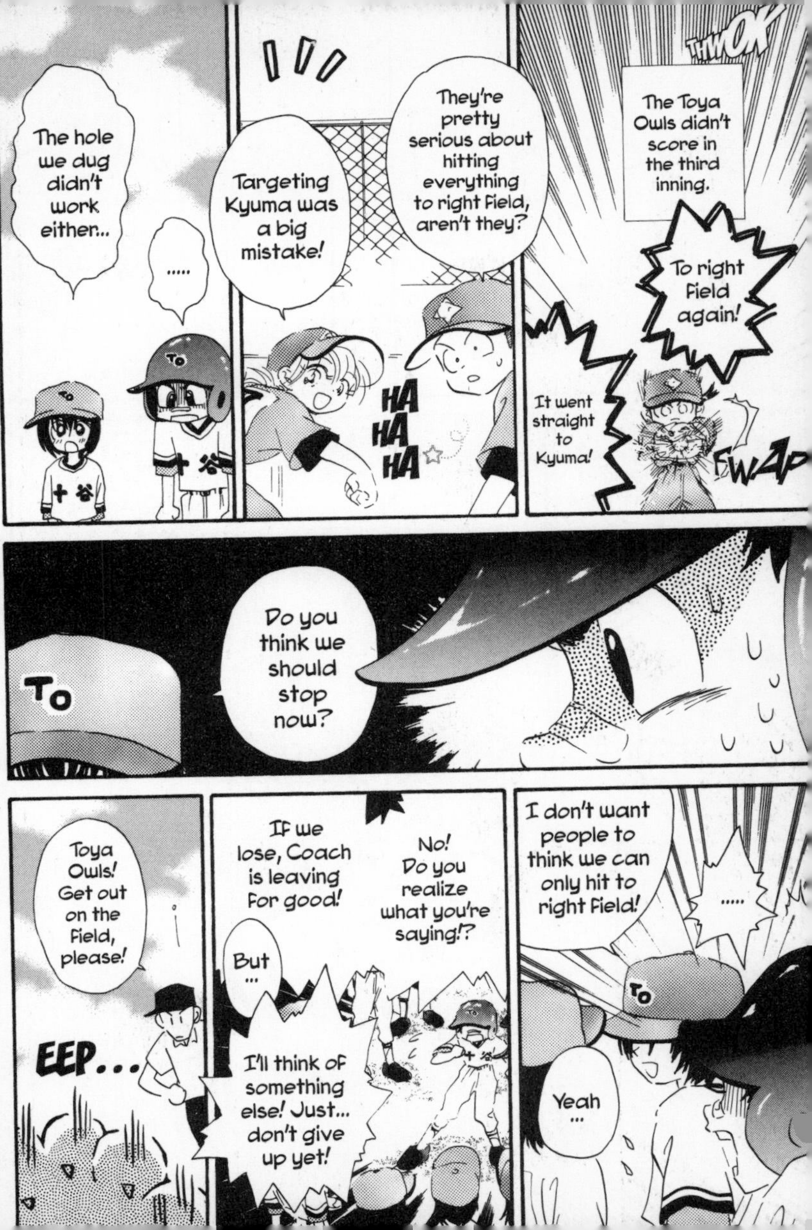
THWOK
The Toya Owls didn't score in the third inning.
To right field again!
It went straight to Kyuma!
FWAP
They're pretty serious about hitting everything to right field, aren't they?
Targeting Kyuma was a big mistake!
HA HA HA
The hole we dug didn't work either...
.....
Do you think we should stop now?
I don't want people to think we can only hit to right field!
.....
Yeah ...
No! Do you realize what you're saying!?
If we lose, Coach is leaving for good!
But ...
I'll think of something else! Just... don't give up yet!
Toya Owls! Get out on the field, please!
EEP...

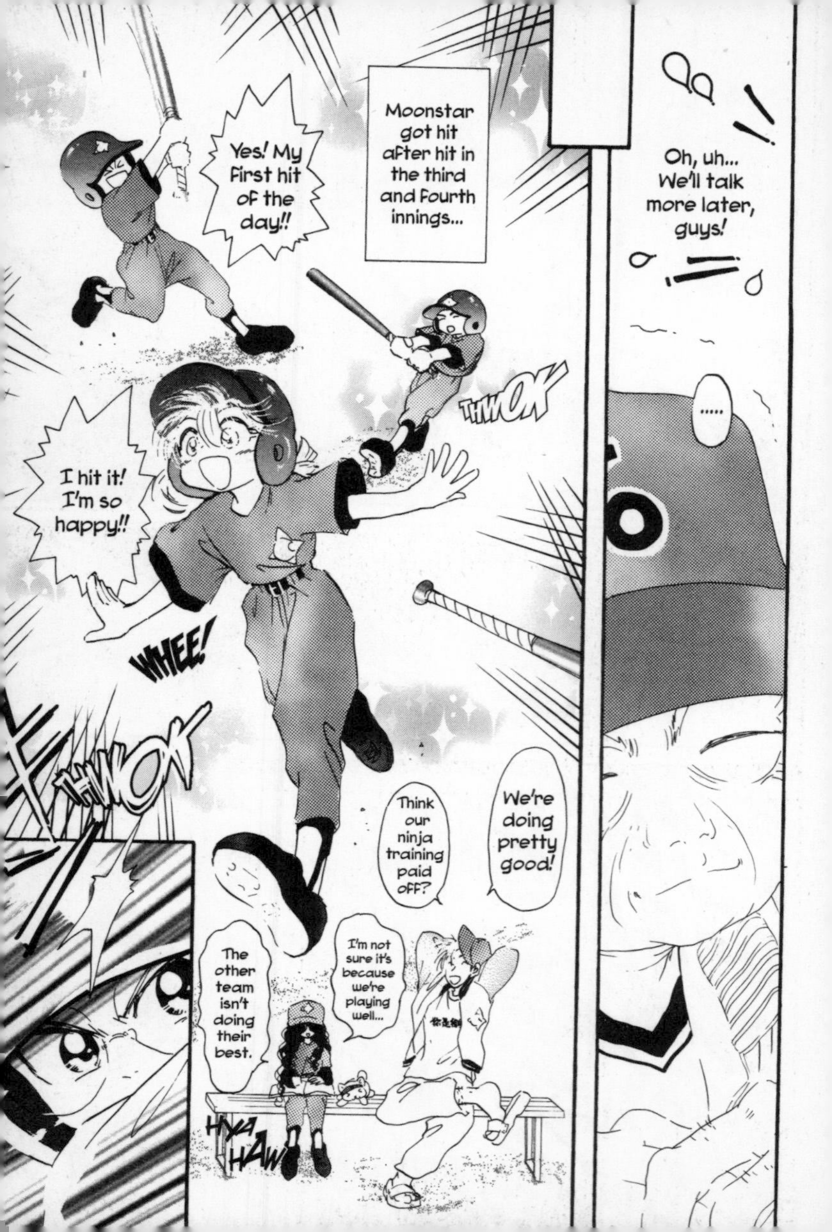
Oh, uh... We'll talk more later, guys!
......
Moonstar got hit after hit in the third and fourth innings...
Yes! My first hit of the day!!
THWOK
I hit it! I'm so happy!!
WHEE!
THWOK
We're doing pretty good!
Think our ninja training paid off?
I'm not sure it's because we're playing well...
The other team isn't doing their best.
HYA HAW

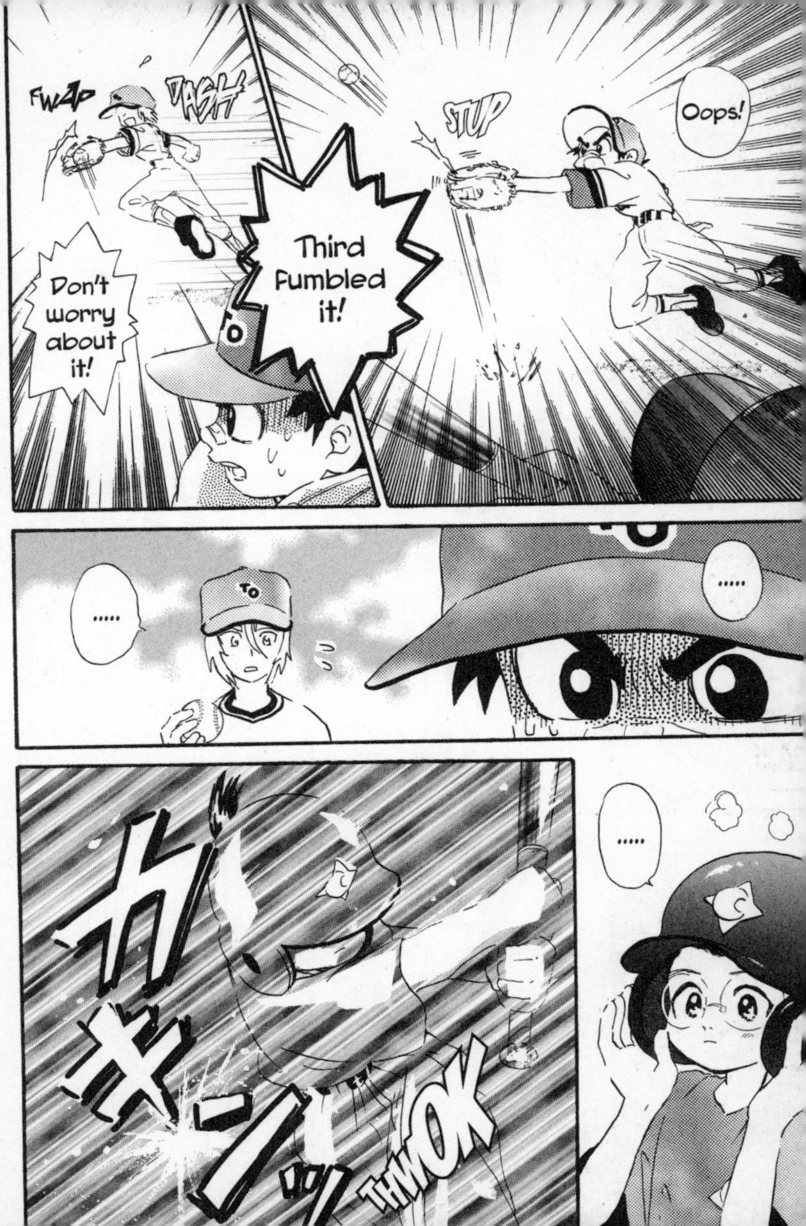
Oops!
STUP
Third fumbled it!
DASH
FWAP
Don't worry about it!
......
......
......
THWOK

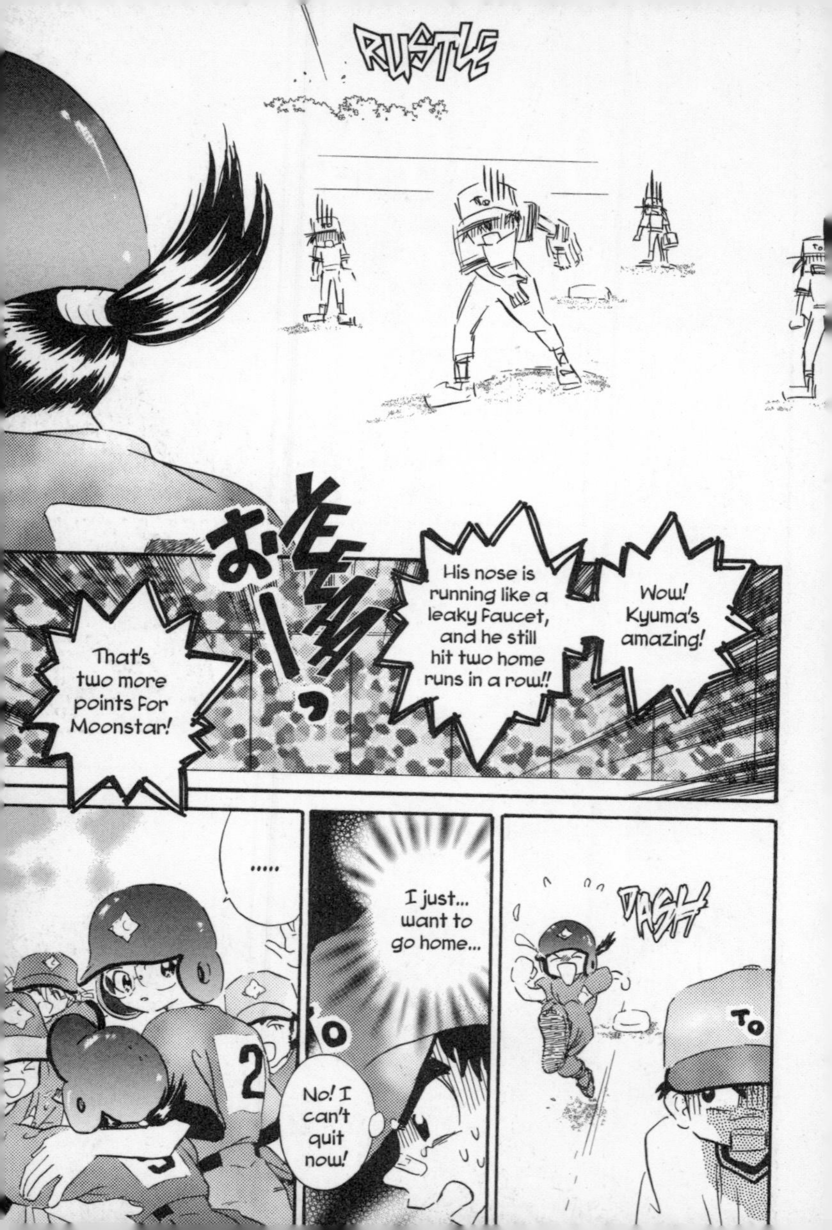
RUSTLE
Wow! Kyuma's amazing!
His nose is running like a leaky faucet, and he still hit two home runs in a row!!
That's two more points for Moonstar!
DASH
I just... want to go home...
.....
No! I can't quit now!

1	2	3	4	5		
0	0	0	0	0	0	
0	1	0	2	0		

At the top of the sixth inning, the score was 3 to 0 for Moonstar.

It's just... three points...

.....

NERVOUS

We have to win... We have to...

MMRR

Yeah, the three point lead must be putting some serious pressure on Toya.

さ
ざ
わ

What a one-sided game! Is this all we can expect from the third round of the Platinum Bat Cup?

Moonstar's got this game in the bag...

MMRR
MMRR

If you focus too much on your desire to win...

Doesn't that make it harder to do your best?

Um... I don't mean to overstep my bounds, but...

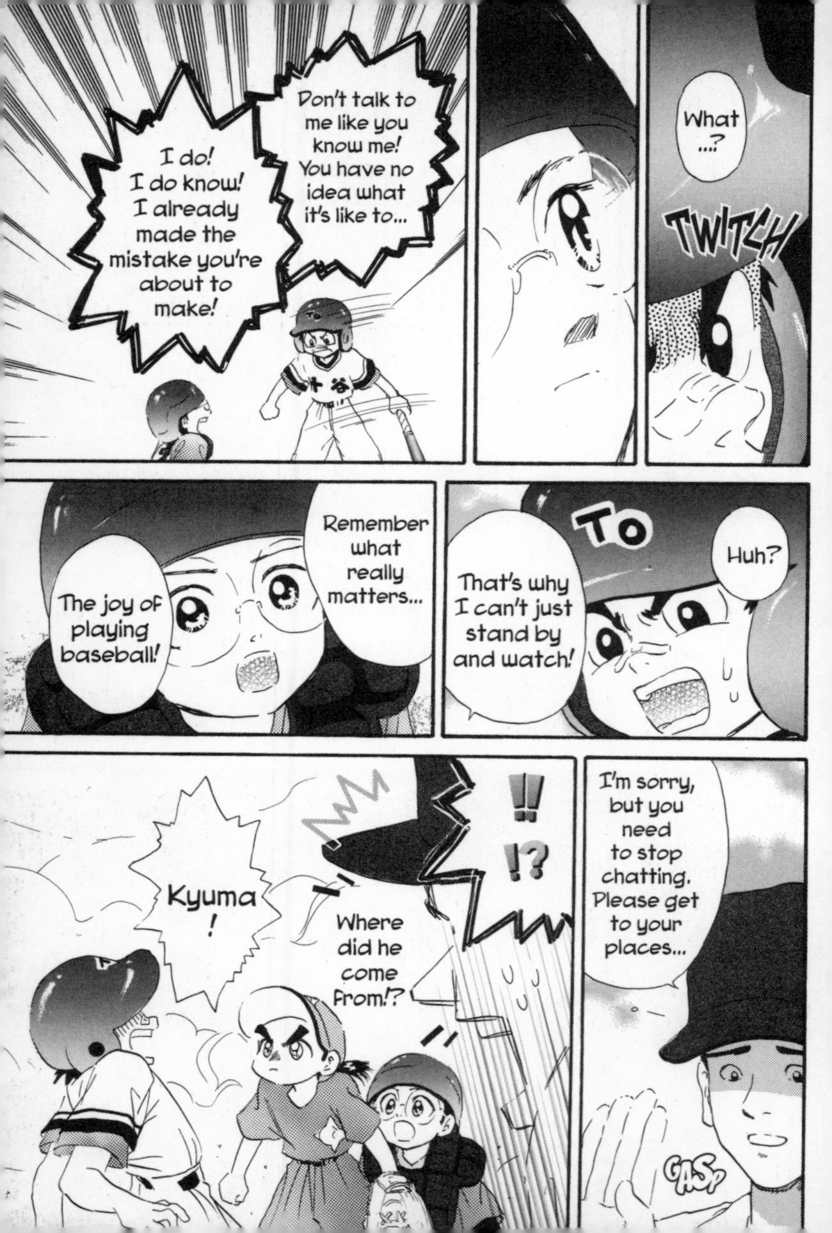
What ...?
TWITCH
Don't talk to me like you know me! You have no idea what it's like to...
I do! I do know! I already made the mistake you're about to make!
Huh?
TO
That's why I can't just stand by and watch!
Remember what really matters...
The joy of playing baseball!
I'm sorry, but you need to stop chatting. Please get to your places...
GASP
!!
!?
Where did he come from!?
Kyuma!

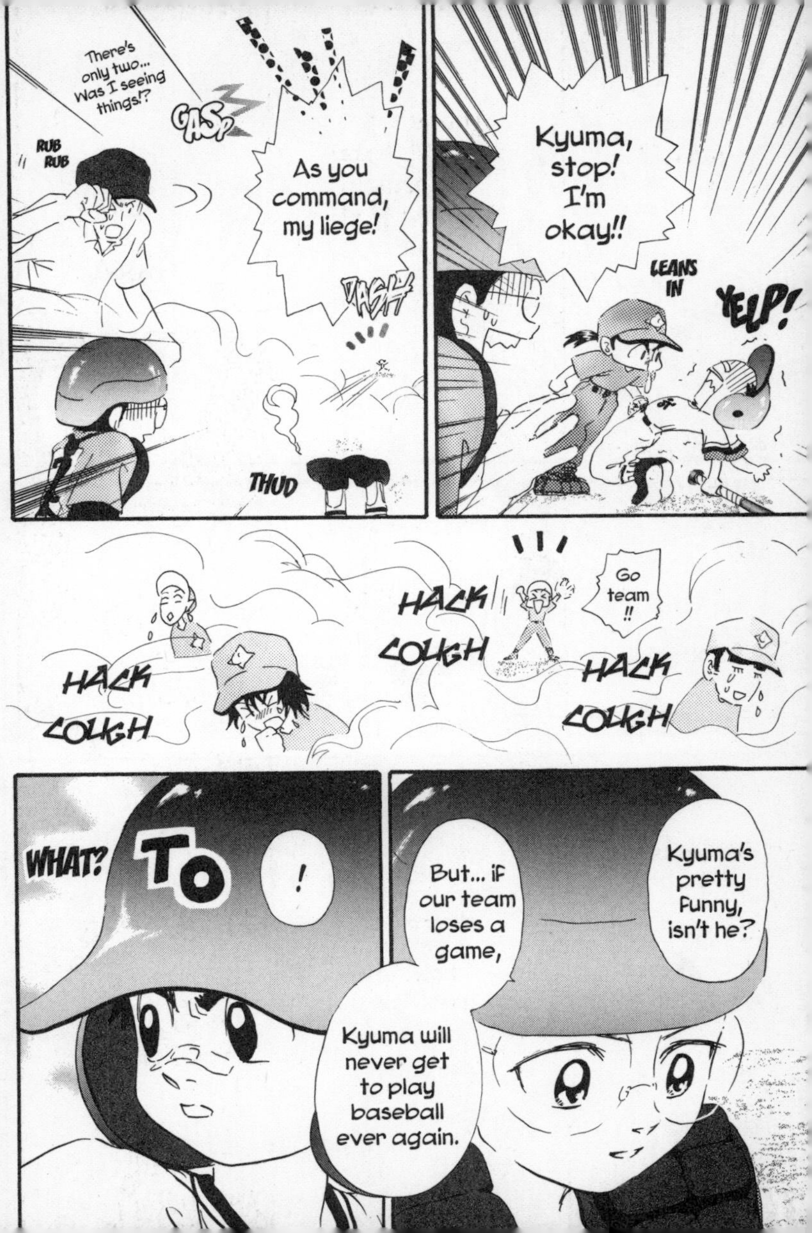

Kyuma, stop! I'm okay!!
LEANS IN
YELP!
As you command, my liege!
There's only two... Was I seeing things!?
GASP
RUB RUB
DASH
THUD
HACK
COUGH
Go team !!
HACK
COUGH
HACK
COUGH
Kyuma's pretty funny, isn't he?
But... if our team loses a game,
Kyuma will never get to play baseball ever again.
!
TO
WHAT?

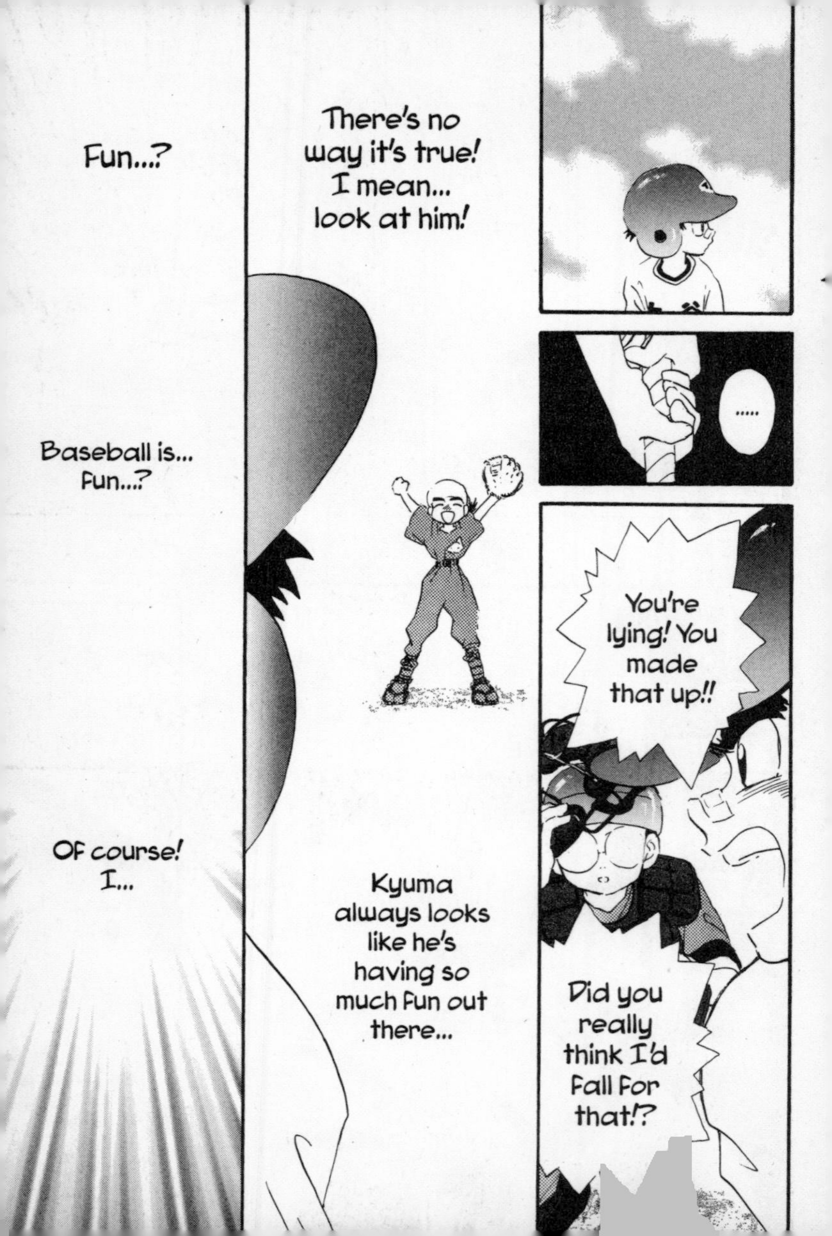

.....
You're lying! You made that up!!
Did you really think I'd fall for that!?
There's no way it's true! I mean... look at him!
Kyuma always looks like he's having so much fun out there...
Fun...?
Baseball is... fun...?
Of course! I...

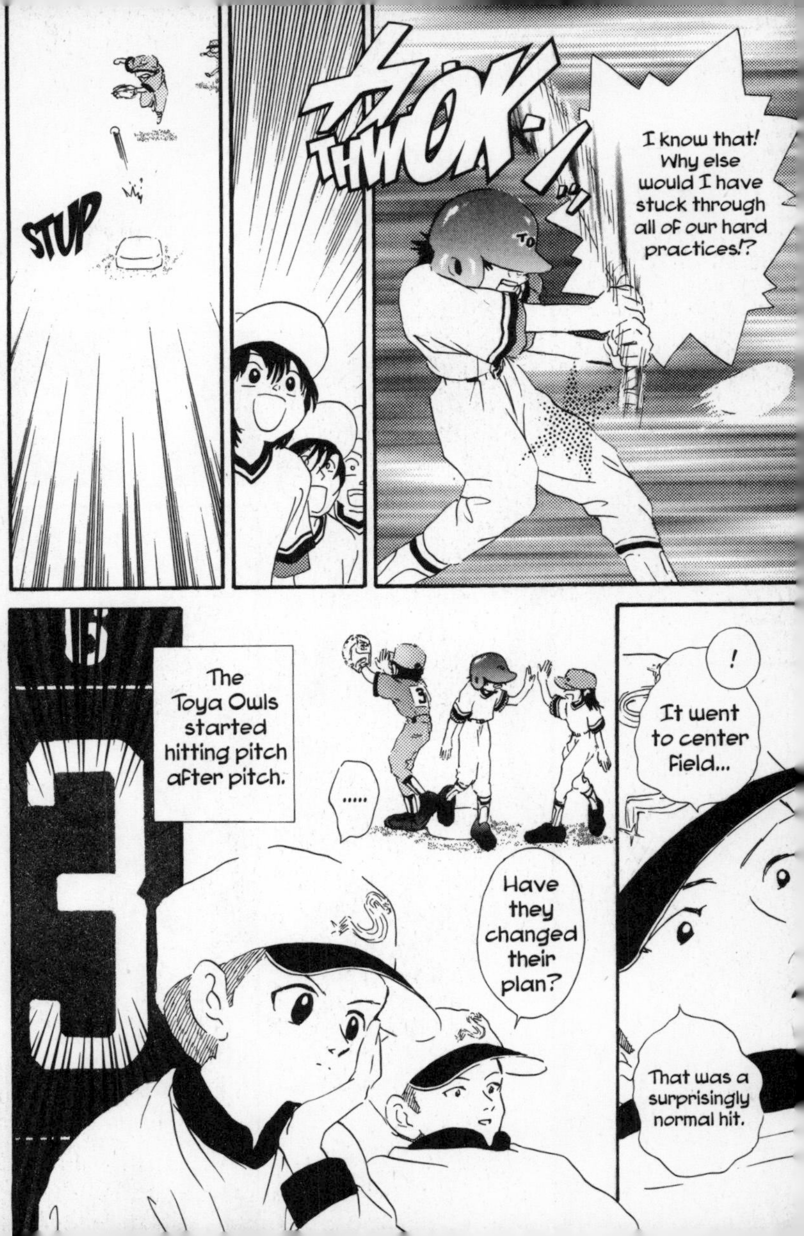
THWOK
I know that! Why else would I have stuck through all of our hard practices!?
STUP
!
It went to center field...
That was a surprisingly normal hit.
.....
The Toya Owls started hitting pitch after pitch.
Have they changed their plan?

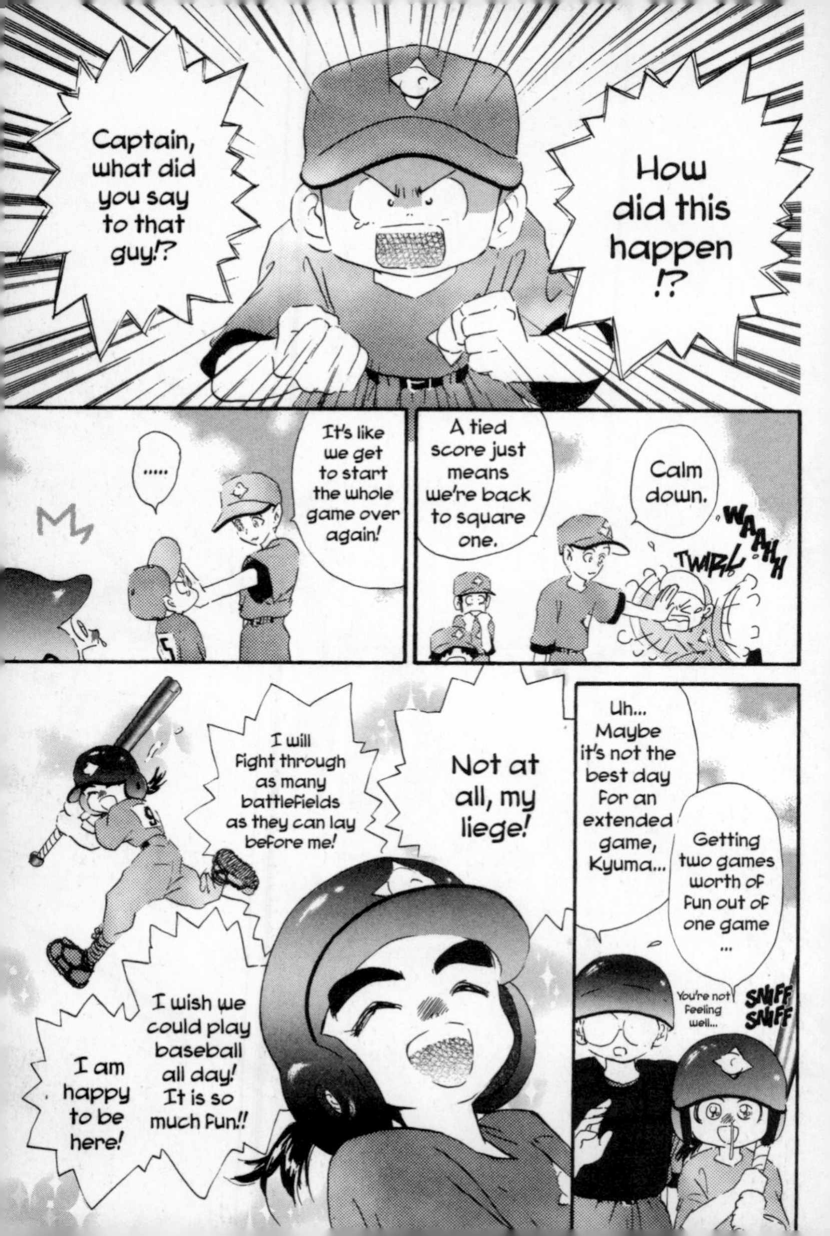
How did this happen!?
Captain, what did you say to that guy!?
Calm down.
A tied score just means we're back to square one.
WAAHH
TWIRL
It's like we get to start the whole game over again!
.....
Uh... Maybe it's not the best day for an extended game, Kyuma...
Getting two games worth of fun out of one game ...
You're not feeling well...
SNIFF SNIFF
Not at all, my liege!
I will fight through as many battlefields as they can lay before me!
I wish we could play baseball all day! It is so much fun!!
I am happy to be here!

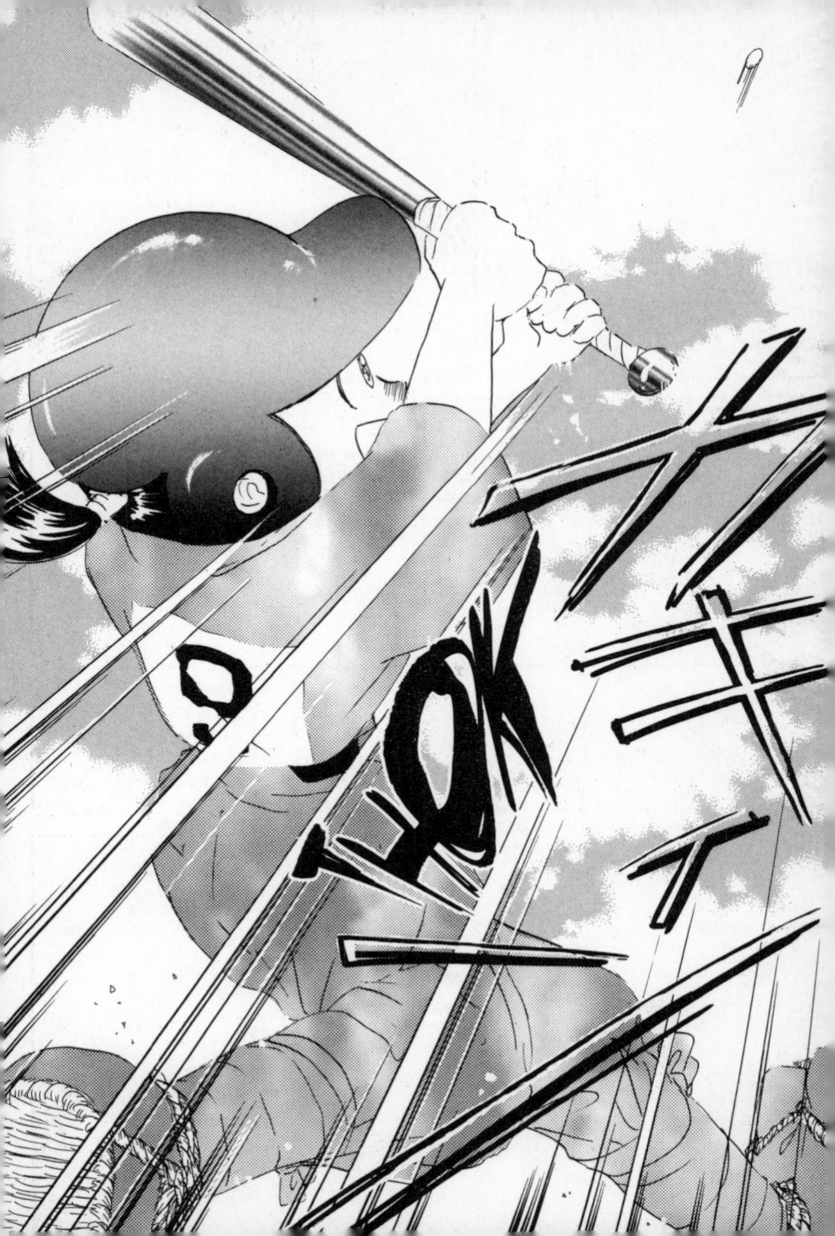
カキイー

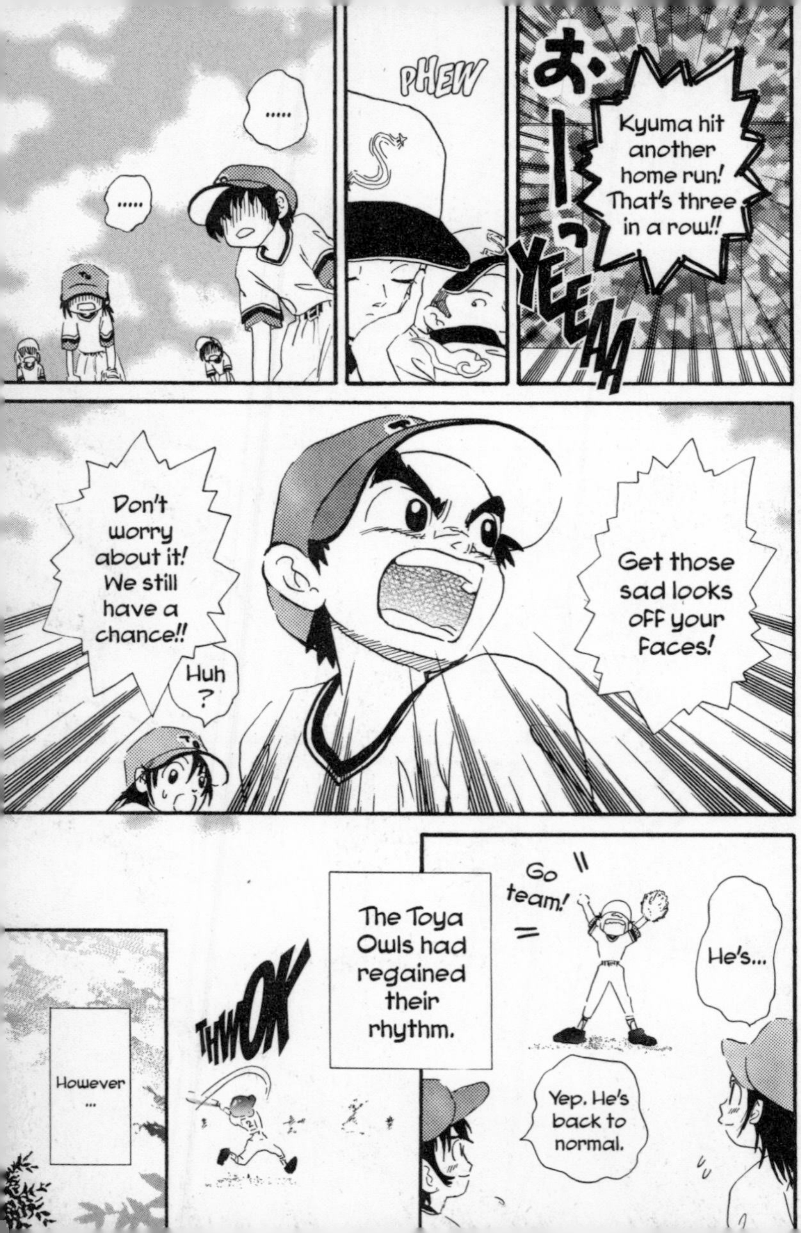
おーっ
Kyuma hit another home run! That's three in a row!!
YEEAAA
PHEW
......
......
Get those sad looks off your faces!
Don't worry about it! We still have a chance!!
Huh?
He's...
Go team!
Yep. He's back to normal.
The Toya Owls had regained their rhythm.
THWOK
However ...

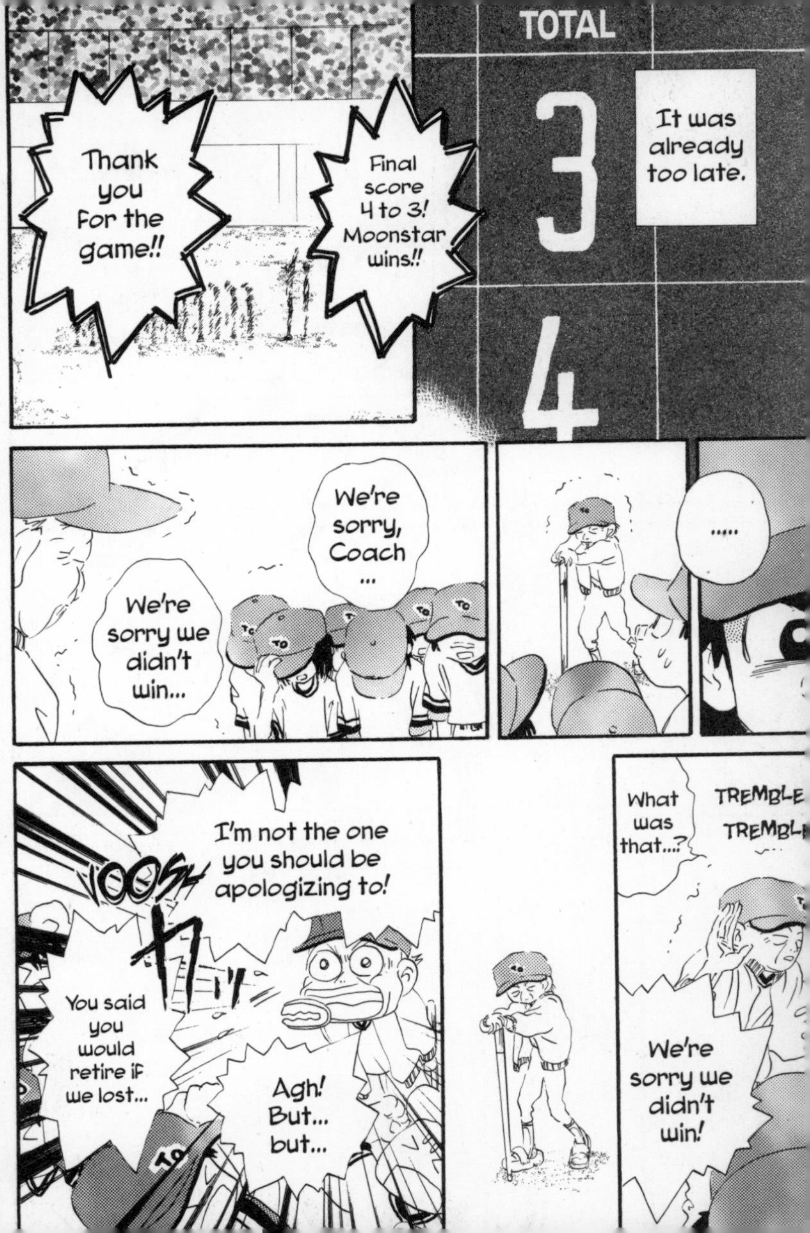
TOTAL
3
4
It was already too late.
Final score 4 to 3! Moonstar wins!!
Thank you for the game!!
.....
We're sorry, Coach...
We're sorry we didn't win...
TREMBLE
TREMBL
What was that...?
We're sorry we didn't win!
I'm not the one you should be apologizing to!
You said you would retire if we lost...
Agh! But... but...

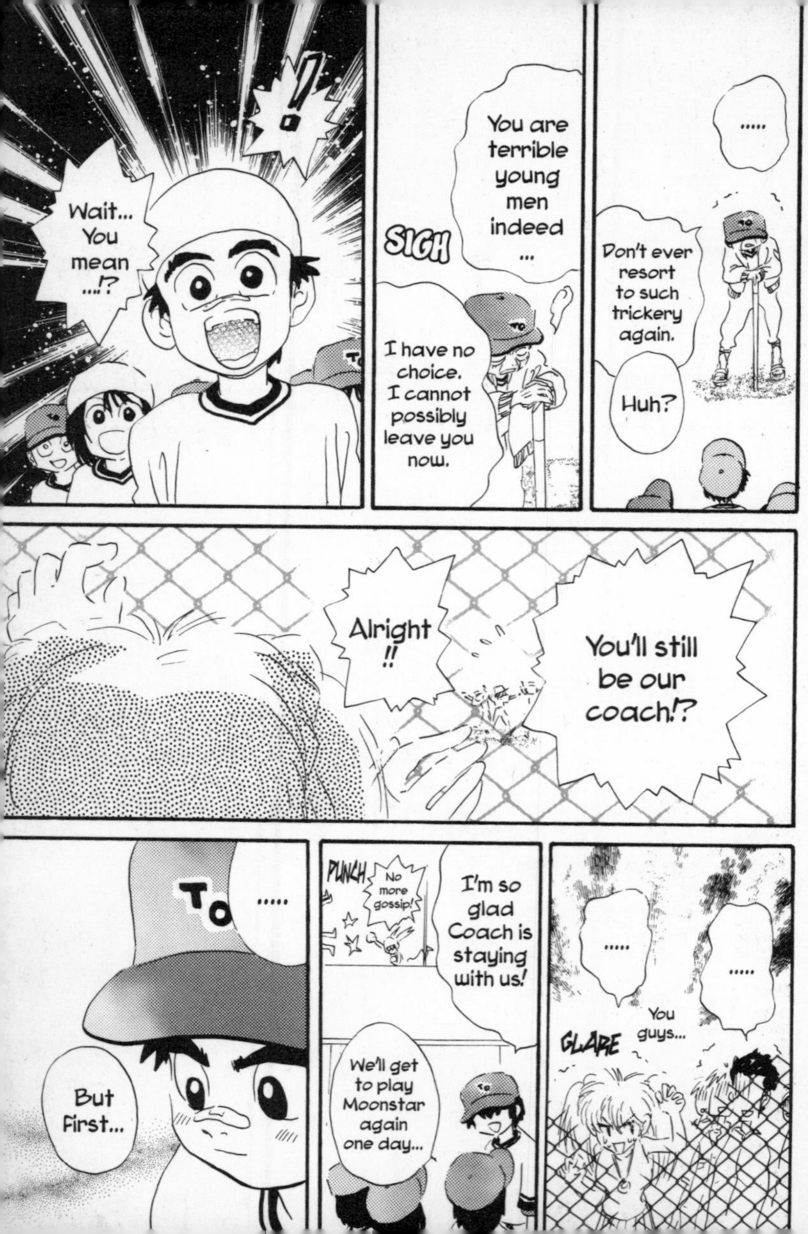
.....
Don't ever resort to such trickery again.
Huh?
You are terrible young men indeed ...
SIGH
I have no choice. I cannot possibly leave you now.
!
Wait... You mean ...!?
You'll still be our coach!?
Alright !!
.....
.....
You guys...
GLARE
I'm so glad Coach is staying with us!
No more gossip!
PUNCH
We'll get to play Moonstar again one day...
.....
But first...

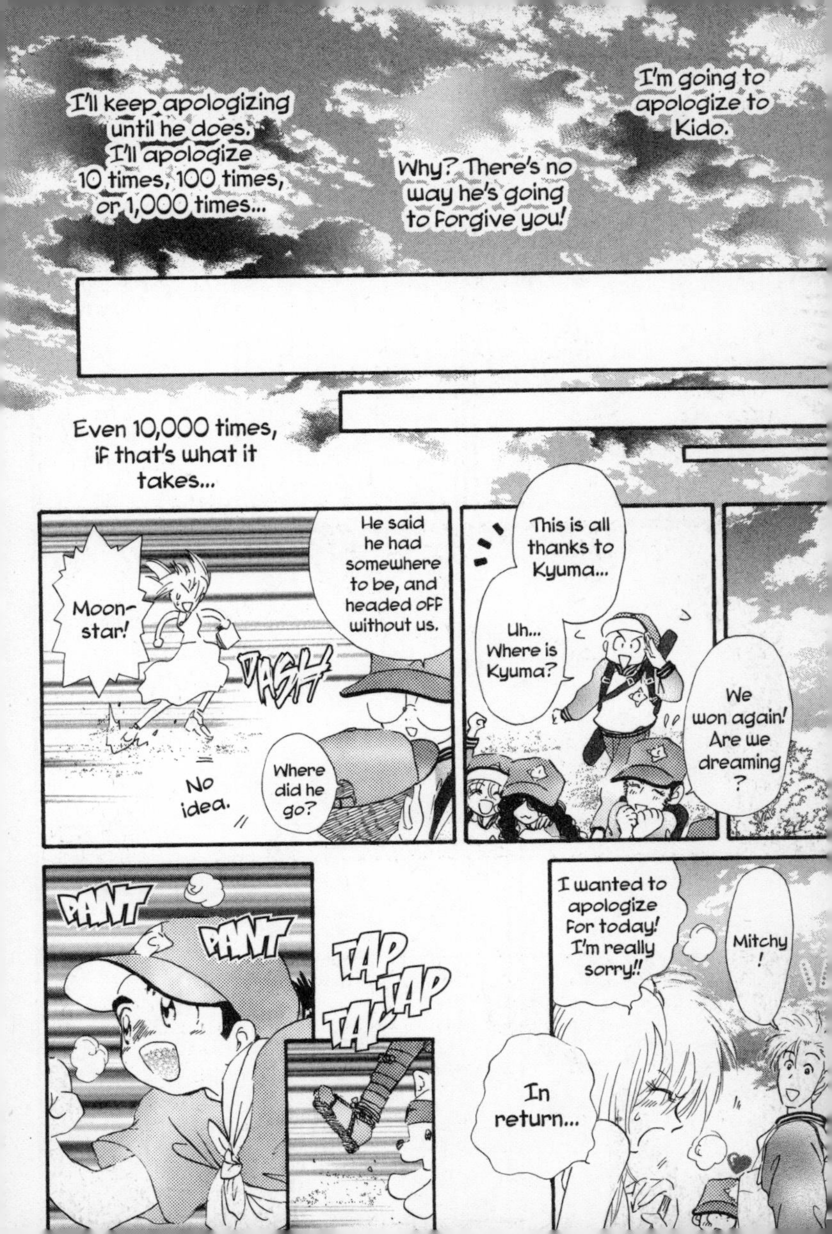
I'm going to apologize to Kido.
Why? There's no way he's going to forgive you!
I'll keep apologizing until he does. I'll apologize 10 times, 100 times, or 1,000 times...
Even 10,000 times, if that's what it takes...
We won again! Are we dreaming?
This is all thanks to Kyuma...
Uh... Where is Kyuma?
He said he had somewhere to be, and headed off without us.
Where did he go?
No idea.
Moon-star!
DASH
Mitchy!
I wanted to apologize for today! I'm really sorry!!
In return...
TAP
TAP
TAP
PANT
PANT

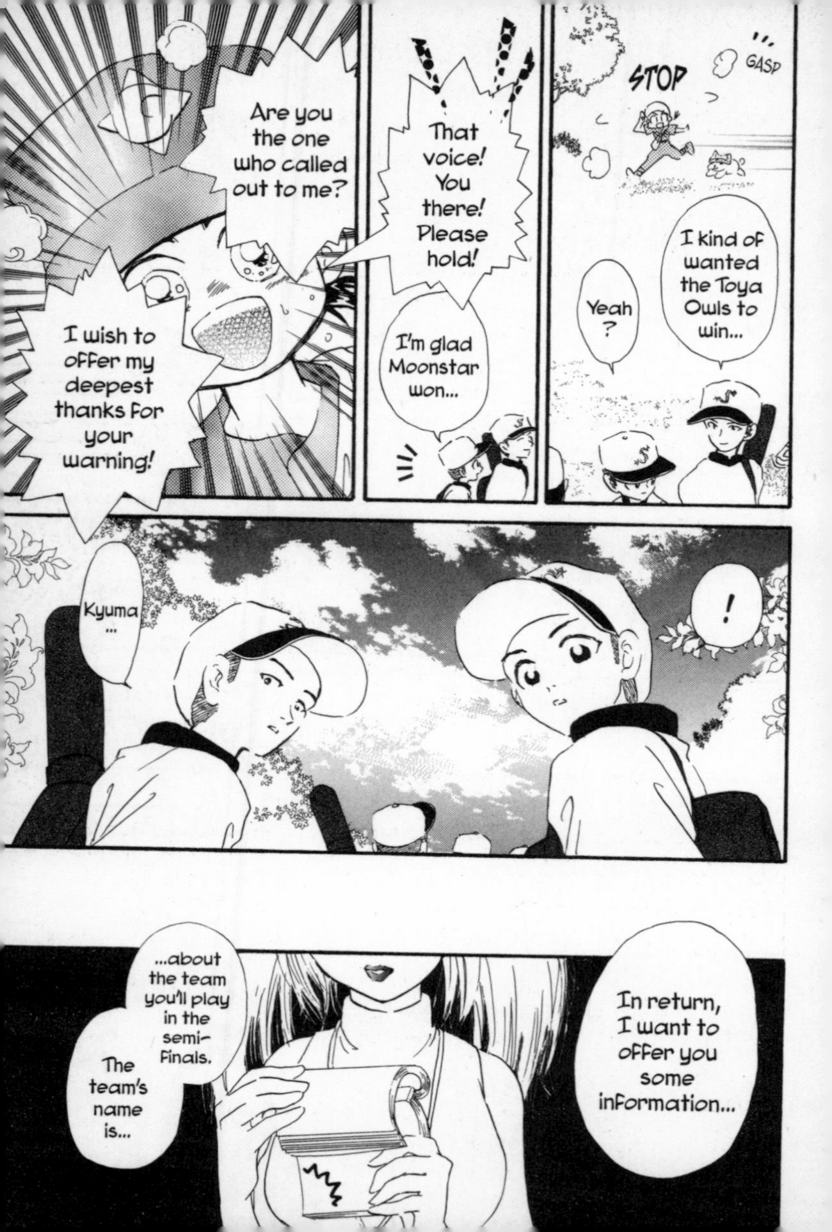
GASP
STOP
I kind of wanted the Toya Owls to win...
Yeah?
I'm glad Moonstar won...
That voice! You there! Please hold!
Are you the one who called out to me?
I wish to offer my deepest thanks for your warning!
!
Kyuma...
In return, I want to offer you some information...
...about the team you'll play in the semi-finals.
The team's name is...

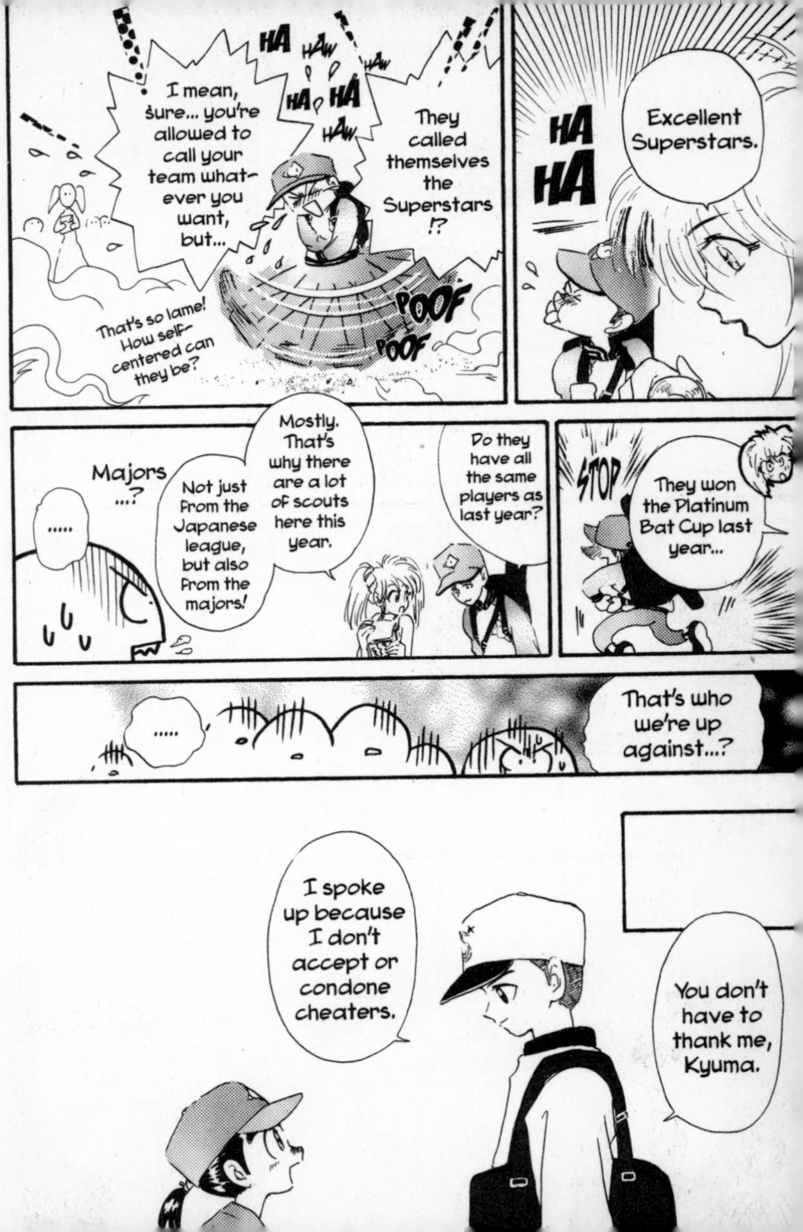
HA
HA
Excellent Superstars.
They called themselves the Superstars !?
HA HAW HAW HA HA HAW
I mean, sure... you're allowed to call your team whatever you want, but...
POOF
POOF
That's so lame! How self-centered can they be?
STOP
They won the Platinum Bat Cup last year...
Do they have all the same players as last year?
Mostly. That's why there are a lot of scouts here this year.
Not just from the Japanese league, but also from the majors!
Majors ...?
.....
That's who we're up against...?
.....
You don't have to thank me, Kyuma.
I spoke up because I don't accept or condone cheaters.

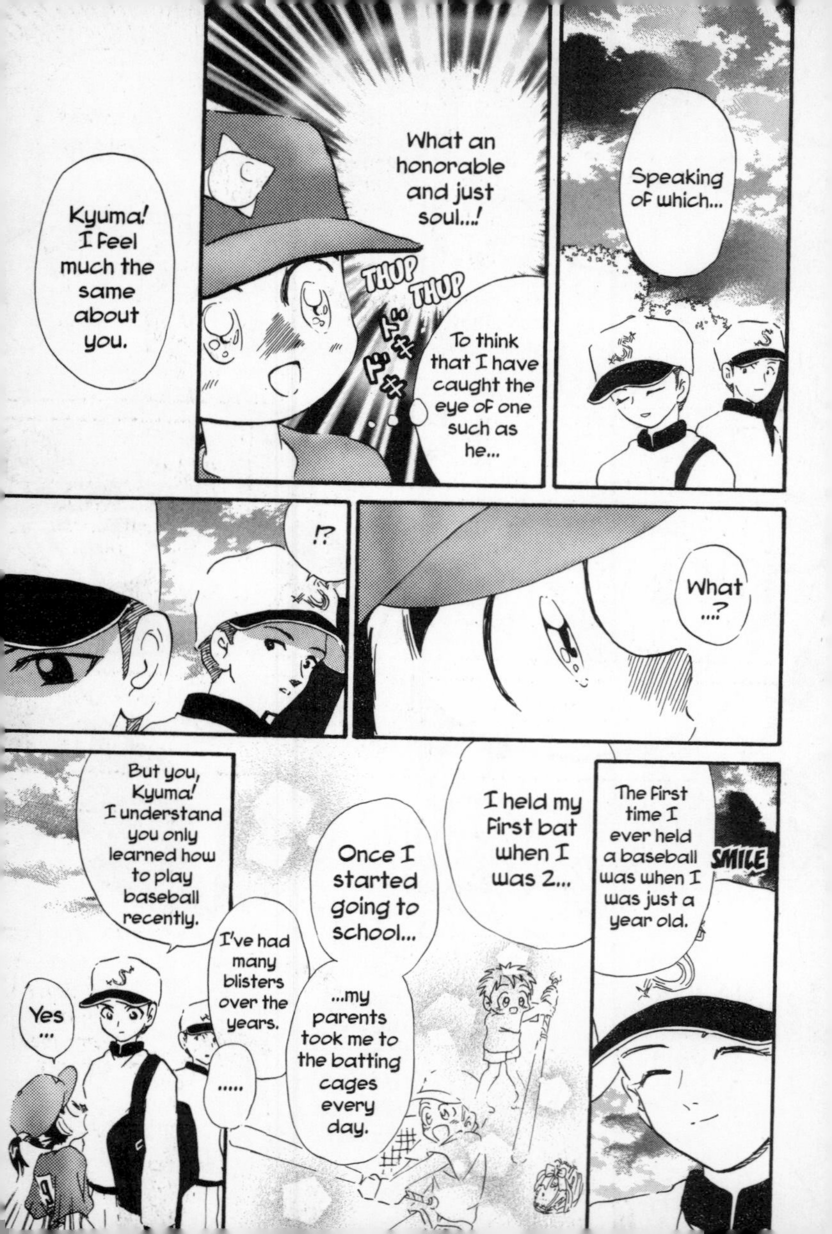
Speaking of which...
What an honorable and just soul...!
THUP THUP
ドキドキ
To think that I have caught the eye of one such as he...
Kyuma! I feel much the same about you.
What ...?
!?
SMILE
The first time I ever held a baseball was when I was just a year old.
I held my first bat when I was 2...
Once I started going to school...
...my parents took me to the batting cages every day.
I've had many blisters over the years.
But you, Kyuma! I understand you only learned how to play baseball recently.
Yes ...
.....

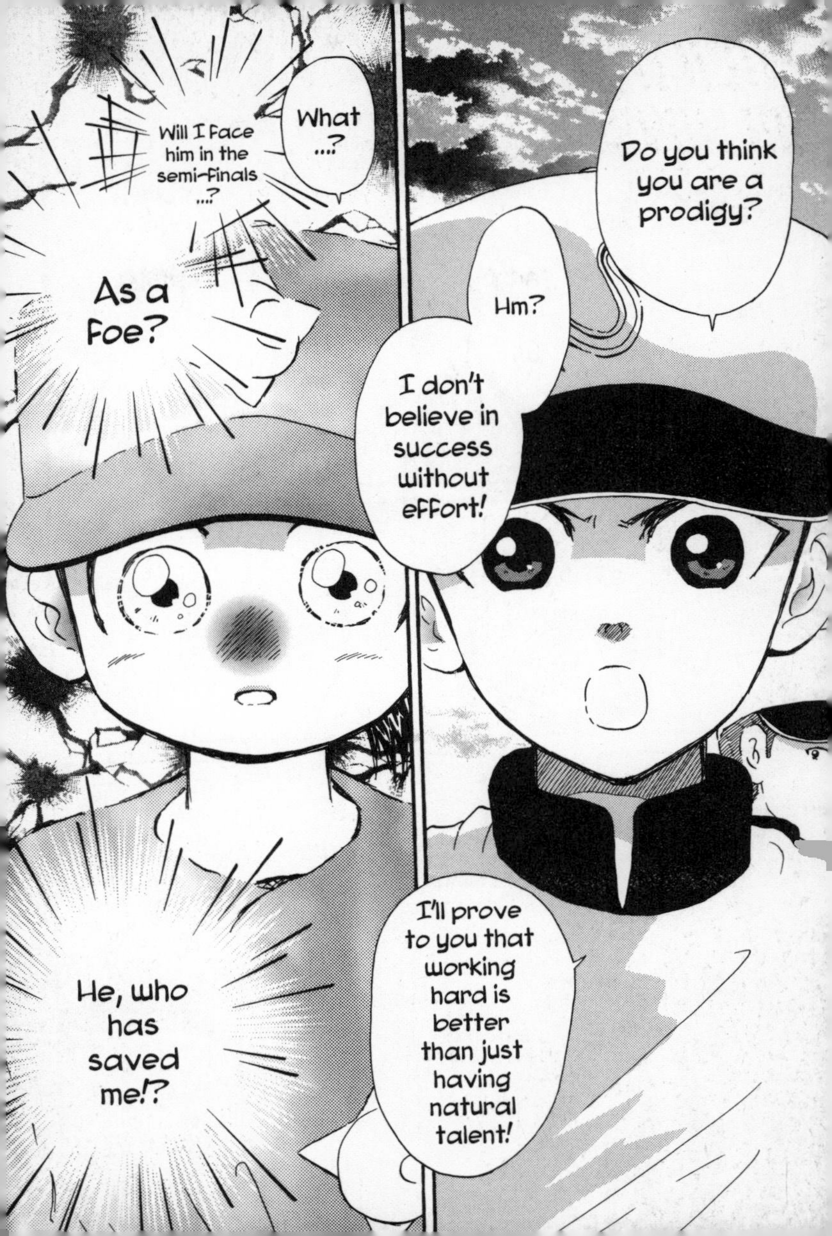
Do you think you are a prodigy?
Hm?
I don't believe in success without effort!
I'll prove to you that working hard is better than just having natural talent!
What ...?
Will I face him in the semi-finals ...?
As a foe?
He, who has saved me!?

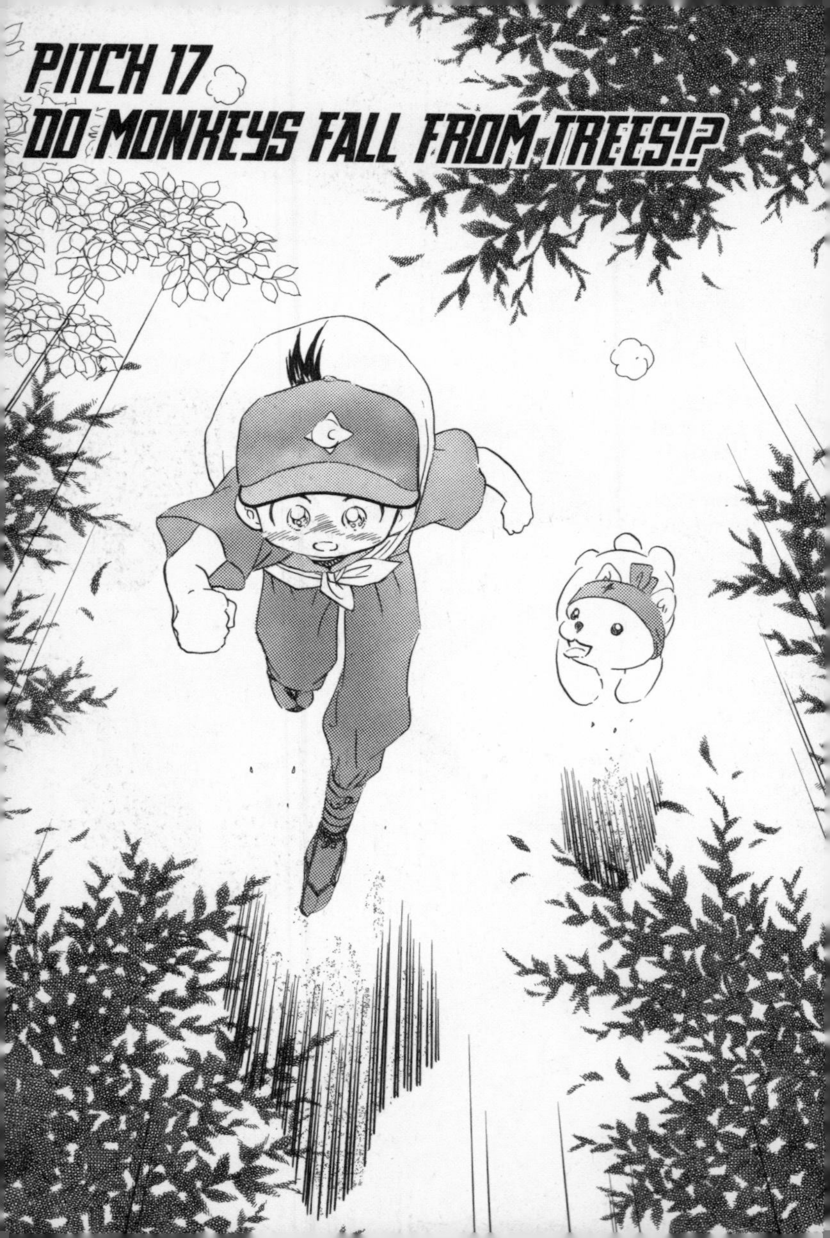
PITCH 17
DO MONKEYS FALL FROM TREES!?

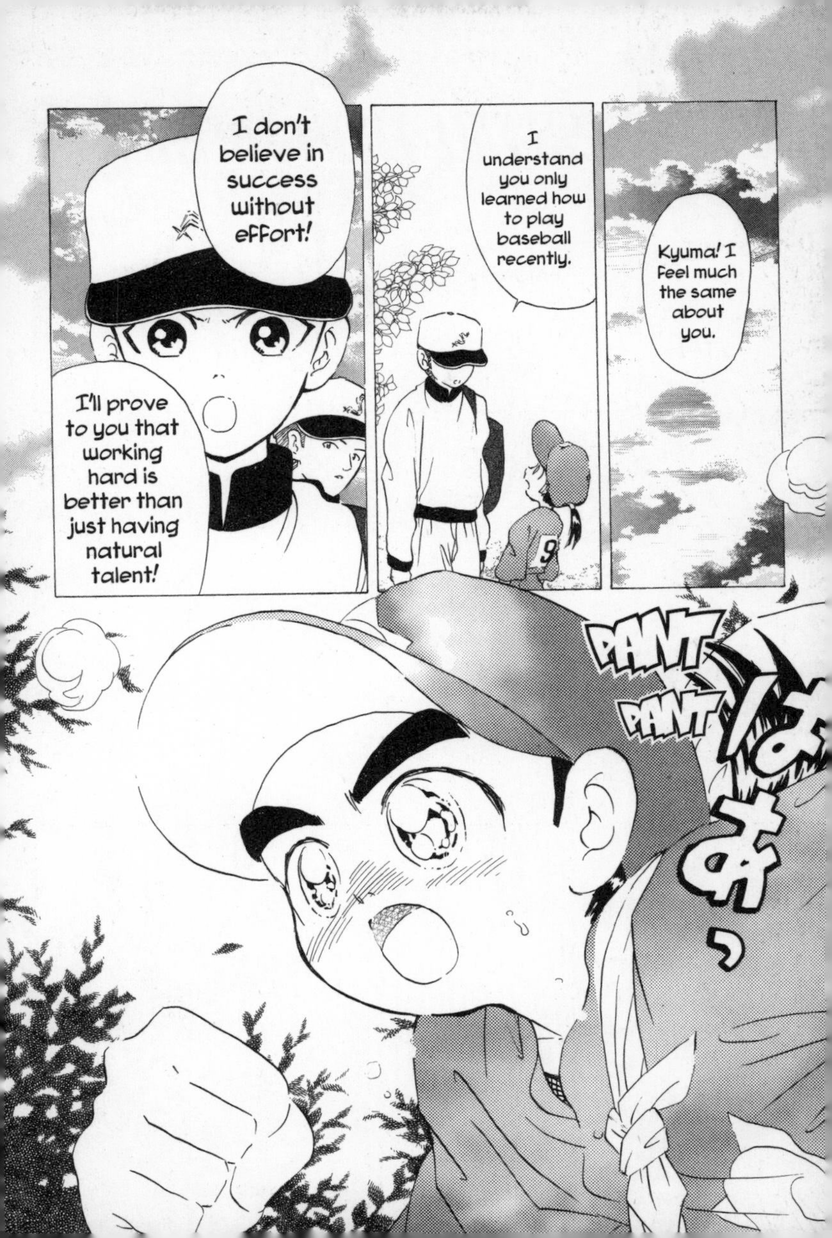
Kyuma! I feel much the same about you.
I understand you only learned how to play baseball recently.
I don't believe in success without effort!
I'll prove to you that working hard is better than just having natural talent!
PANT
PANT
はあっ

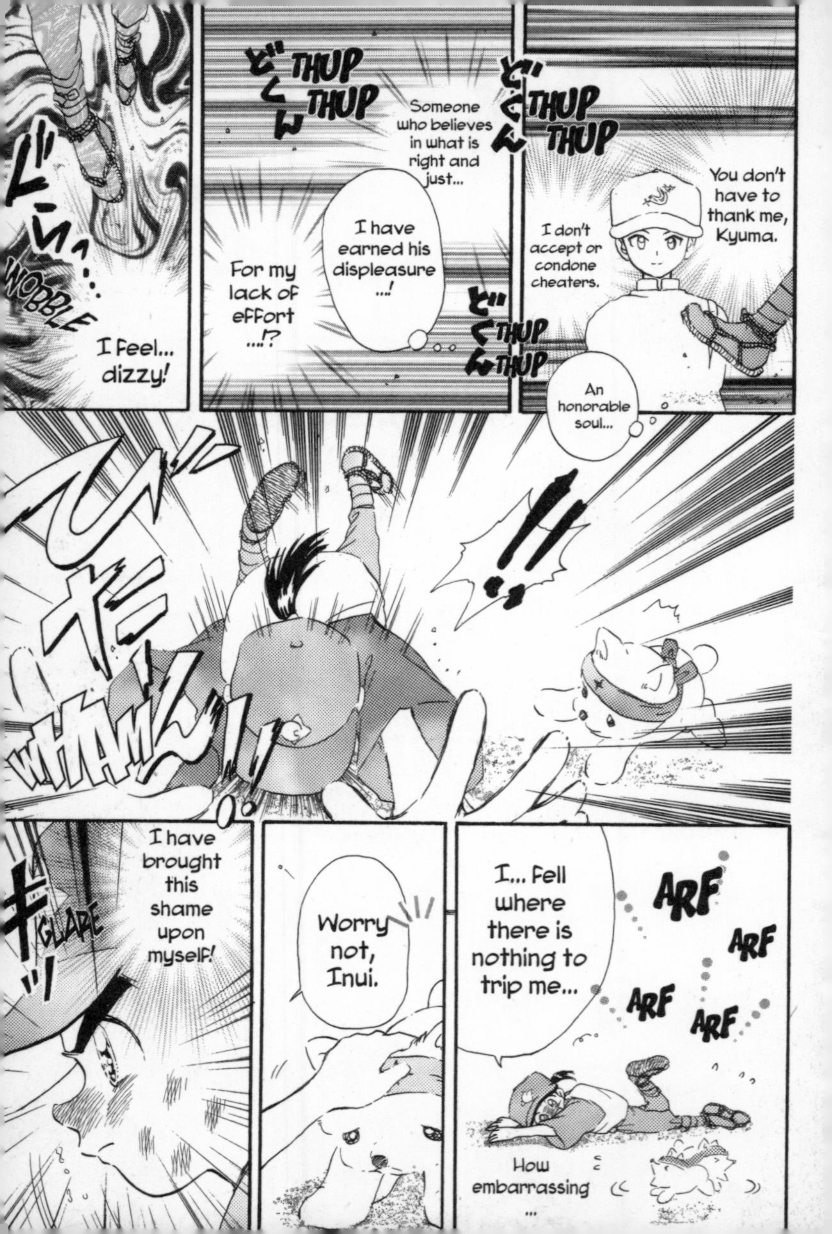

どくん THUP THUP
You don't have to thank me, Kyuma.
I don't accept or condone cheaters.
どくん THUP THUP
An honorable soul...
どくん THUP THUP
Someone who believes in what is right and just...
I have earned his displeasure ...!
For my lack of effort ...!?
WOBBLE
I feel... dizzy!
!!..
WHAM!!
ARF ARF ARF ARF
I... fell where there is nothing to trip me...
How embarrassing ...
Worry not, Inui.
GLARE
I have brought this shame upon myself!

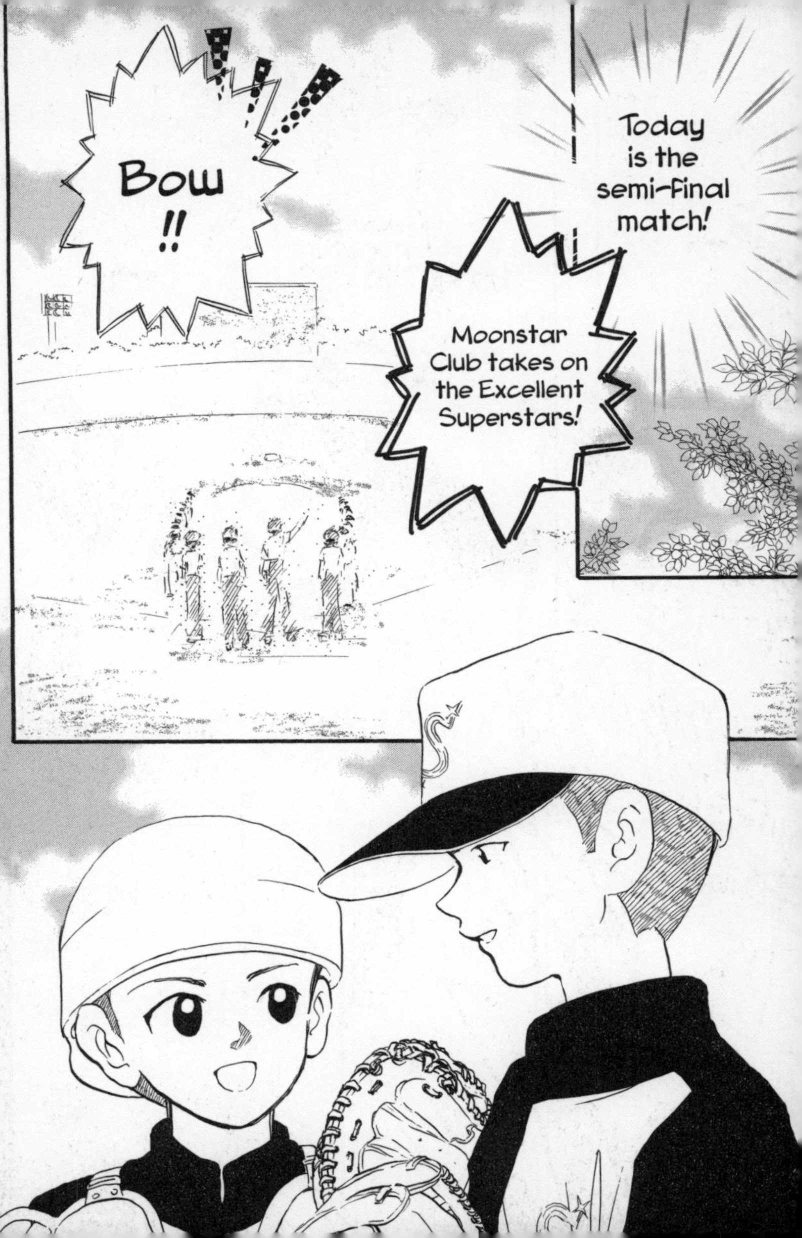
Today is the semi-final match!
Moonstar Club takes on the Excellent Superstars!
Bow !!

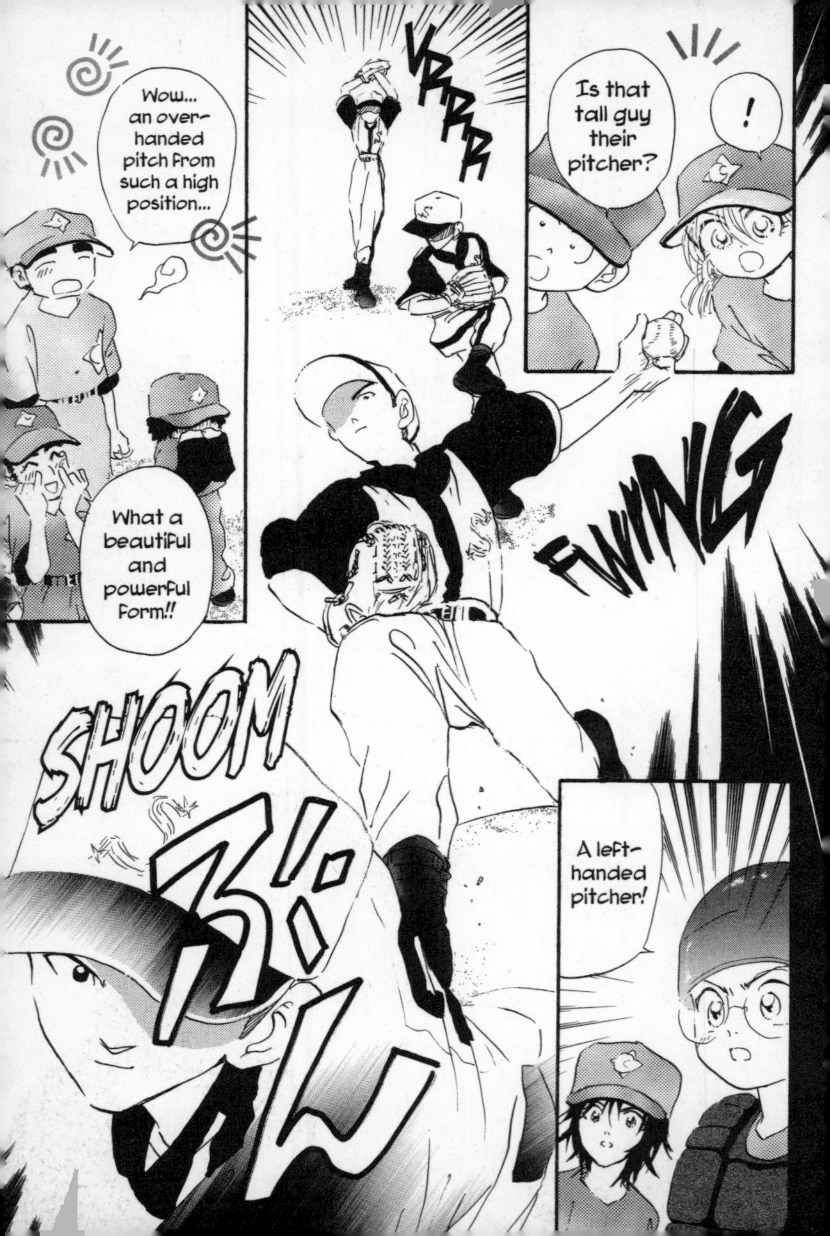
!
Is that tall guy their pitcher?
Wow... an over-handed pitch from such a high position...
What a beautiful and powerful form!!
FWING
A left-handed pitcher!
SHOOM

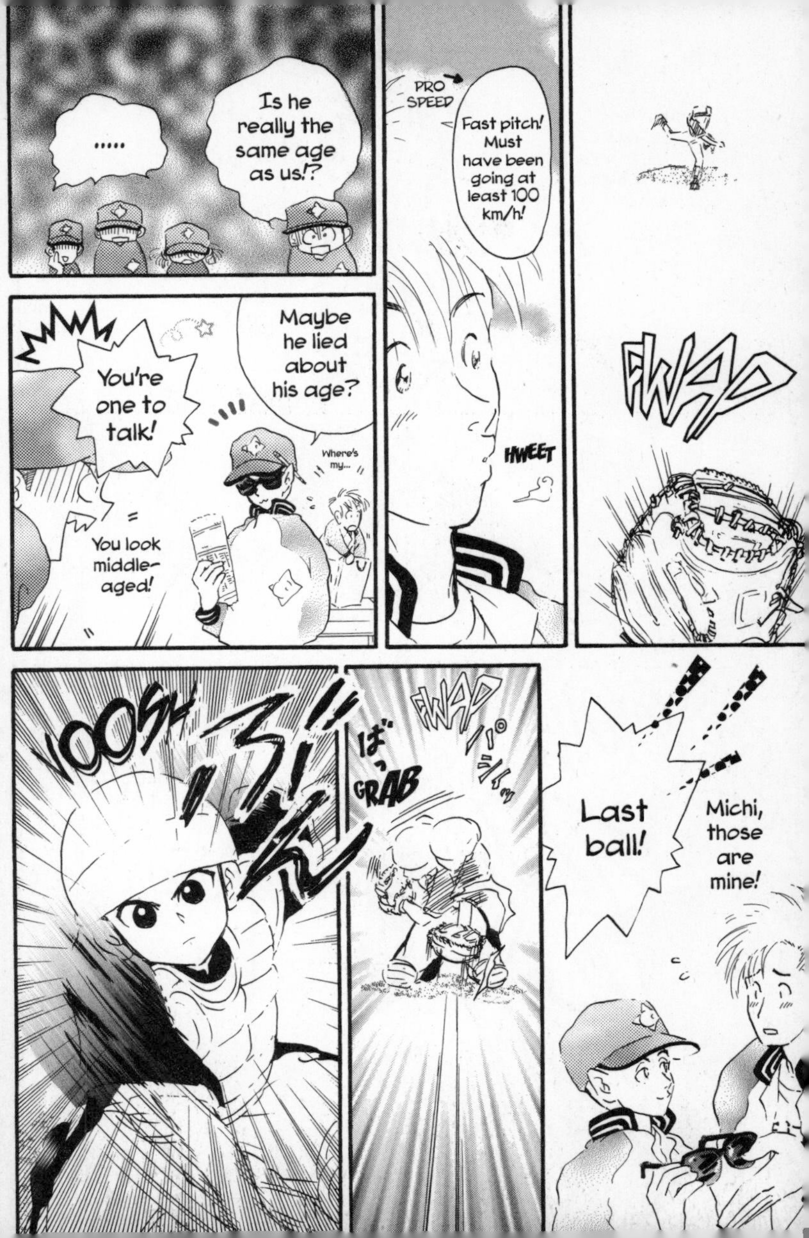
FWAP
PRO SPEED
Fast pitch! Must have been going at least 100 km/h!
HWEET
Is he really the same age as us!?
.....
Maybe he lied about his age?
You're one to talk!
Where's my...
= You look middle-aged!
Michi, those are mine!
Last ball!
FWAP
ばっ
GRAB
VOOSH

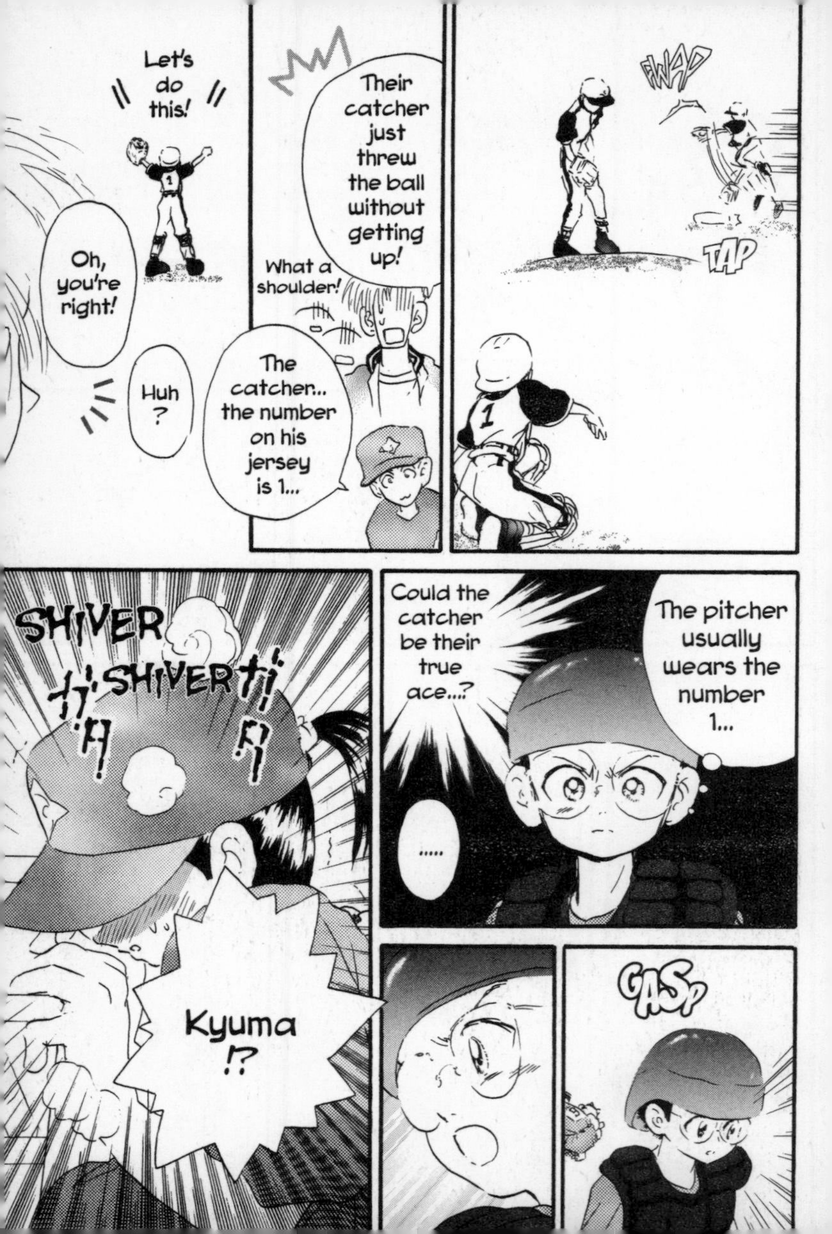

WAP
TAP
Their catcher just threw the ball without getting up!
What a shoulder!
The catcher... the number on his jersey is 1...
Let's do this!
Oh, you're right!
Huh?
The pitcher usually wears the number 1...
Could the catcher be their true ace...?
.....
GASP
SHIVER
SHIVER
Kyuma!?

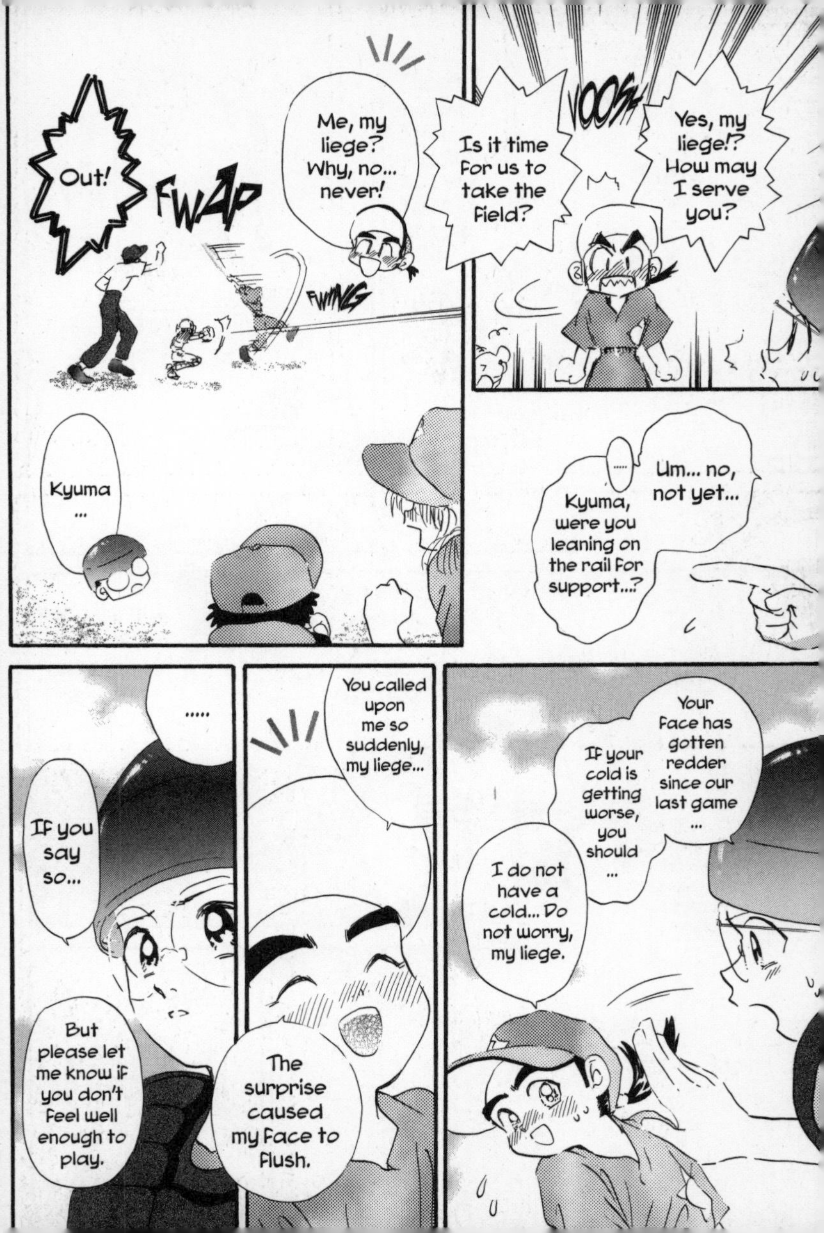
Yes, my liege!? How may I serve you?
VOOSH
Is it time for us to take the field?
Me, my liege? Why, no... never!
FWAP
Out!
FWING
Um... no, not yet...
.....
Kyuma, were you leaning on the rail for support...?
Kyuma ...
Your face has gotten redder since our last game ...
If your cold is getting worse, you should ...
I do not have a cold... Do not worry, my liege.
You called upon me so suddenly, my liege...
The surprise caused my face to flush.
.....
If you say so...
But please let me know if you don't feel well enough to play.

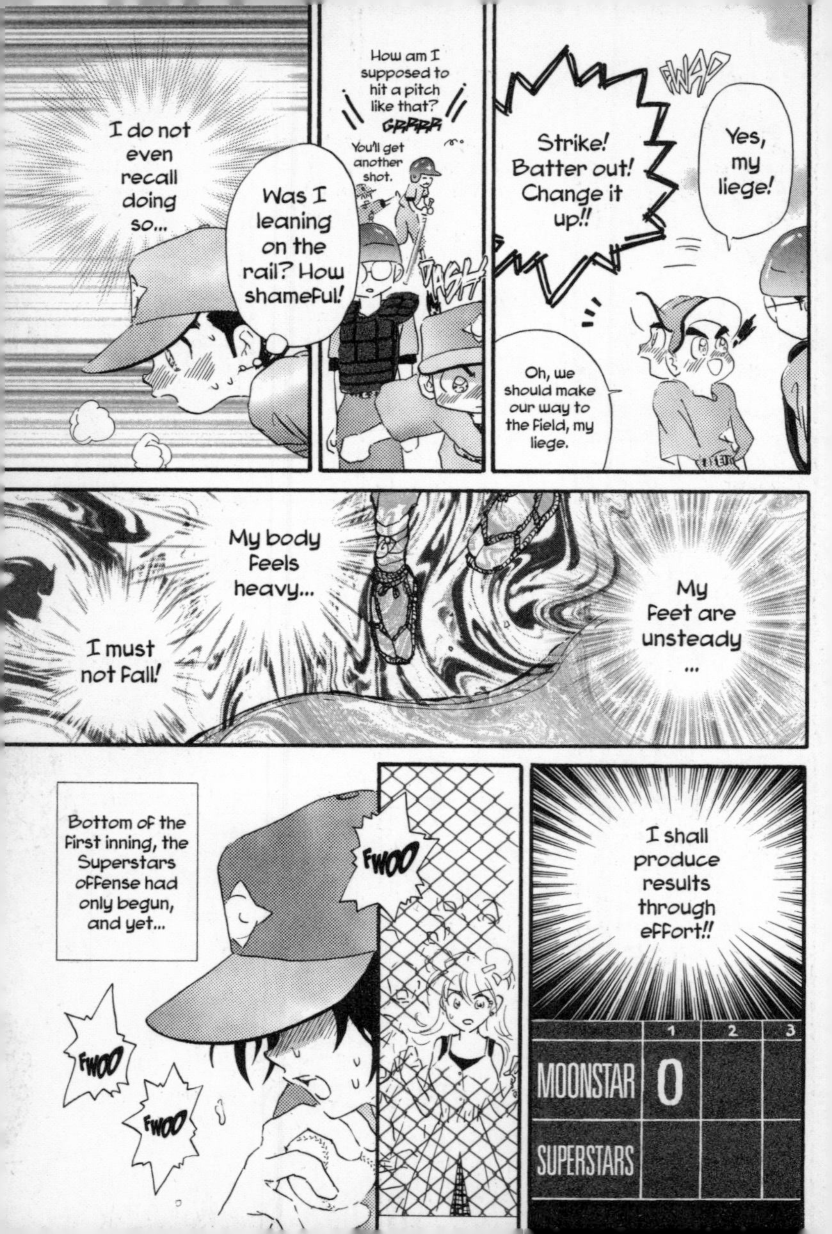
FWAP
Strike! Batter out! Change it up!!
Yes, my liege!
Oh, we should make our way to the field, my liege.
How am I supposed to hit a pitch like that?
GRRRR
You'll get another shot.
Was I leaning on the rail? How shameful!
DASH
I do not even recall doing so...
My feet are unsteady ...
My body feels heavy...
I must not fall!
I shall produce results through effort!!
1 2 3
MOONSTAR 0
SUPERSTARS
FWOO
Bottom of the first inning, the Superstars offense had only begun, and yet...
FWOO
FWOO

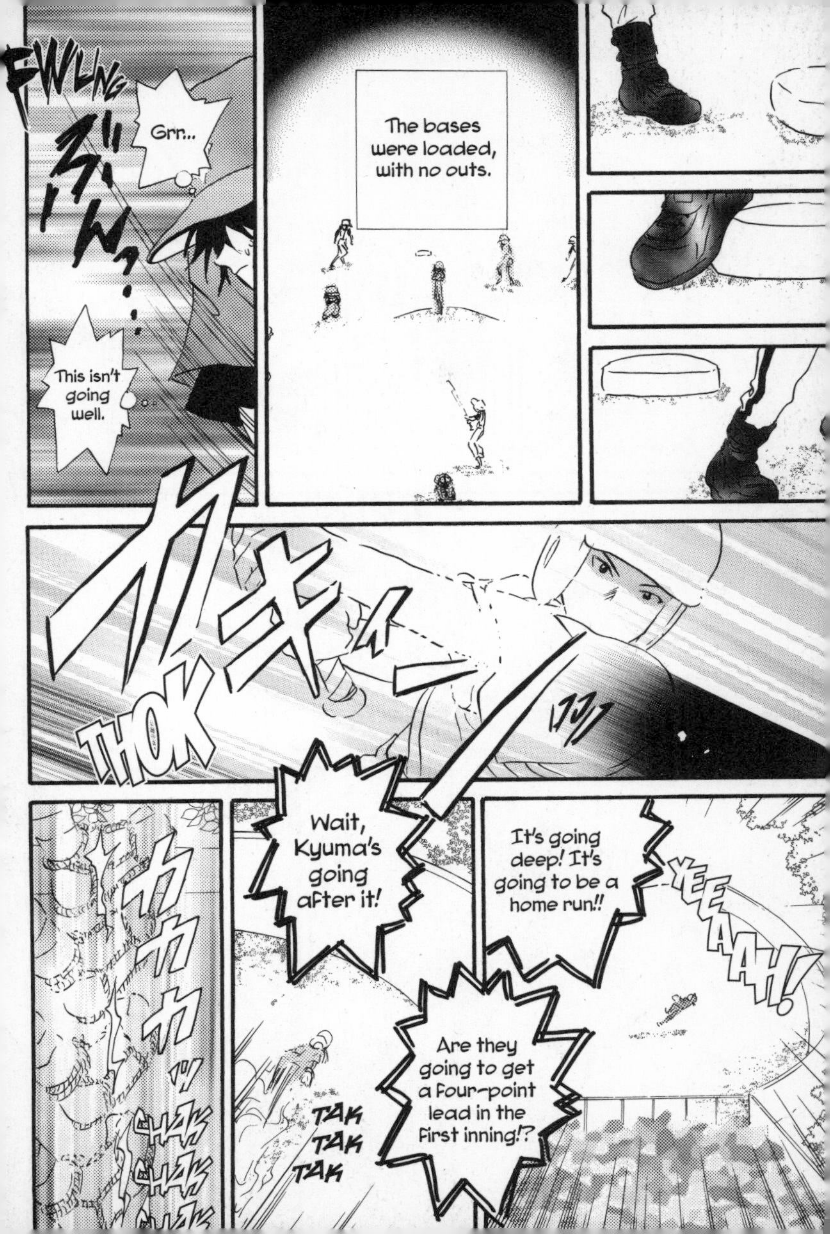
The bases were loaded, with no outs.
FWUNG
Grr...
This isn't going well.
THOK
It's going deep! It's going to be a home run!!
YEEAAAH!
Wait, Kyuma's going after it!
Are they going to get a four-point lead in the first inning!?
TAK TAK TAK
CHAK CHAK

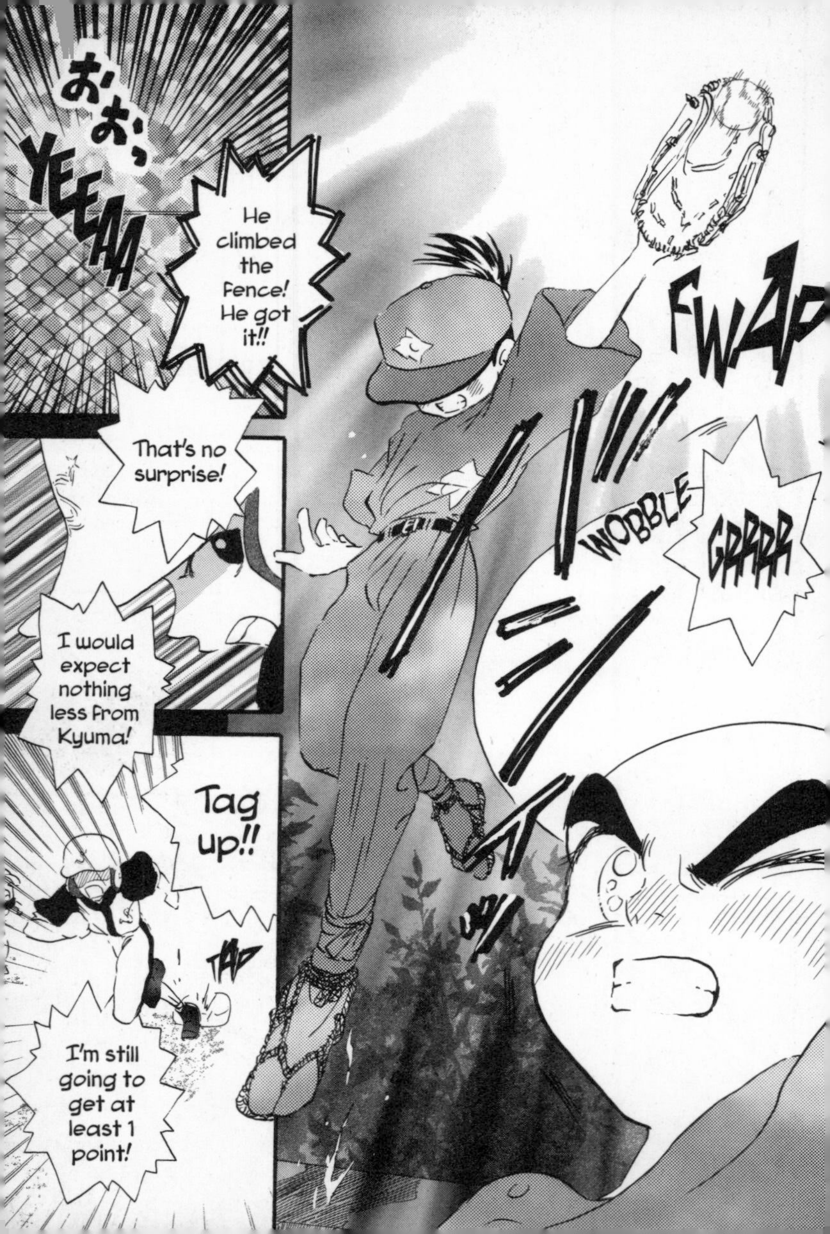
FWAP
WOBBLE
GRRRR
おおっ
YEEAAA
He climbed the fence! He got it!!
That's no surprise!
I would expect nothing less from Kyuma!
Tag up!!
TAP
I'm still going to get at least 1 point!

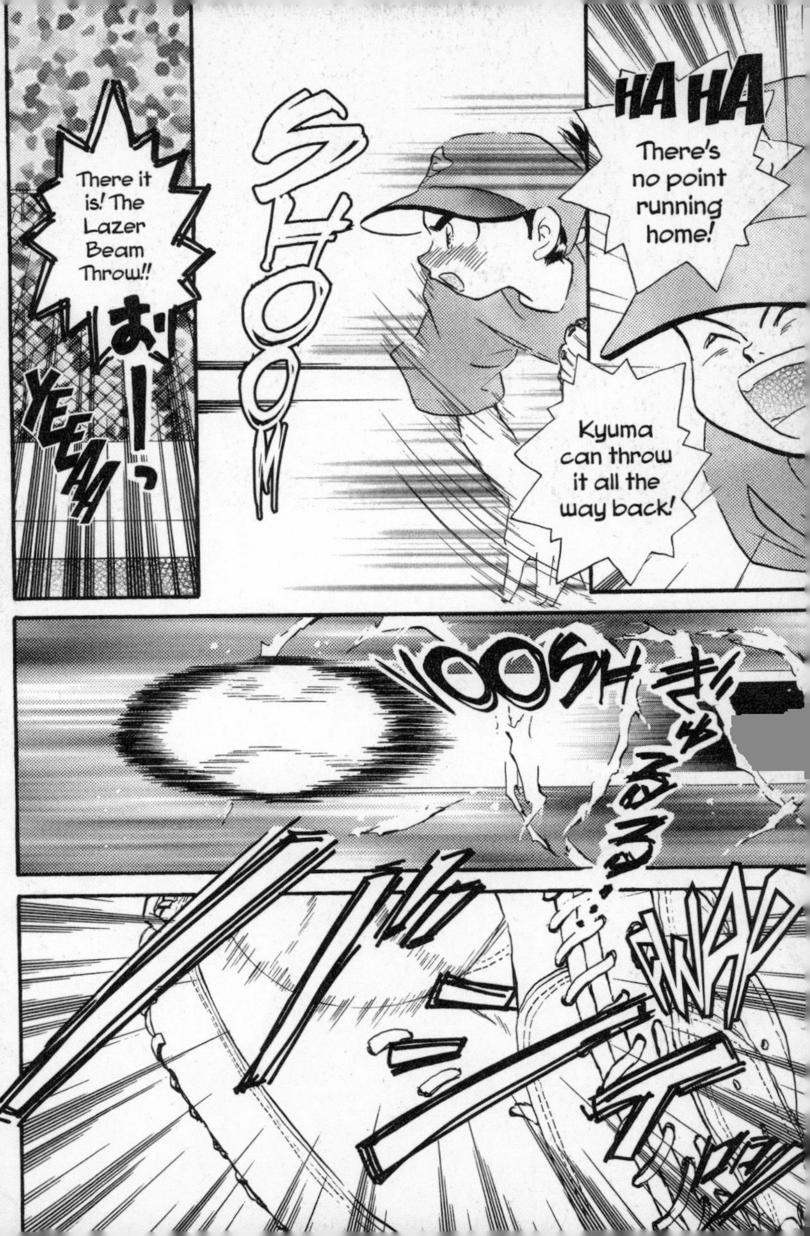
HA HA
There's no point running home!
Kyuma can throw it all the way back!
SHOOOM
There it is! The Lazer Beam Throw!!
YEEAAH
WOOSH

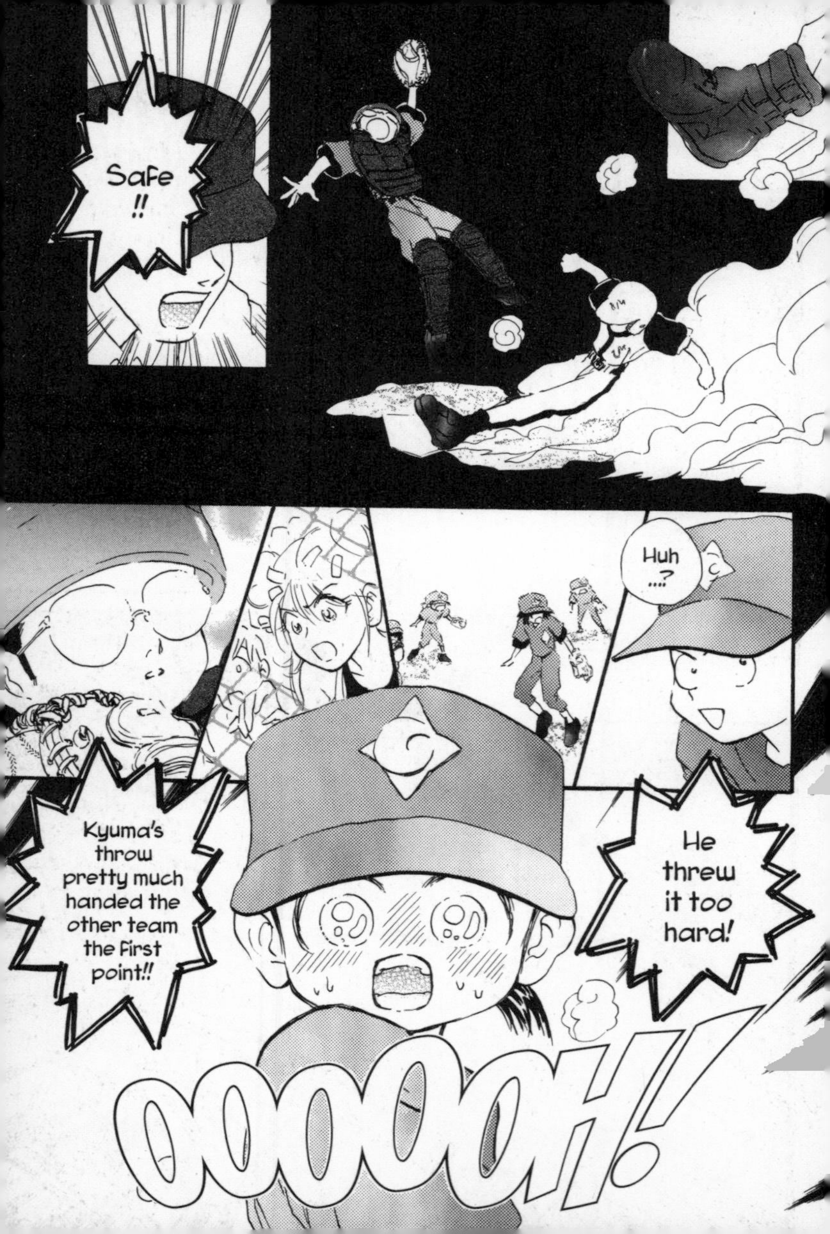
Safe !!
Huh ...?
He threw it too hard!
Kyuma's throw pretty much handed the other team the first point!!
OOOOOH!

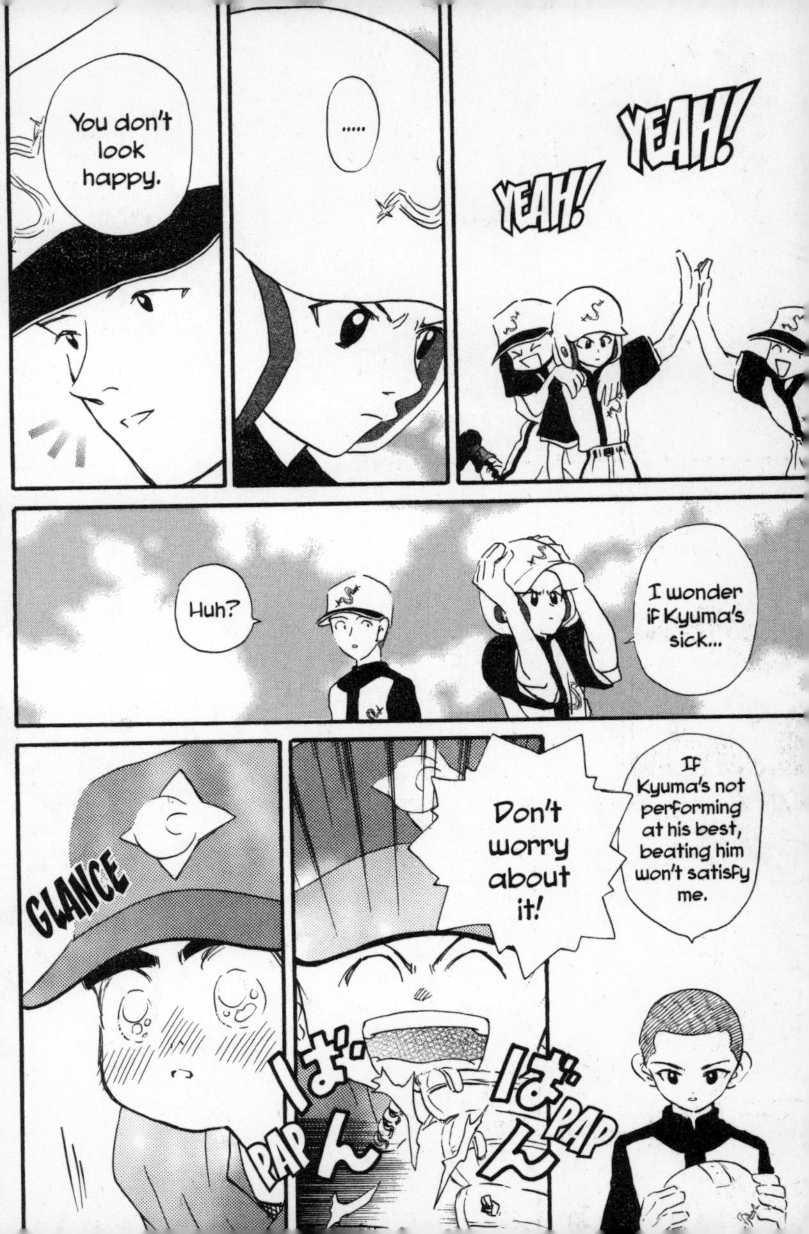
YEAH!
YEAH!
.....
You don't look happy.
I wonder if Kyuma's sick...
Huh?
If Kyuma's not performing at his best, beating him won't satisfy me.
Don't worry about it!
ばん
PAP
ばん
PAP
GLANCE

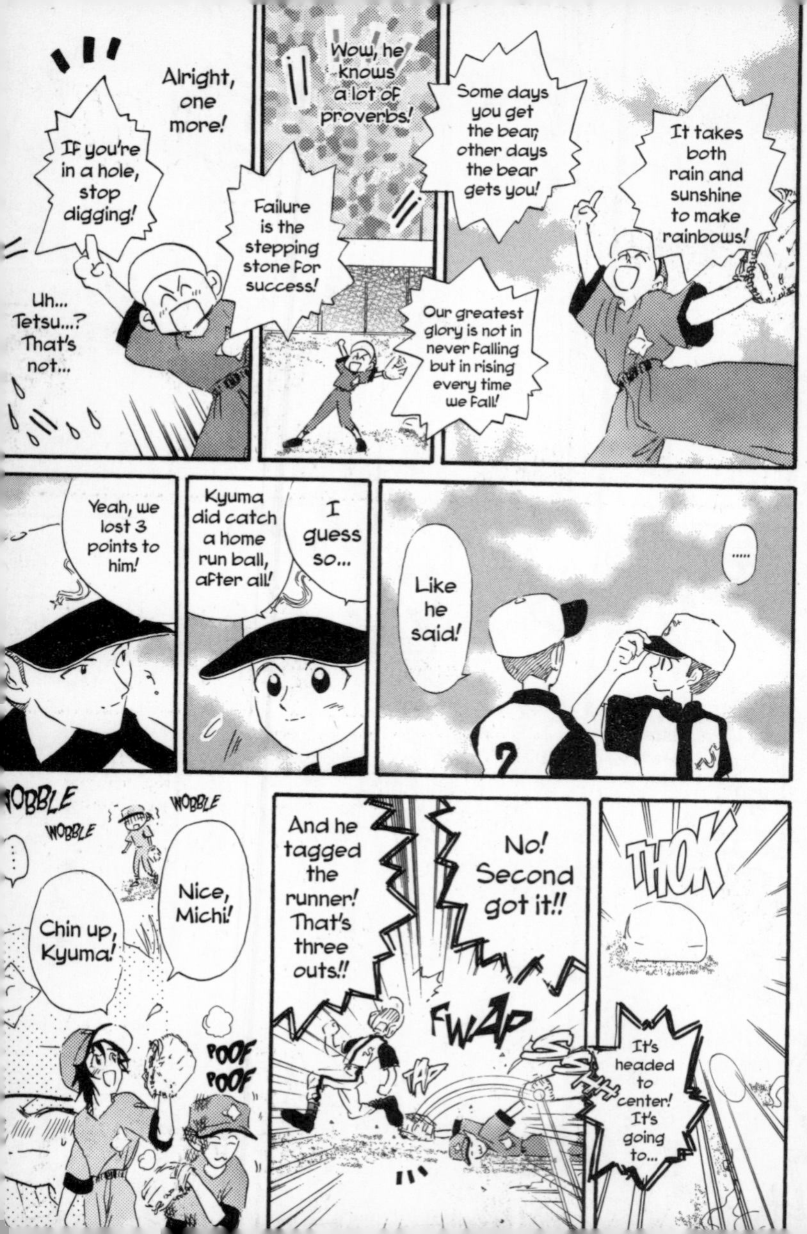
It takes both rain and sunshine to make rainbows!
Some days you get the bear, other days the bear gets you!
Our greatest glory is not in never falling but in rising every time we fall!
Wow, he knows a lot of proverbs!
Failure is the stepping stone for success!
Alright, one more!
If you're in a hole, stop digging!
Uh... Tetsu...? That's not...
.....
Like he said!
I guess so...
Kyuma did catch a home run ball, after all!
Yeah, we lost 3 points to him!
THOK
It's headed to center! It's going to...
No! Second got it!!
And he tagged the runner! That's three outs!!
FWAP
TAP
WOBBLE
WOBBLE
WOBBLE
Nice, Michi!
...
Chin up, Kyuma!
POOF POOF

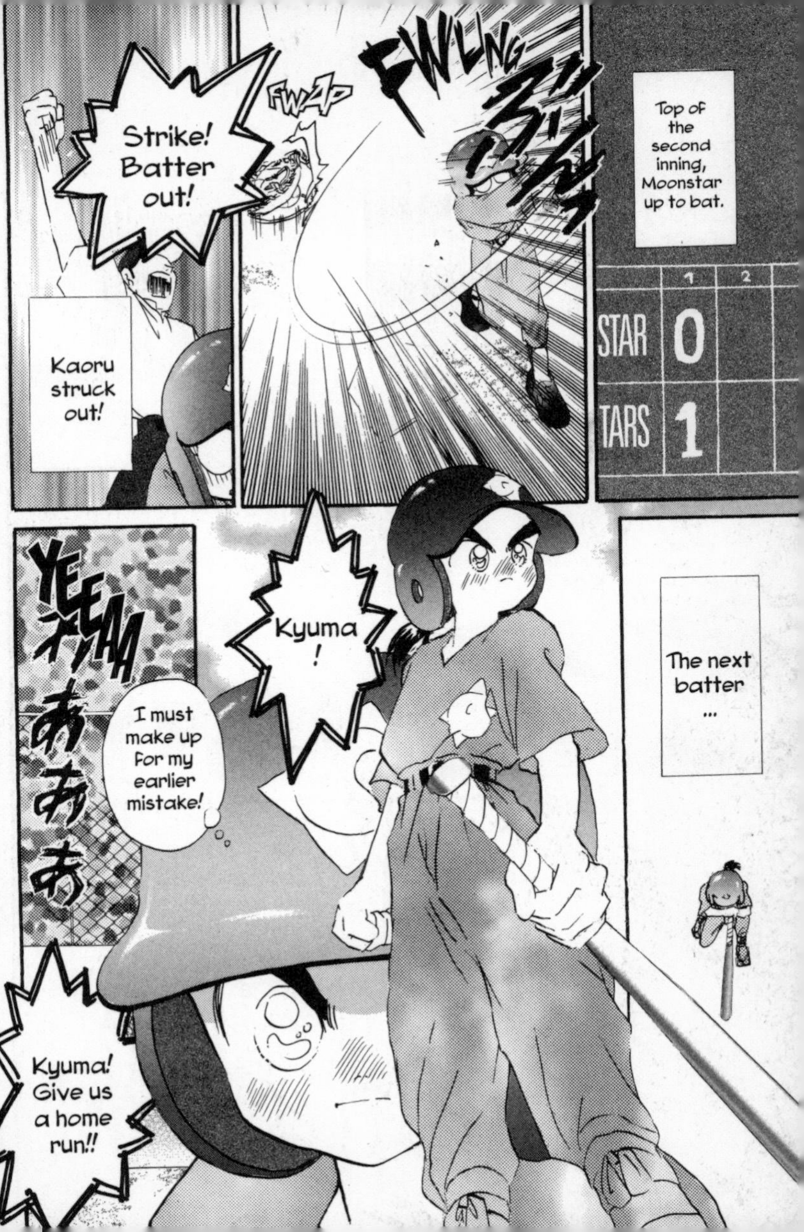
Top of the second inning, Moonstar up to bat.
1
2
STAR
0
TARS
1
FWUNG
FWAP
Strike! Batter out!
Kaoru struck out!
The next batter ...
Kyuma!
I must make up for my earlier mistake!
YEEAAA
Kyuma! Give us a home run!!

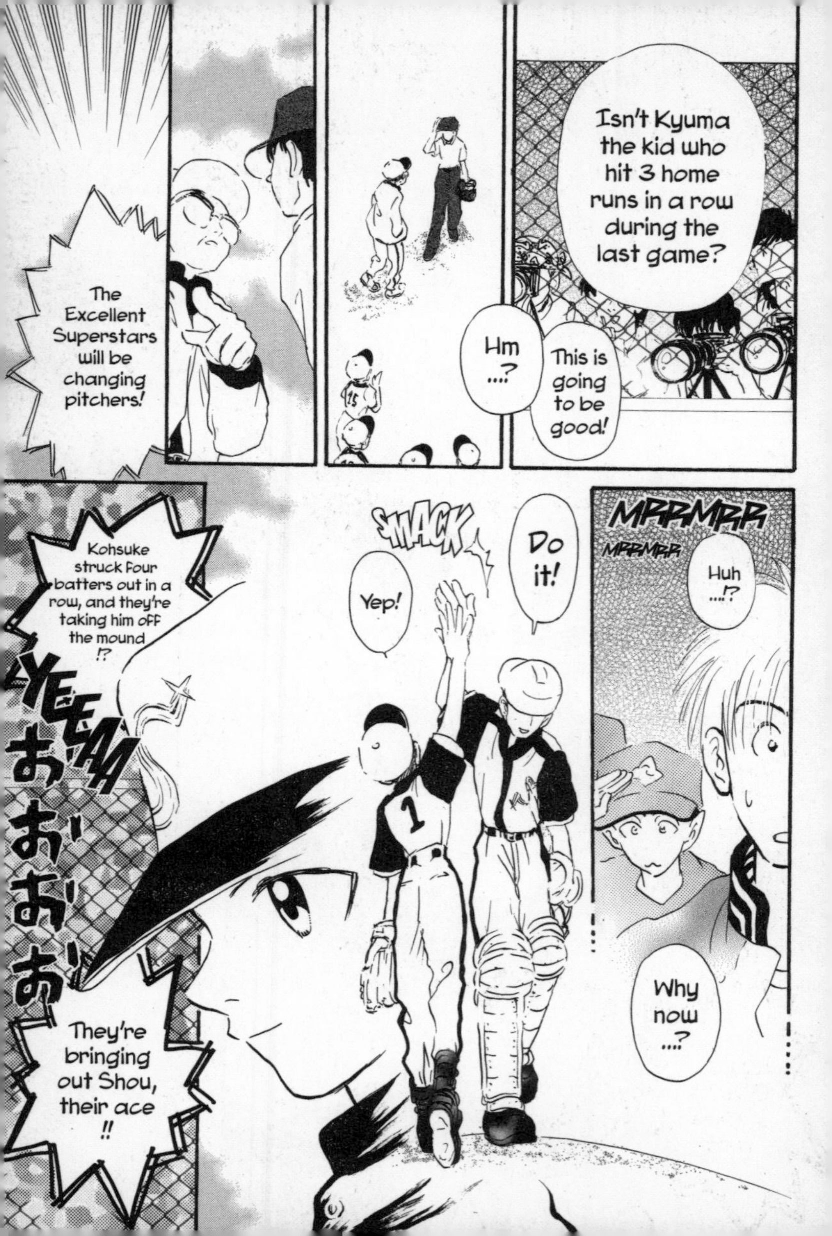
Isn't Kyuma the kid who hit 3 home runs in a row during the last game?
This is going to be good!
Hm ...?
The Excellent Superstars will be changing pitchers!
MRRMRR
MRRMRR
Huh ...!?
Why now ...?
Do it!
SMACK
Yep!
Kohsuke struck four batters out in a row, and they're taking him off the mound !?
YEEAAA
おおおお
They're bringing out Shou, their ace !!

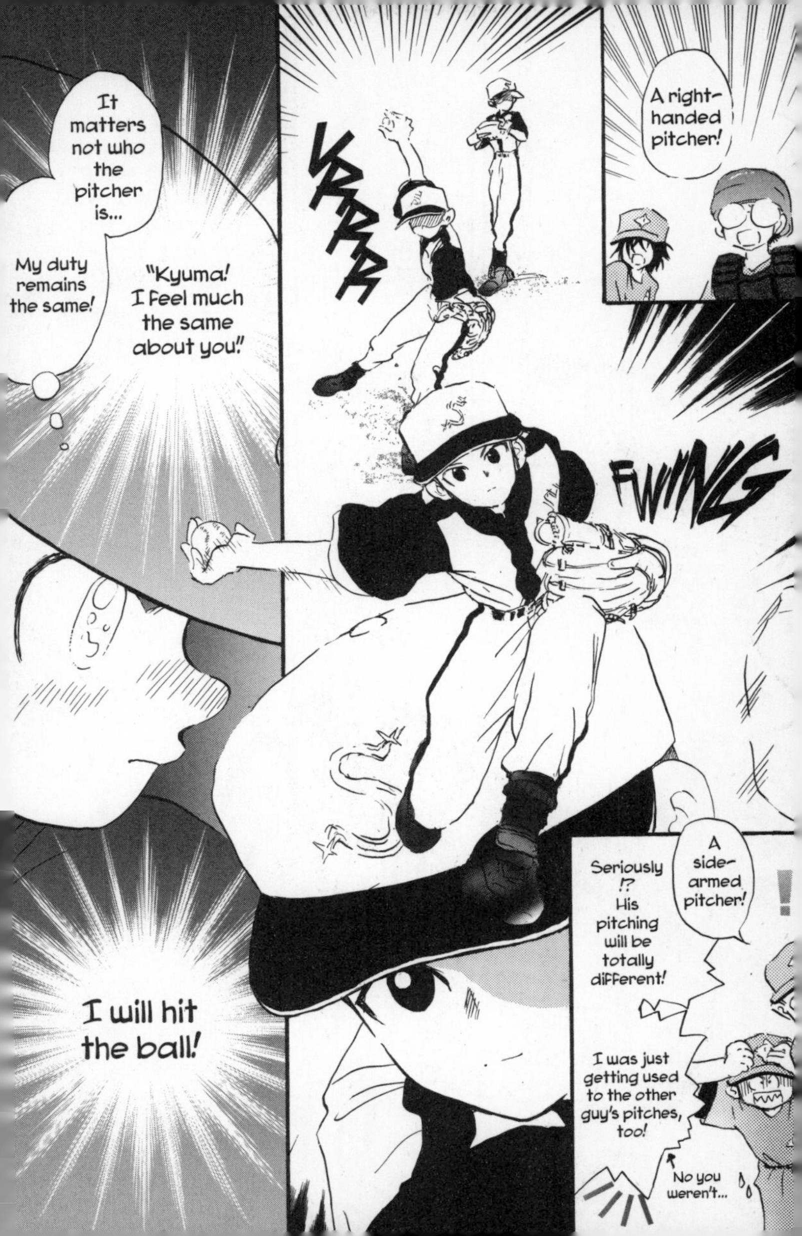
A right-handed pitcher!
VRRRR
FWING
A side-armed pitcher!
Seriously!? His pitching will be totally different!
I was just getting used to the other guy's pitches, too!
No you weren't...
It matters not who the pitcher is...
My duty remains the same!
"Kyuma! I feel much the same about you!"
I will hit the ball!

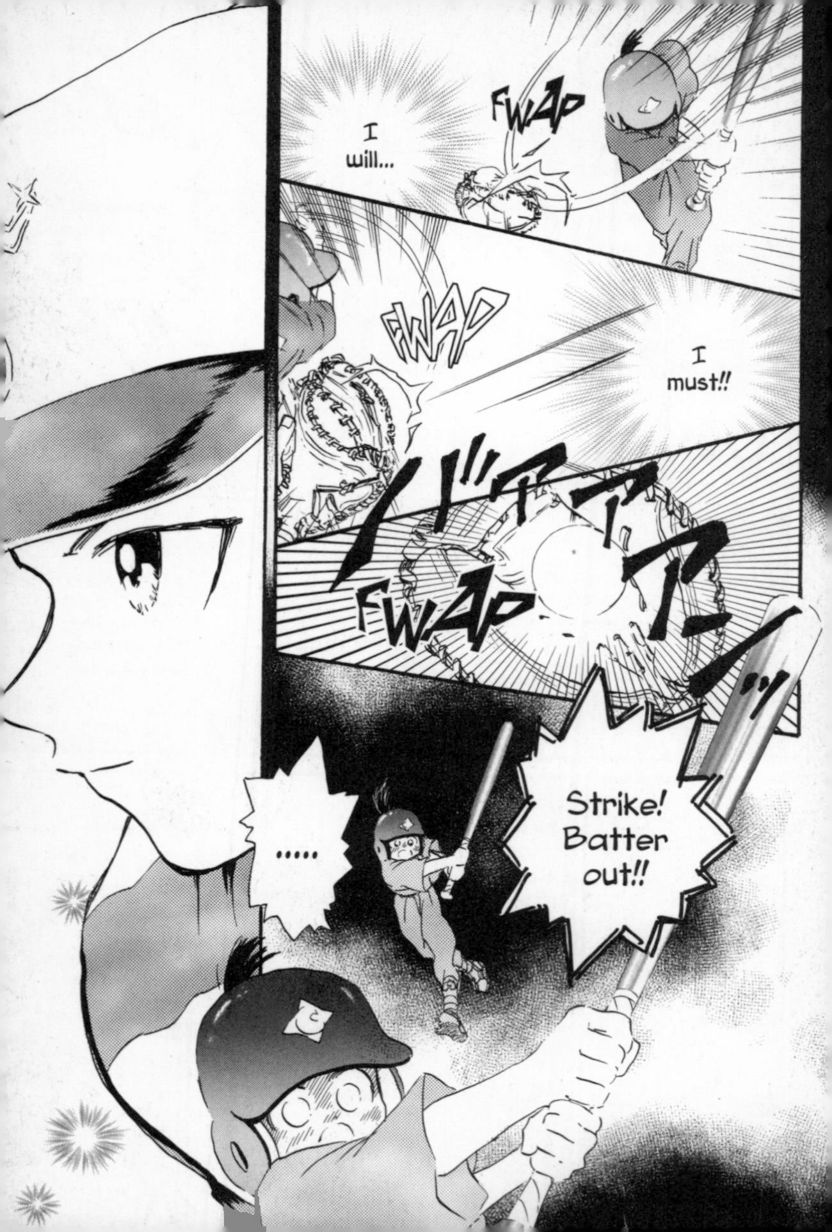
FWAP
I will...
FWAP
I must!!
FWAP
Strike! Batter out!!
.....

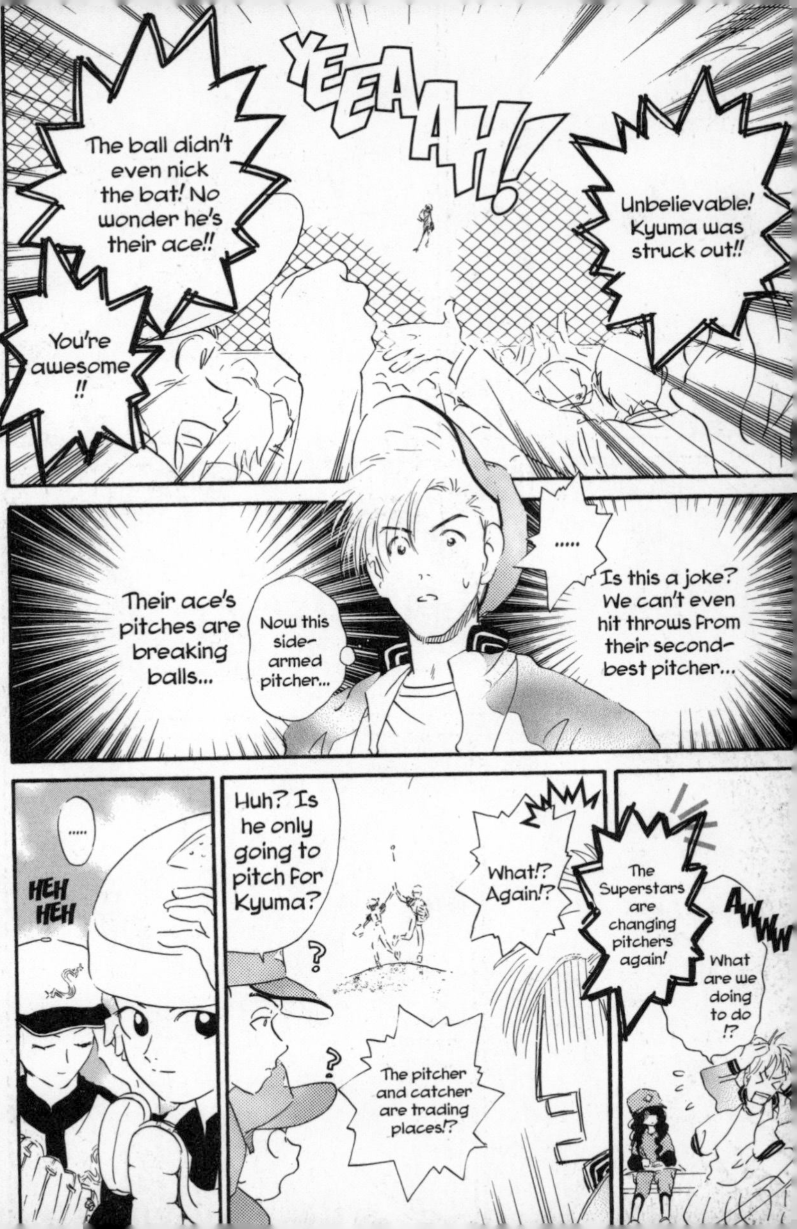
YEEAAH!
Unbelievable! Kyuma was struck out!!
The ball didn't even nick the bat! No wonder he's their ace!!
You're awesome !!
.....
Is this a joke? We can't even hit throws from their second-best pitcher...
Now this side-armed pitcher...
Their ace's pitches are breaking balls...
The Superstars are changing pitchers again!
AWWW
What are we doing to do !?
What!? Again!?
Huh? Is he only going to pitch for Kyuma?
?
?
The pitcher and catcher are trading places!?
.....
HEH HEH

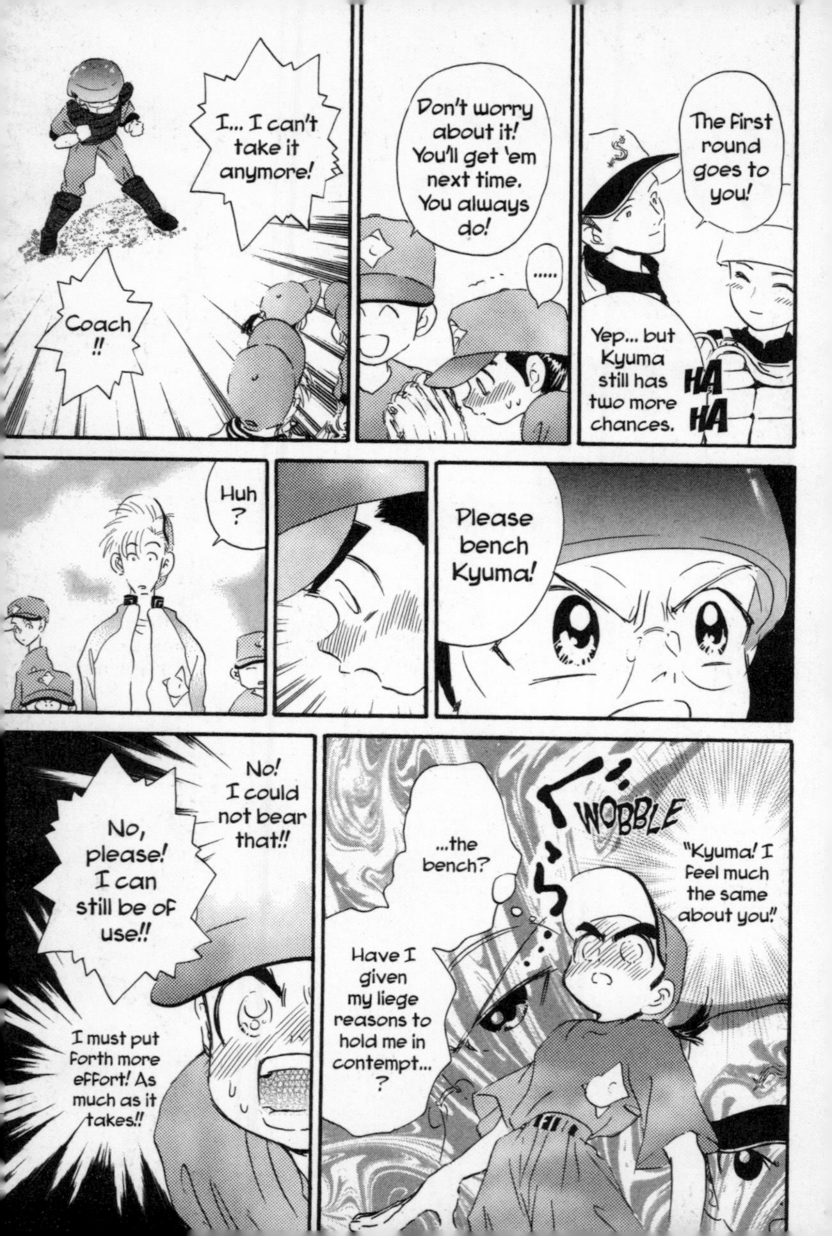
The first round goes to you!
Yep... but Kyuma still has two more chances.
HA HA
Don't worry about it! You'll get 'em next time. You always do!
.....
I... I can't take it anymore!
Coach!!
Please bench Kyuma!
Huh?
WOBBLE
"Kyuma! I feel much the same about you!"
...the bench?
Have I given my liege reasons to hold me in contempt...?
No! I could not bear that!!
No, please! I can still be of use!!
I must put forth more effort! As much as it takes!!

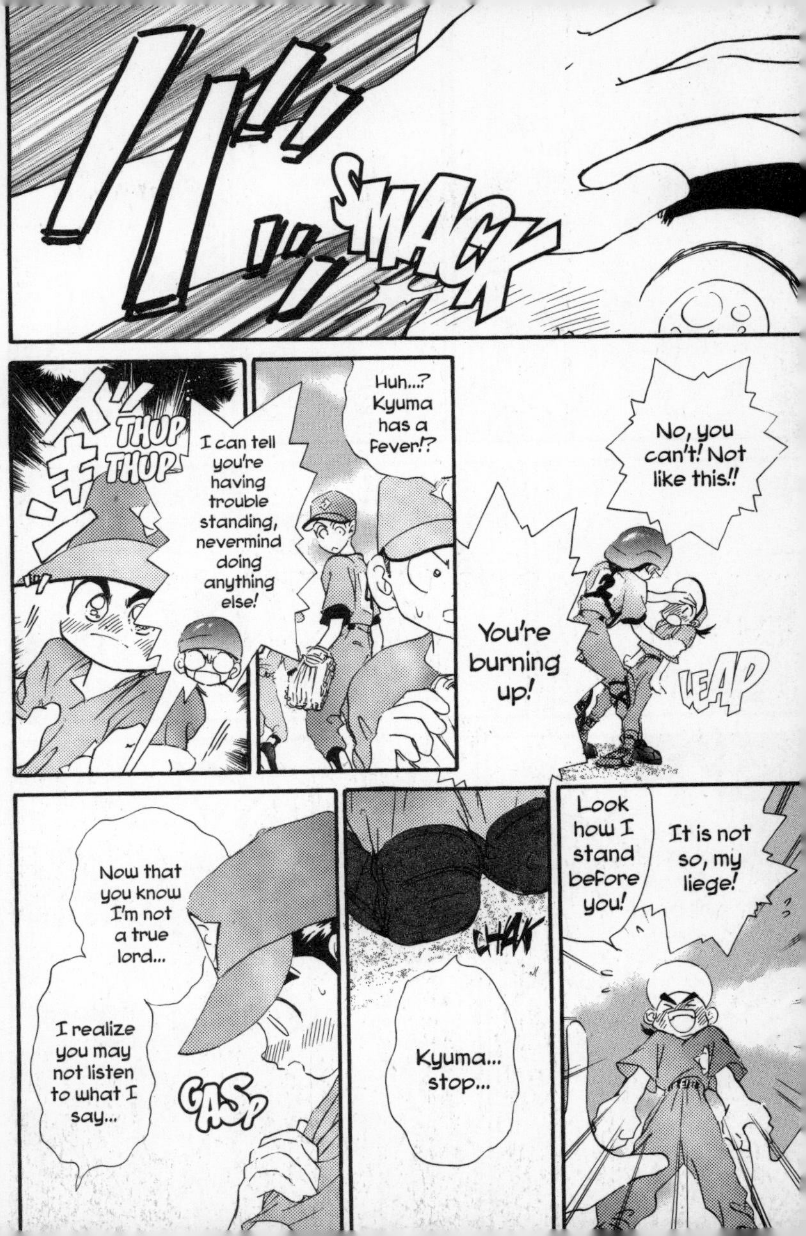
SWACK
No, you can't! Not like this!!
LEAP
You're burning up!
Huh...? Kyuma has a fever!?
THUP THUP
I can tell you're having trouble standing, nevermind doing anything else!
It is not so, my liege!
Look how I stand before you!
CHAK
Kyuma... stop...
Now that you know I'm not a true lord...
I realize you may not listen to what I say...
GASP

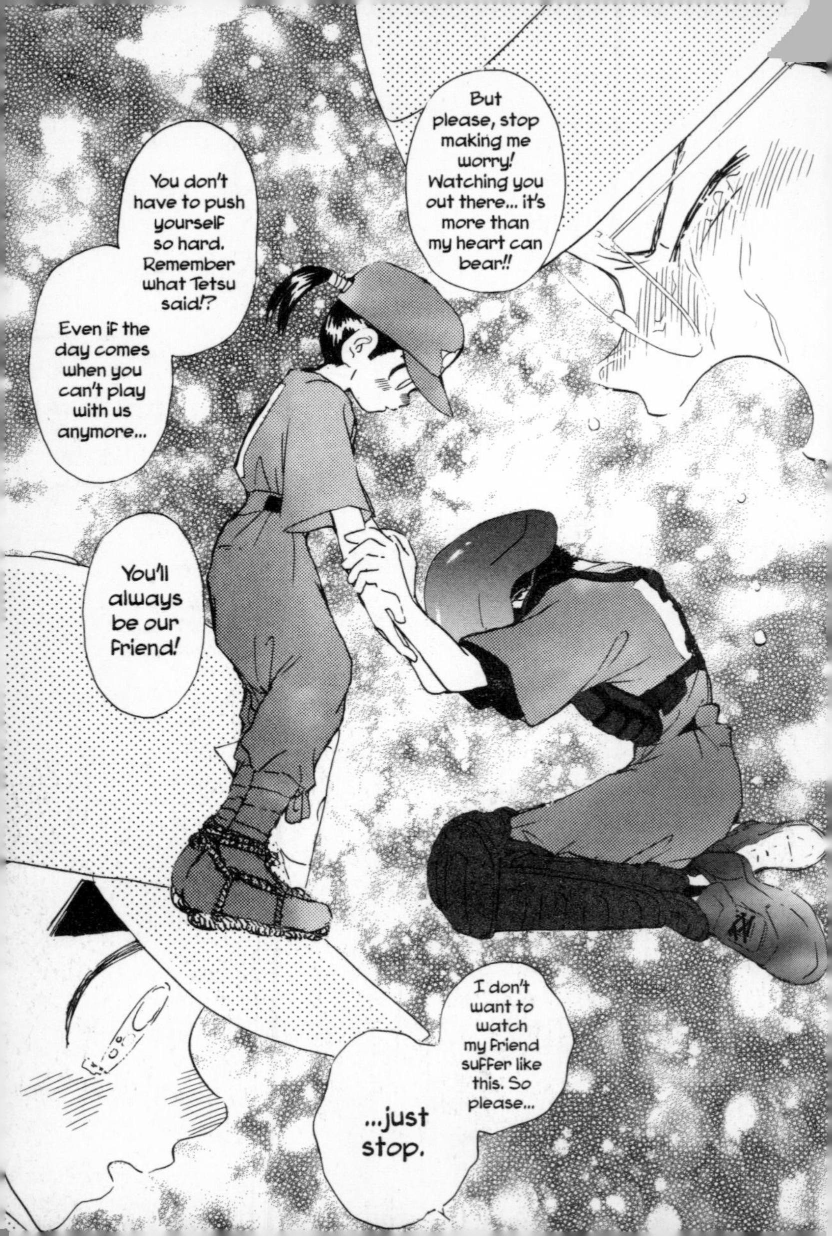
But please, stop making me worry! Watching you out there... it's more than my heart can bear!!
You don't have to push yourself so hard. Remember what Tetsu said!?
Even if the day comes when you can't play with us anymore...
You'll always be our friend!
I don't want to watch my friend suffer like this. So please...
...just stop.

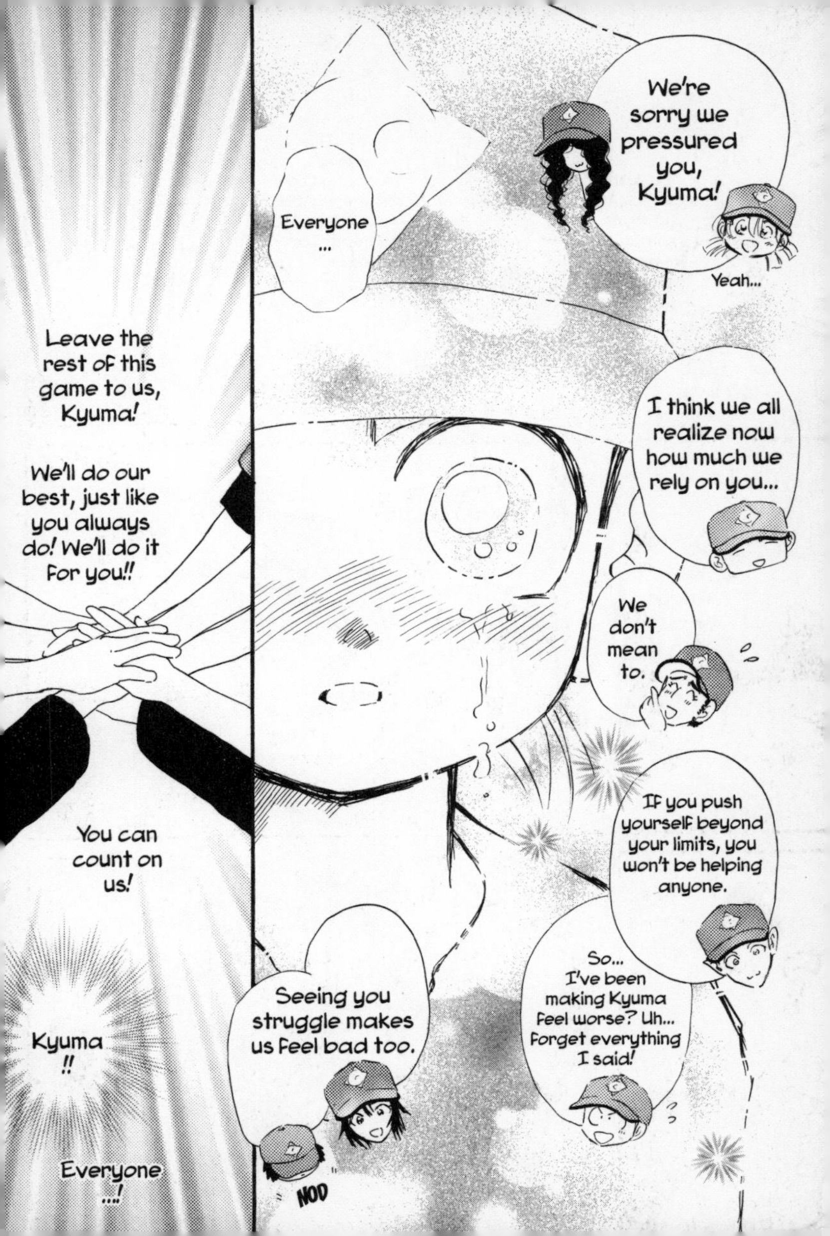
We're sorry we pressured you, Kyuma!
Yeah...
Everyone ...
I think we all realize now how much we rely on you...
We don't mean to.
If you push yourself beyond your limits, you won't be helping anyone.
So... I've been making Kyuma feel worse? Uh... Forget everything I said!
Seeing you struggle makes us feel bad too.
NOD
Leave the rest of this game to us, Kyuma!
We'll do our best, just like you always do! We'll do it for you!!
You can count on us!
Kyuma !!
Everyone ...!

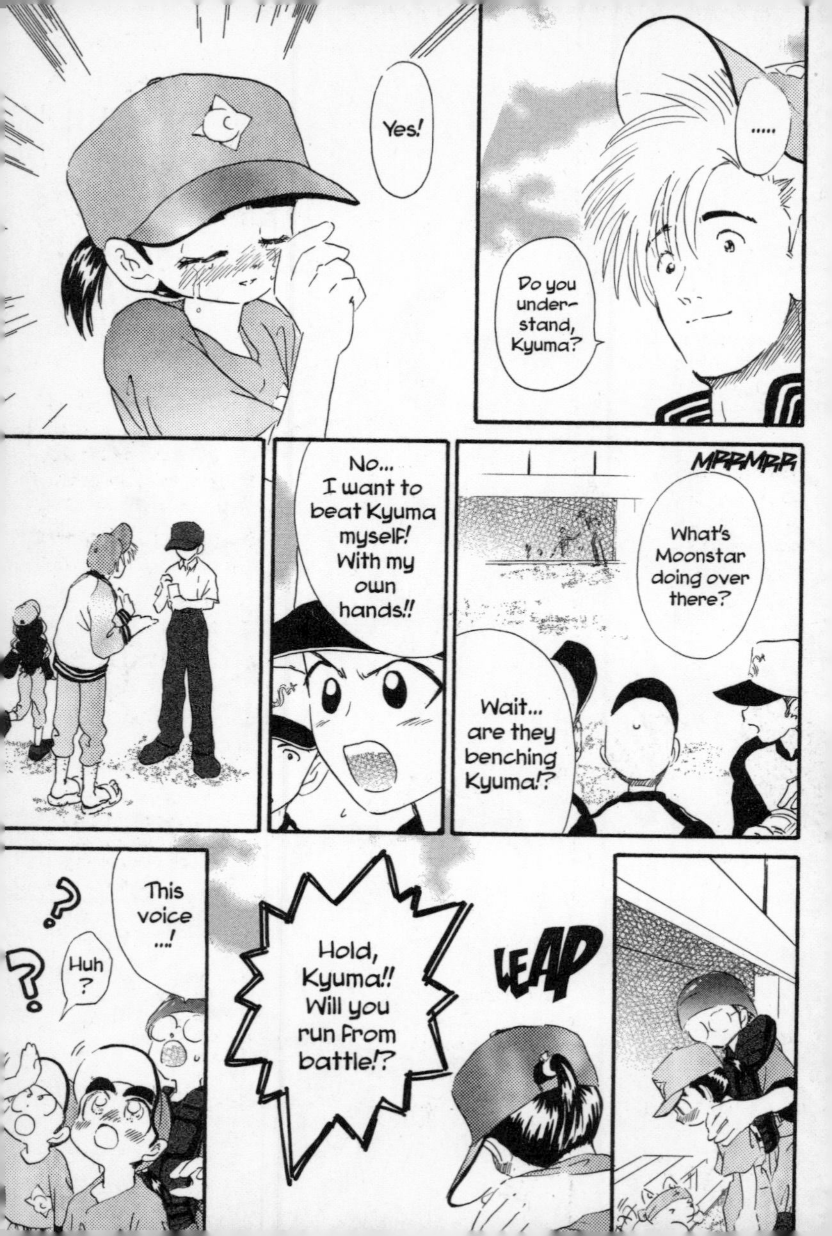
.....
Do you under-stand, Kyuma?
Yes!
MRRMRR
What's Moonstar doing over there?
Wait... are they benching Kyuma!?
No... I want to beat Kyuma myself! With my own hands!!
LEAP
Hold, Kyuma!! Will you run from battle!?
This voice ...!
Huh?
?
?

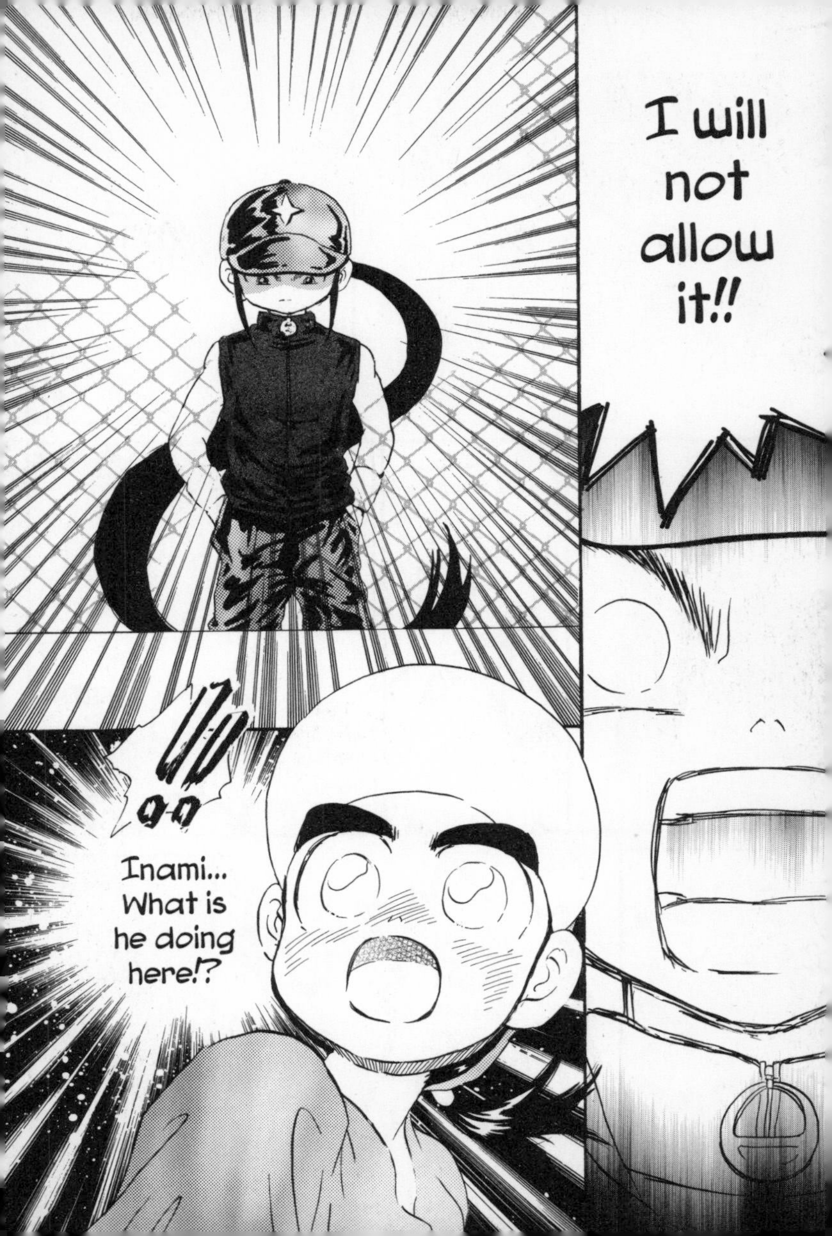
I will not allow it!!
Inami... What is he doing here!?

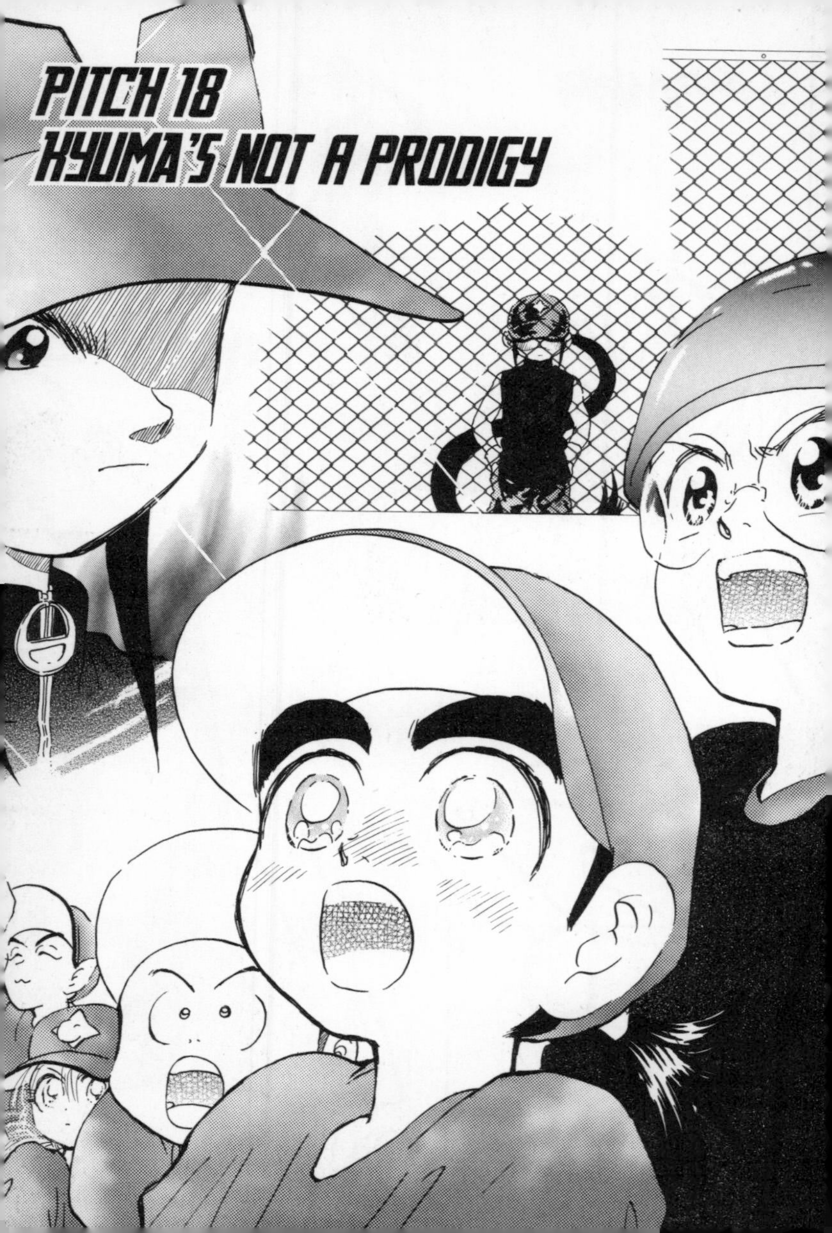
PITCH 18
KYUMA'S NOT A PRODIGY

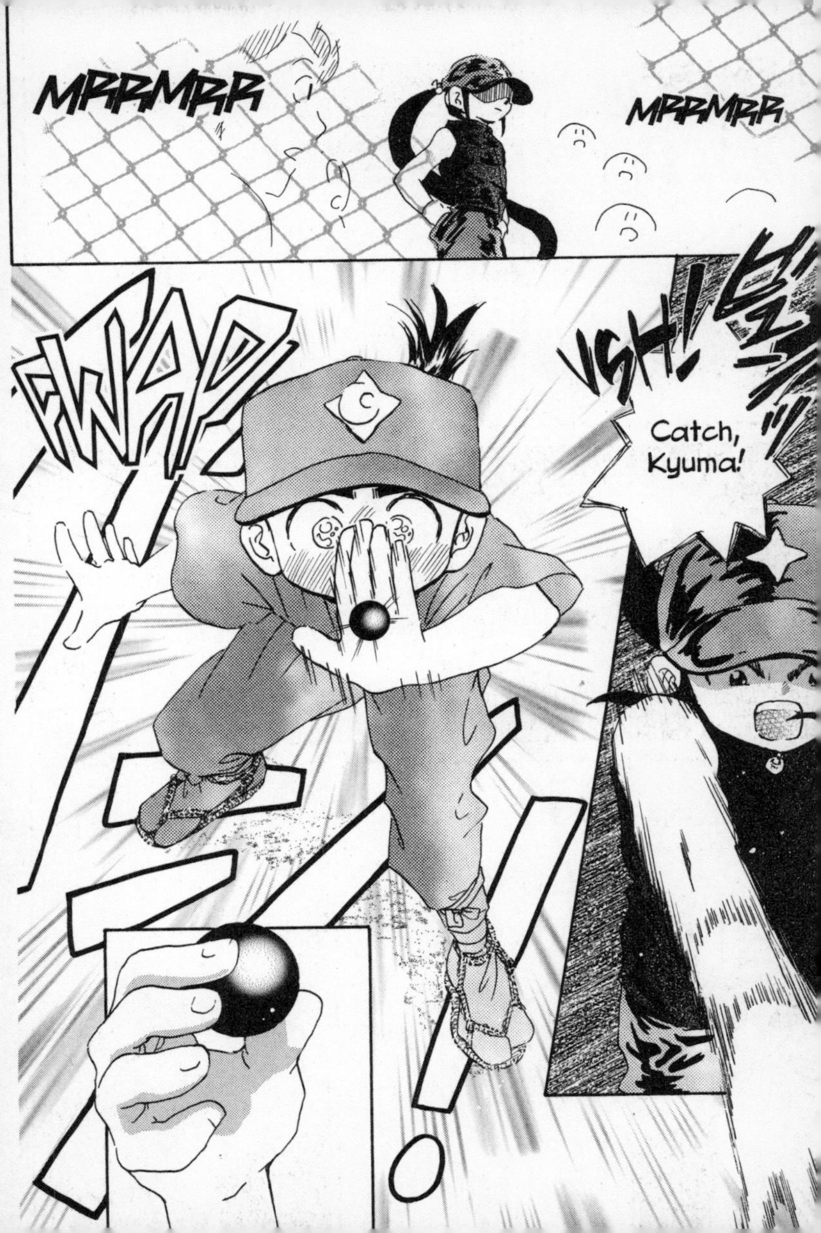
MRRMRR
MRRMRR
VSH!
Catch, Kyuma!
FWAP

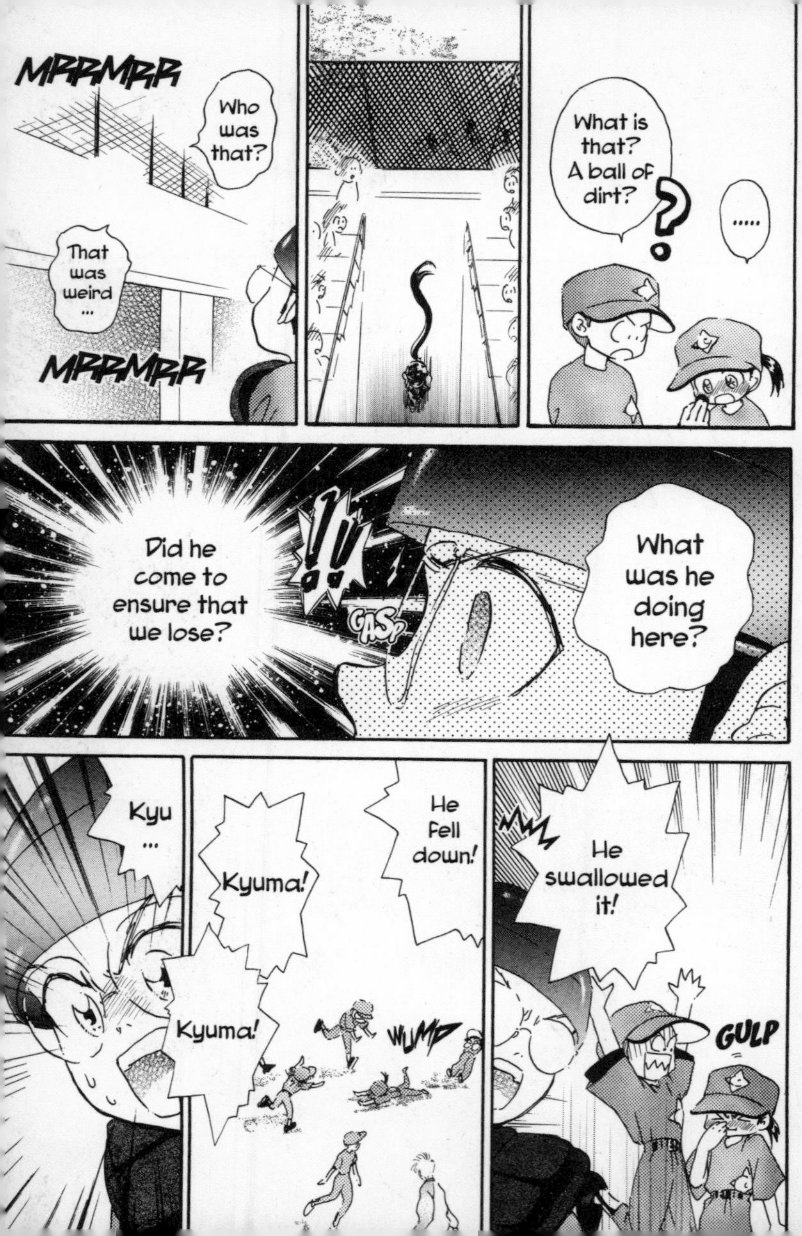

What is that? A ball of dirt?
?
.....
Who was that?
MRRMRR
That was weird ...
MRRMRR
What was he doing here?
!!
GASP
Did he come to ensure that we lose?
He swallowed it!
GULP
He fell down!
Kyuma!
WUMP
Kyu ...
Kyuma!

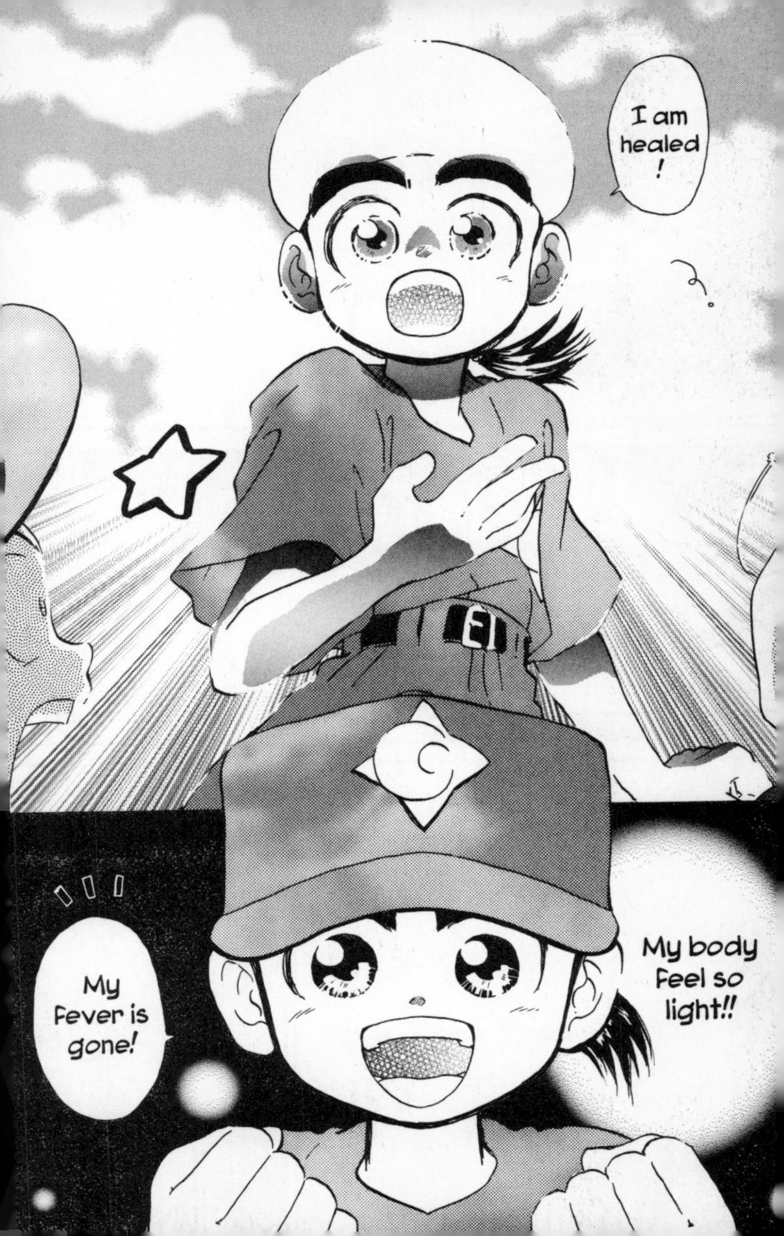
I am healed!
My body feel so light!!
My fever is gone!

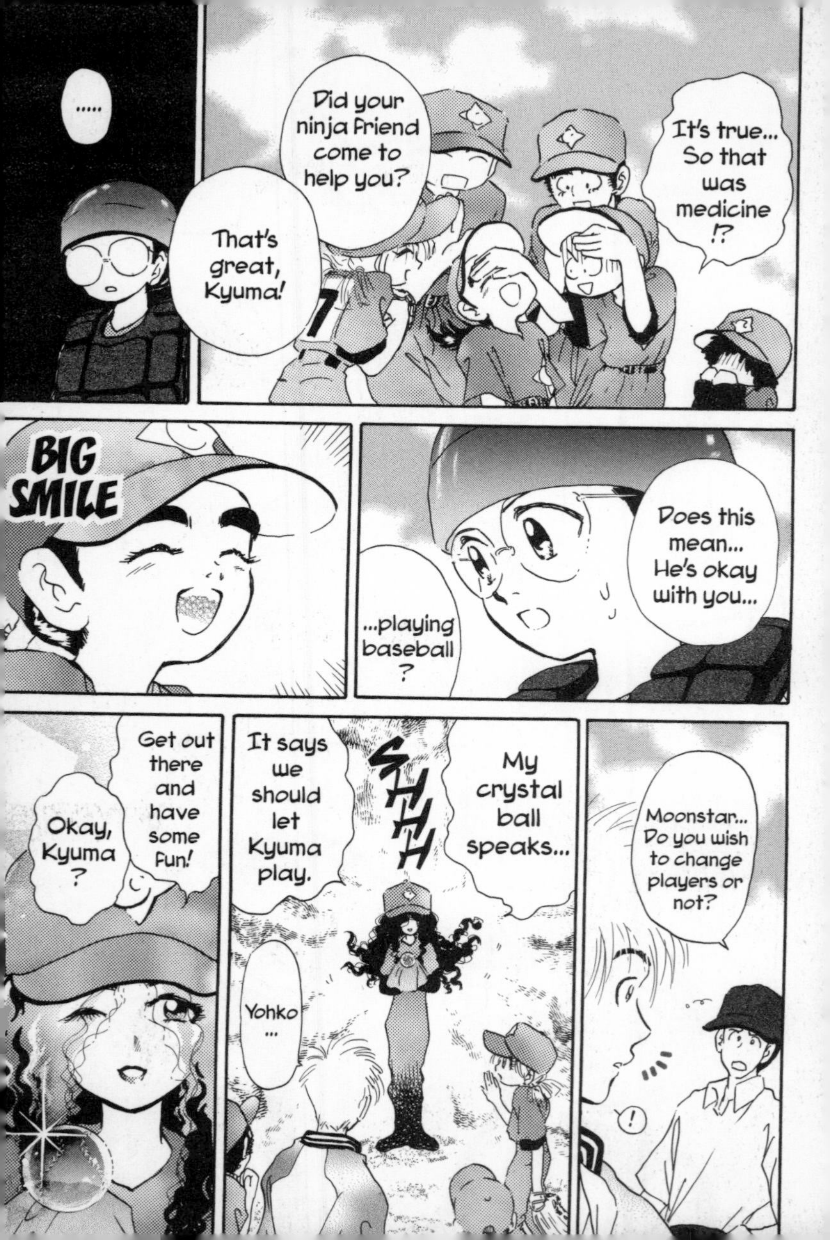
It's true... So that was medicine !?
Did your ninja friend come to help you?
That's great, Kyuma!
......
Does this mean... He's okay with you...
...playing baseball ?
BIG SMILE
Moonstar... Do you wish to change players or not?
!
My crystal ball speaks...
SHHH
It says we should let Kyuma play.
Yohko ...
Get out there and have some fun!
Okay, Kyuma ?

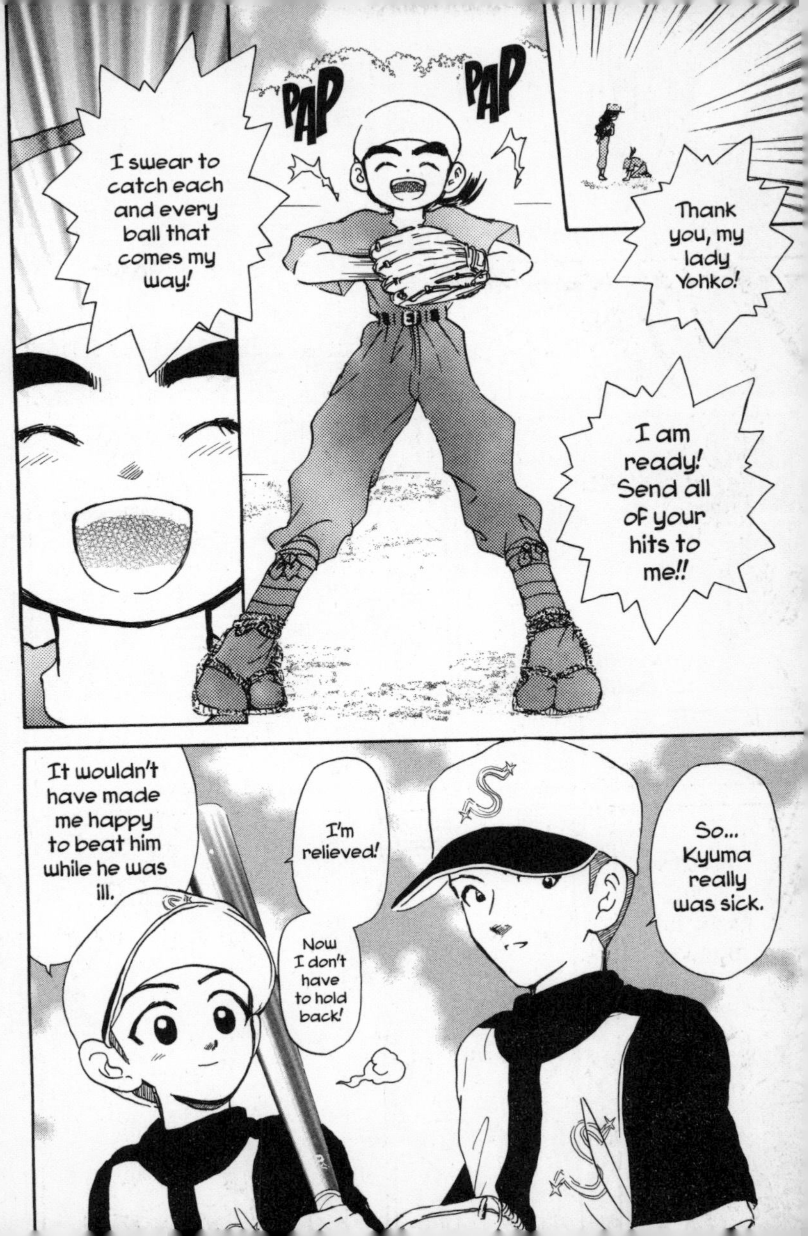
Thank you, my lady Yohko!
PAP
PAP
I am ready! Send all of your hits to me!!
I swear to catch each and every ball that comes my way!
So... Kyuma really was sick.
I'm relieved!
Now I don't have to hold back!
It wouldn't have made me happy to beat him while he was ill.

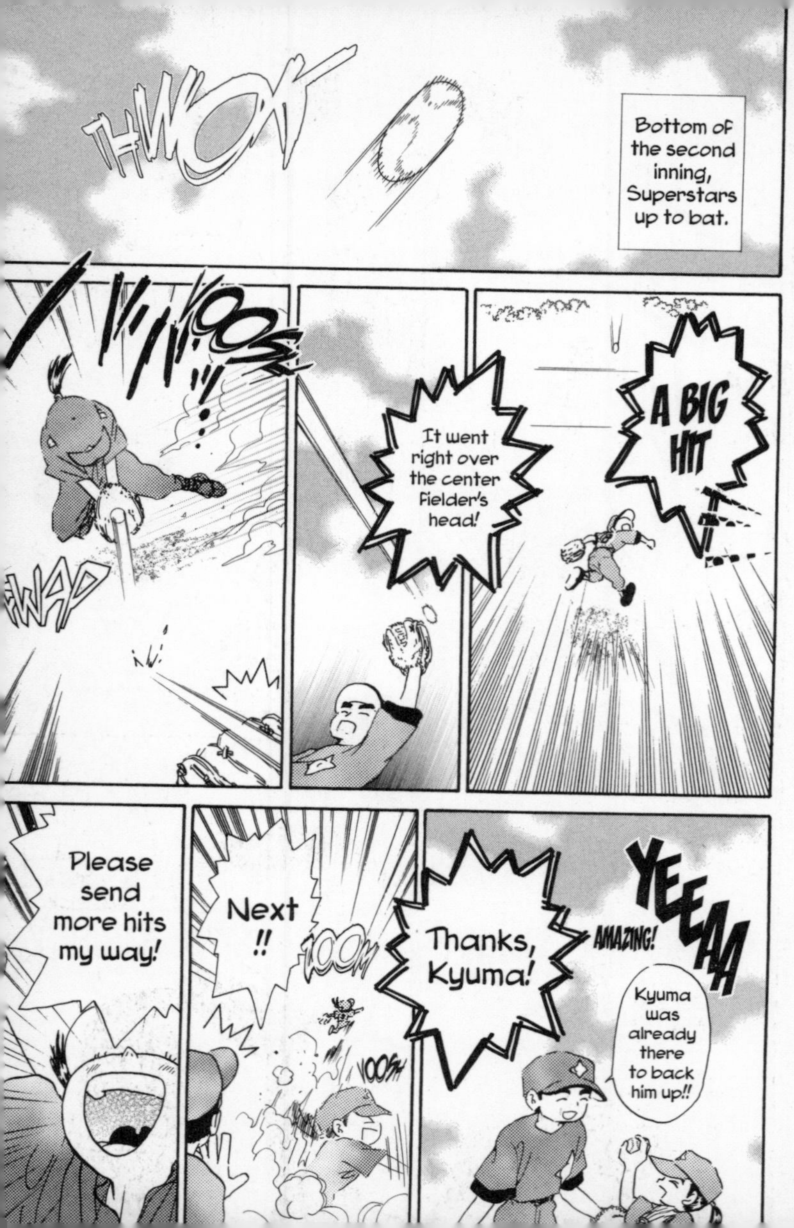

Bottom of the second inning, Superstars up to bat.
THWOCK
A BIG HIT
It went right over the center fielder's head!
WAP
YEEAAA
Thanks, Kyuma!
AMAZING!
Kyuma was already there to back him up!!
Next!!
ZOOM
VOOSH
Please send more hits my way!

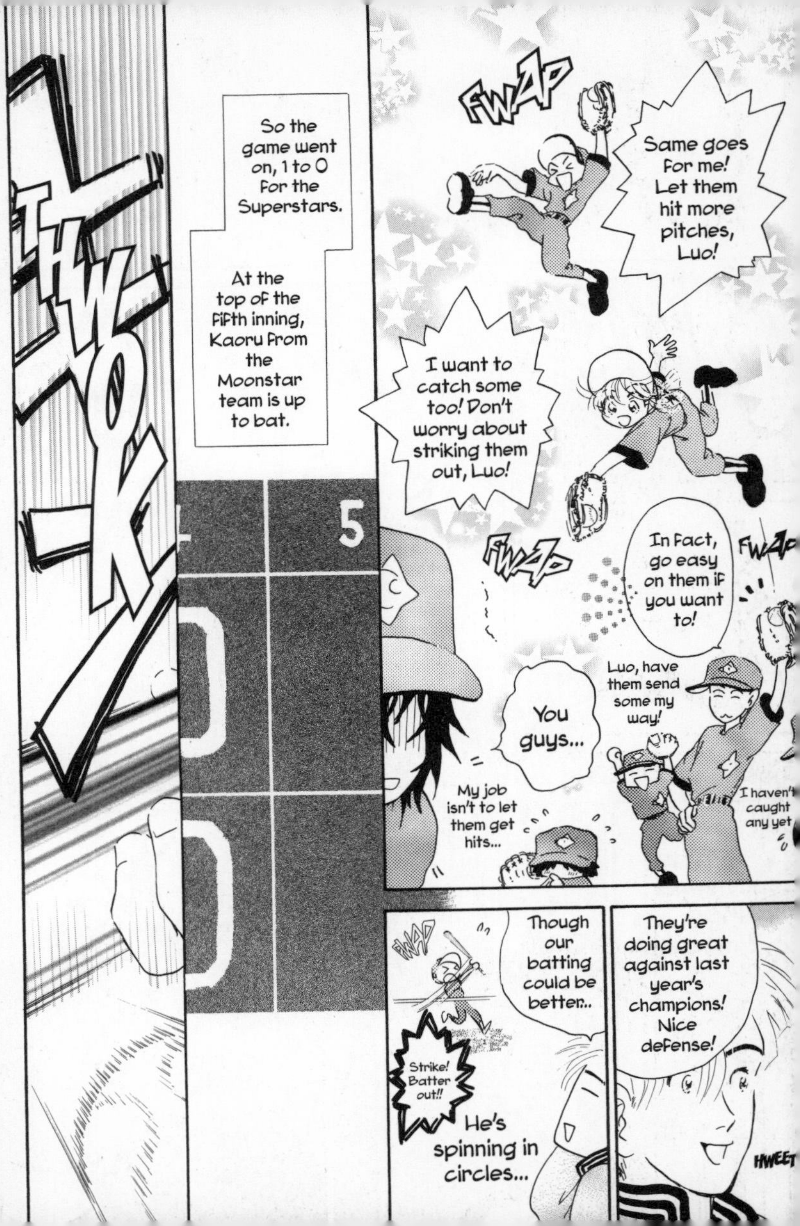
FWAP
Same goes for me! Let them hit more pitches, Luo!
I want to catch some too! Don't worry about striking them out, Luo!
FWAP
In fact, go easy on them if you want to!
FWAP
Luo, have them send some my way!
I haven't caught any yet
You guys...
My job isn't to let them get hits...
They're doing great against last year's champions! Nice defense!
HWEET
Though our batting could be better...
FWAP
Strike! Batter out!!
He's spinning in circles...
So the game went on, 1 to 0 for the Superstars.
At the top of the fifth inning, Kaoru from the Moonstar team is up to bat.
5
0
0
THWOK

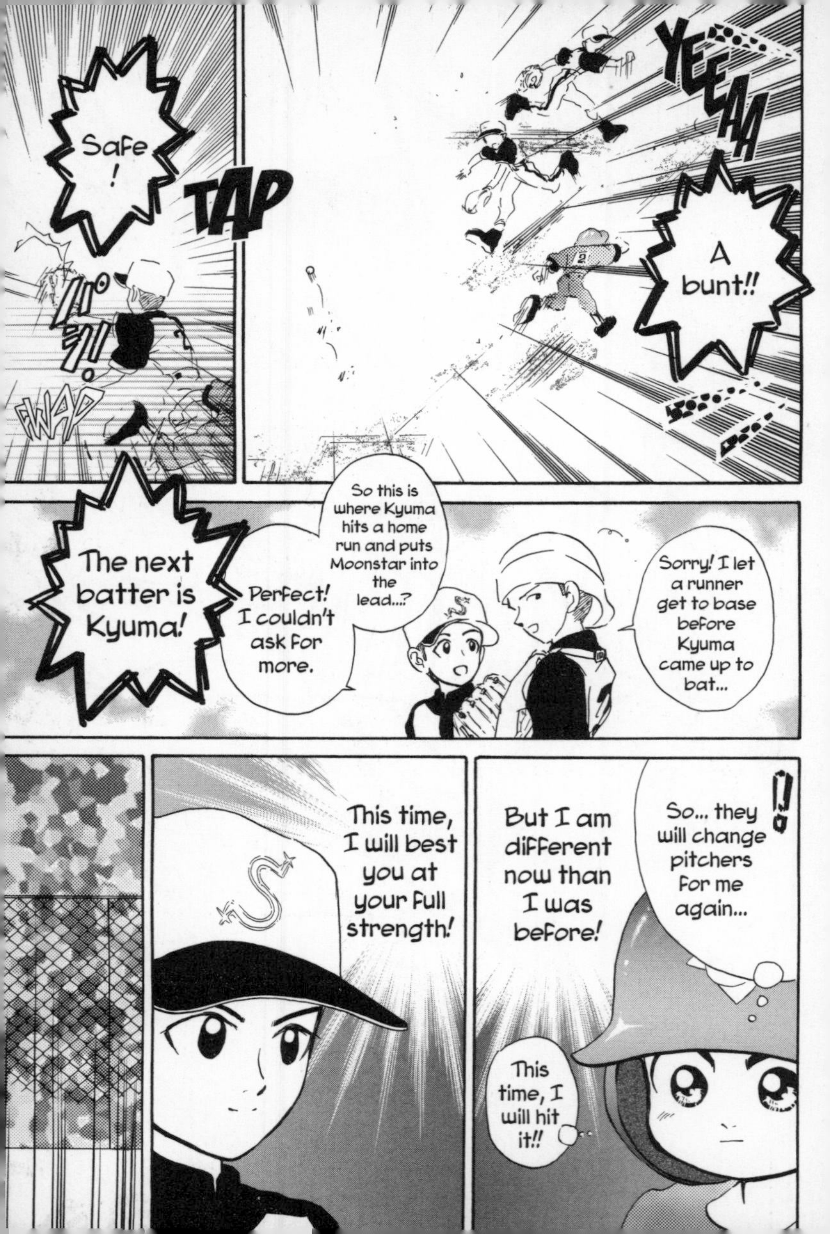
YEEAA
A bunt!!
Safe!
TAP
FWAP
Sorry! I let a runner get to base before Kyuma came up to bat...
So this is where Kyuma hits a home run and puts Moonstar into the lead...?
Perfect! I couldn't ask for more.
The next batter is Kyuma!
So... they will change pitchers for me again...
!!
But I am different now than I was before!
This time, I will hit it!!
This time, I will best you at your full strength!

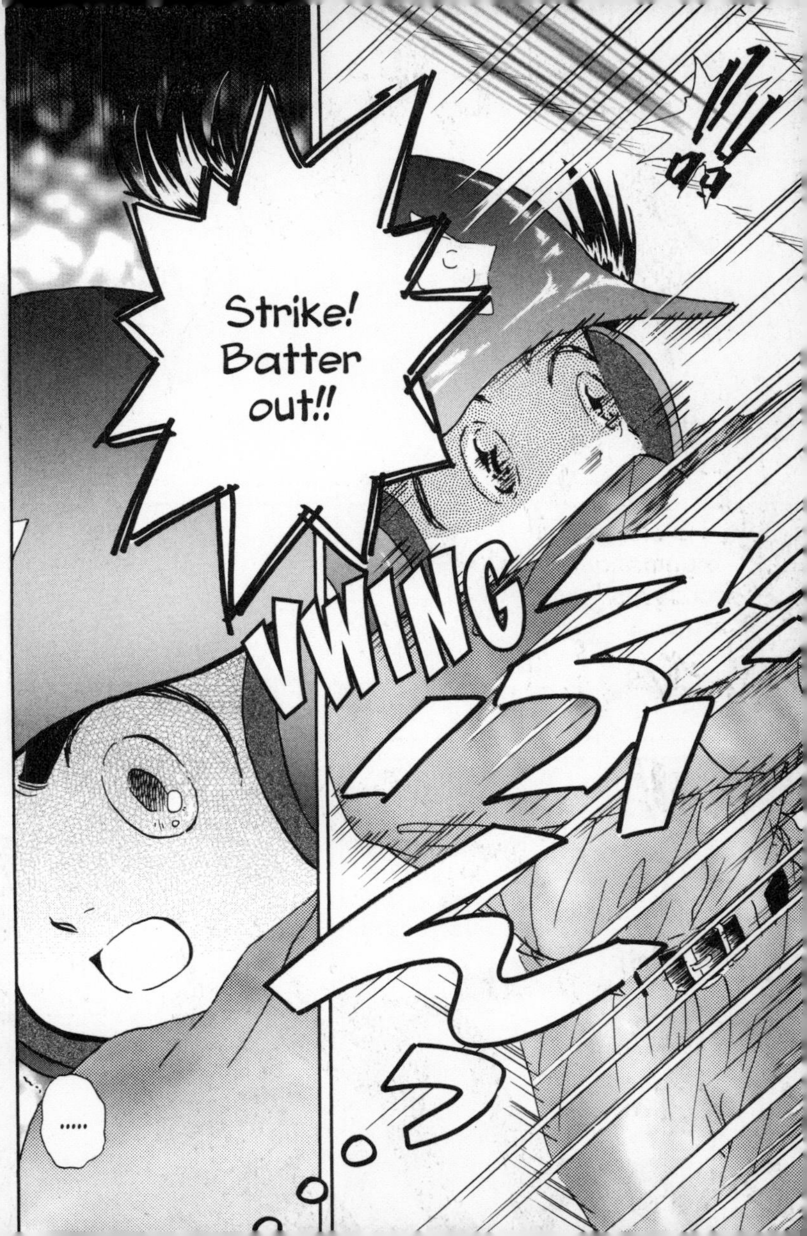
Strike! Batter out!!
VWING
......

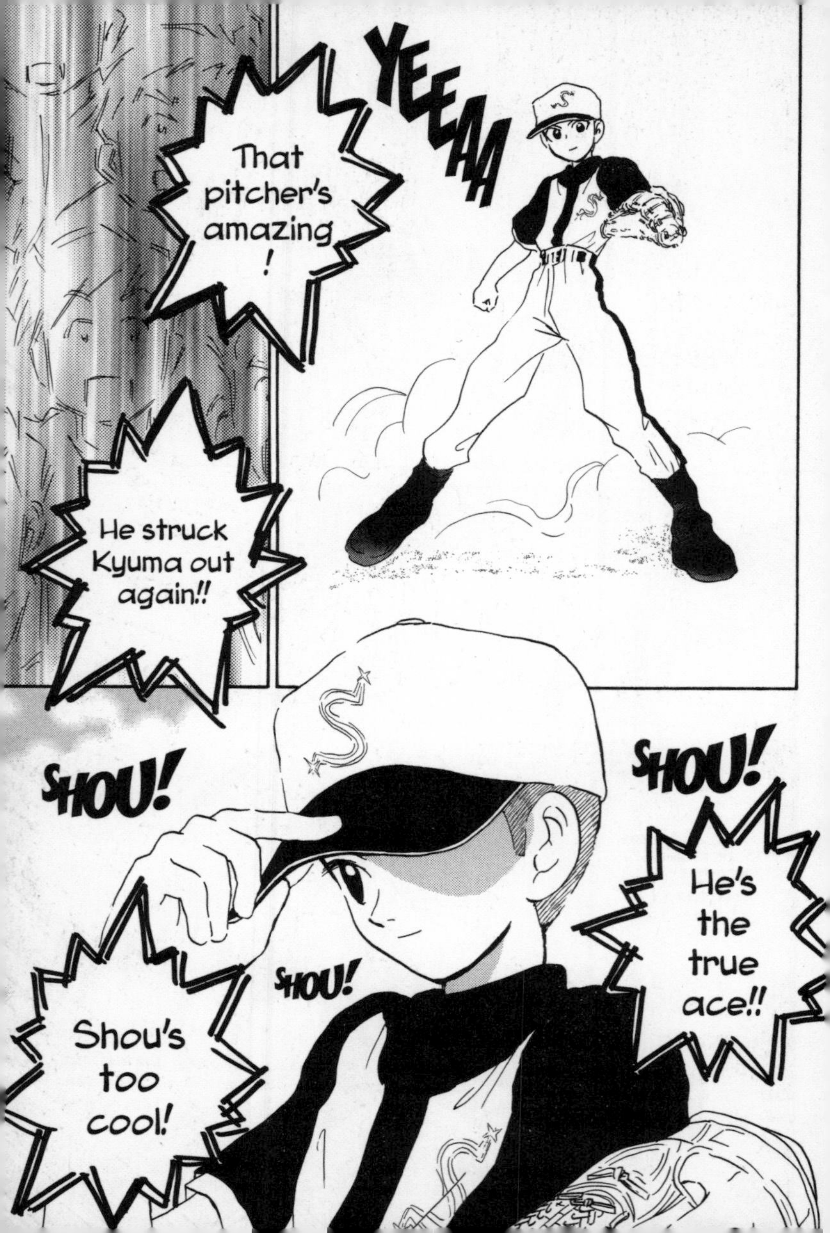

YEEAAA
That pitcher's amazing!
He struck Kyuma out again!!
SHOU!
SHOU!
He's the true ace!!
SHOU!
Shou's too cool!

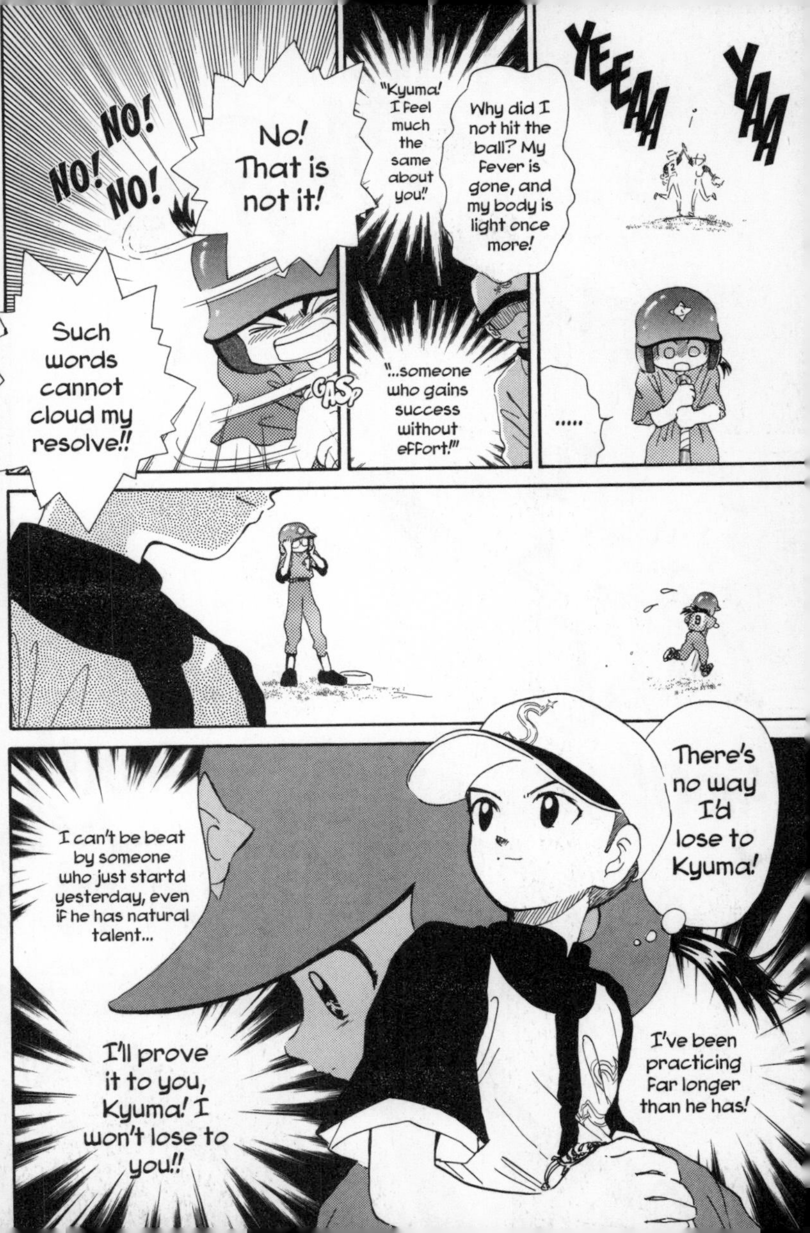
YEEAAA YAAA
.....
Why did I not hit the ball? My fever is gone, and my body is light once more!
"Kyuma! I feel much the same about you!"
"...someone who gains success without effort!"
No! That is not it!
NO! NO! NO!
GASP
Such words cannot cloud my resolve!!
There's no way I'd lose to Kyuma!
I can't be beat by someone who just startd yesterday, even if he has natural talent...
I've been practicing far longer than he has!
I'll prove it to you, Kyuma! I won't lose to you!!

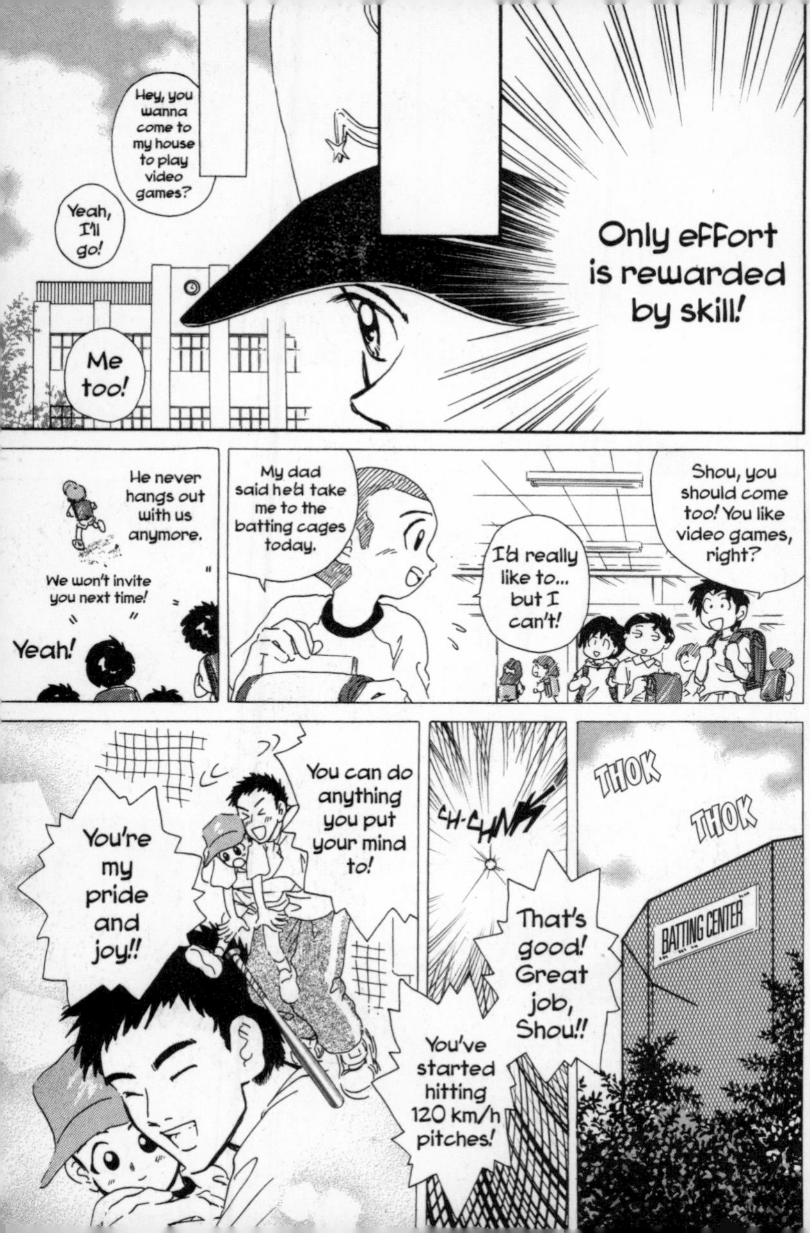
Only effort is rewarded by skill!
Hey, you wanna come to my house to play video games?
Yeah, I'll go!
Me too!
Shou, you should come too! You like video games, right?
I'd really like to... but I can't!
My dad said he'd take me to the batting cages today.
He never hangs out with us anymore.
We won't invite you next time!
Yeah!
THOK
THOK
BATTING CENTER
CH-CHINK
That's good! Great job, Shou!!
You've started hitting 120 km/h pitches!
You can do anything you put your mind to!
You're my pride and joy!!

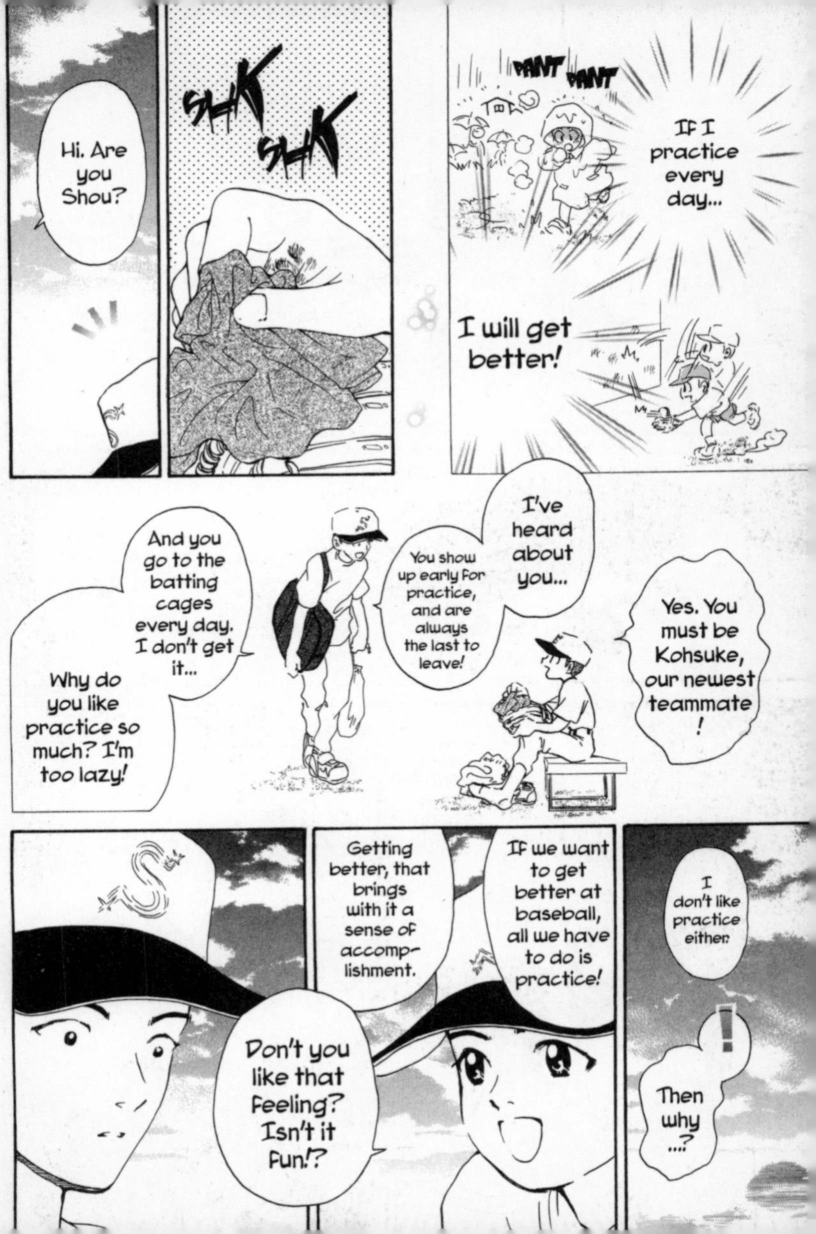
PANT PANT
If I practice every day...
I will get better!
SLIK SLIK
Hi. Are you Shou?
Yes. You must be Kohsuke, our newest teammate!
I've heard about you...
You show up early for practice, and are always the last to leave!
And you go to the batting cages every day. I don't get it...
Why do you like practice so much? I'm too lazy!
I don't like practice either.
!
Then why ...?
If we want to get better at baseball, all we have to do is practice!
Getting better, that brings with it a sense of accomplishment.
Don't you like that feeling? Isn't it fun!?

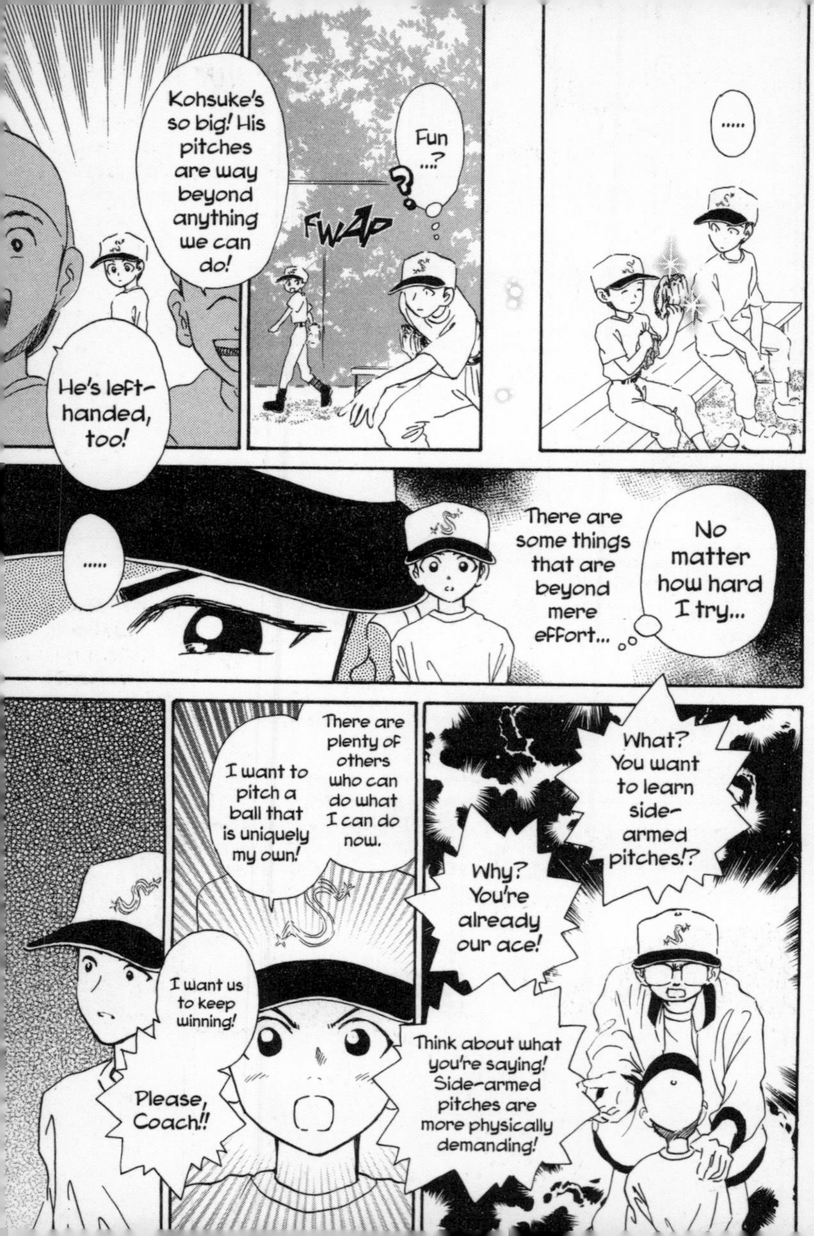
......
Fun ...?
FWAP
Kohsuke's so big! His pitches are way beyond anything we can do!
He's left-handed, too!
No matter how hard I try...
There are some things that are beyond mere effort...
......
What? You want to learn side-armed pitches!?
Why? You're already our ace!
Think about what you're saying! Side-armed pitches are more physically demanding!
There are plenty of others who can do what I can do now.
I want to pitch a ball that is uniquely my own!
I want us to keep winning!
Please, Coach!!

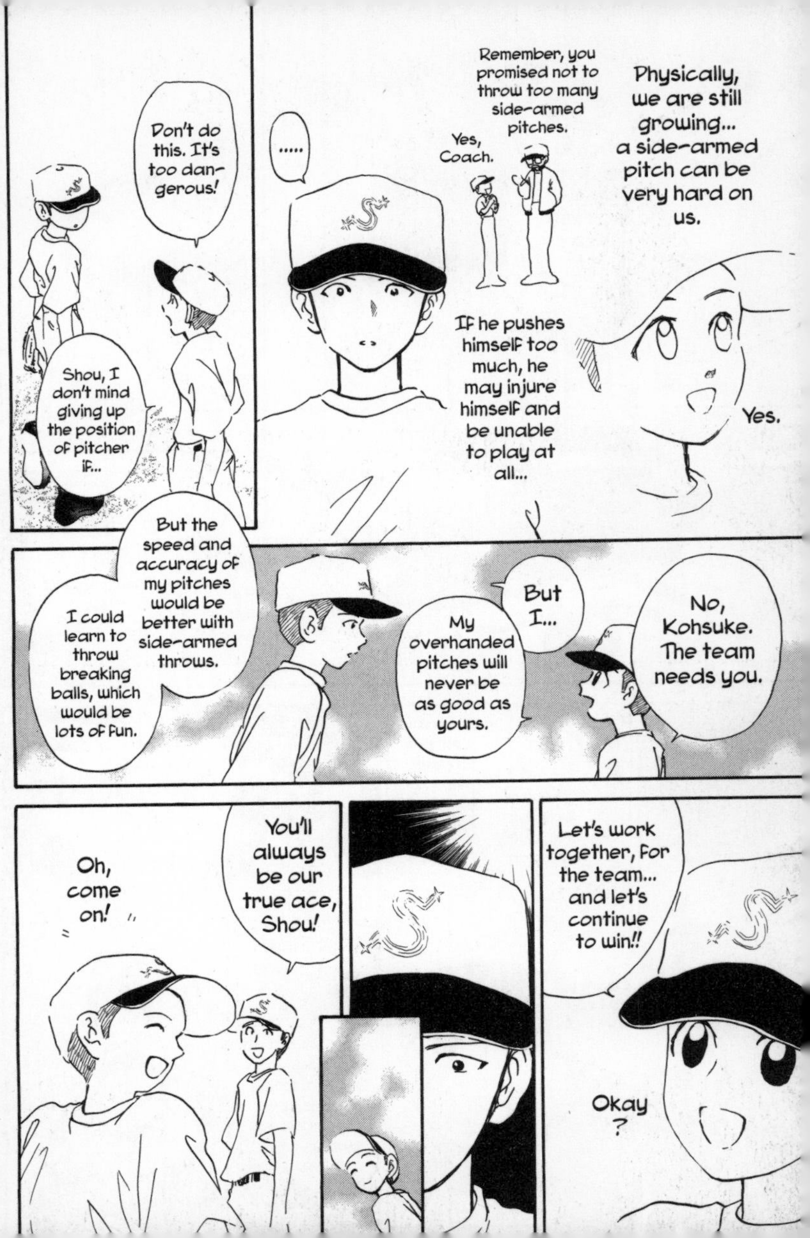
Physically, we are still growing... a side-armed pitch can be very hard on us.
Remember, you promised not to throw too many side-armed pitches.
Yes, Coach.
Yes.
If he pushes himself too much, he may injure himself and be unable to play at all...
.....
Don't do this. It's too dangerous!
Shou, I don't mind giving up the position of pitcher if...
No, Kohsuke. The team needs you.
But I...
My overhanded pitches will never be as good as yours.
But the speed and accuracy of my pitches would be better with side-armed throws.
I could learn to throw breaking balls, which would be lots of fun.
Let's work together, for the team... and let's continue to win!!
Okay?
You'll always be our true ace, Shou!
Oh, come on!

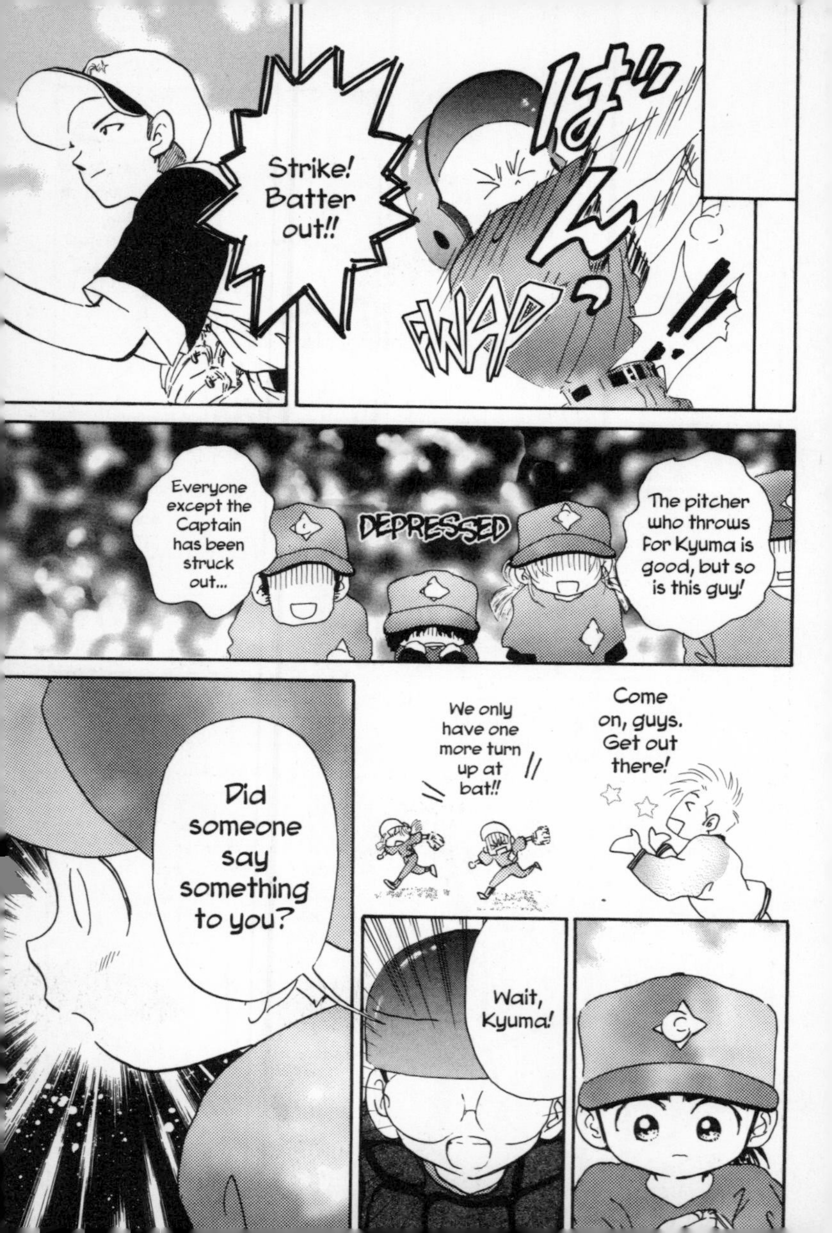
ばん
FWAP
Strike! Batter out!!
The pitcher who throws for Kyuma is good, but so is this guy!
DEPRESSED
Everyone except the Captain has been struck out...
Come on, guys. Get out there!
We only have one more turn up at bat!!
Wait, Kyuma!
Did someone say something to you?

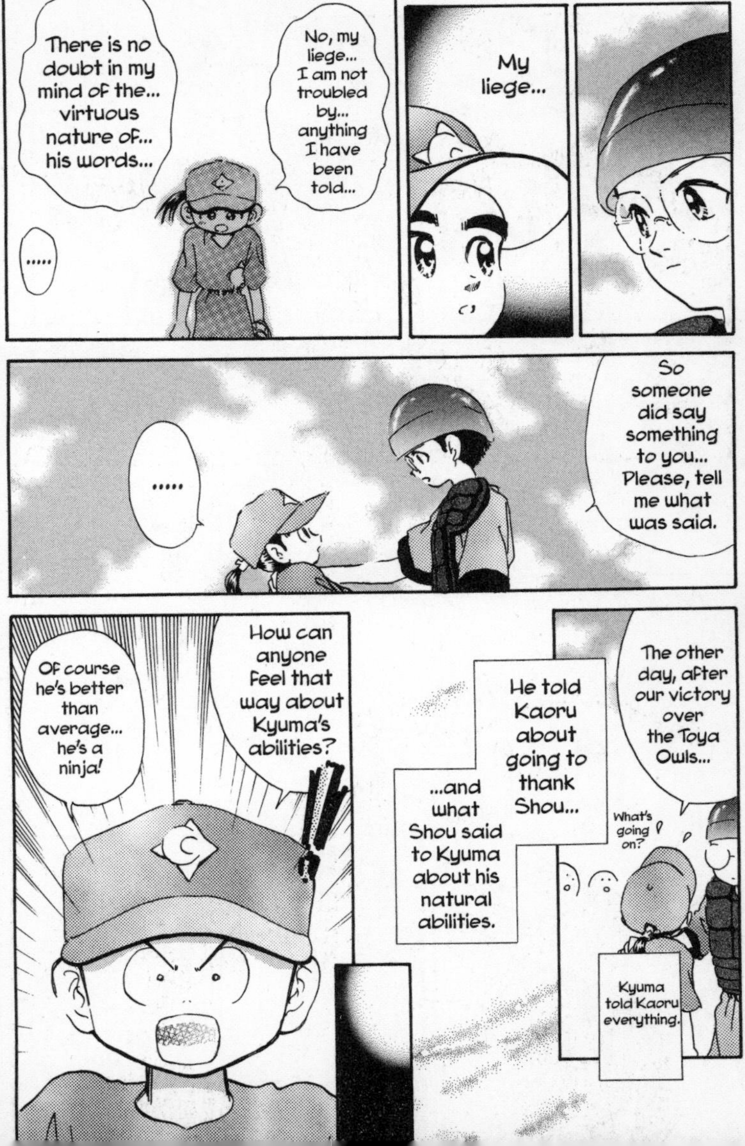
My liege...
No, my liege... I am not troubled by... anything I have been told...
There is no doubt in my mind of the... virtuous nature of... his words...
......
So someone did say something to you... Please, tell me what was said.
......
The other day, after our victory over the Toya Owls...
What's going on?
He told Kaoru about going to thank Shou...
...and what Shou said to Kyuma about his natural abilities.
Kyuma told Kaoru everything.
How can anyone feel that way about Kyuma's abilities?
Of course he's better than average... he's a ninja!
!

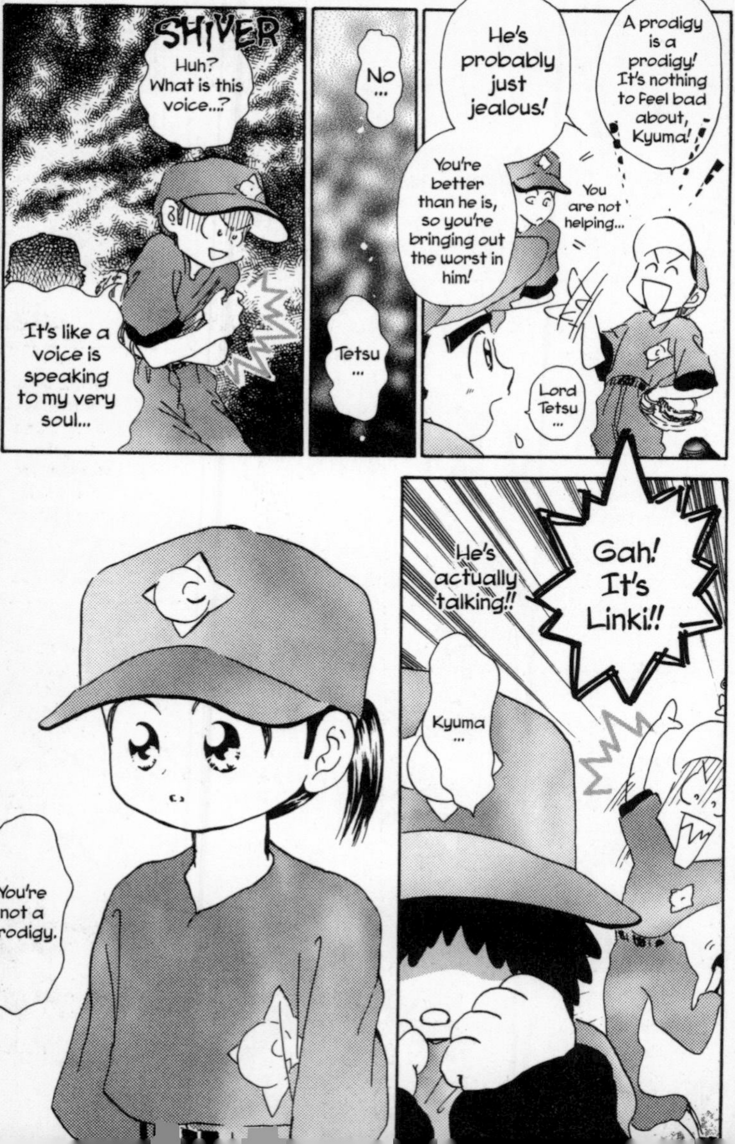
A prodigy is a prodigy! It's nothing to feel bad about, Kyuma!
He's probably just jealous!
You're better than he is, so you're bringing out the worst in him!
You are not helping...
Lord Tetsu ...
No ...
Tetsu ...
SHIVER
Huh? What is this voice...?
It's like a voice is speaking to my very soul...
Gah! It's Linki!!
He's actually talking!!
Kyuma ...
You're not a prodigy.

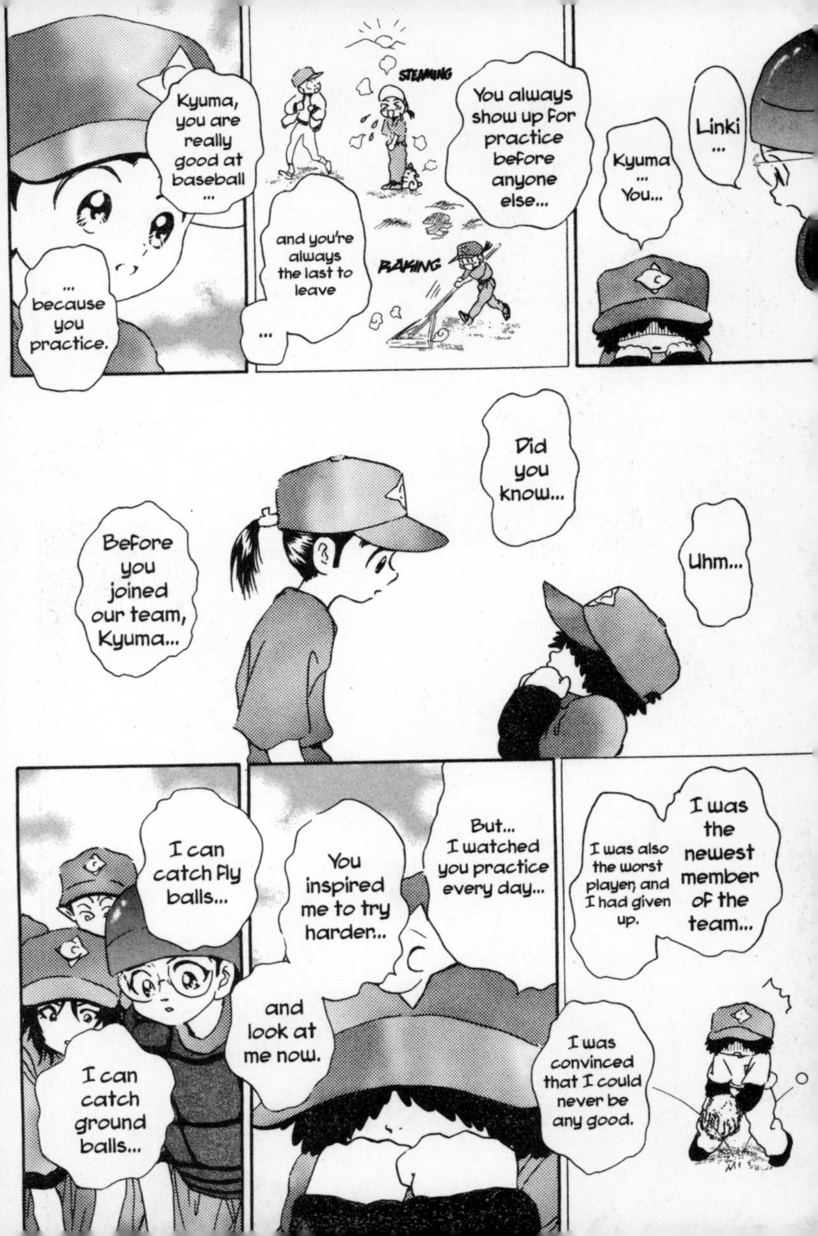
Linki ...
Kyuma ... You...
You always show up for practice before anyone else...
STEAMING
RAKING
and you're always the last to leave
...
Kyuma, you are really good at baseball ...
... because you practice.
Did you know...
Uhm...
Before you joined our team, Kyuma...
I was the newest member of the team...
I was also the worst player, and I had given up.
I was convinced that I could never be any good.
But... I watched you practice every day...
You inspired me to try harder...
and look at me now.
I can catch fly balls...
I can catch ground balls...

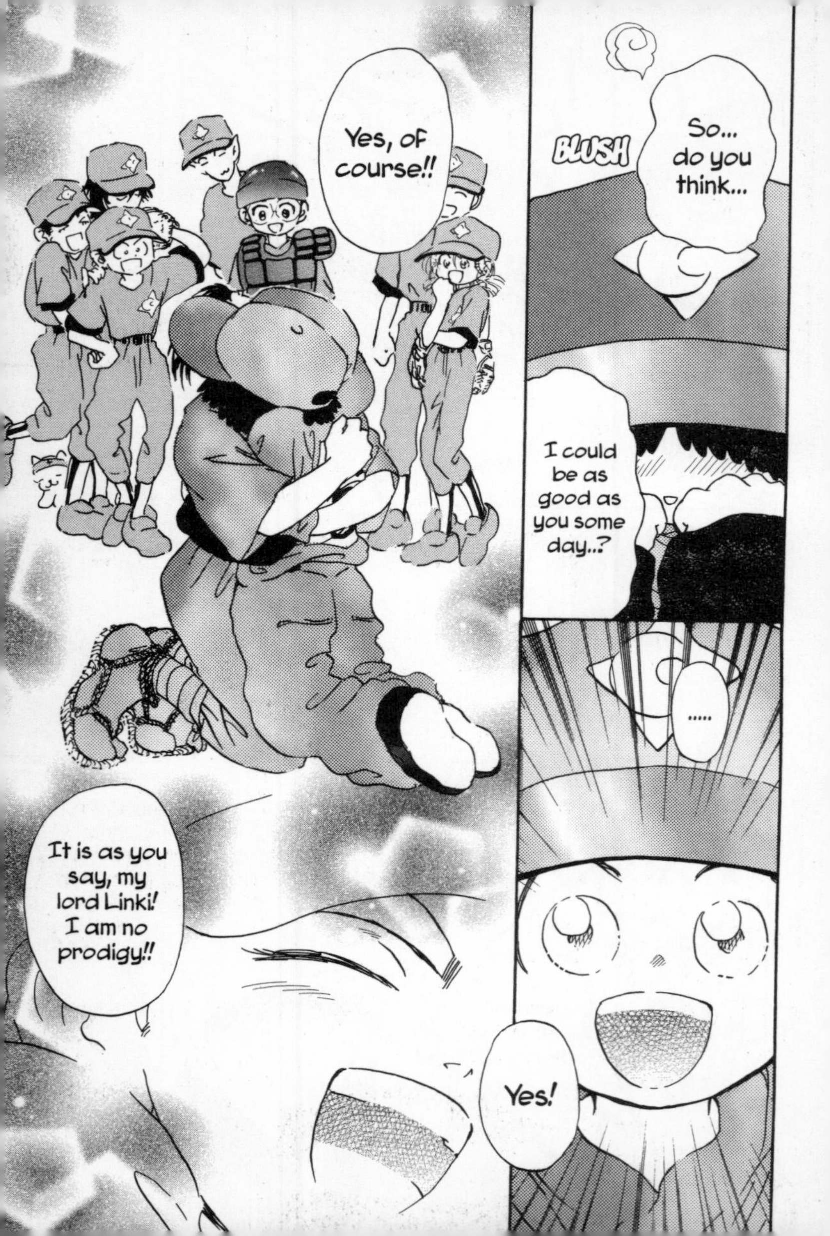

So... do you think...
BLUSH
I could be as good as you some day..?
.....
Yes!
Yes, of course!!
It is as you say, my lord Linki! I am no prodigy!!

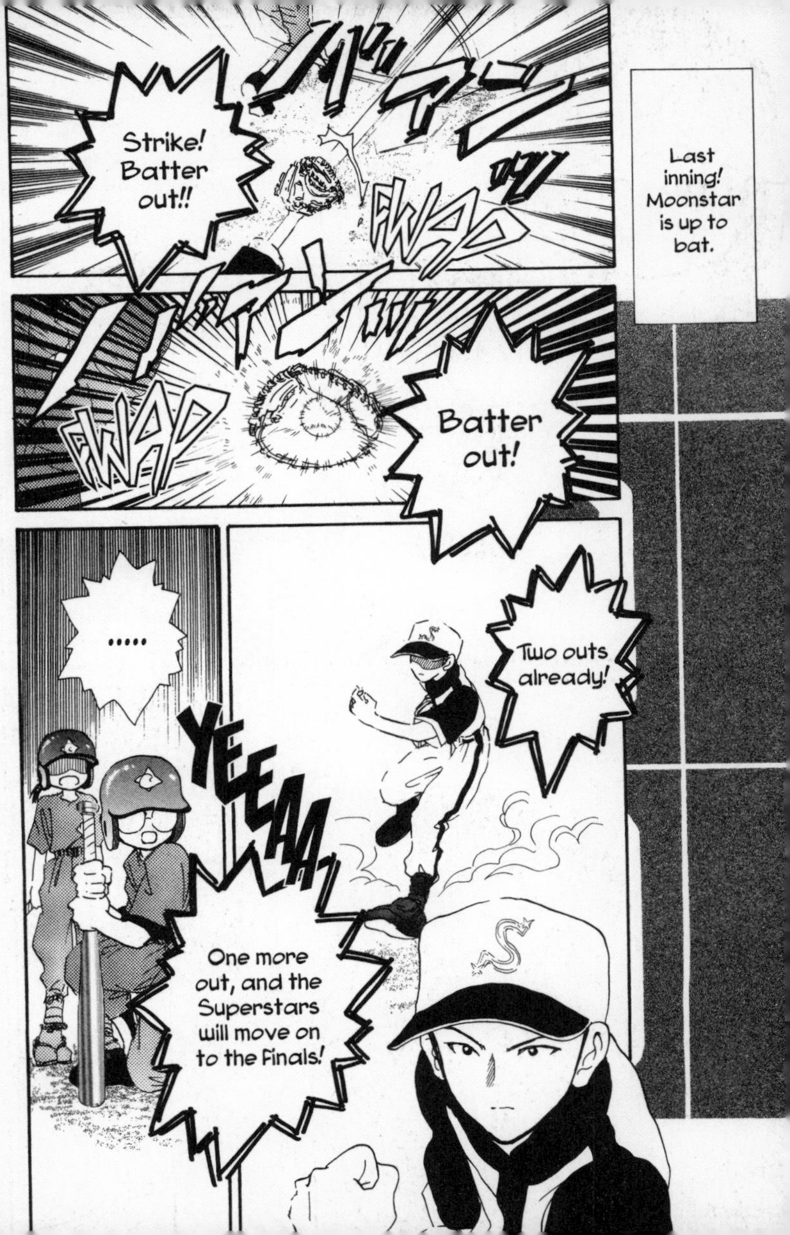
Last inning! Moonstar is up to bat.
Strike! Batter out!!
FWAP
FWAP
Batter out!
Two outs already!
YEEAAA
One more out, and the Superstars will move on to the Finals!
.....

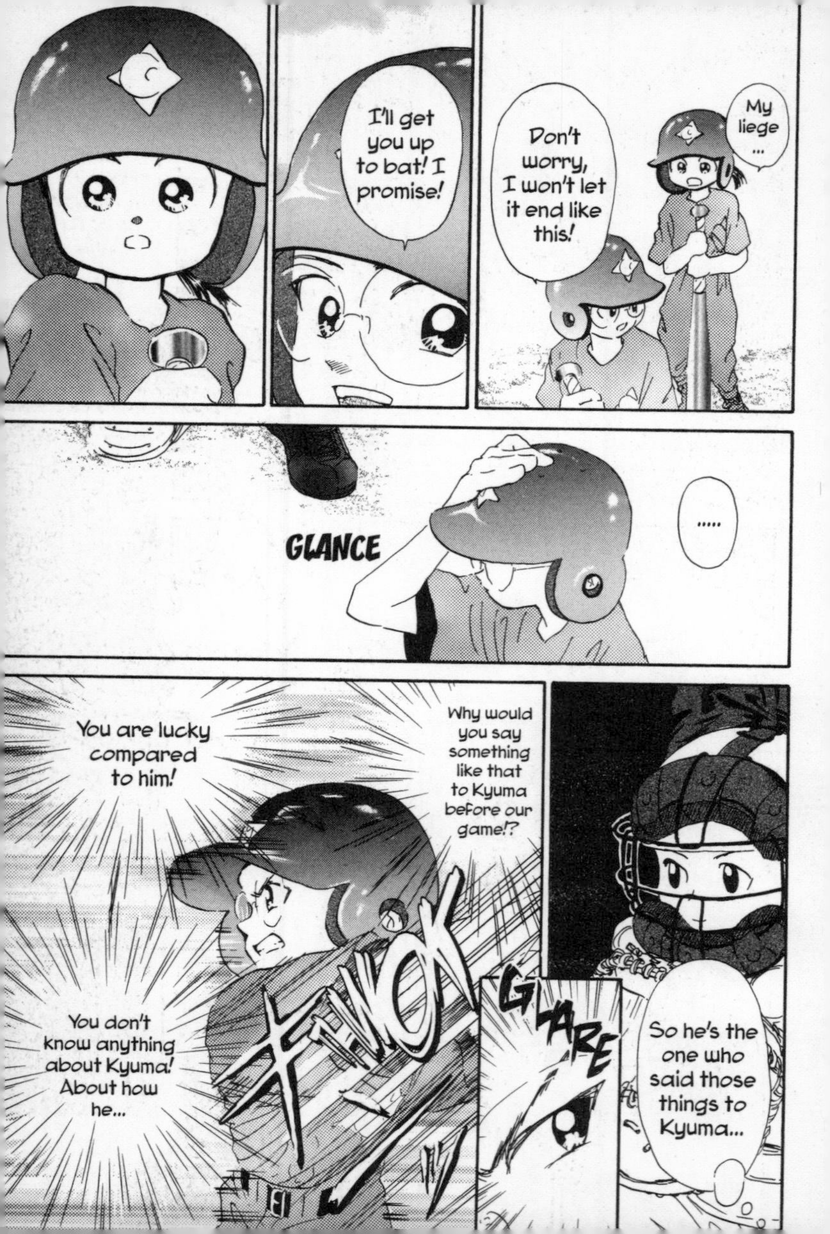
My liege ...
Don't worry, I won't let it end like this!
I'll get you up to bat! I promise!
.....
GLANCE
So he's the one who said those things to Kyuma...
GLARE
Why would you say something like that to Kyuma before our game!?
You are lucky compared to him!
THWOK
You don't know anything about Kyuma! About how he...

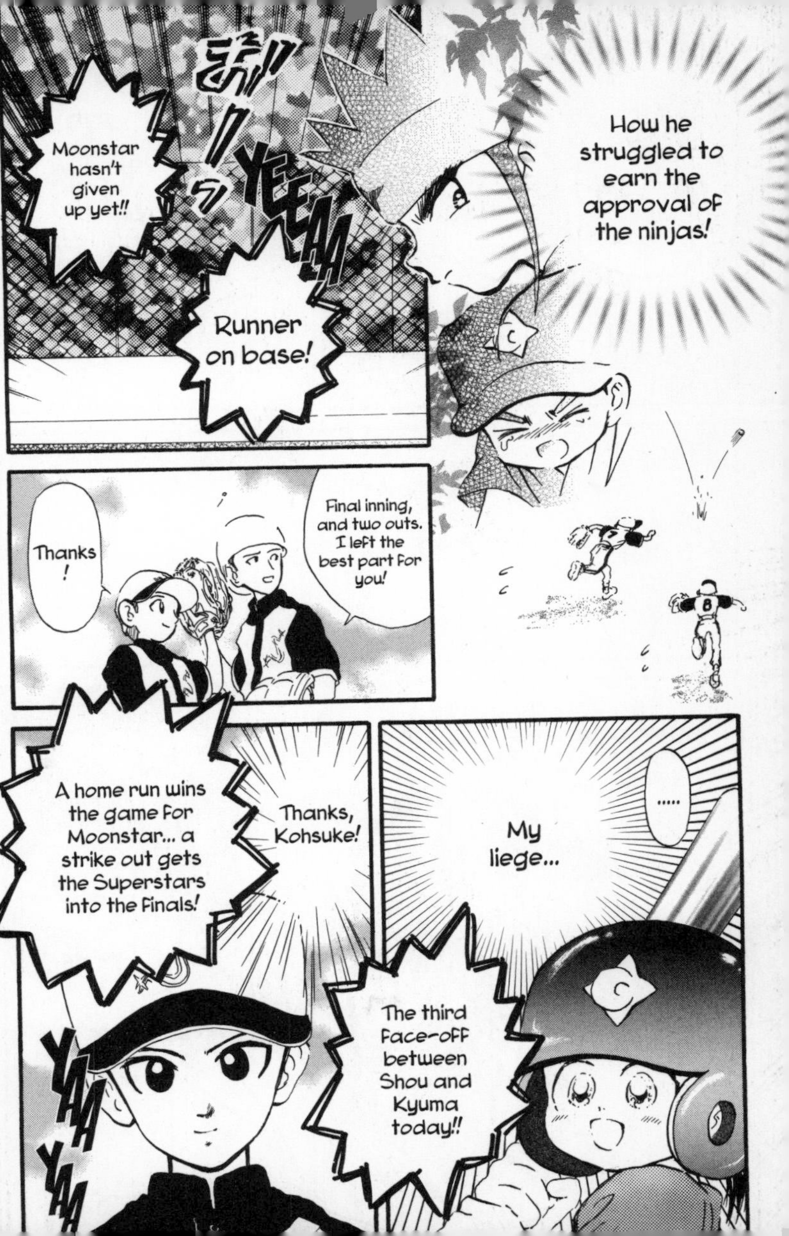

How he struggled to earn the approval of the ninjas!
YEEAAA
Moonstar hasn't given up yet!!
Runner on base!
Final inning, and two outs. I left the best part for you!
Thanks!
.....
My liege...
The third face-off between Shou and Kyuma today!!
Thanks, Kohsuke!
A home run wins the game for Moonstar... a strike out gets the Superstars into the finals!
YAAA YAAA

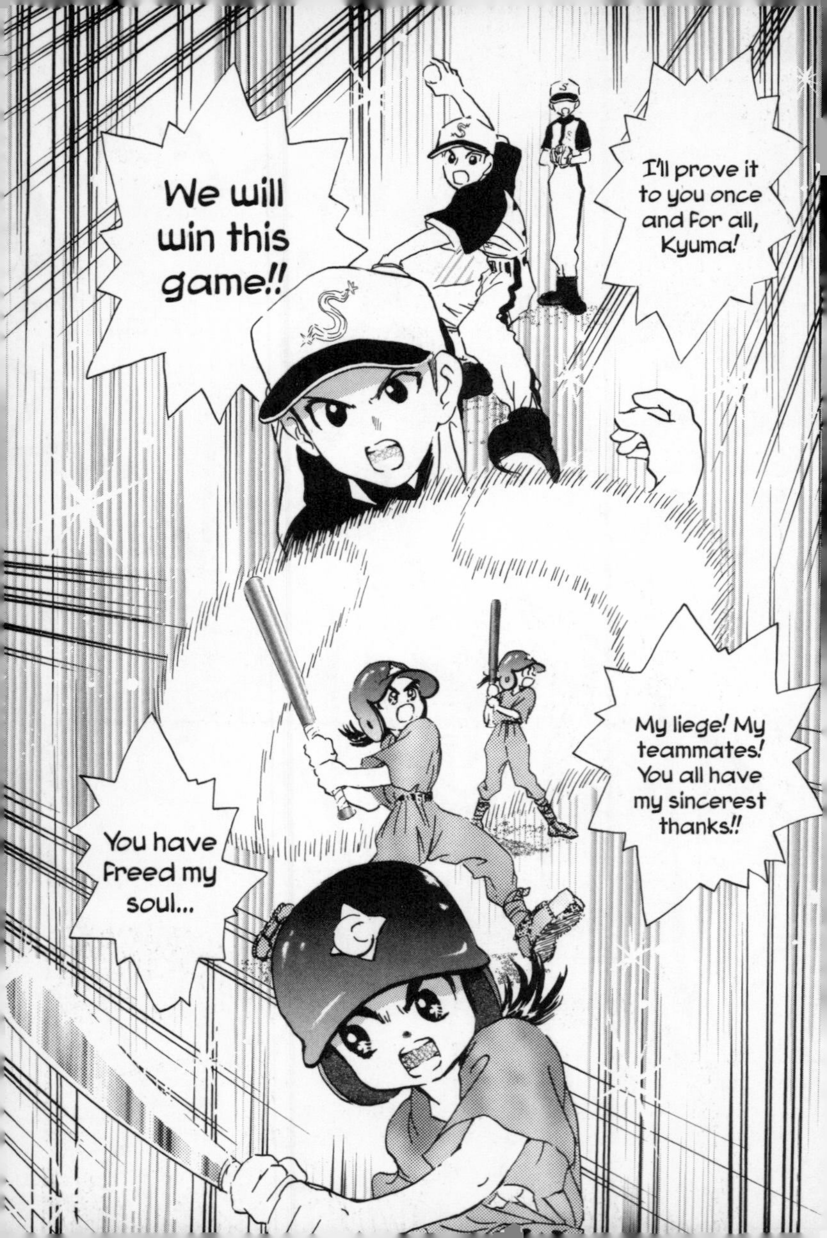
I'll prove it to you once and for all, Kyuma!
We will win this game!!
My liege! My teammates! You all have my sincerest thanks!!
You have freed my soul...

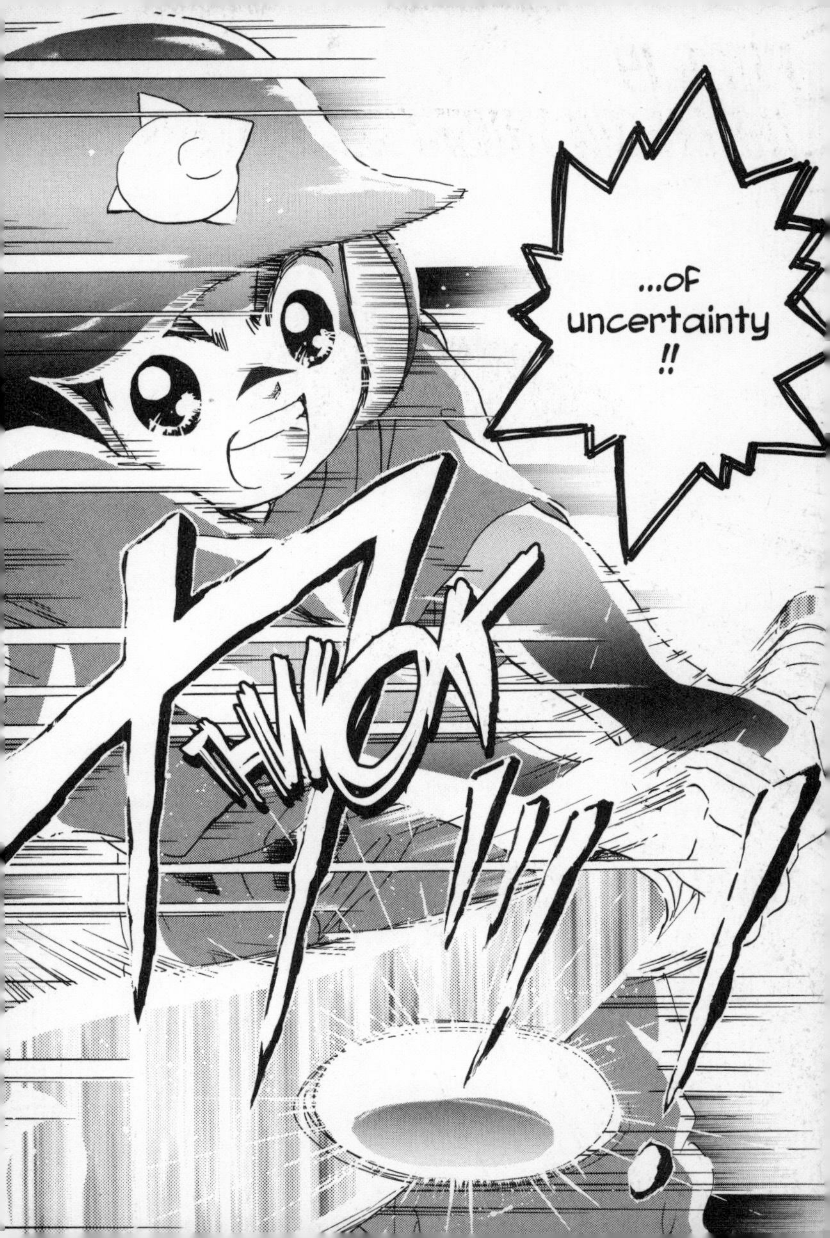
...of uncertainty !!
TWOK !!!

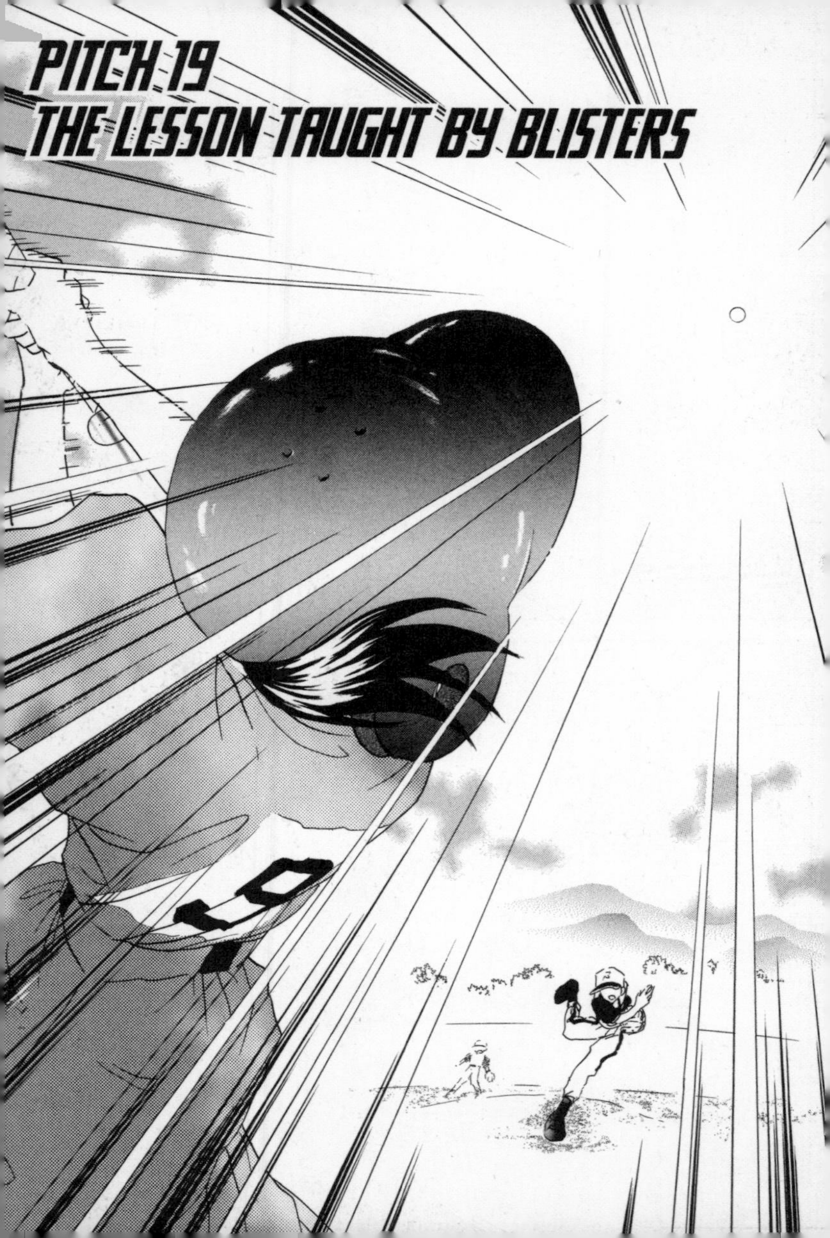
PITCH 19
THE LESSON TAUGHT BY BLISTERS

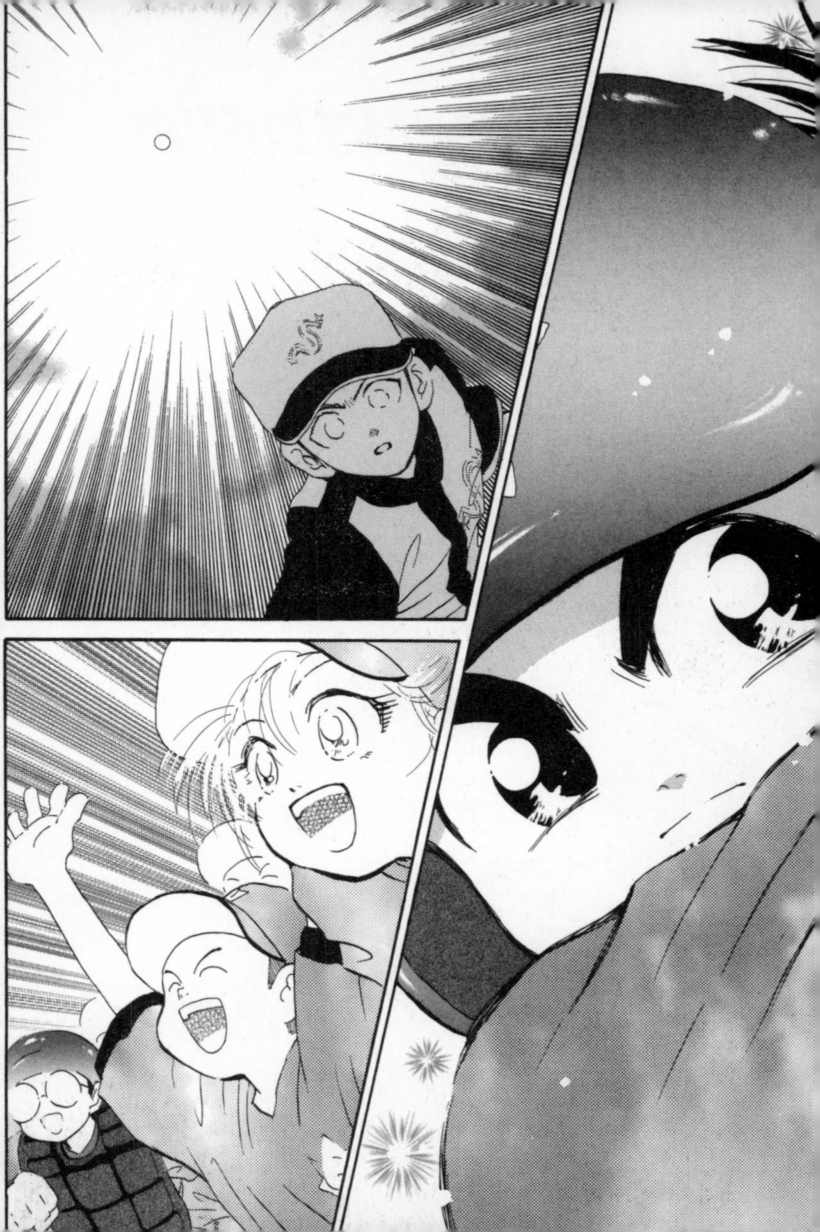

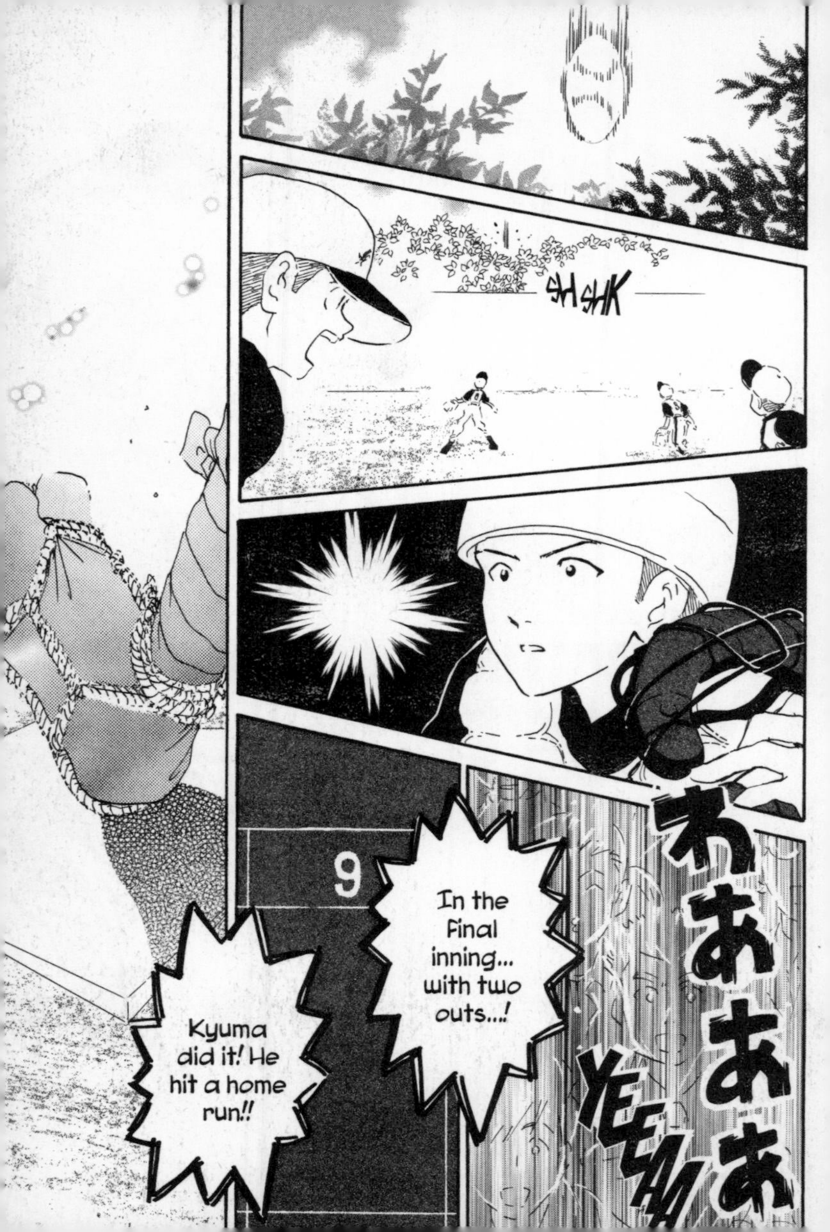
SHASHIK
わあああ
YEEAH
In the final inning... with two outs...!
Kyuma did it! He hit a home run!!

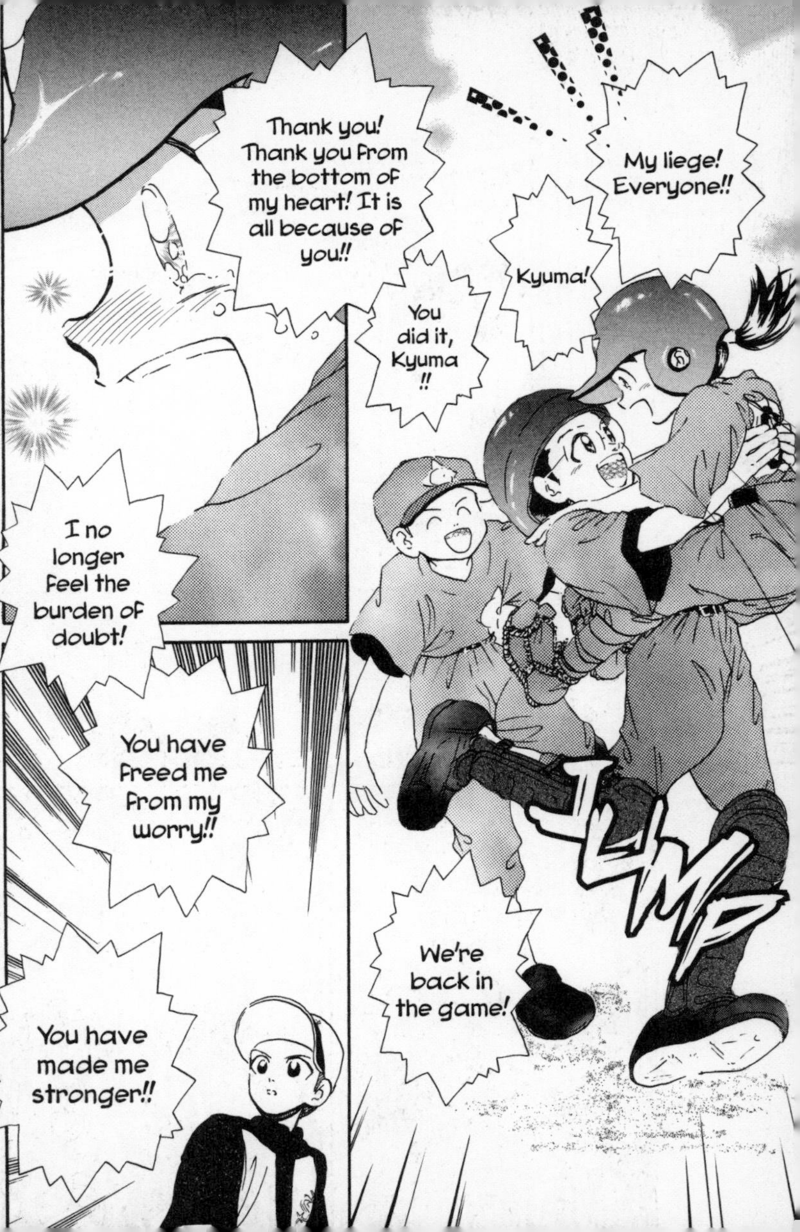
My liege! Everyone!!
Kyuma!
You did it, Kyuma!!
JUMP
We're back in the game!
Thank you! Thank you from the bottom of my heart! It is all because of you!!
I no longer feel the burden of doubt!
You have freed me from my worry!!
You have made me stronger!!

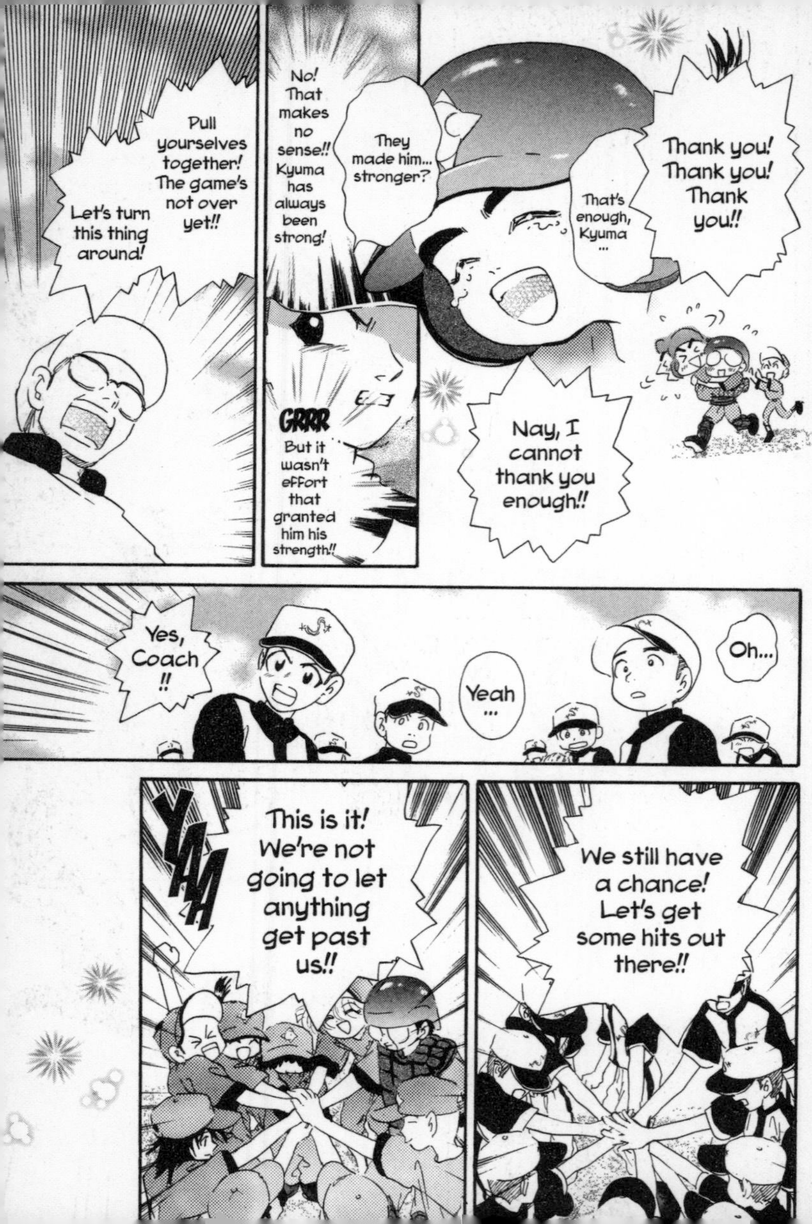
Thank you! Thank you! Thank you!!
That's enough, Kyuma ...
Nay, I cannot thank you enough!!
They made him... stronger?
No! That makes no sense!! Kyuma has always been strong!
GRRR
But it wasn't effort that granted him his strength!!
Pull yourselves together! The game's not over yet!!
Let's turn this thing around!
Oh...
Yeah ...
Yes, Coach !!
We still have a chance! Let's get some hits out there!!
This is it! We're not going to let anything get past us!!
YAA

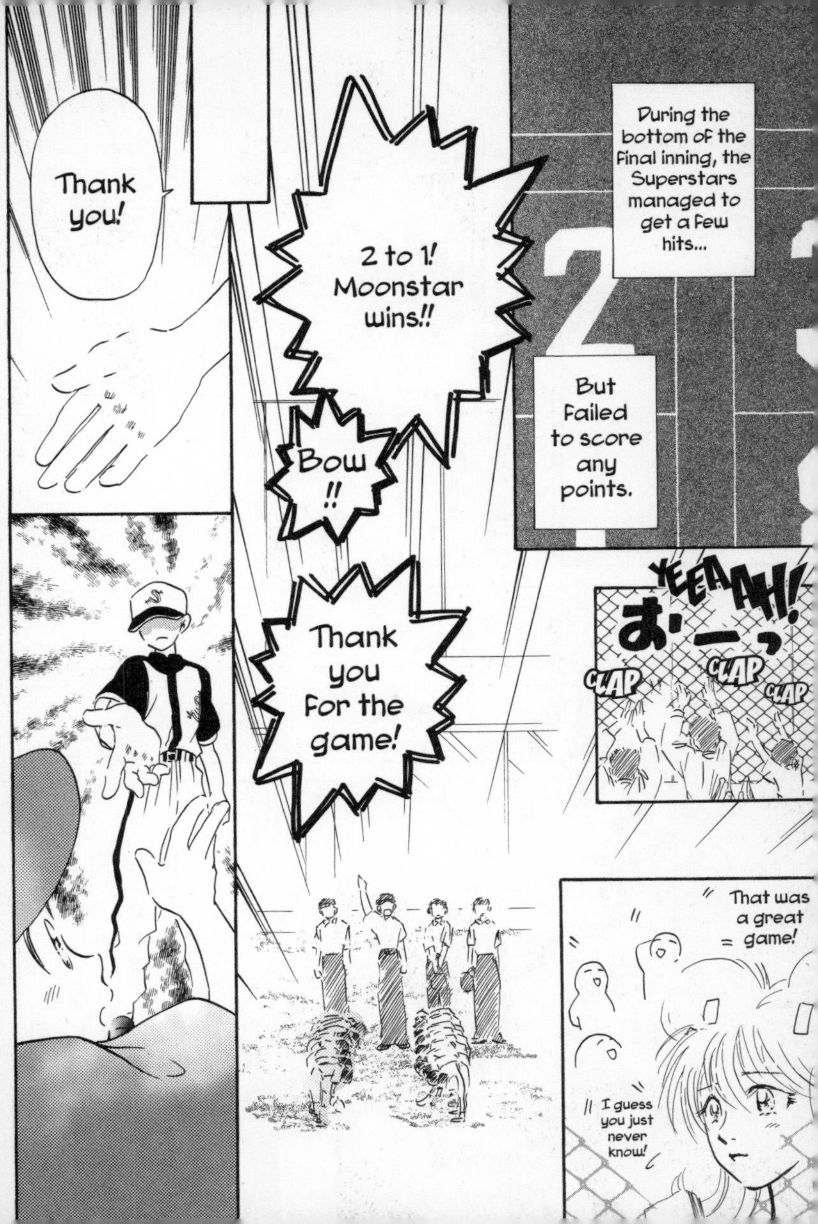
During the bottom of the final inning, the Superstars managed to get a few hits...
But failed to score any points.
2 to 1! Moonstar wins!!
Bow !!
Thank you!
YEEAAH!
おーっ
CLAP
CLAP
CLAP
Thank you for the game!
That was a great game!
I guess you just never know!

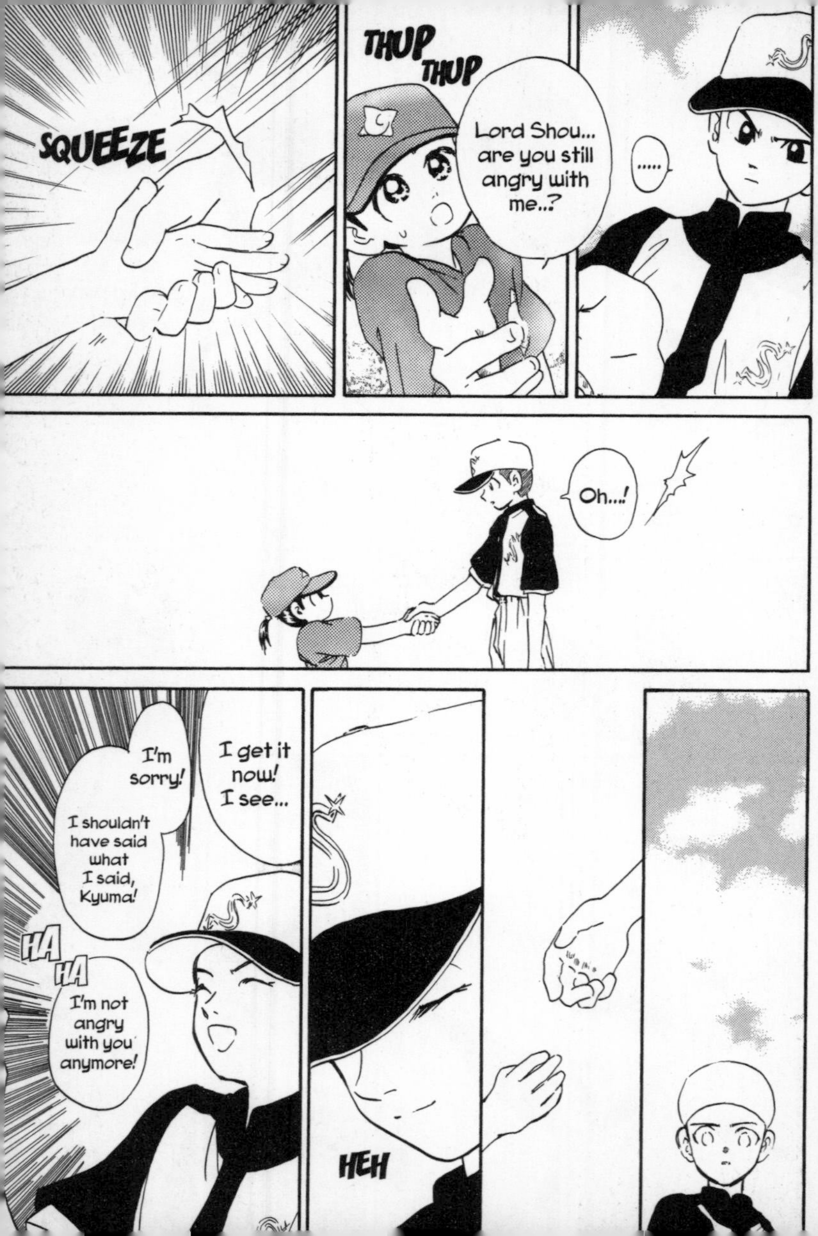
.....
THUP THUP
Lord Shou... are you still angry with me..?
SQUEEZE
Oh...!
HEH
I get it now! I see...
I'm sorry!
I shouldn't have said what I said, Kyuma!
HA HA
I'm not angry with you anymore!

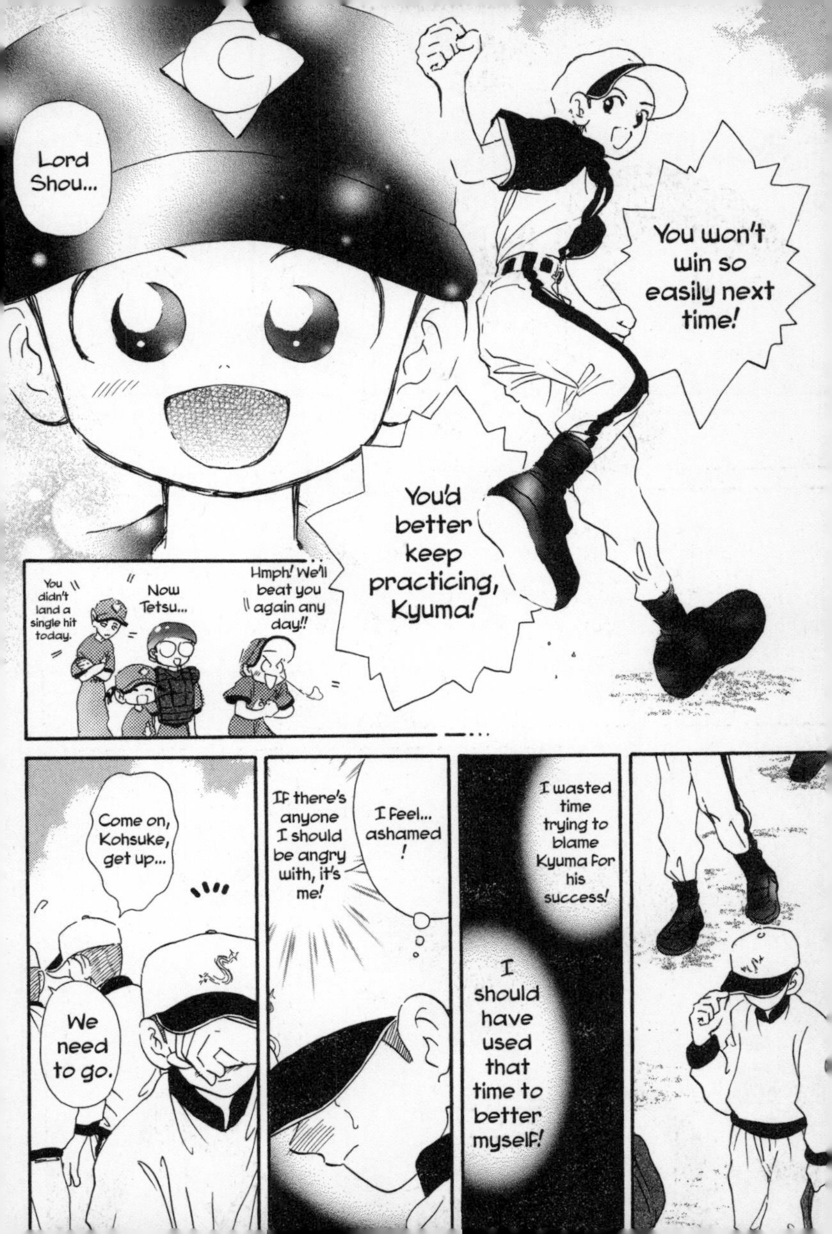
You won't win so easily next time!
You'd better keep practicing, Kyuma!
Lord Shou...
Hmph! We'll beat you again any day!!
Now Tetsu...
You didn't land a single hit today.
I wasted time trying to blame Kyuma for his success!
I should have used that time to better myself!
I feel... ashamed!
If there's anyone I should be angry with, it's me!
Come on, Kohsuke, get up...
We need to go.

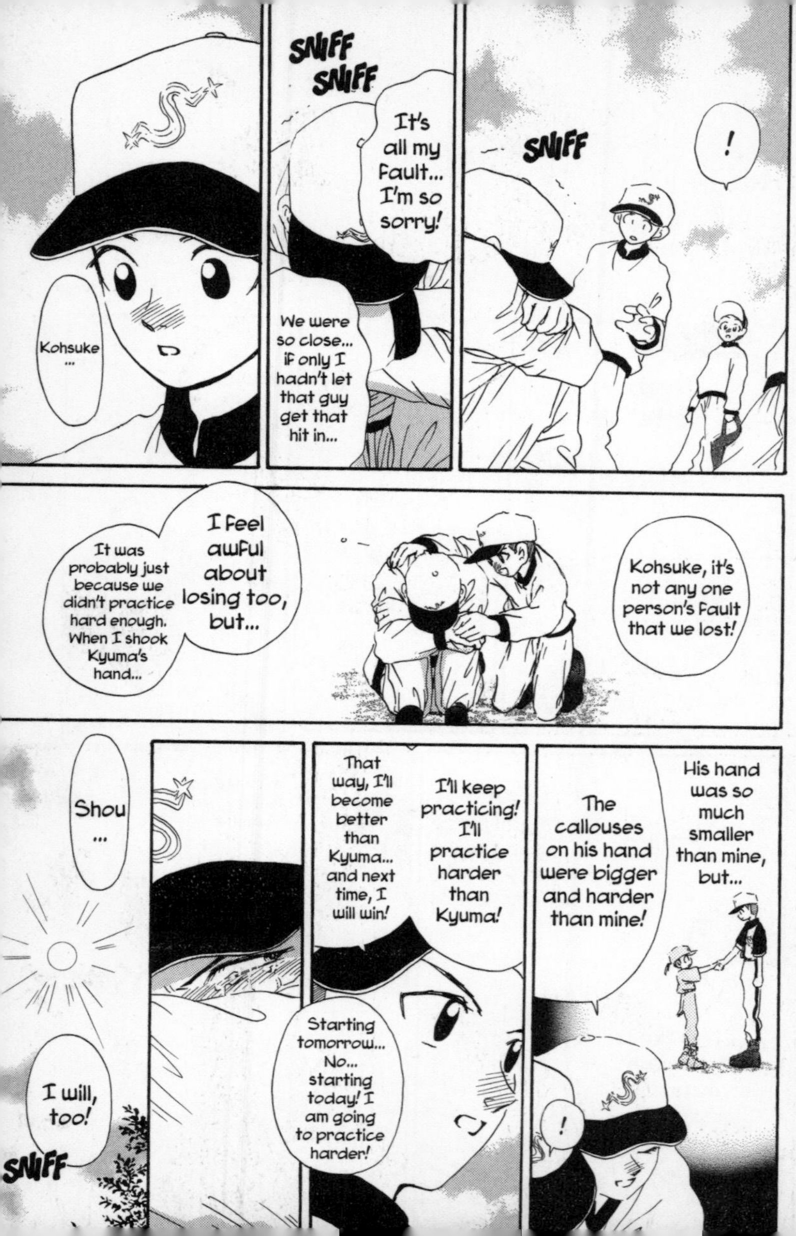
!
SNIFF
SNIFF SNIFF
It's all my fault... I'm so sorry!
We were so close... if only I hadn't let that guy get that hit in...
Kohsuke ...
Kohsuke, it's not any one person's fault that we lost!
I feel awful about losing too, but...
It was probably just because we didn't practice hard enough. When I shook Kyuma's hand...
His hand was so much smaller than mine, but...
The callouses on his hand were bigger and harder than mine!
!
I'll keep practicing! I'll practice harder than Kyuma!
That way, I'll become better than Kyuma... and next time, I will win!
Starting tomorrow... No... starting today! I am going to practice harder!
Shou ...
I will, too!
SNIFF

Hey Coach!
Coach!!
We made it to the finals...
HAW HAW
Is he okay...?
HAW
Is this a dream...?
Go, Nana!
Yeee-aaah!
KICK
EEK!
That hurts!!
AAAK!
GASP
Wait... that means it's not a dream!
WAAH!
I have to go!!
VOOSH
Where's he going?
No idea...
But you know, it is a little hard to believe...
Hmm...
Yeah! I don't think any of us expected to beat last year's champions!
Could that mean we're going to be this year's champs!?
Tetsu...
I feel like nothing can stand in my way now!

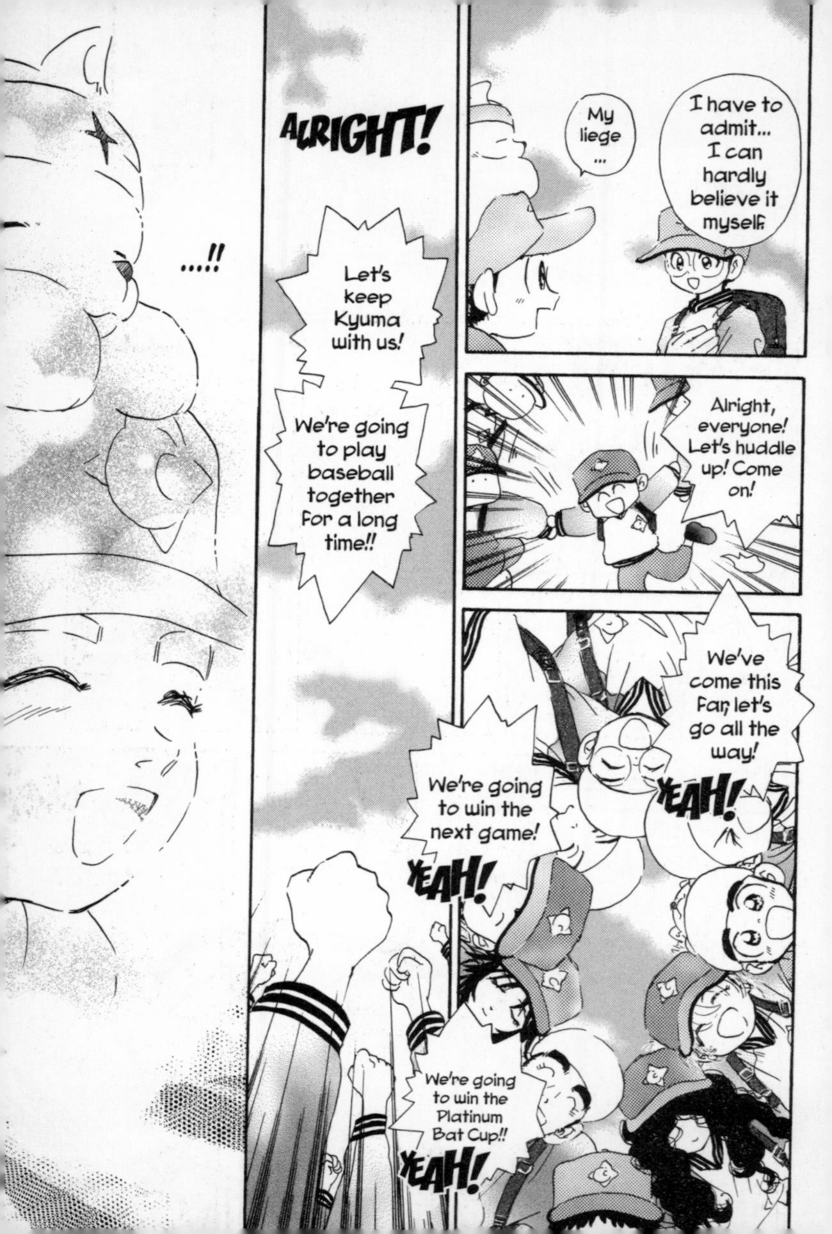
I have to admit... I can hardly believe it myself.
My liege ...
Alright, everyone! Let's huddle up! Come on!
We've come this far, let's go all the way!
YEAH!
We're going to win the next game!
YEAH!
We're going to win the Platinum Bat Cup!!
YEAH!
ALRIGHT!
Let's keep Kyuma with us!
We're going to play baseball together for a long time!!
....!!

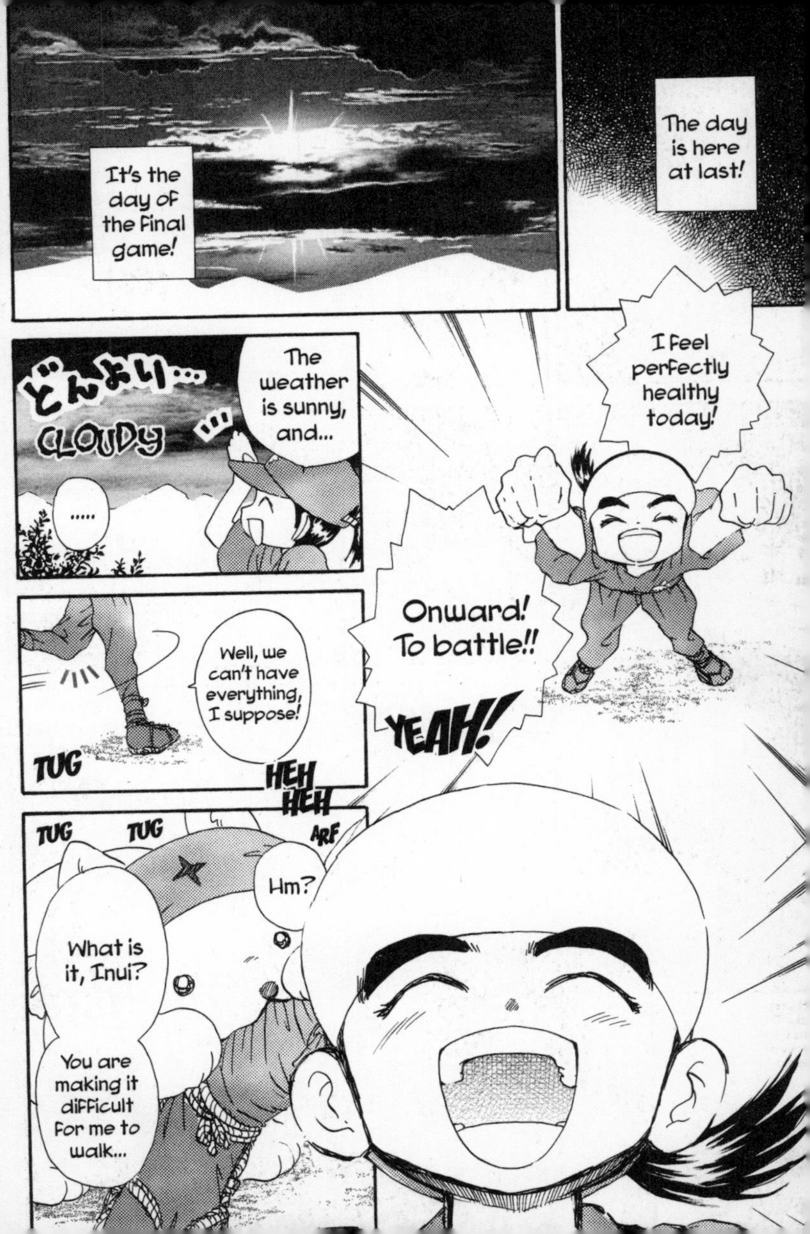
The day is here at last!
It's the day of the final game!
I feel perfectly healthy today!
Onward! To battle!!
YEAH!
The weather is sunny, and...
どんより…
CLOUDY
...
.....
Well, we can't have everything, I suppose!
TUG
HEH HEH
TUG
TUG
ARF
Hm?
What is it, Inui?
You are making it difficult for me to walk...

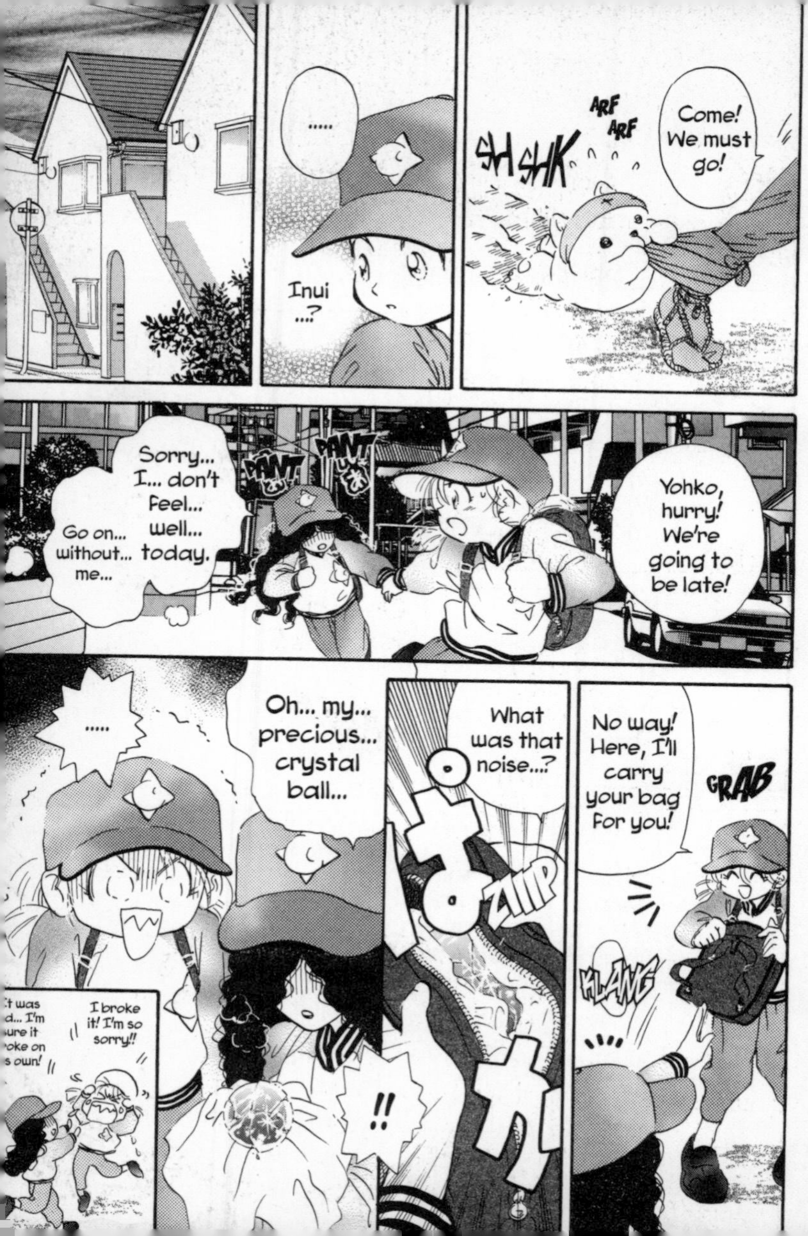
Come! We must go!
ARF ARF
SHSHK
.....
Inui ...?
Yohko, hurry! We're going to be late!
PANT PANT
Sorry... I... don't feel... well... today.
Go on... without... me...
No way! Here, I'll carry your bag for you!
GRAB
KLANG
....
What was that noise...?
ZIIIP
Oh... my... precious... crystal ball...
.....
!!
I broke it! I'm so sorry!!

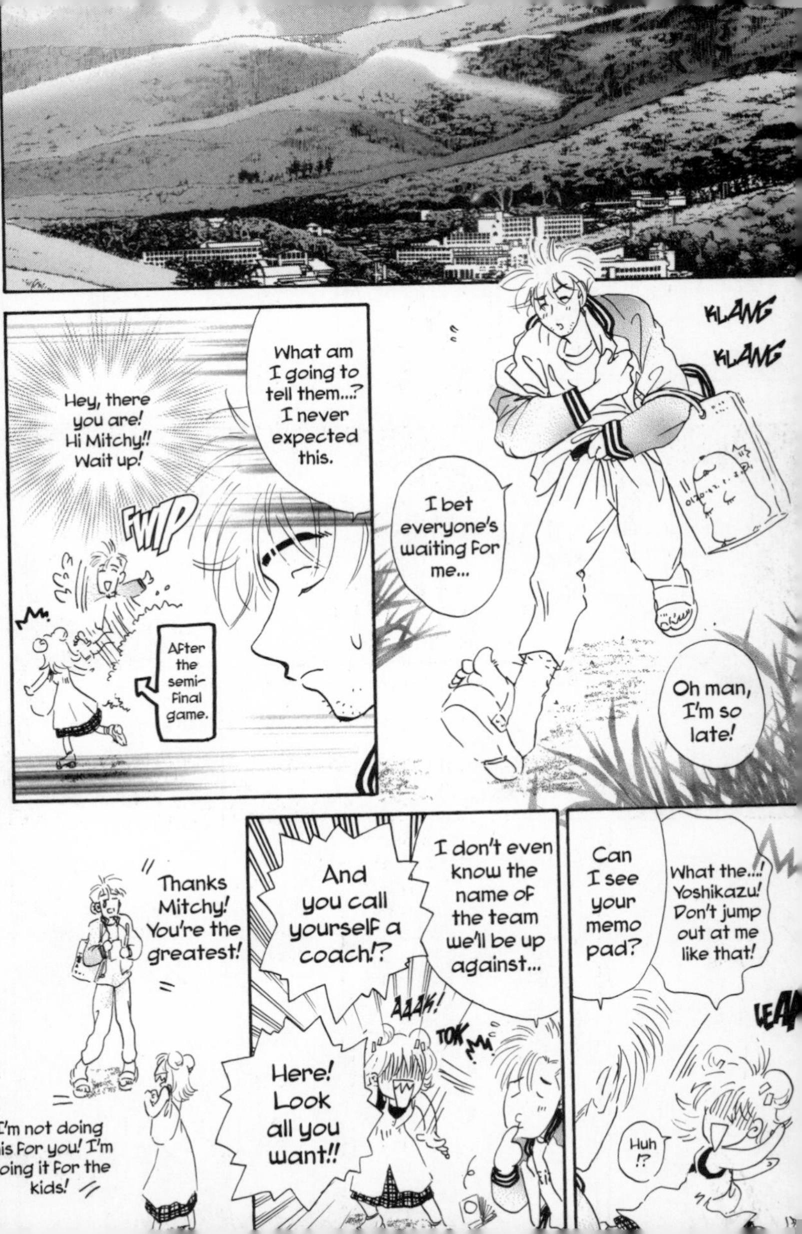
KLANG
KLANG
I bet everyone's waiting for me...
Oh man, I'm so late!
What am I going to tell them...? I never expected this.
Hey, there you are! Hi Mitchy!! Wait up!
FWIP
After the semi-final game.
What the...! Yoshikazu! Don't jump out at me like that!
Can I see your memo pad?
Huh !?
I don't even know the name of the team we'll be up against...
And you call yourself a coach!?
AAAK!
TOK
Here! Look all you want!!
Thanks Mitchy! You're the greatest!
I'm not doing this for you! I'm doing it for the kids!

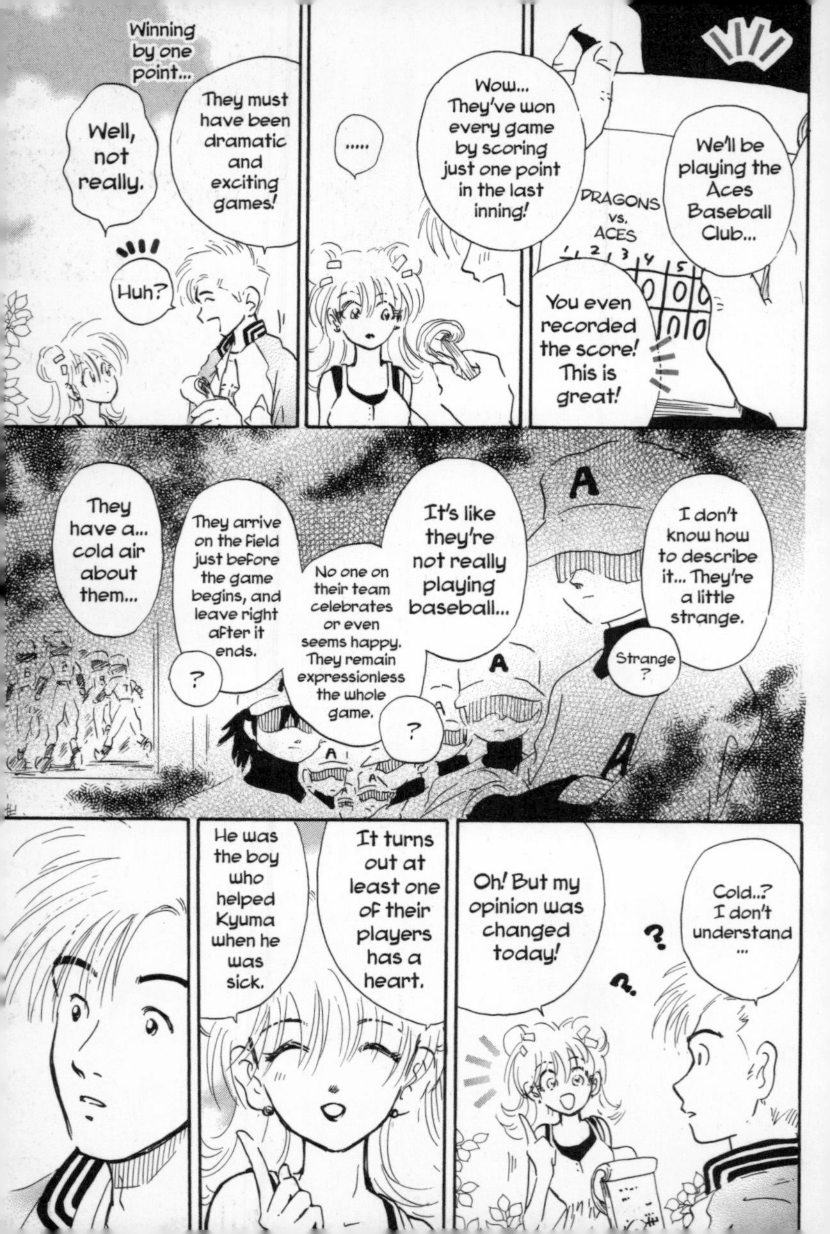
We'll be playing the Aces Baseball Club...
DRAGONS vs. ACES
You even recorded the score! This is great!
Wow... They've won every game by scoring just one point in the last inning!
.....
They must have been dramatic and exciting games!
Winning by one point...
Well, not really.
Huh?
I don't know how to describe it... They're a little strange.
Strange?
It's like they're not really playing baseball...
No one on their team celebrates or even seems happy. They remain expressionless the whole game.
?
They arrive on the field just before the game begins, and leave right after it ends.
They have a... cold air about them...
?
Cold..? I don't understand ...
Oh! But my opinion was changed today!
It turns out at least one of their players has a heart.
He was the boy who helped Kyuma when he was sick.

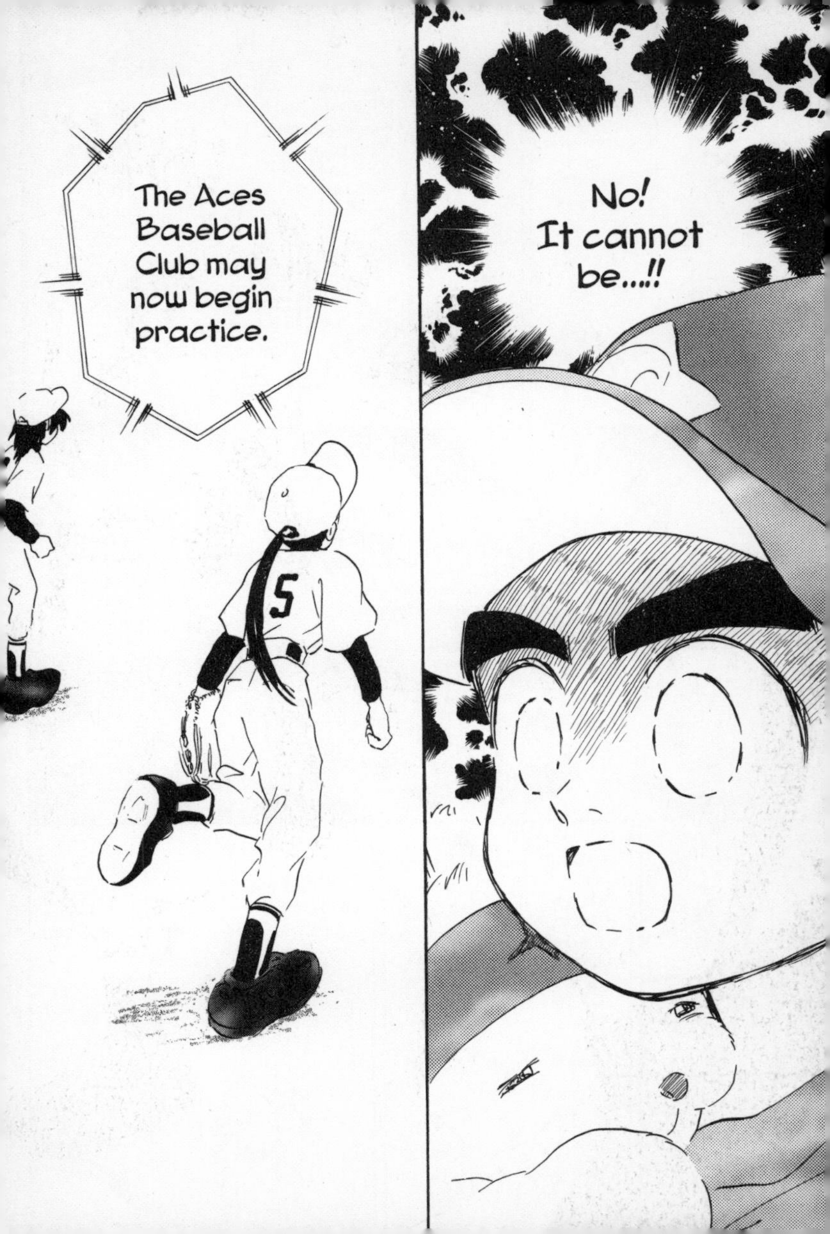
No! It cannot be...!!
The Aces Baseball Club may now begin practice.

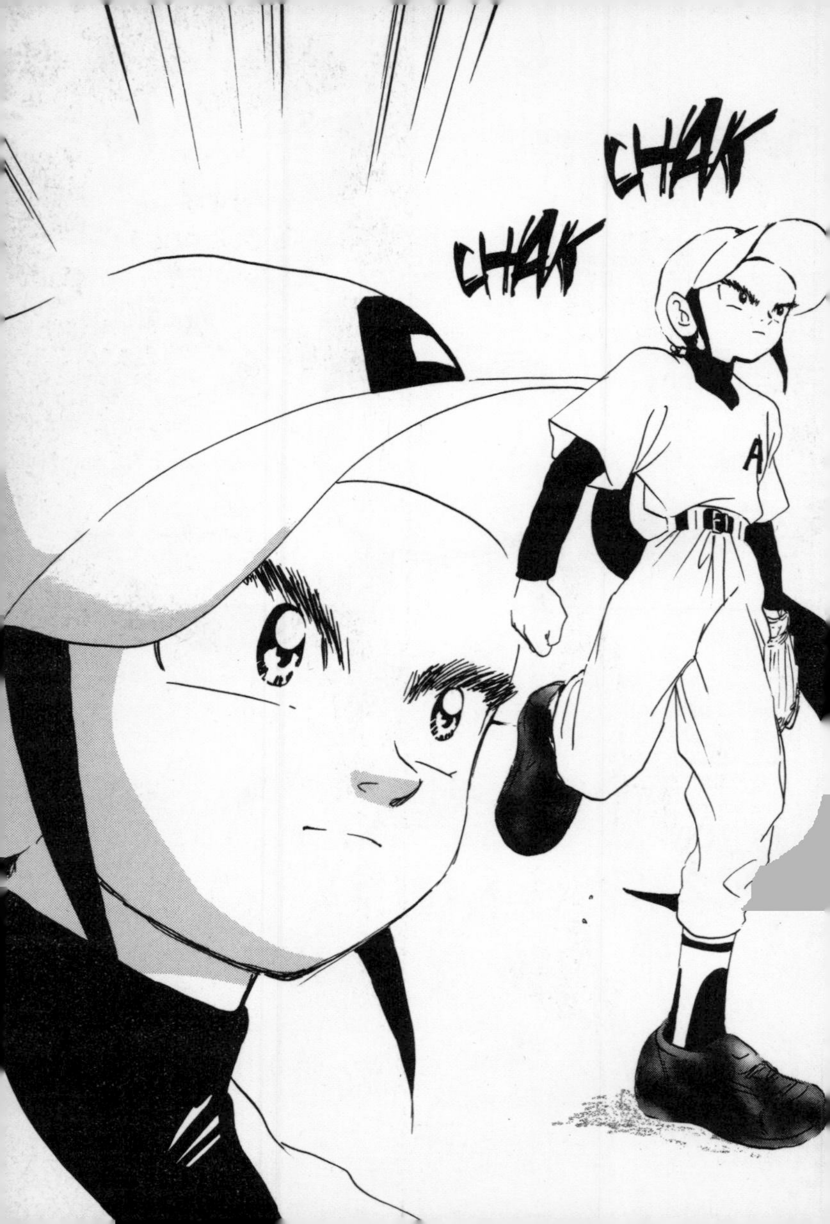
CHAK
CHAK

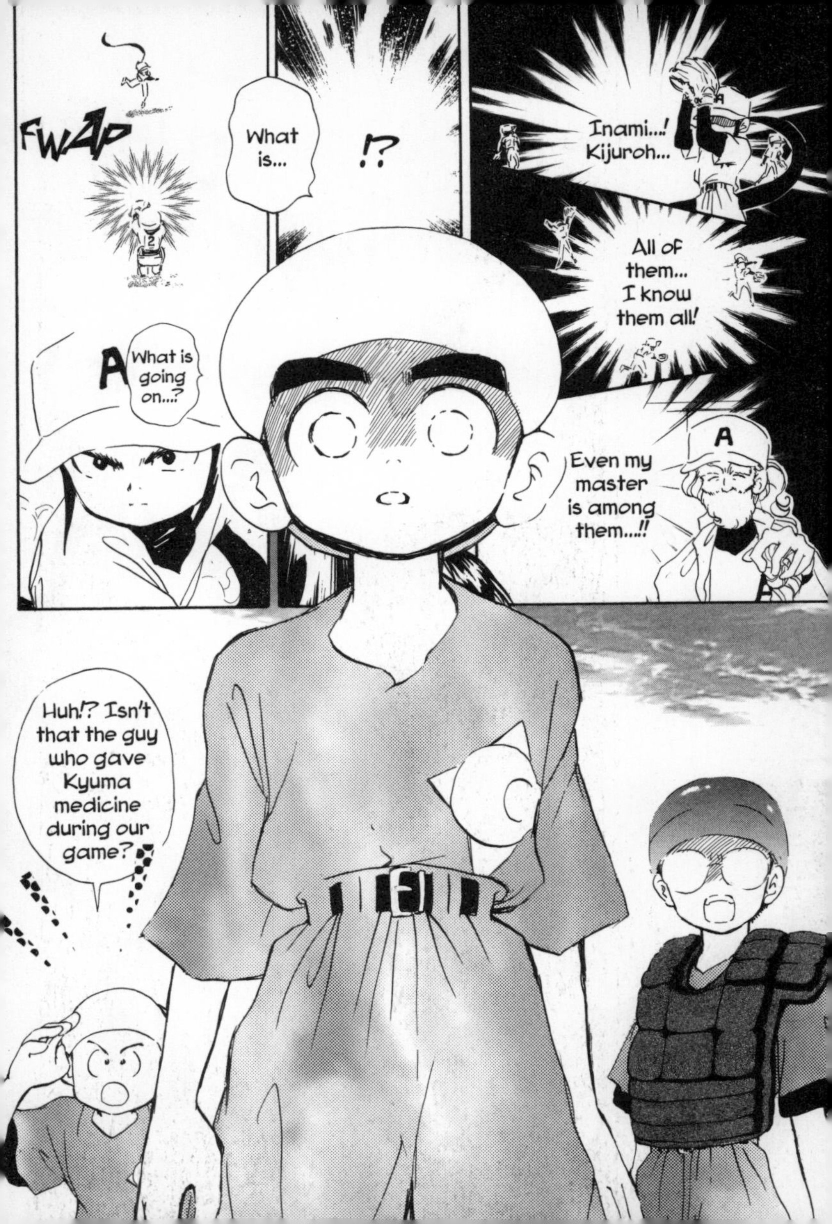

Inami...! Kijuroh...
All of them... I know them all!
Even my master is among them...!!
What is...
!?
FWAP
What is going on...?
Huh!? Isn't that the guy who gave Kyuma medicine during our game?

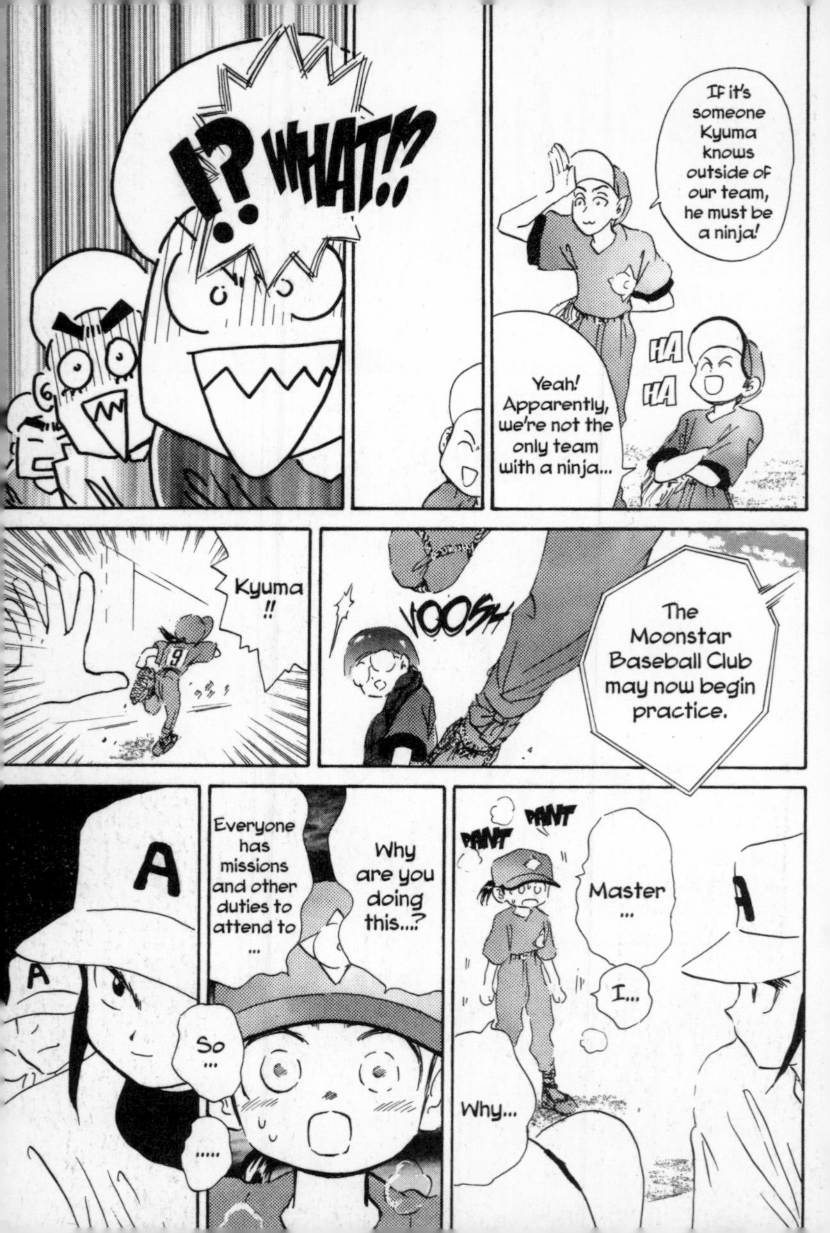
If it's someone Kyuma knows outside of our team, he must be a ninja!
HA HA
Yeah! Apparently, we're not the only team with a ninja...
!? WHAT!?
The Moonstar Baseball Club may now begin practice.
VOOSH
Kyuma !!
PANT PANT
Master ...
I...
Why...
Why are you doing this...?
Everyone has missions and other duties to attend to ...
So ...
.....

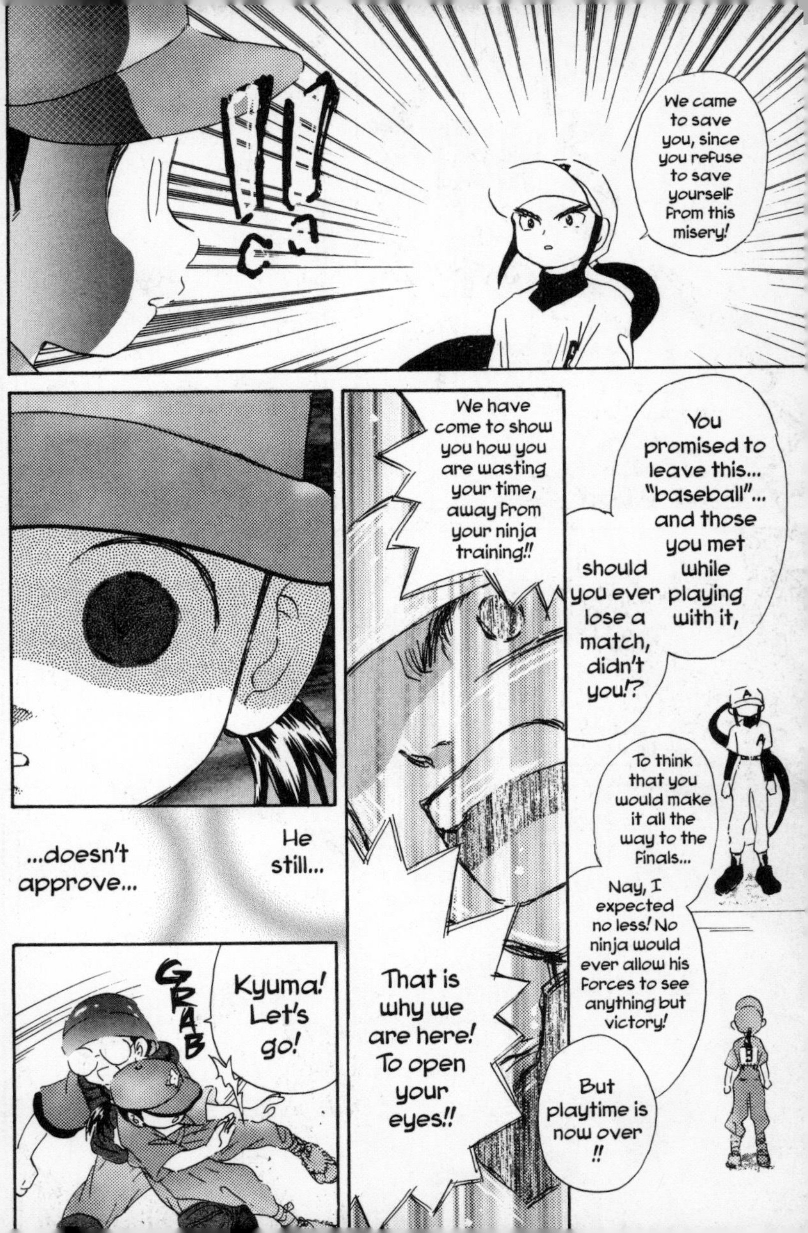

We came to save you, since you refuse to save yourself from this misery!
We have come to show you how you are wasting your time, away from your ninja training!!
You promised to leave this... "baseball"... and those you met while playing with it, should you ever lose a match, didn't you!?
To think that you would make it all the way to the finals...
Nay, I expected no less! No ninja would ever allow his forces to see anything but victory!
But playtime is now over !!
That is why we are here! To open your eyes!!
He still...
...doesn't approve...
GRAB
Kyuma! Let's go!

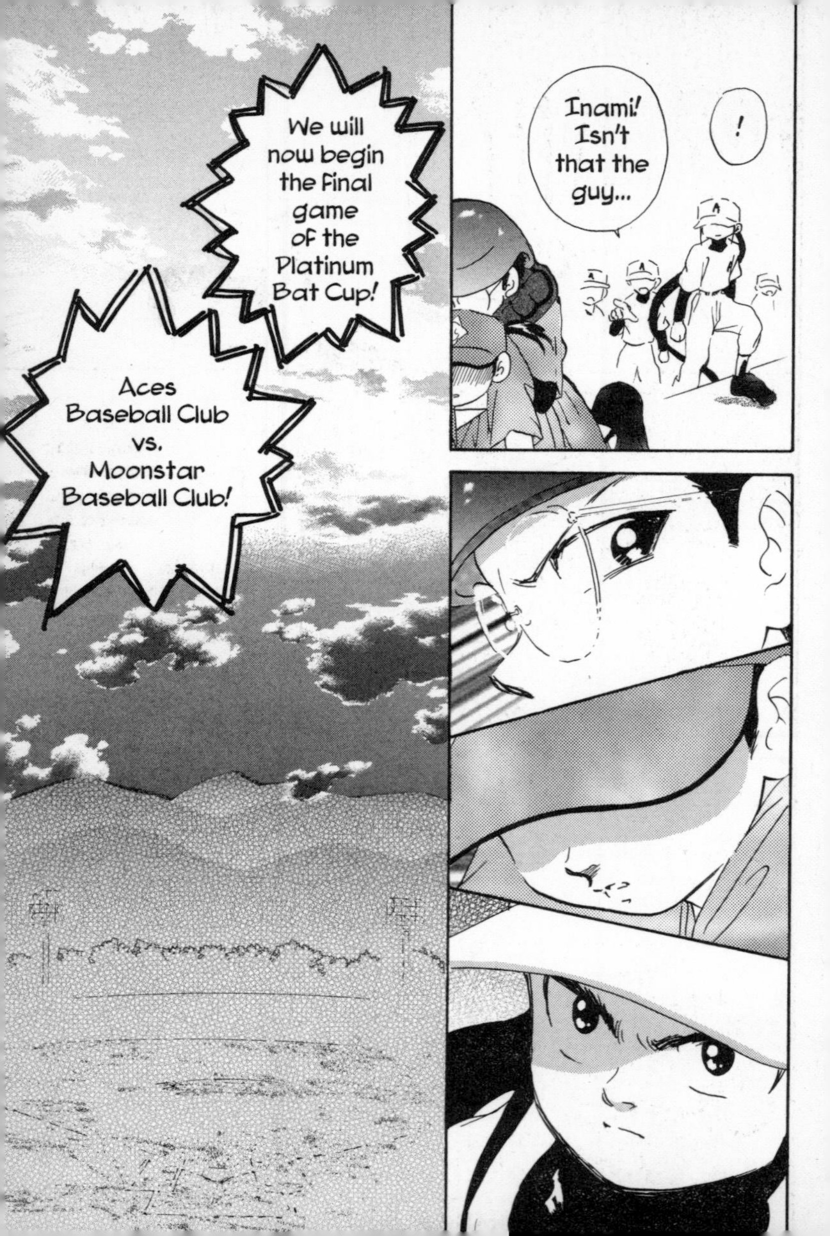
!
Inami! Isn't that the guy...
We will now begin the final game of the Platinum Bat Cup!
Aces Baseball Club vs. Moonstar Baseball Club!

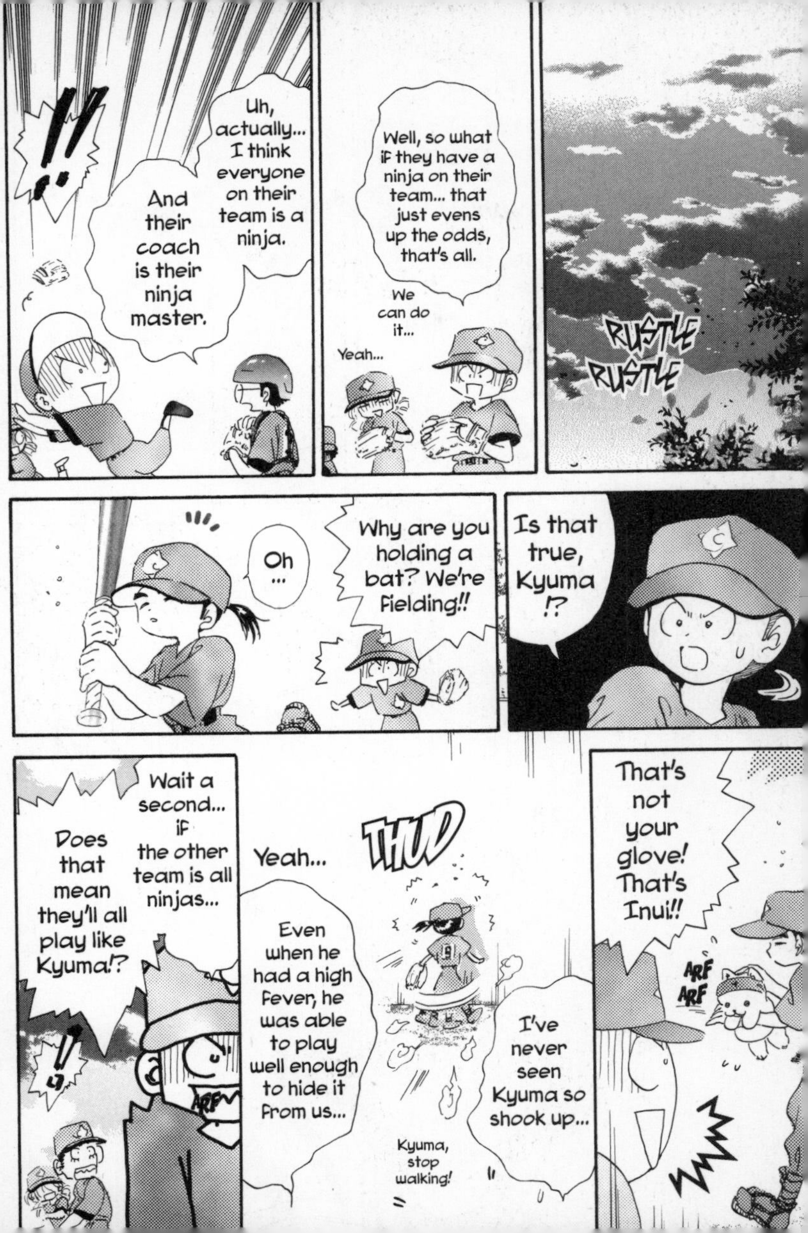
RUSTLE
RUSTLE
Well, so what if they have a ninja on their team... that just evens up the odds, that's all.
We can do it...
Yeah...
Uh, actually... I think everyone on their team is a ninja.
And their coach is their ninja master.
Is that true, Kyuma!?
Why are you holding a bat? We're fielding!!
Oh ...
That's not your glove! That's Inui!!
ARF ARF
THUD
Yeah...
Even when he had a high fever, he was able to play well enough to hide it from us...
I've never seen Kyuma so shook up...
Kyuma, stop walking!
Wait a second... if the other team is all ninjas...
Does that mean they'll all play like Kyuma!?
ARF

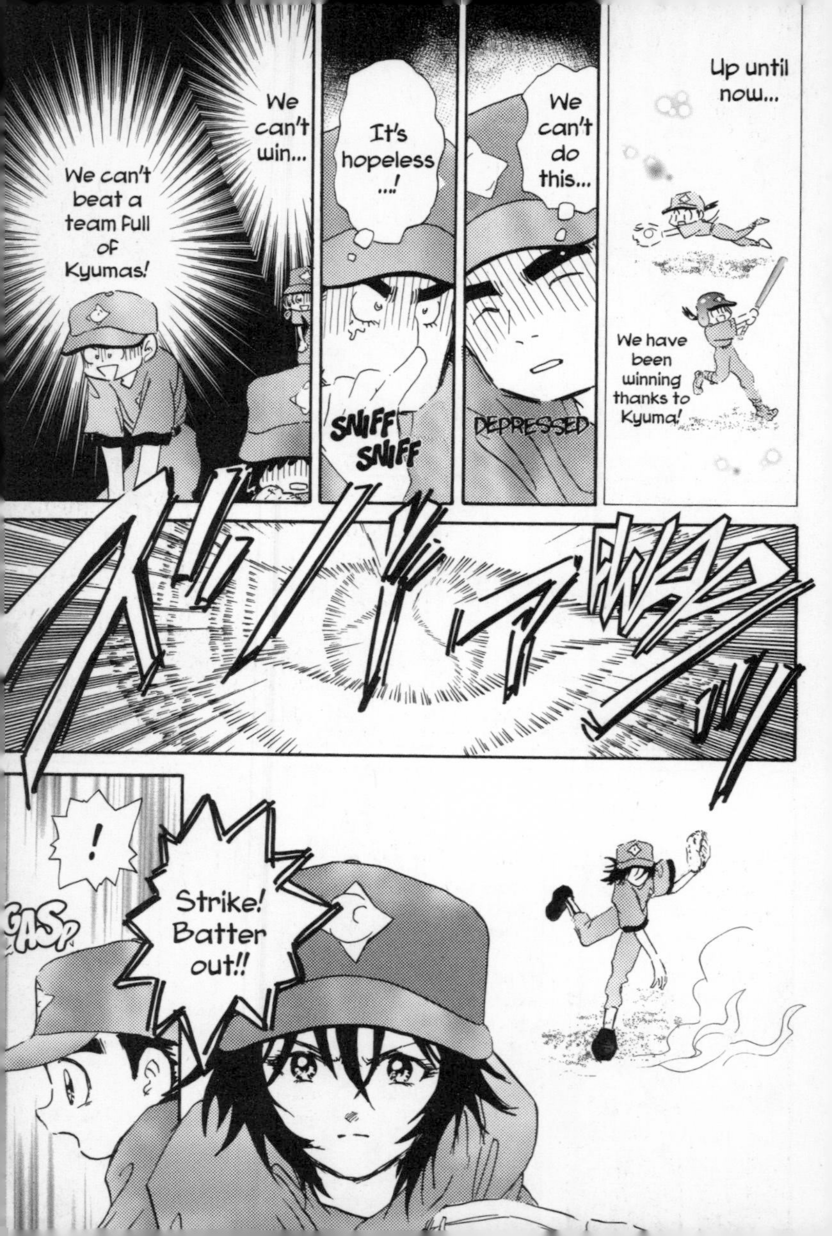
Up until now...
We have been winning thanks to Kyuma!
We can't do this...
DEPRESSED
It's hopeless...!
SNIFF SNIFF
We can't win...
We can't beat a team full of Kyumas!
Strike! Batter out!!
!
GASP

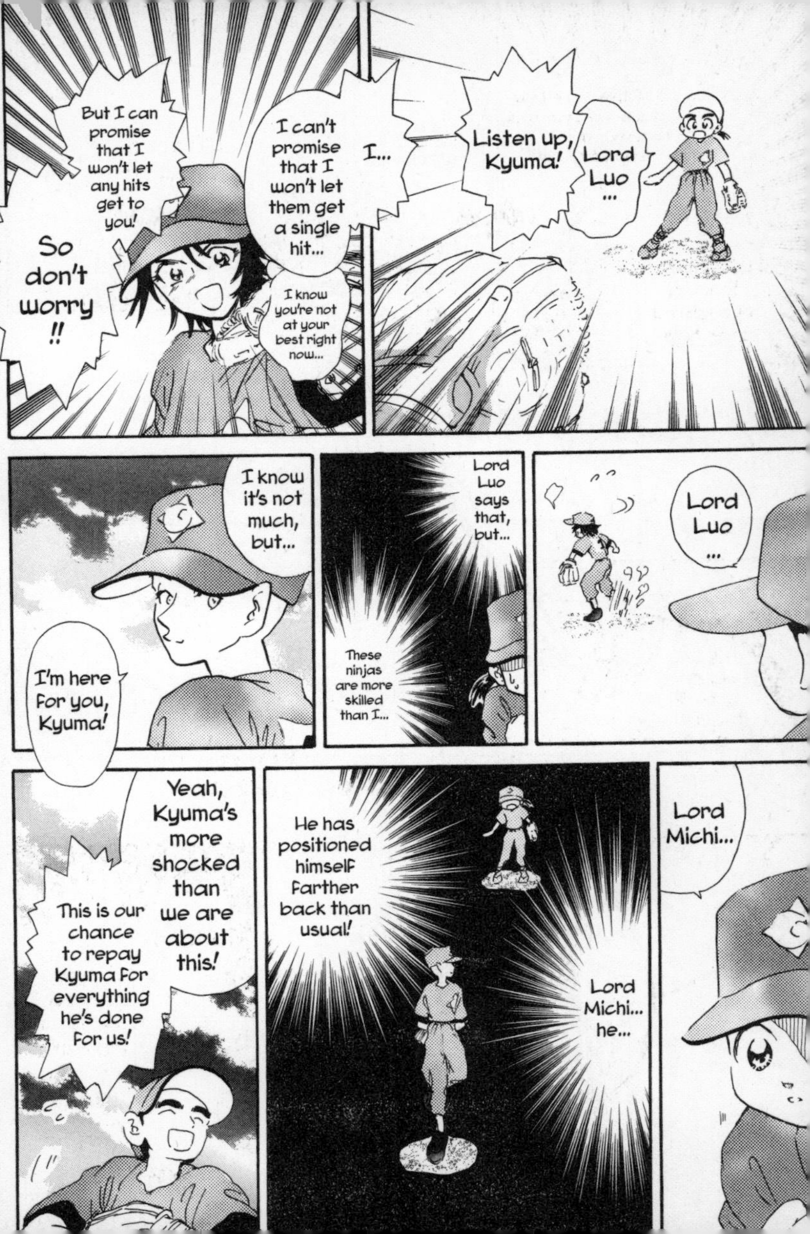
Lord Luo ...
Listen up, Kyuma!
I...
I can't promise that I won't let them get a single hit...
I know you're not at your best right now...
But I can promise that I won't let any hits get to you!
So don't worry !!
Lord Luo ...
Lord Luo says that, but...
These ninjas are more skilled than I...
I know it's not much, but...
I'm here for you, Kyuma!
Lord Michi...
He has positioned himself farther back than usual!
Lord Michi... he...
Yeah, Kyuma's more shocked than we are about this!
This is our chance to repay Kyuma for everything he's done for us!

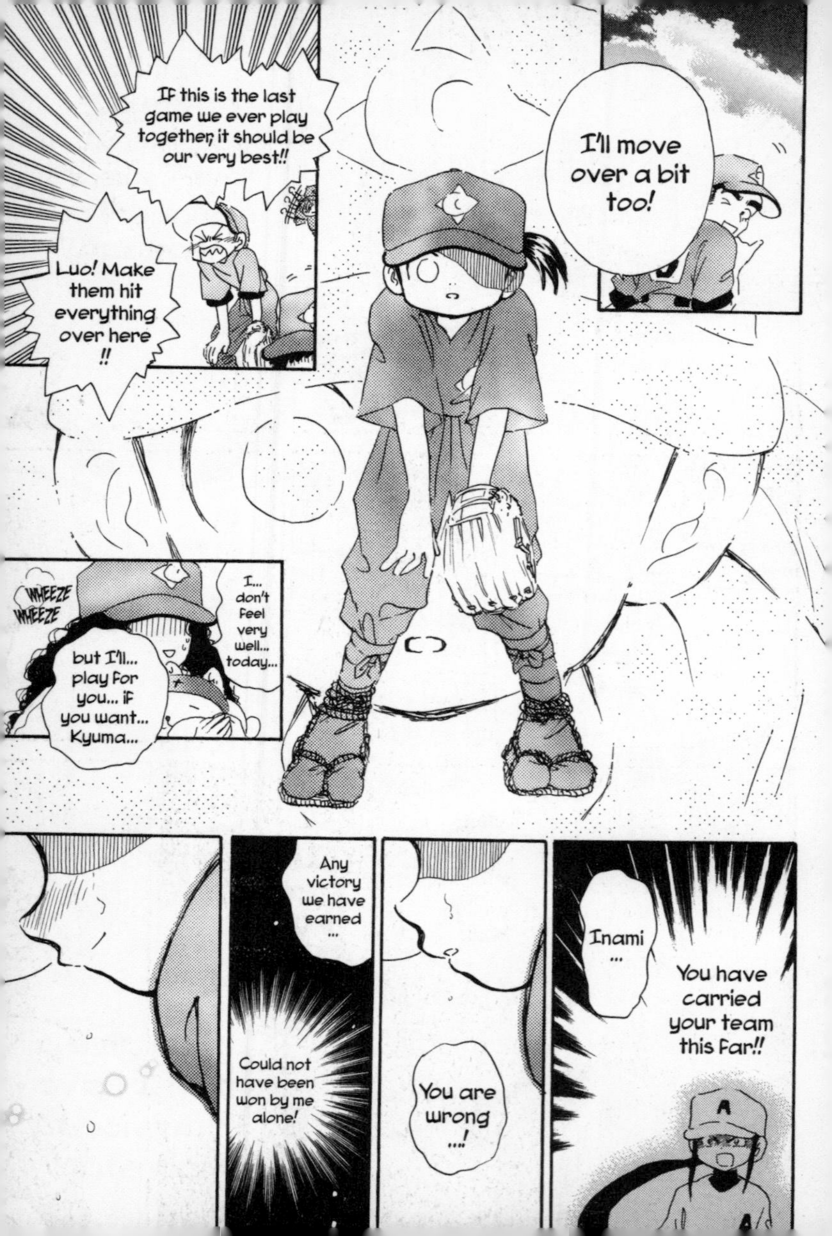
I'll move over a bit too!
If this is the last game we ever play together, it should be our very best!!
Luo! Make them hit everything over here !!
I... don't feel very well... today...
WHEEZE WHEEZE
but I'll... play for you... if you want... Kyuma...
Inami ...
You have carried your team this far!!
You are wrong ...!
Any victory we have earned ...
Could not have been won by me alone!

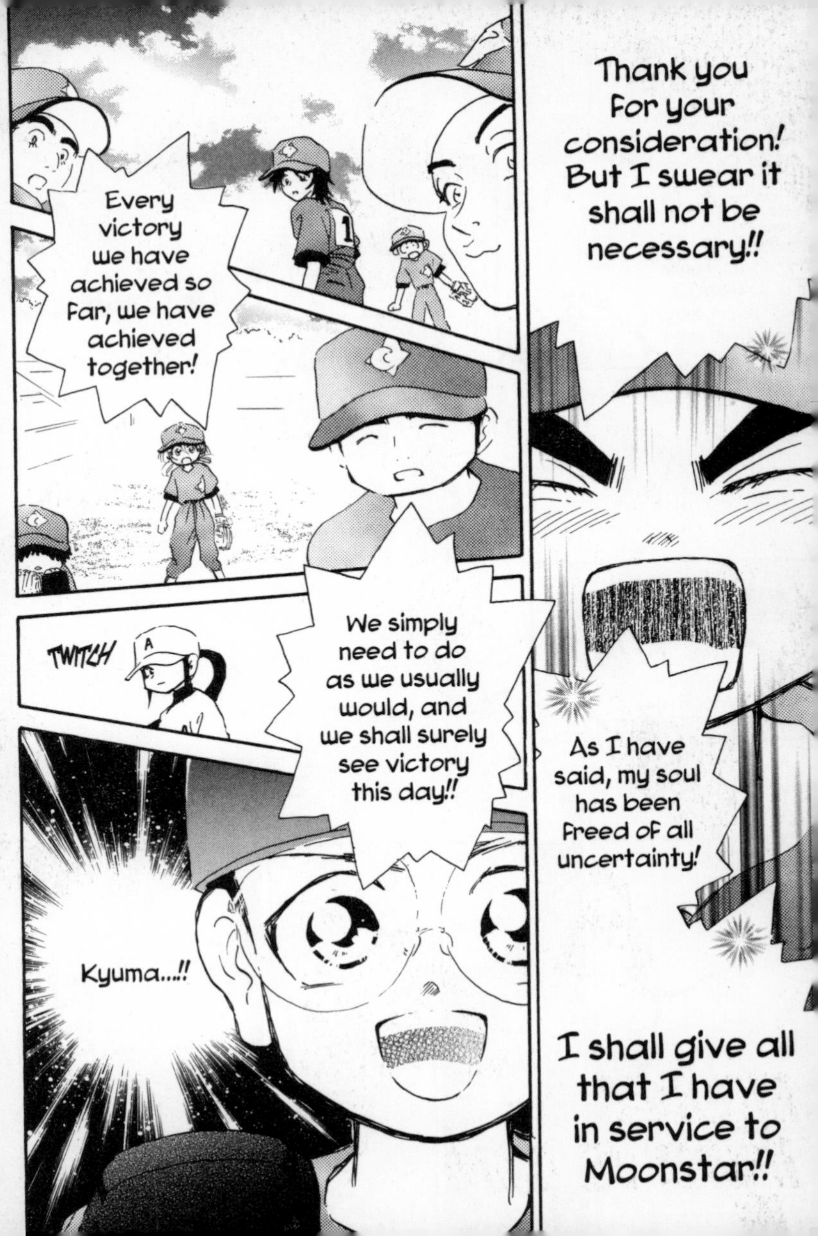
Thank you for your consideration! But I swear it shall not be necessary!!
As I have said, my soul has been freed of all uncertainty!
I shall give all that I have in service to Moonstar!!
Every victory we have achieved so far, we have achieved together!
TWITCH
We simply need to do as we usually would, and we shall surely see victory this day!!
Kyuma...!!

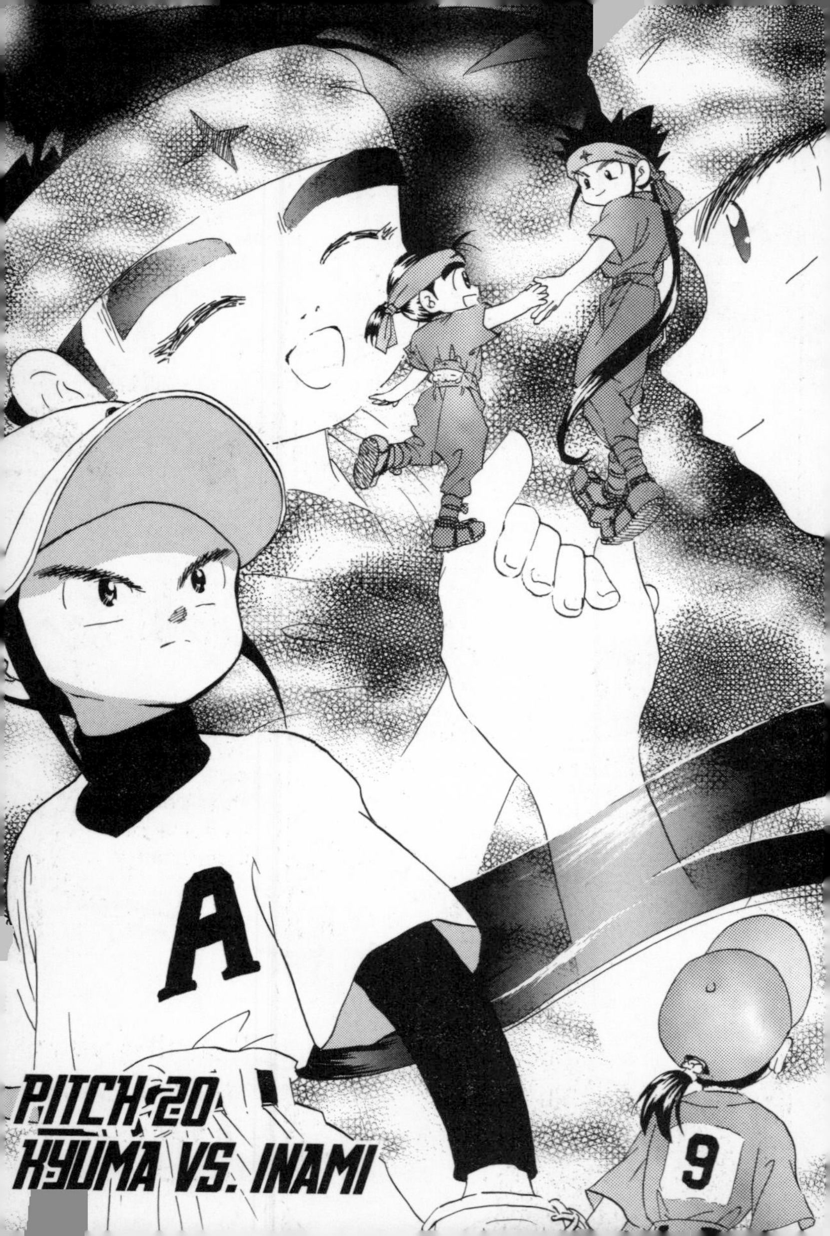
PITCH 20
KYUMA VS. INAMI
A
9

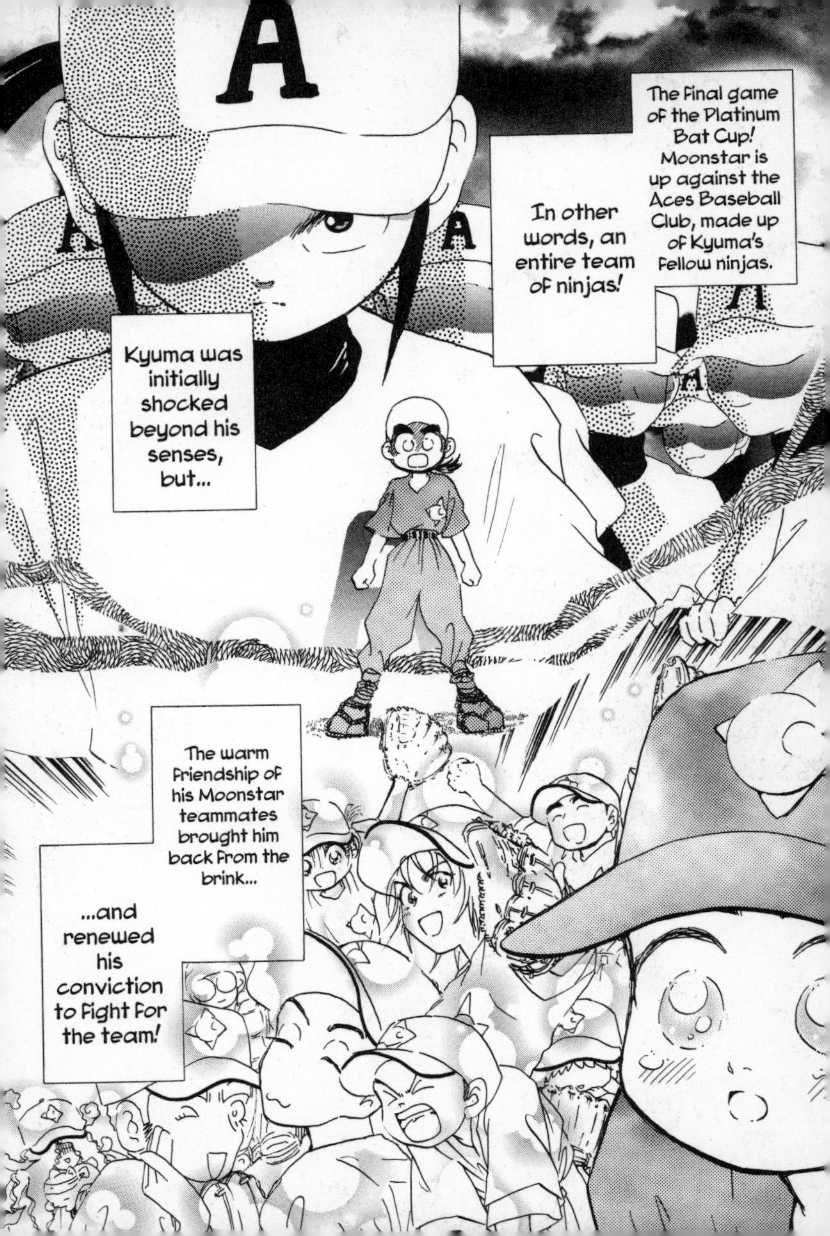
The final game of the Platinum Bat Cup! Moonstar is up against the Aces Baseball Club, made up of Kyuma's fellow ninjas.
In other words, an entire team of ninjas!
Kyuma was initially shocked beyond his senses, but...
The warm friendship of his Moonstar teammates brought him back from the brink...
...and renewed his conviction to fight for the team!

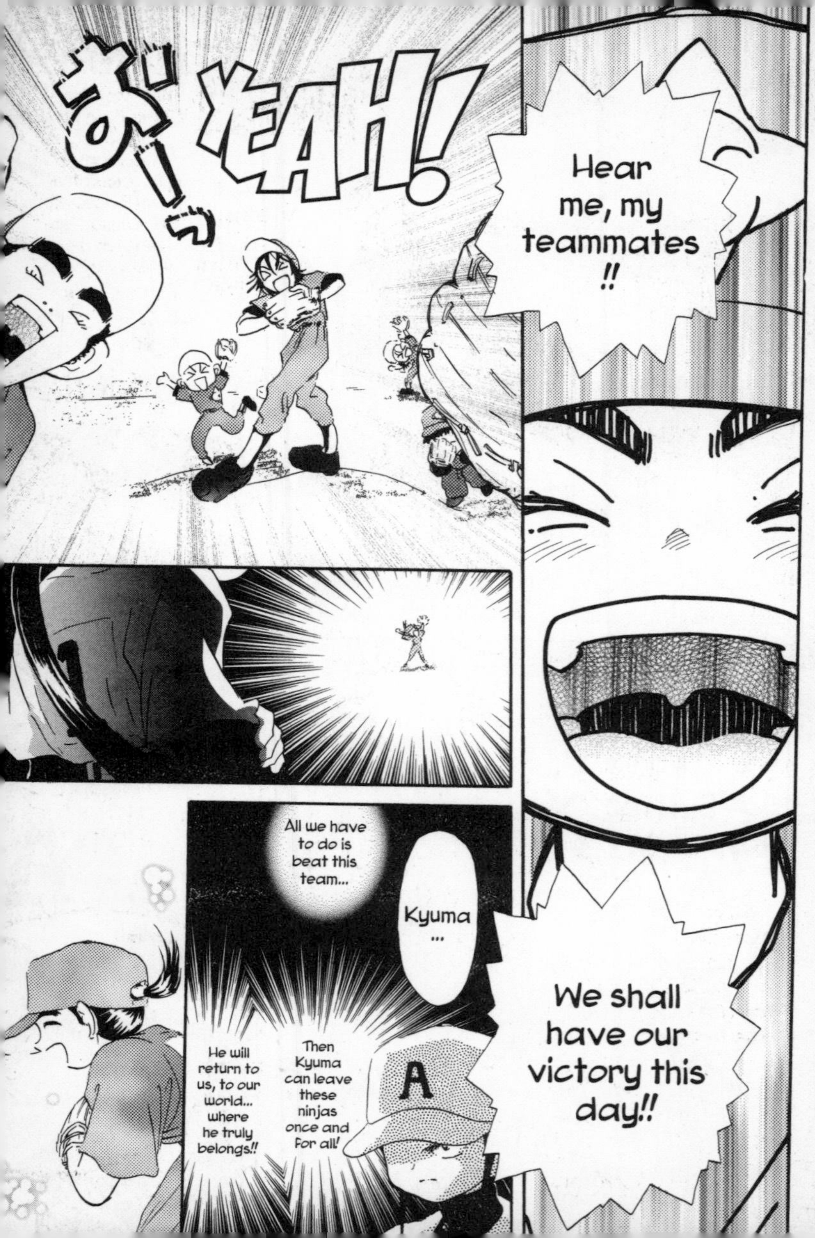
Hear me, my teammates!!
We shall have our victory this day!!
おーっ
YEAH!
All we have to do is beat this team...
Kyuma...
Then Kyuma can leave these ninjas once and for all!
He will return to us, to our world... where he truly belongs!!

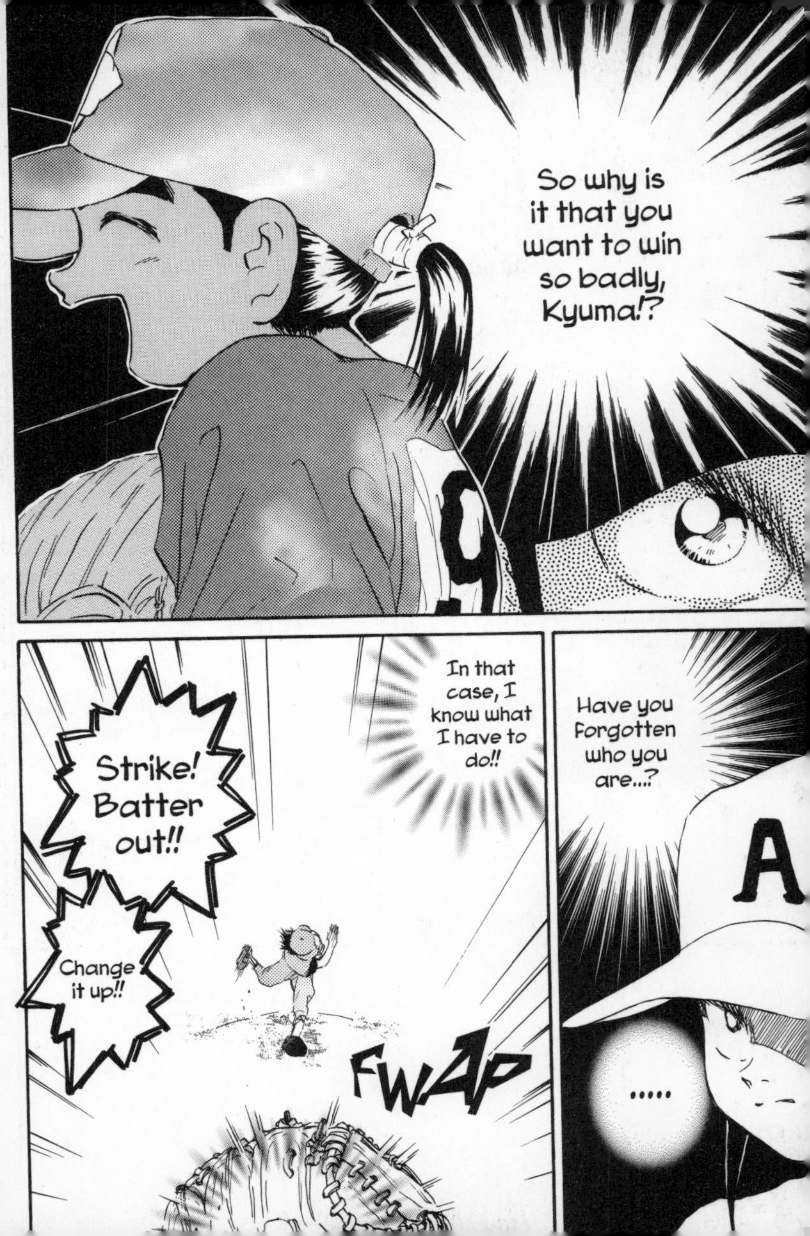

So why is it that you want to win so badly, Kyuma!?
Have you forgotten who you are...?
.....
In that case, I know what I have to do!!
Strike! Batter out!!
FWAP
Change it up!!

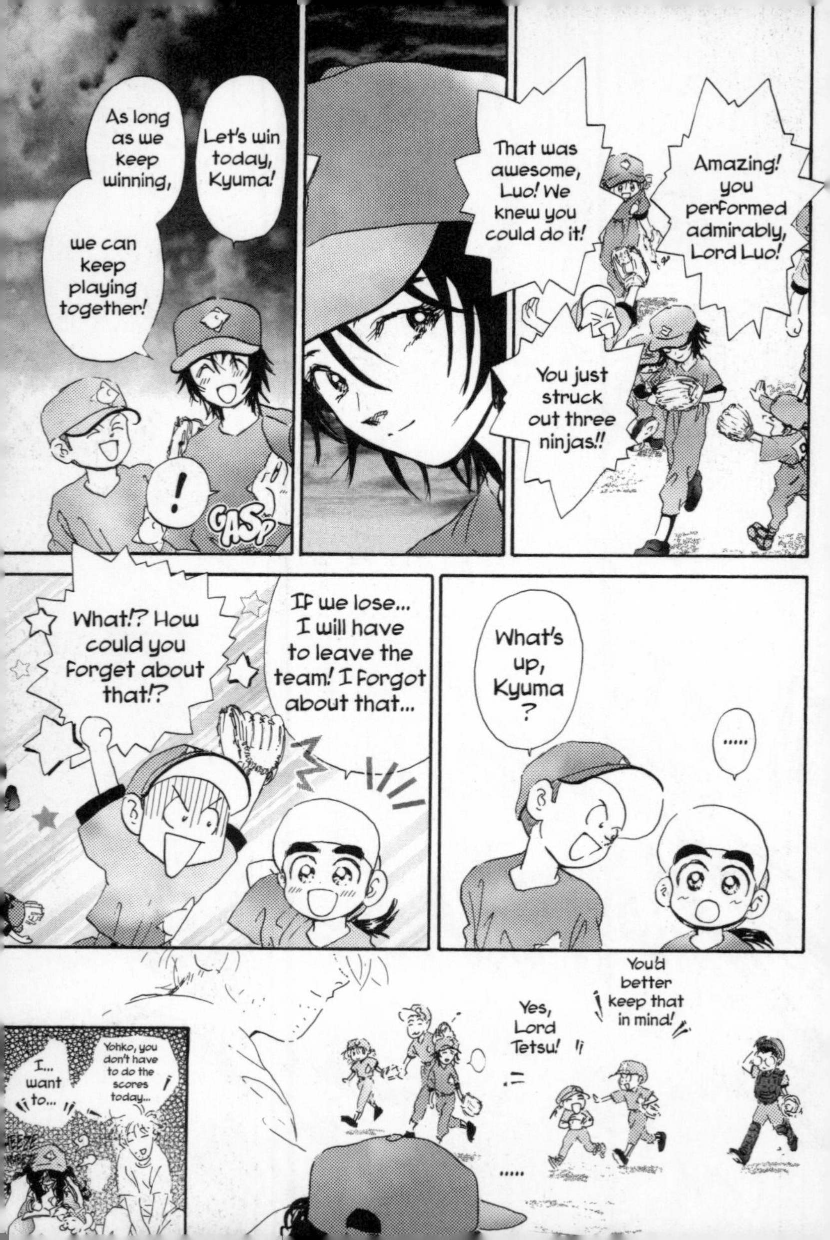
Amazing! you performed admirably, Lord Luo!
That was awesome, Luo! We knew you could do it!
You just struck out three ninjas!!
Let's win today, Kyuma!
As long as we keep winning,
we can keep playing together!
!
GASP
What's up, Kyuma?
.....
If we lose... I will have to leave the team! I forgot about that...
What!? How could you forget about that!?
You'd better keep that in mind!
Yes, Lord Tetsu!
.....
Yohko, you don't have to do the scores today...
I... want to...

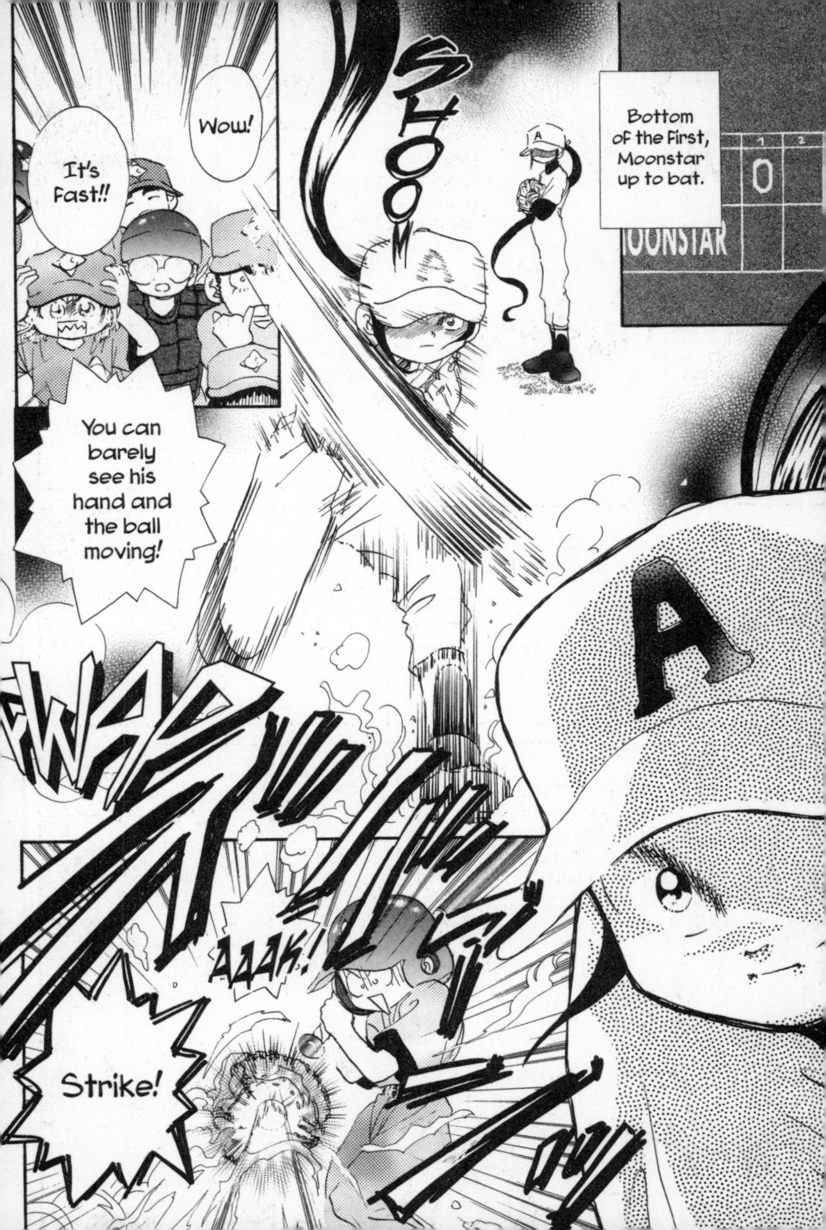

Bottom of the First, Moonstar up to bat.
SHOOM
Wow!
It's Fast!!
You can barely see his hand and the ball moving!
AAAK!
Strike!

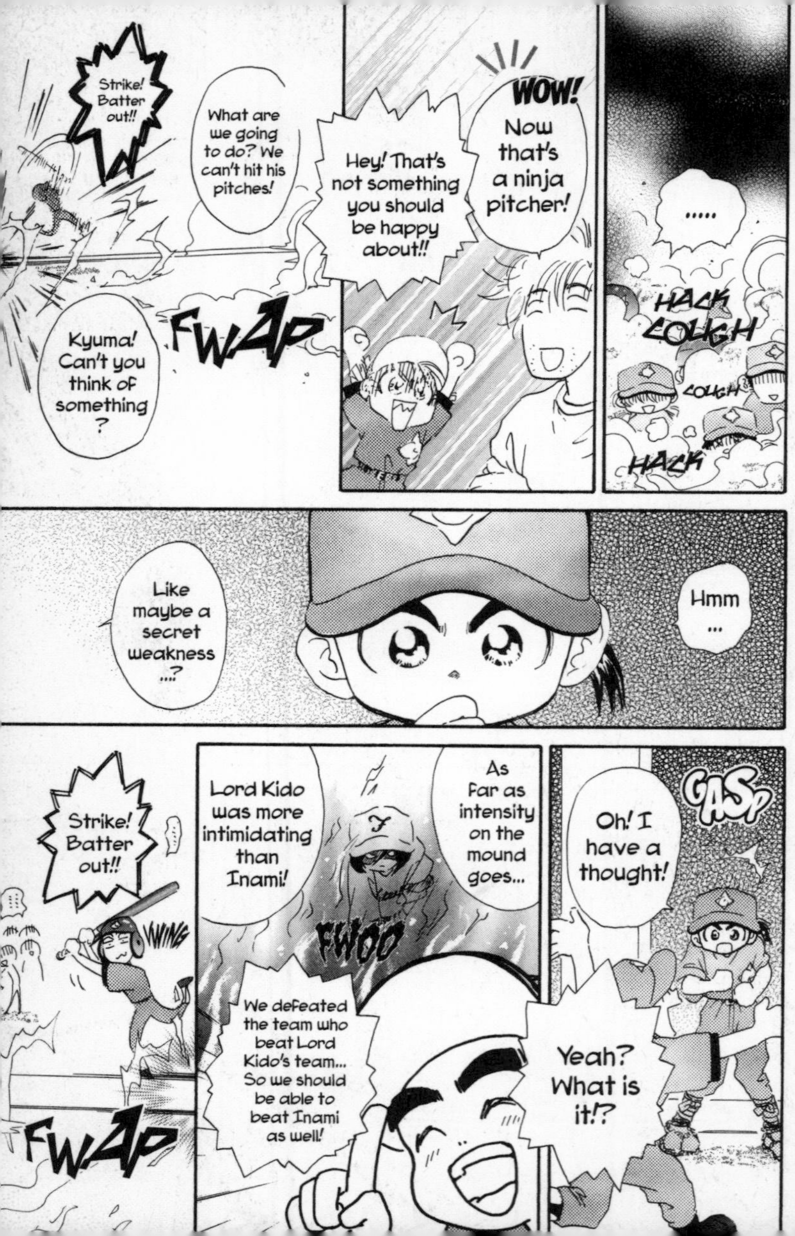
.....
HACK
COUGH
COUGH
HACK
WOW!
Now that's a ninja pitcher!
Hey! That's not something you should be happy about!!
Strike! Batter out!!
What are we going to do? We can't hit his pitches!
FWAP
Kyuma! Can't you think of something?
Hmm...
Like maybe a secret weakness...?
GASP
Oh! I have a thought!
As far as intensity on the mound goes...
Lord Kido was more intimidating than Inami!
FWOO
Yeah? What is it!?
We defeated the team who beat Lord Kido's team... So we should be able to beat Inami as well!
Strike! Batter out!!
VWING
FWAP

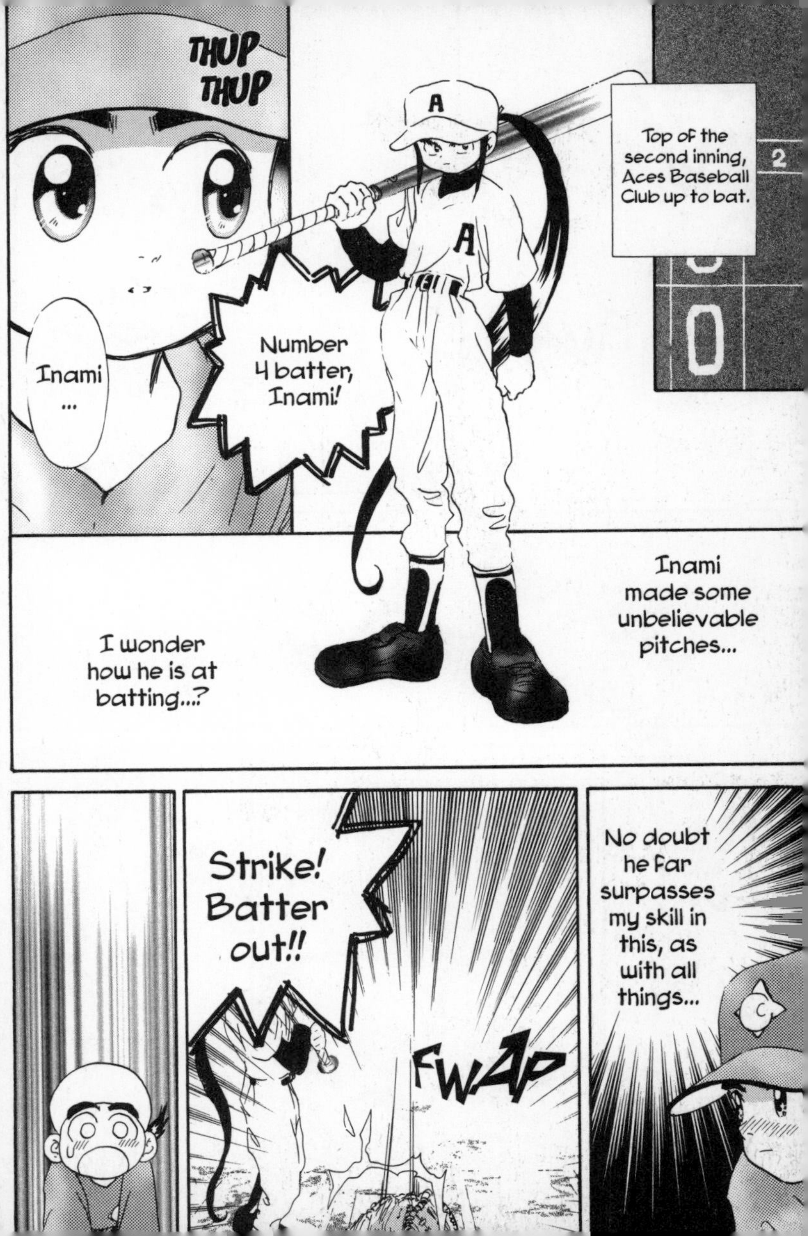
Top of the second inning, Aces Baseball Club up to bat.
2
0
THUP THUP
Number 4 batter, Inami!
Inami ...
Inami made some unbelievable pitches...
I wonder how he is at batting...?
No doubt he far surpasses my skill in this, as with all things...
Strike! Batter out!!
FWAP

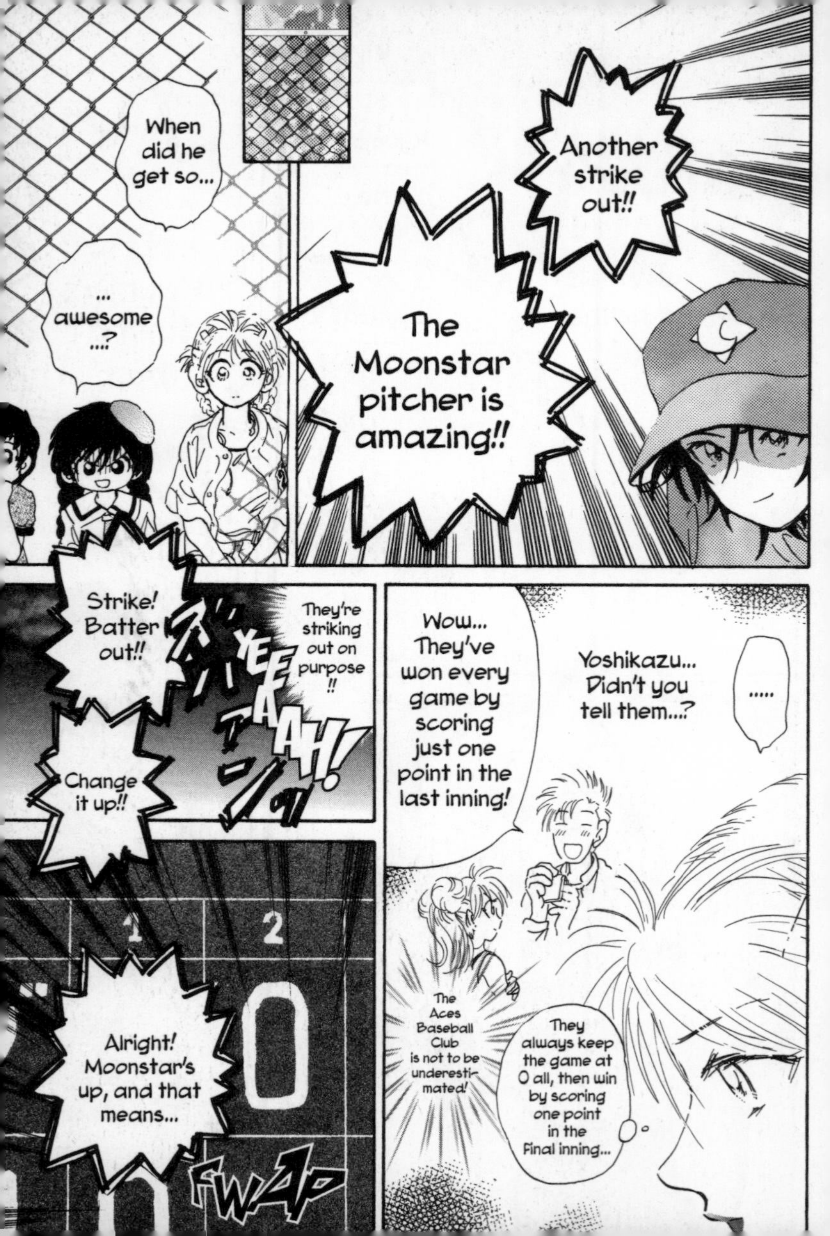
Another strike out!!
The Moonstar pitcher is amazing!!
When did he get so...
... awesome ...?
.....
Yoshikazu... Didn't you tell them...?
Wow... They've won every game by scoring just one point in the last inning!
They always keep the game at 0 all, then win by scoring one point in the final inning...
The Aces Baseball Club is not to be underesti-mated!
They're striking out on purpose!!
YEEAAH!
Strike! Batter out!!
Change it up!!
2
1
0
FWAP
Alright! Moonstar's up, and that means...

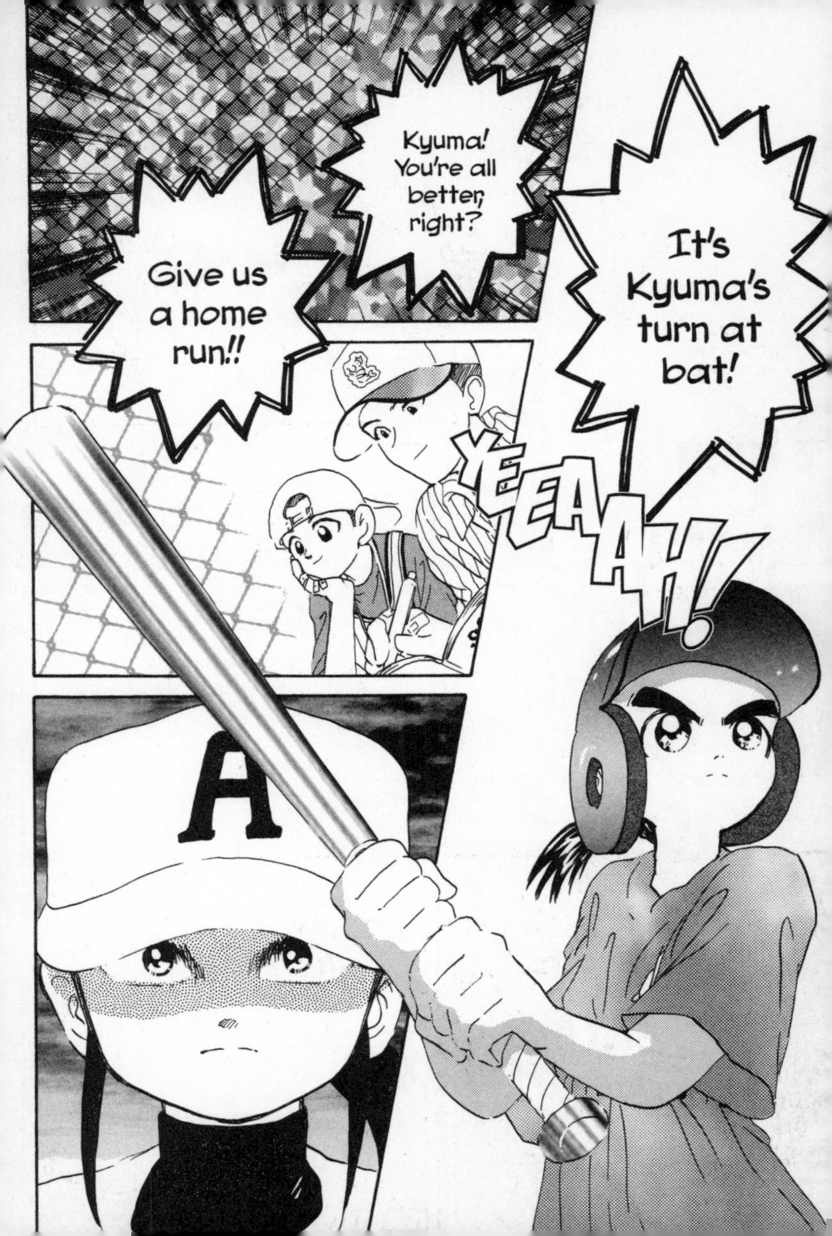
It's Kyuma's turn at bat!
Kyuma! You're all better, right?
Give us a home run!!
YEEAAAH!

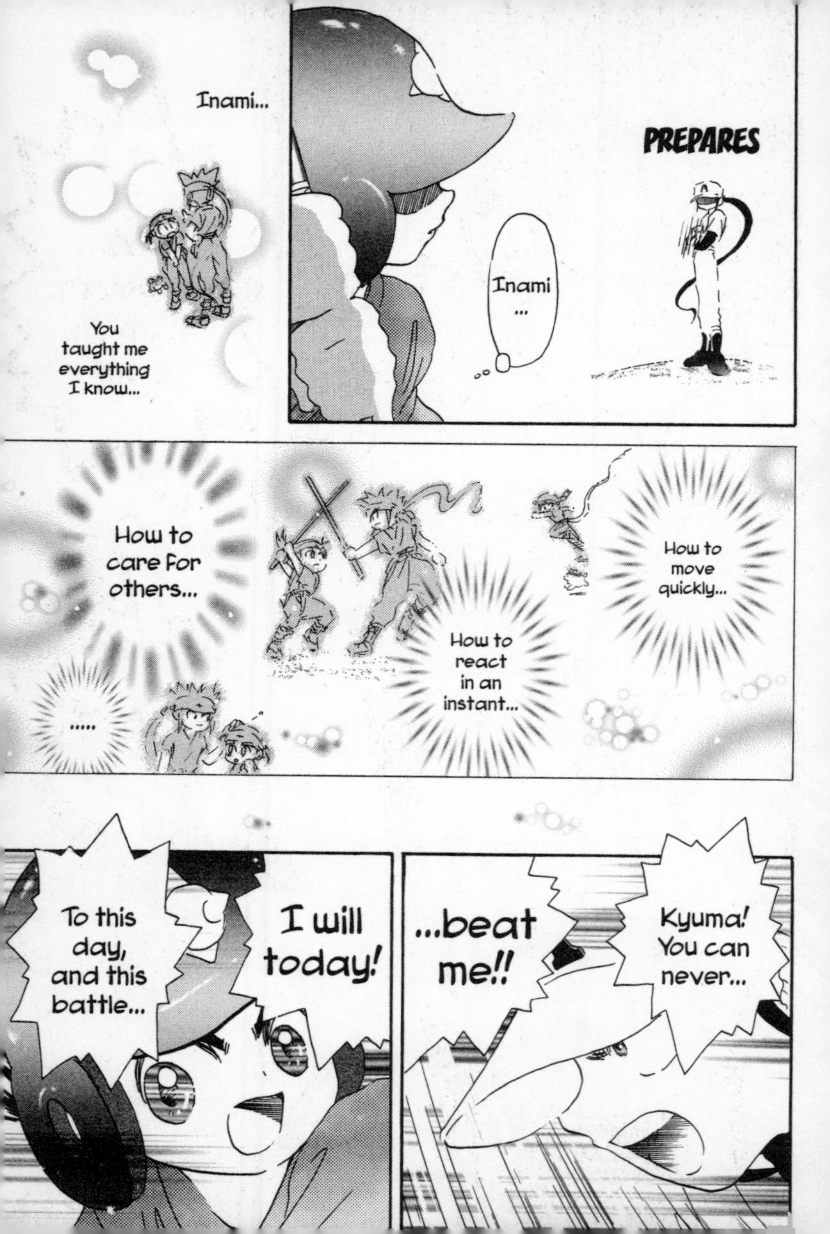
PREPARES
Inami ...
Inami...
You taught me everything I know...
How to move quickly...
How to react in an instant...
How to care for others...
.....
Kyuma! You can never...
...beat me!!
To this day, and this battle...
I will today!

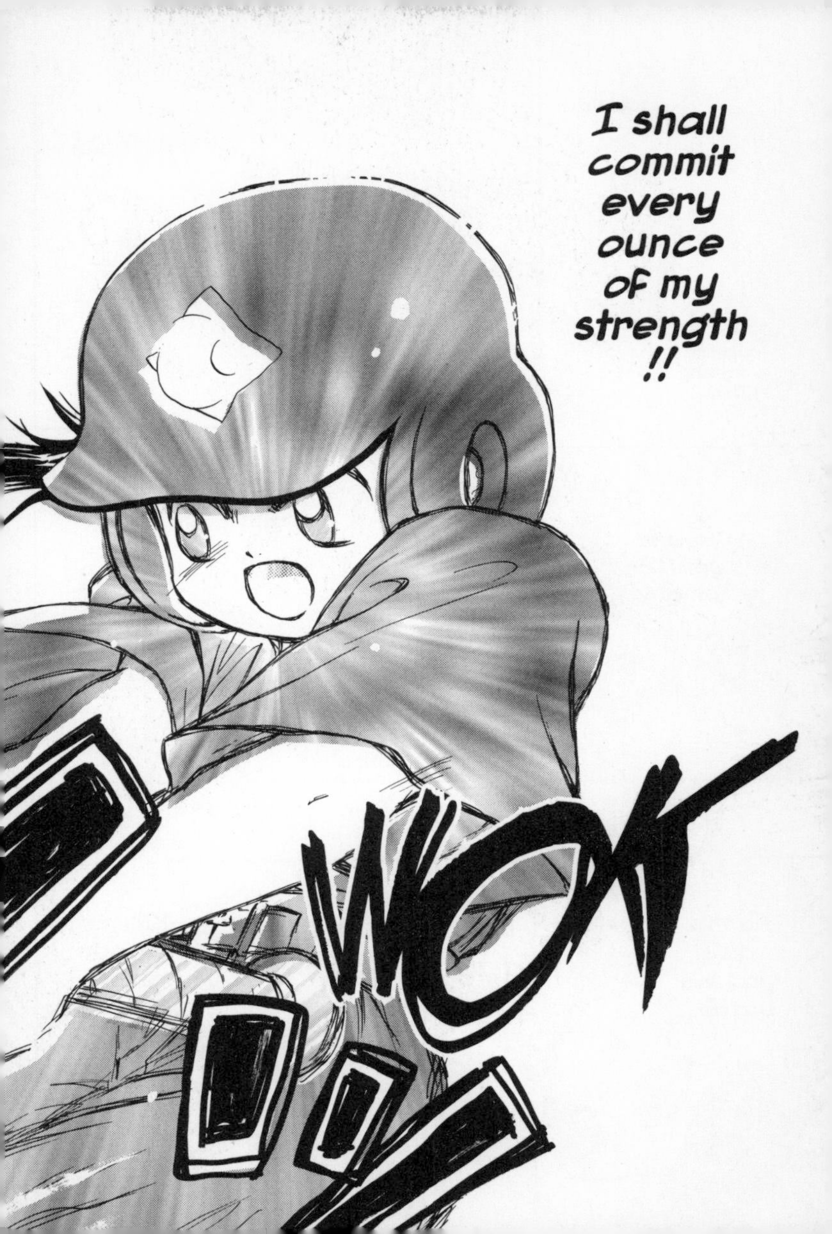
I shall commit every ounce of my strength !!
WOK

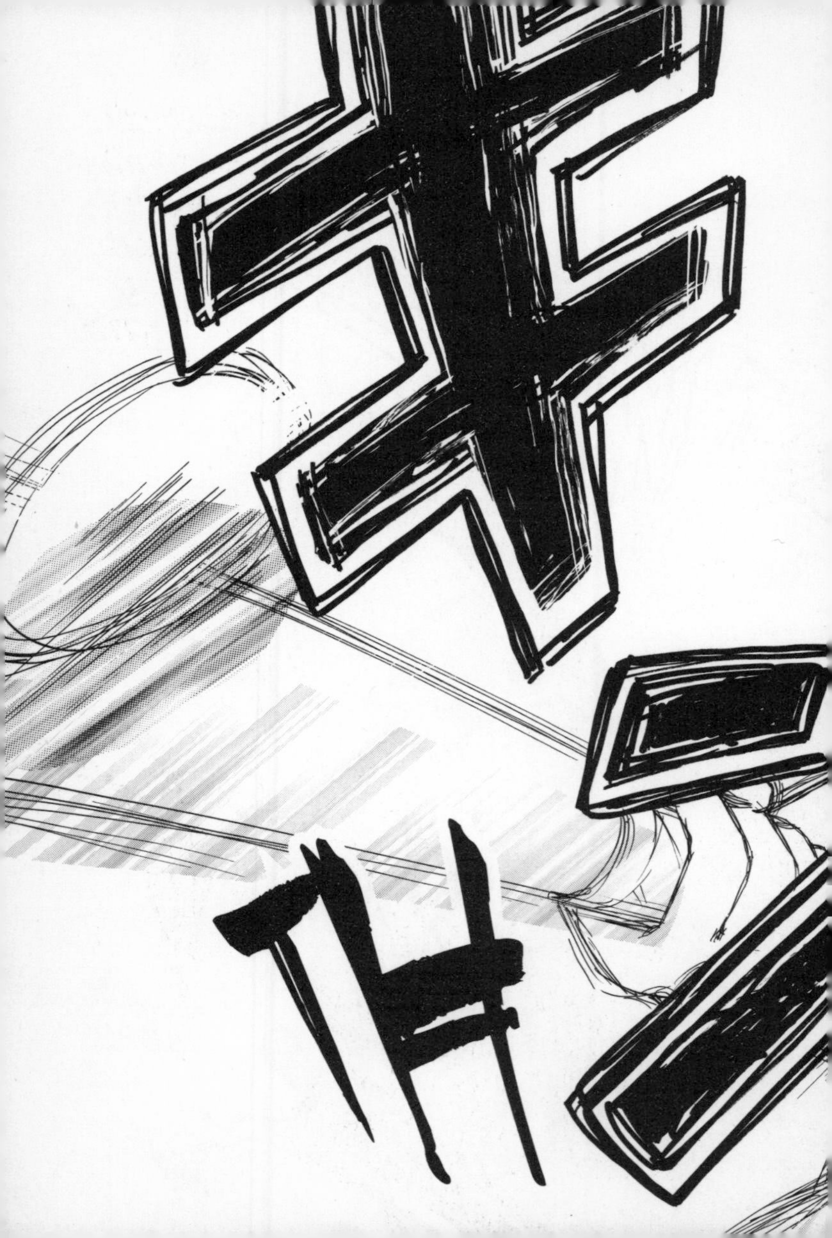

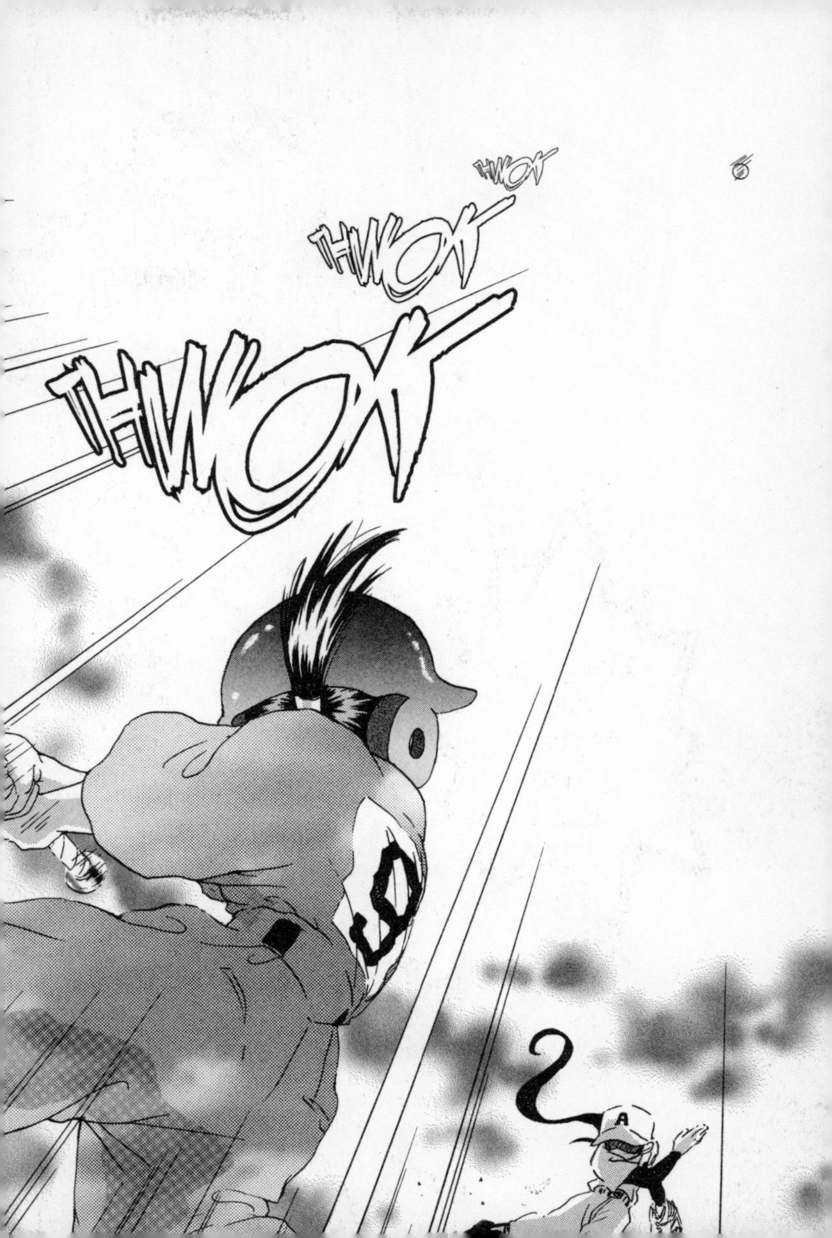
THWOK
THWOK
THWOK

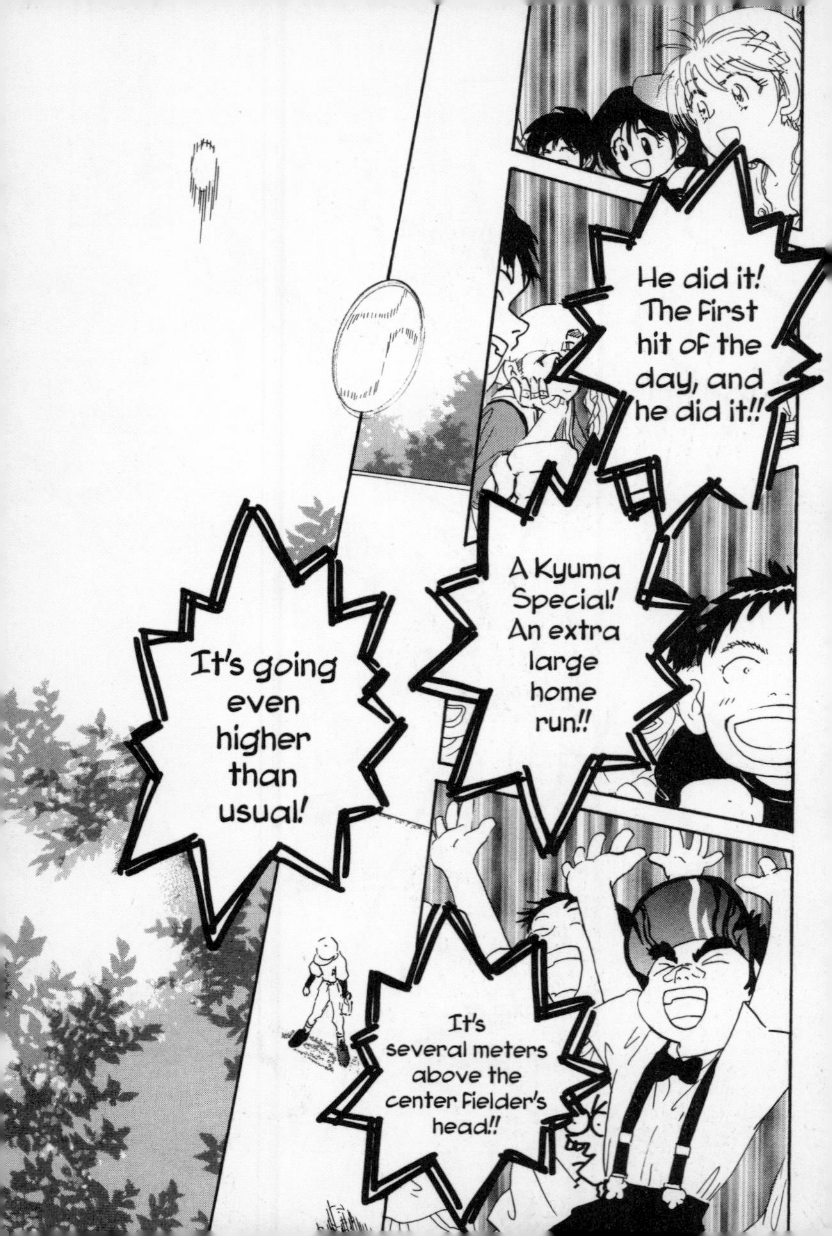
He did it! The first hit of the day, and he did it!!
A Kyuma Special! An extra large home run!!
It's several meters above the center fielder's head!!
It's going even higher than usual!

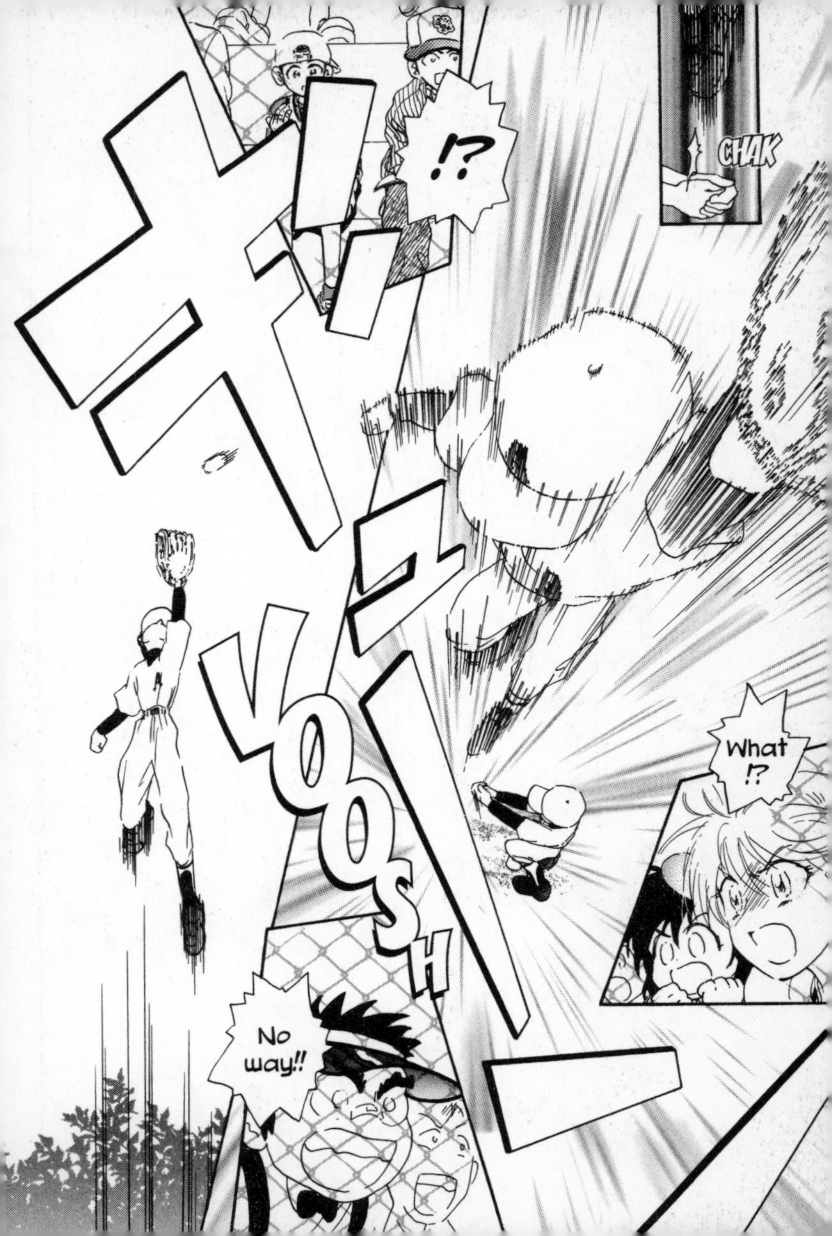
CHAK
!?
VOOSH
What !?
No way!!

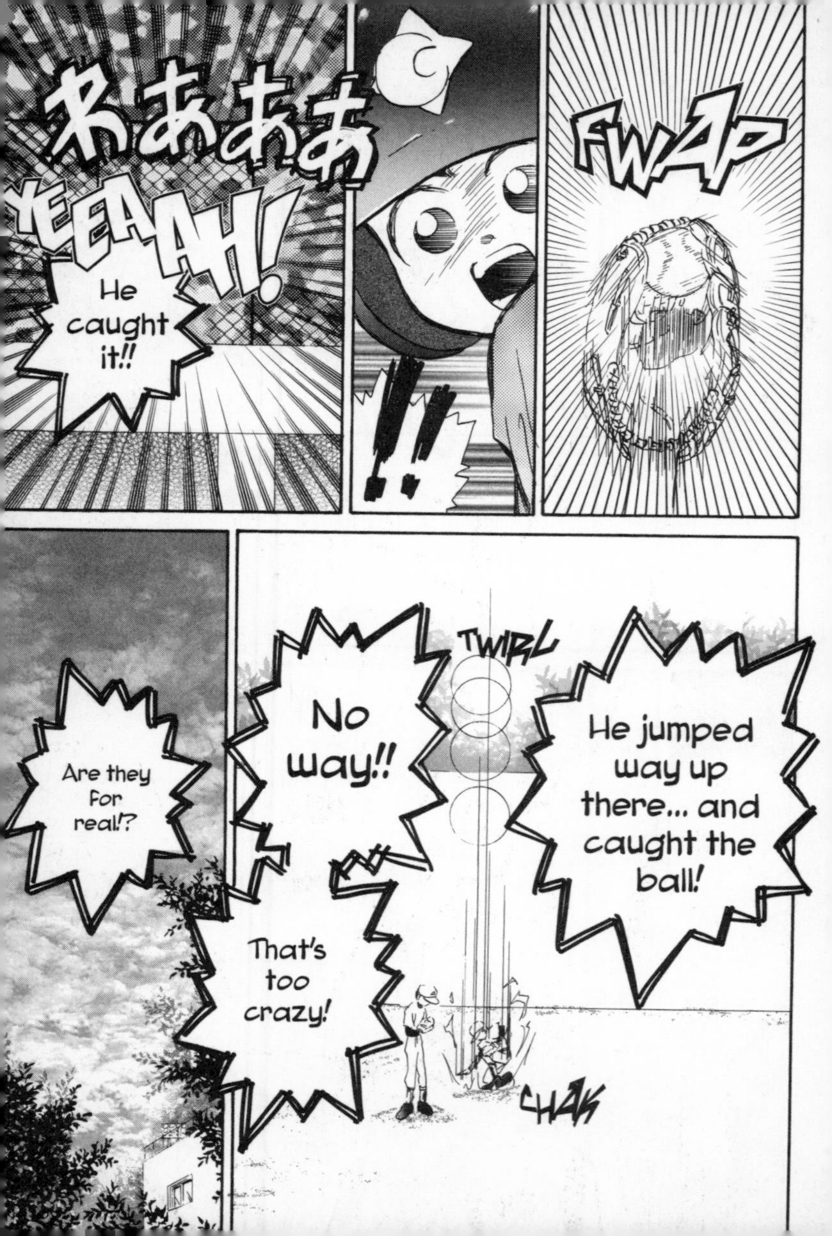

FWAP
!!
おあああ
YEAAH!
He caught it!!
TWIRL
He jumped way up there... and caught the ball!
No way!!
That's too crazy!
CHAK
Are they for real!?

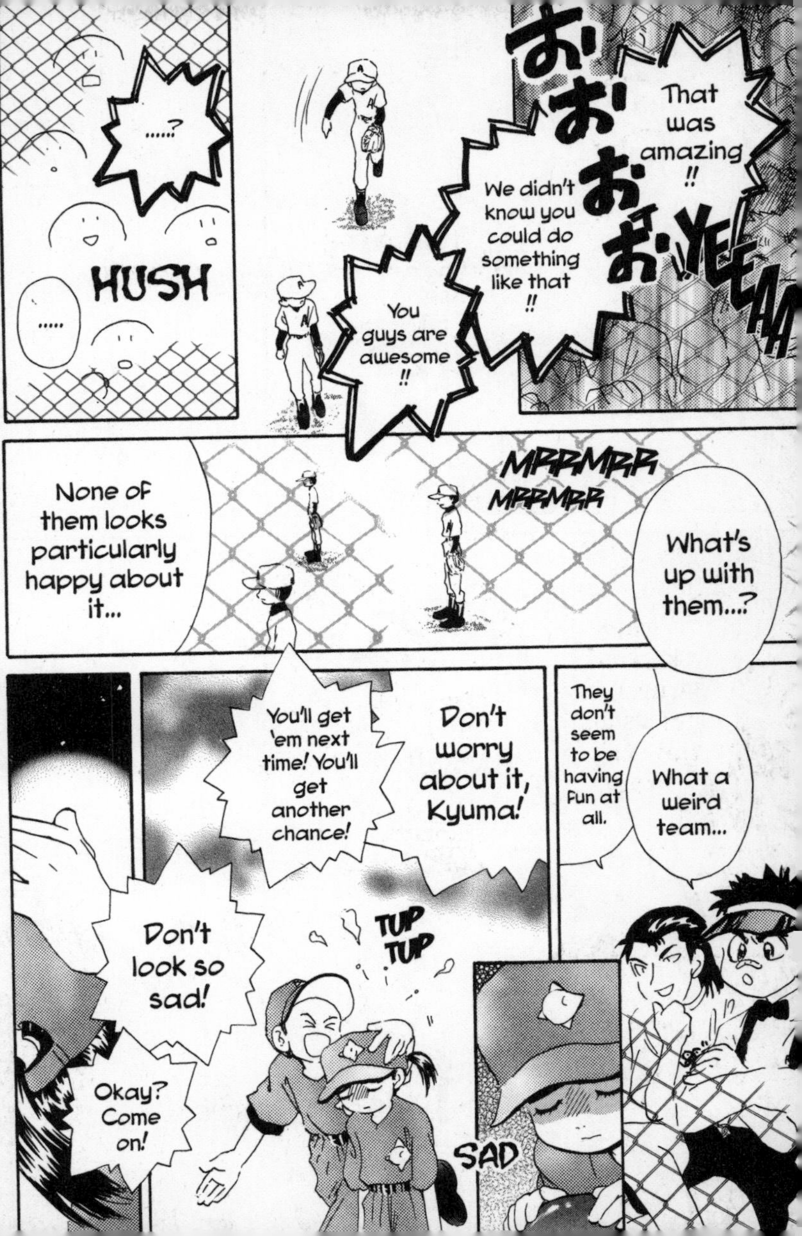
おおおおYEEAAA
That was amazing!!
We didn't know you could do something like that!!
You guys are awesome!!
.....?
HUSH
.....
What's up with them...?
MRRMRR MRRMRR
None of them looks particularly happy about it...
What a weird team...
They don't seem to be having fun at all.
Don't worry about it, Kyuma!
You'll get 'em next time! You'll get another chance!
TUP TUP
Don't look so sad!
Okay? Come on!
SAD

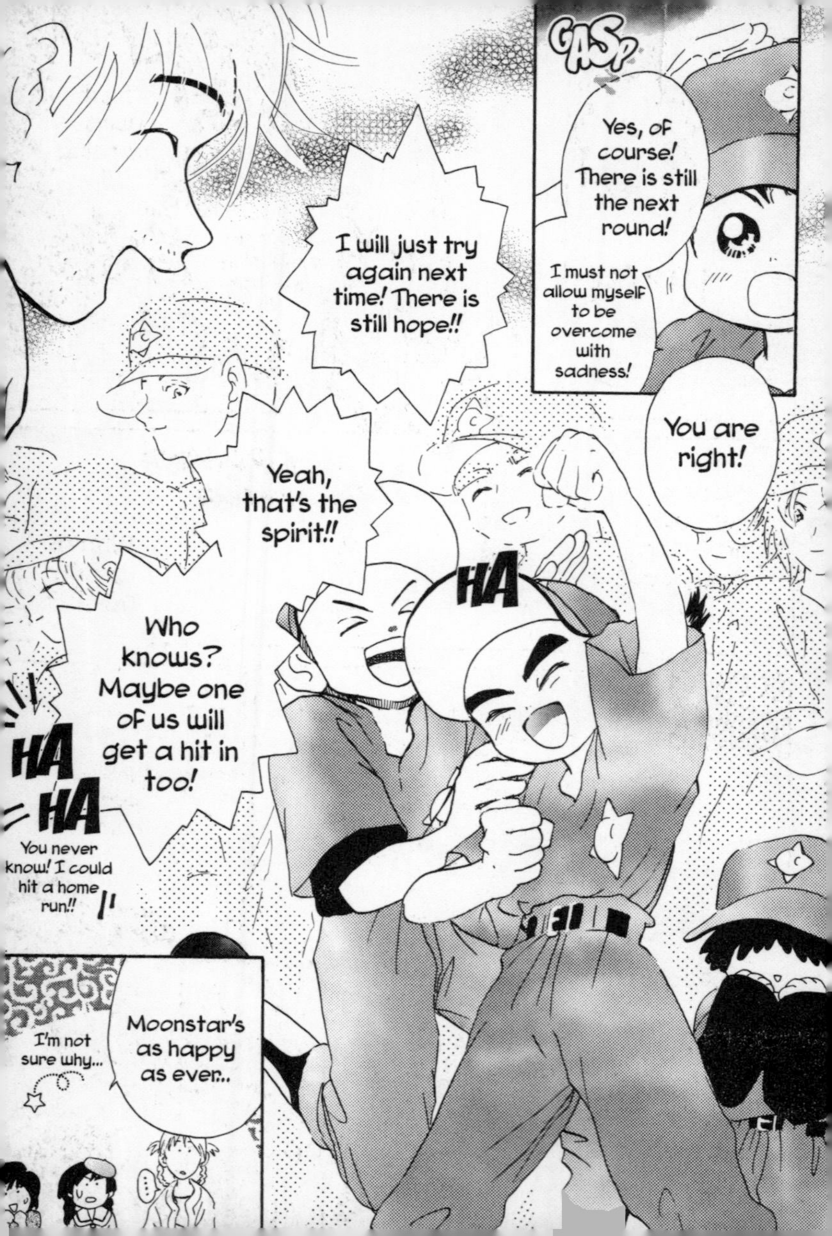
GASP
Yes, of course! There is still the next round!
I must not allow myself to be overcome with sadness!
You are right!
I will just try again next time! There is still hope!!
Yeah, that's the spirit!!
HA
Who knows? Maybe one of us will get a hit in too!
HA HA
You never know! I could hit a home run!!
Moonstar's as happy as ever..
I'm not sure why...
...

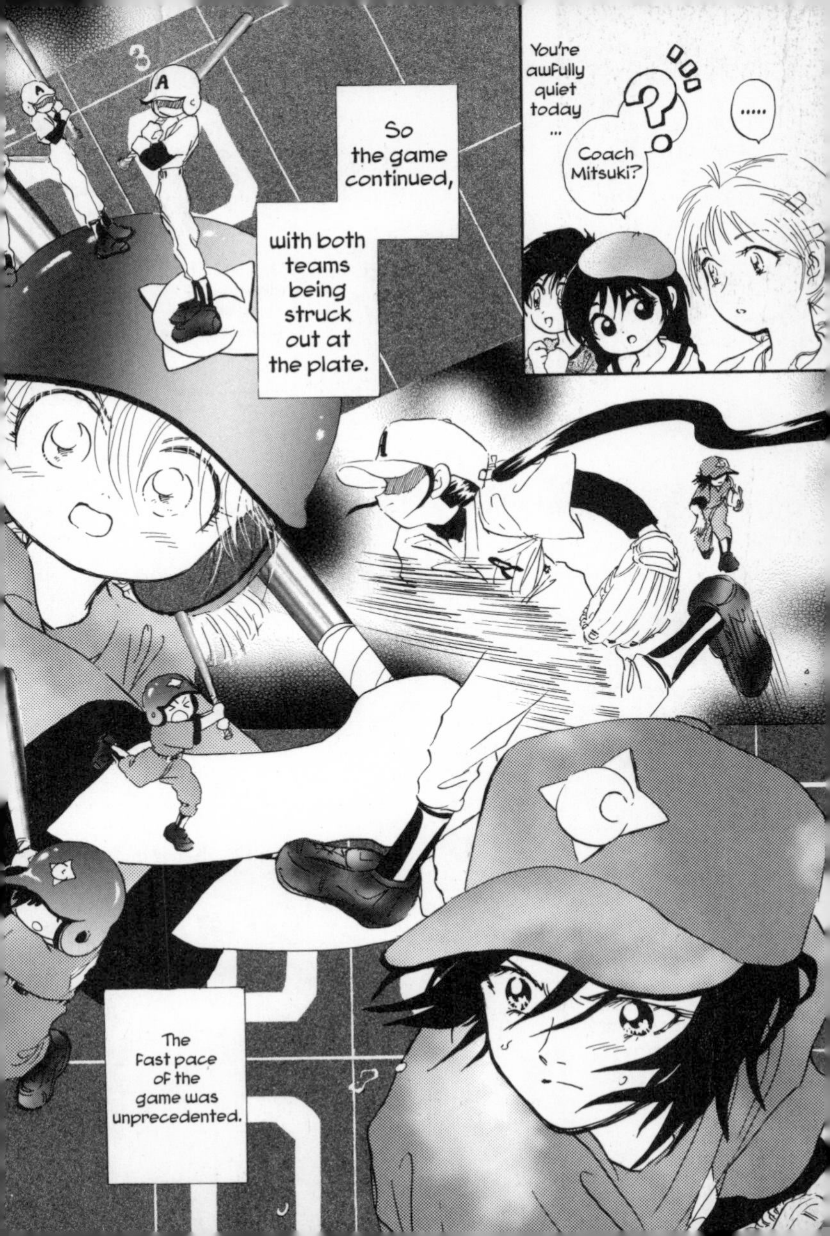
You're awfully quiet today ... Coach Mitsuki?
......
So the game continued,
with both teams being struck out at the plate.
The fast pace of the game was unprecedented.

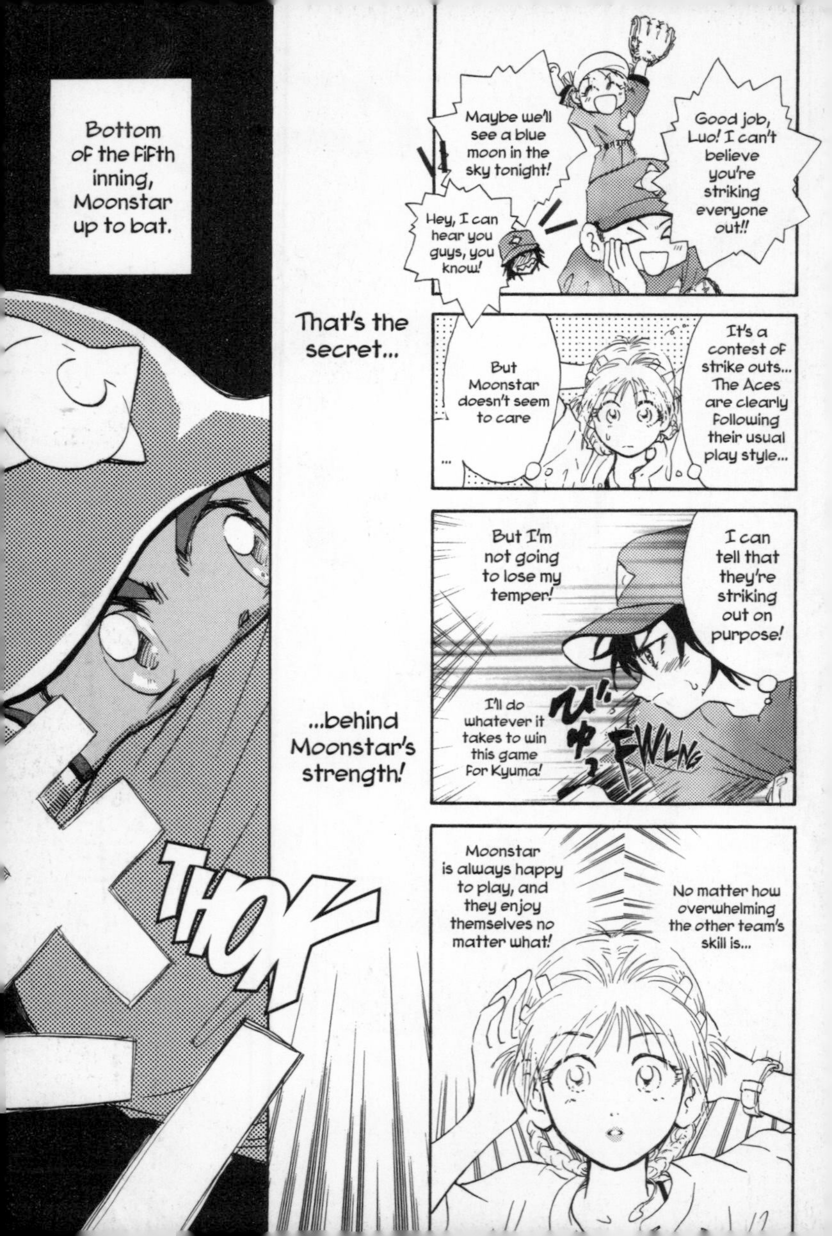
Good job, Luo! I can't believe you're striking everyone out!!
Maybe we'll see a blue moon in the sky tonight!
Hey, I can hear you guys, you know!
It's a contest of strike outs... The Aces are clearly following their usual play style...
But Moonstar doesn't seem to care
...
That's the secret...
I can tell that they're striking out on purpose!
But I'm not going to lose my temper!
I'll do whatever it takes to win this game for Kyuma!
FWUNG
No matter how overwhelming the other team's skill is...
Moonstar is always happy to play, and they enjoy themselves no matter what!
...behind Moonstar's strength!
Bottom of the fifth inning, Moonstar up to bat.
THOK

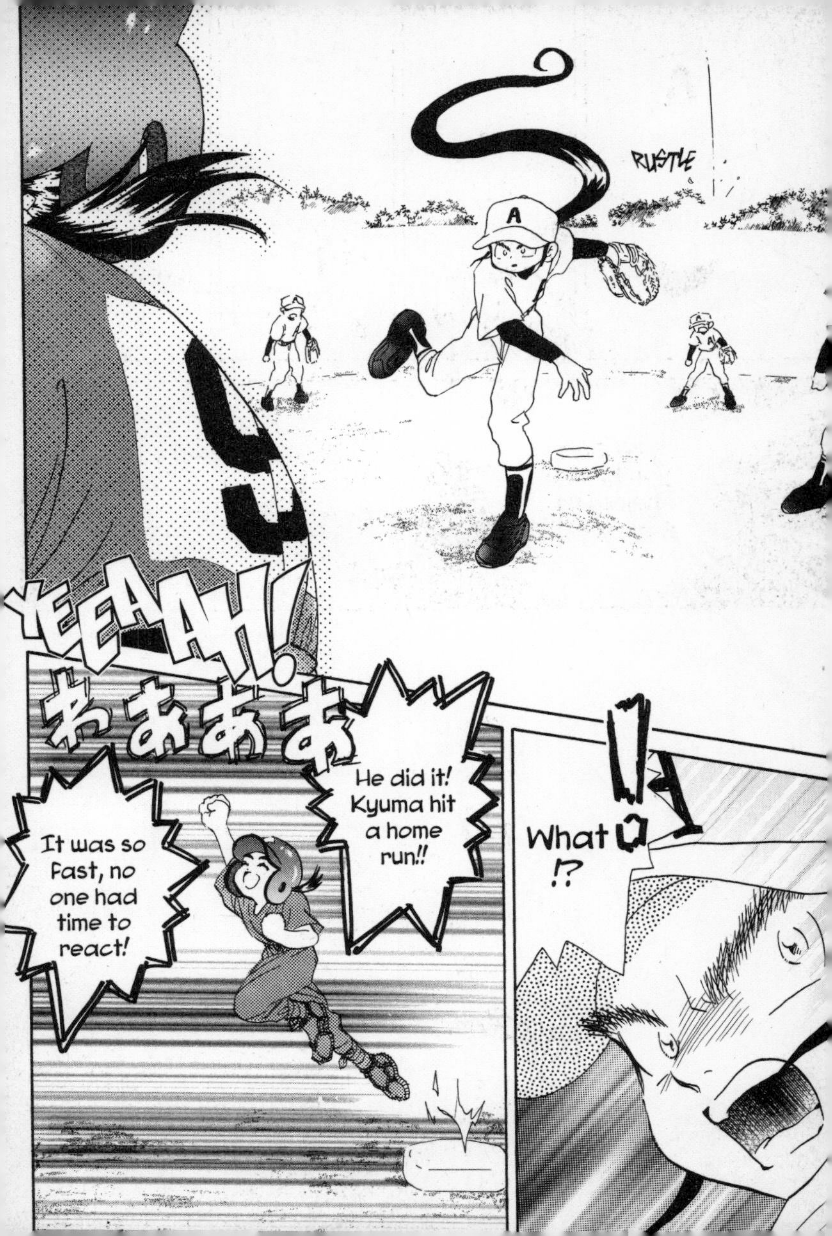
RUSTLE
YEAAH!
おおおお
What!?
He did it! Kyuma hit a home run!!
It was so fast, no one had time to react!

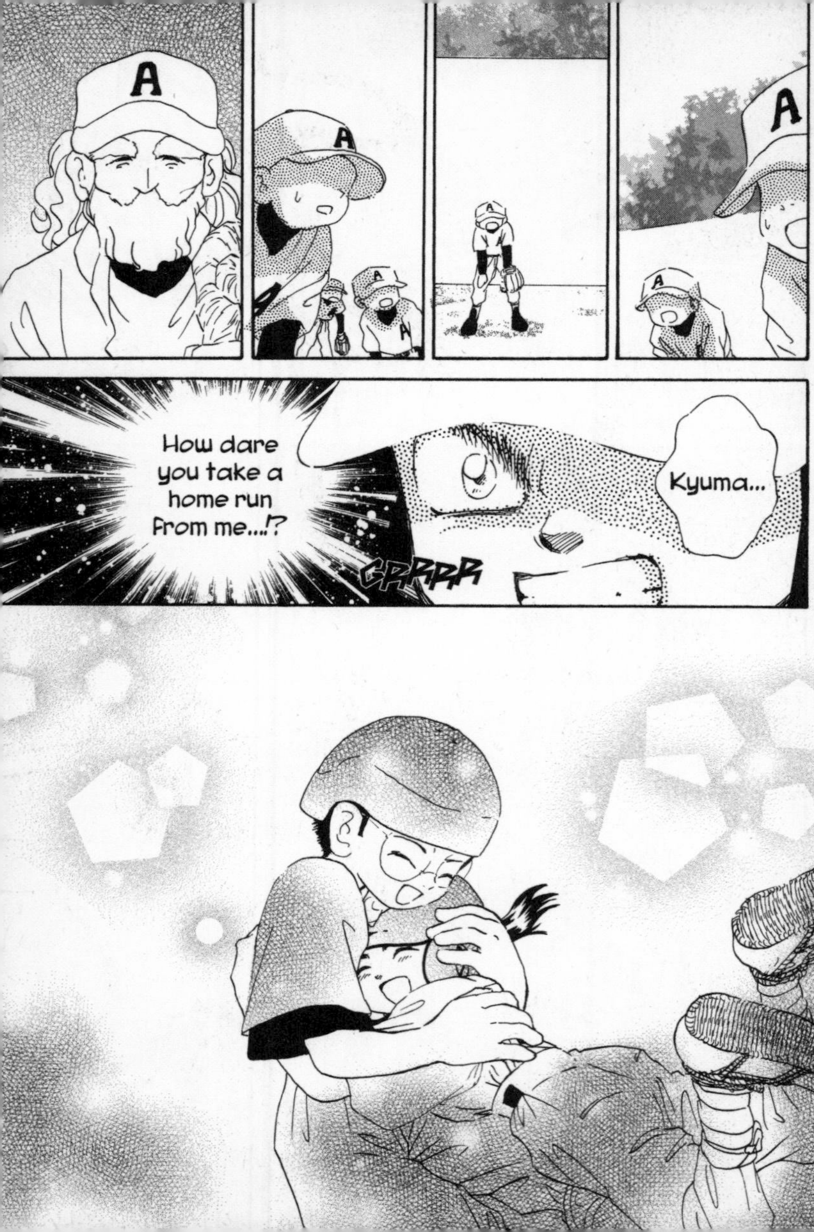
Kyuma...
How dare you take a home run from me...!?
GRRRR

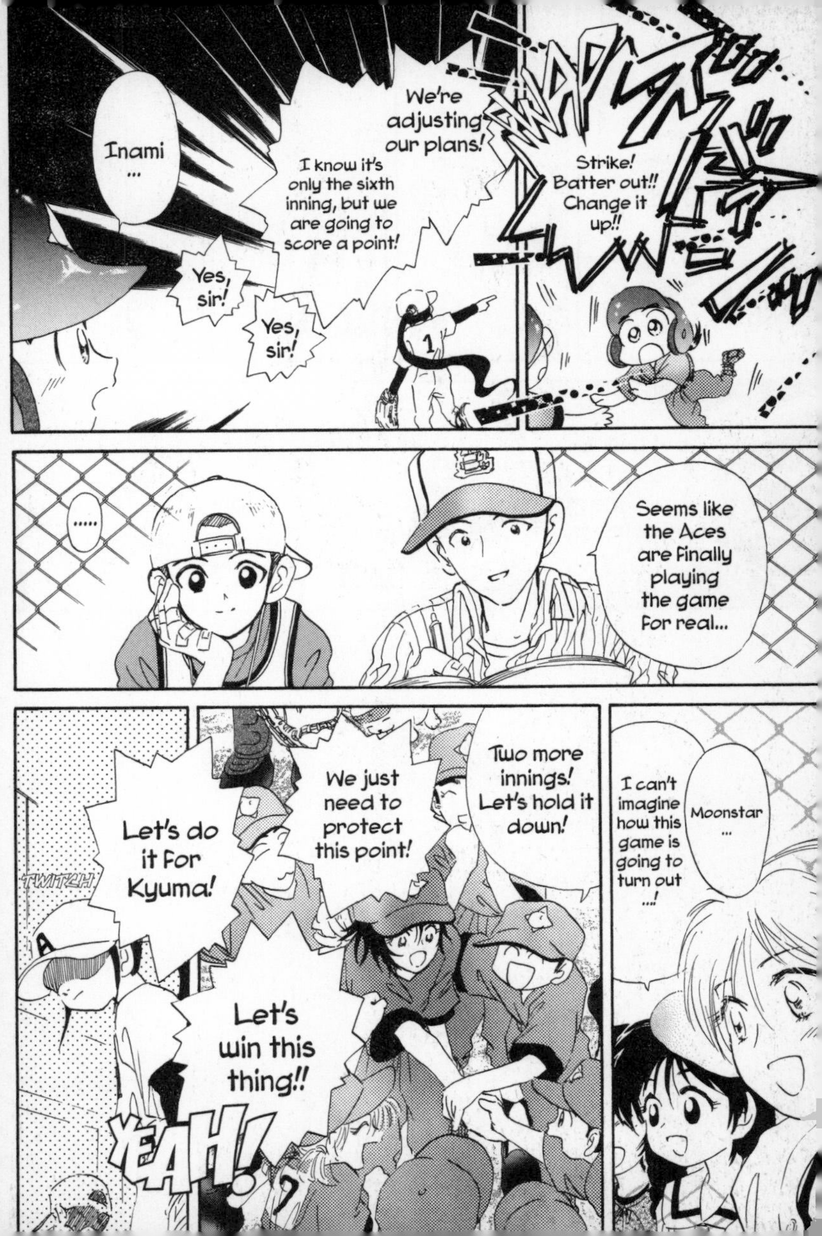
Strike! Batter out!! Change it up!!
We're adjusting our plans!
I know it's only the sixth inning, but we are going to score a point!
Inami ...
Yes, sir!
Yes, sir!
Seems like the Aces are finally playing the game for real...
......
Moonstar ...
I can't imagine how this game is going to turn out ...!
Two more innings! Let's hold it down!
We just need to protect this point!
Let's do it for Kyuma!
TWITCH
Let's win this thing!!
YEAH!

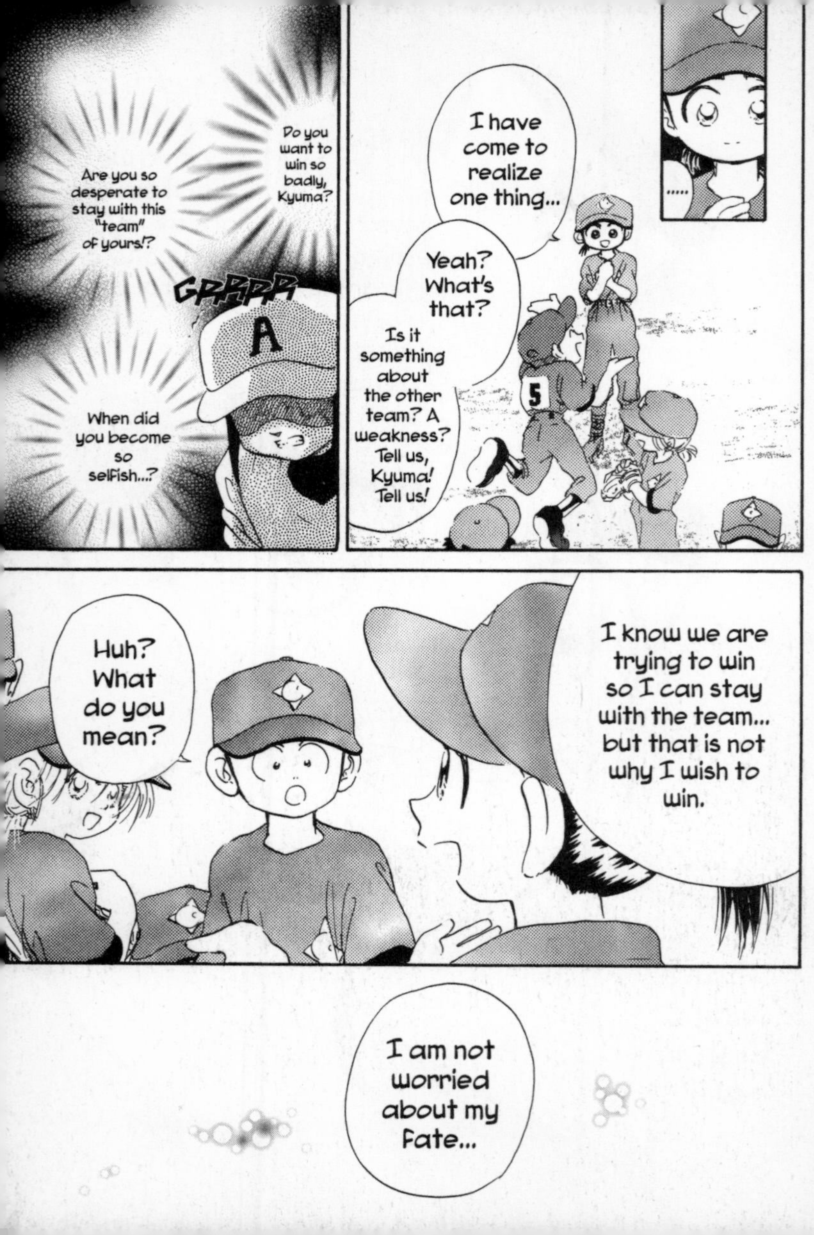
.....
I have come to realize one thing...
Yeah? What's that?
Is it something about the other team? A weakness? Tell us, Kyuma! Tell us!
Do you want to win so badly, Kyuma?
Are you so desperate to stay with this "team" of yours!?
GRRRR
When did you become so selfish...?
I know we are trying to win so I can stay with the team... but that is not why I wish to win.
Huh? What do you mean?
I am not worried about my fate...

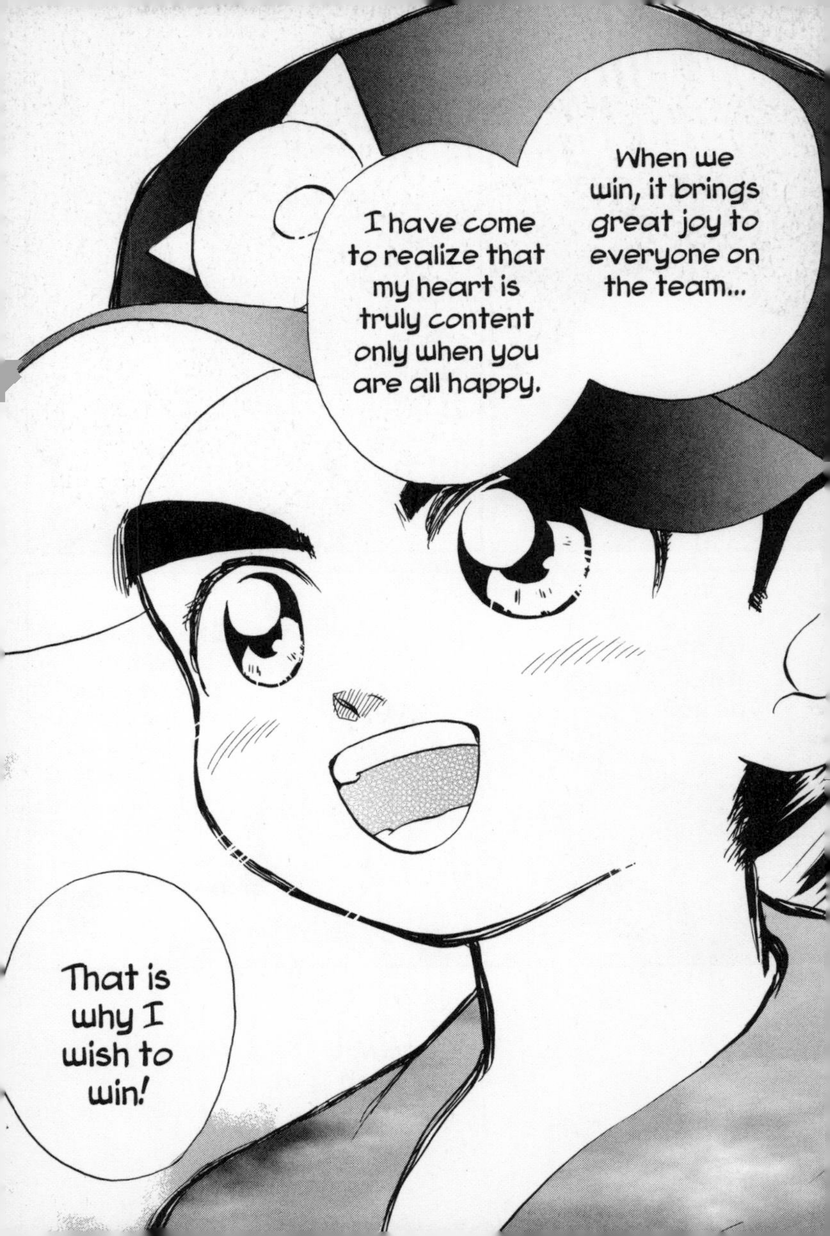
When we win, it brings great joy to everyone on the team...
I have come to realize that my heart is truly content only when you are all happy.
That is why I wish to win!

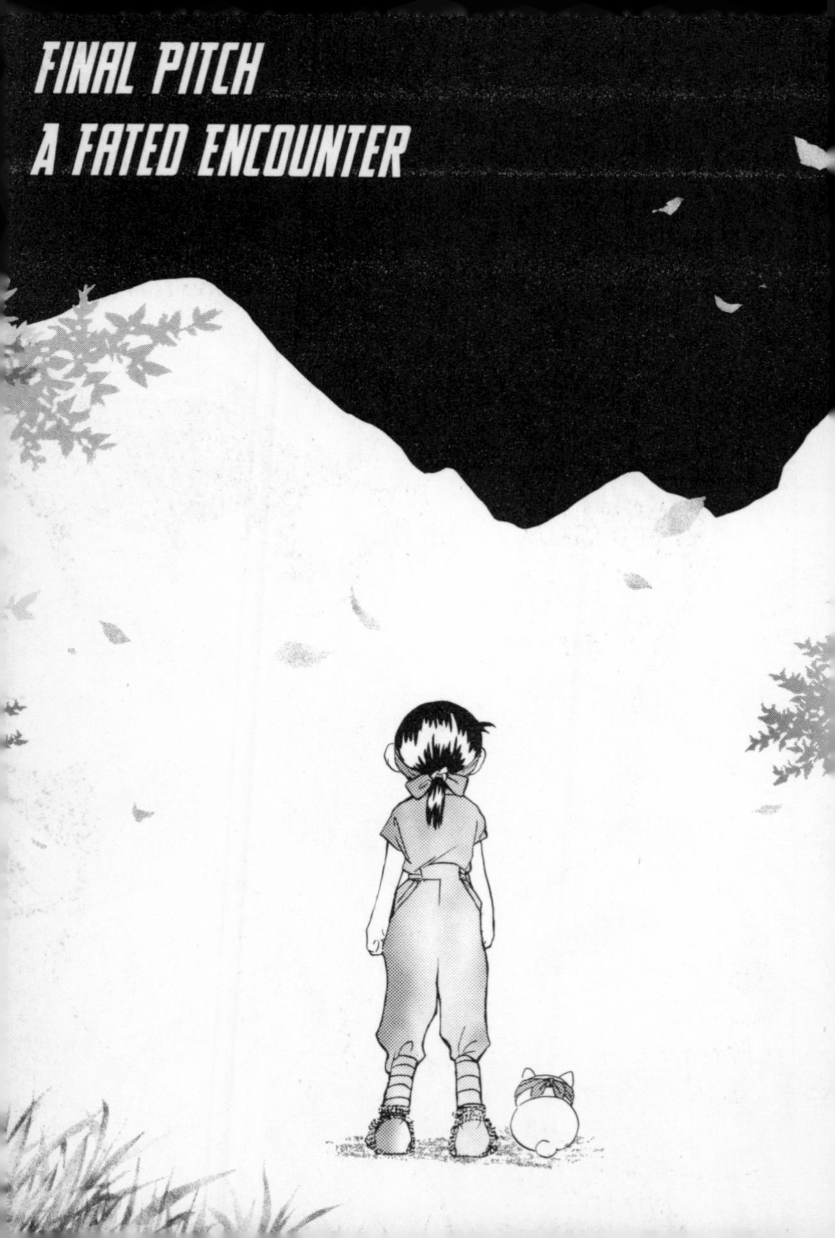
FINAL PITCH
A FATED ENCOUNTER

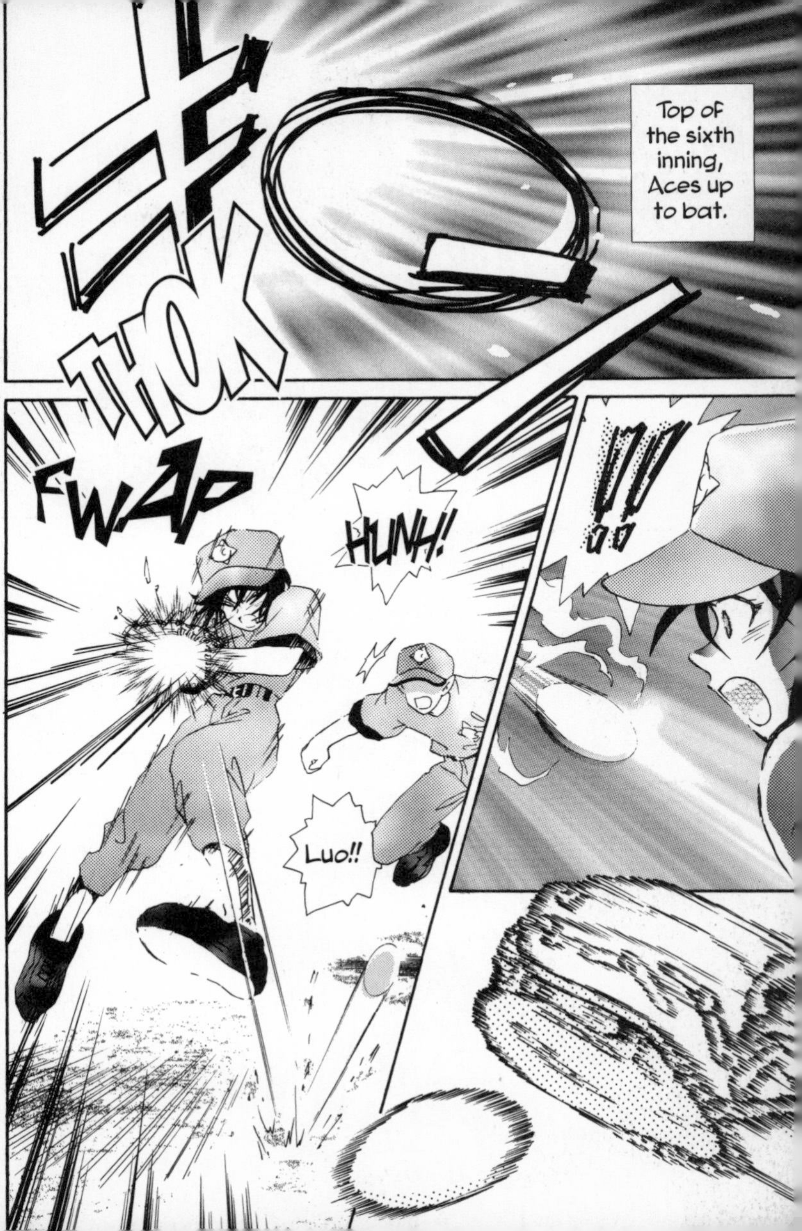
Top of the sixth inning, Aces up to bat.
THOCK
!!
FWAP
HUNH!
Luo!!

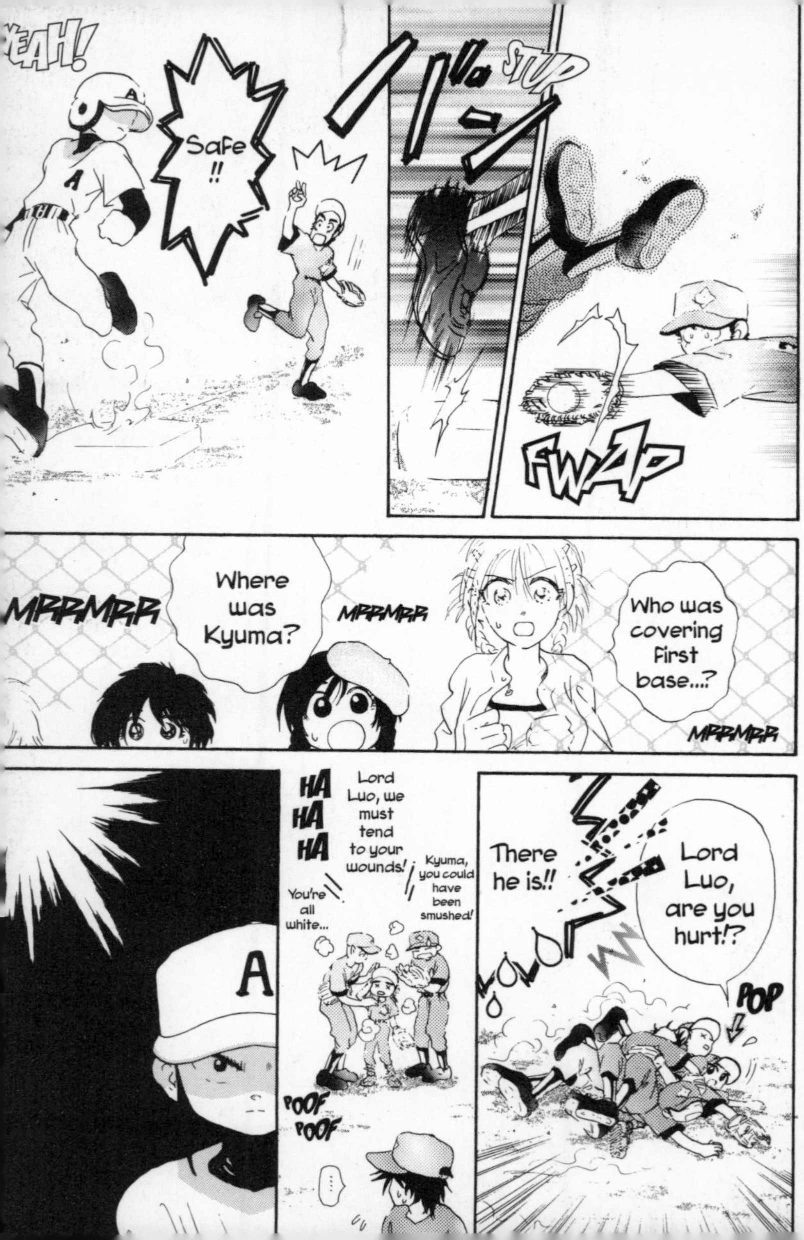
STUP
FWAP
YEAH!
Safe!!
Who was covering first base...?
MRRMRR
Where was Kyuma?
MRRMRR
MRRMRR
Lord Luo, are you hurt!?
There he is!!
POP
Lord Luo, we must tend to your wounds!
Kyuma, you could have been smushed!
HA HA HA
You're all white...
POOF POOF
...

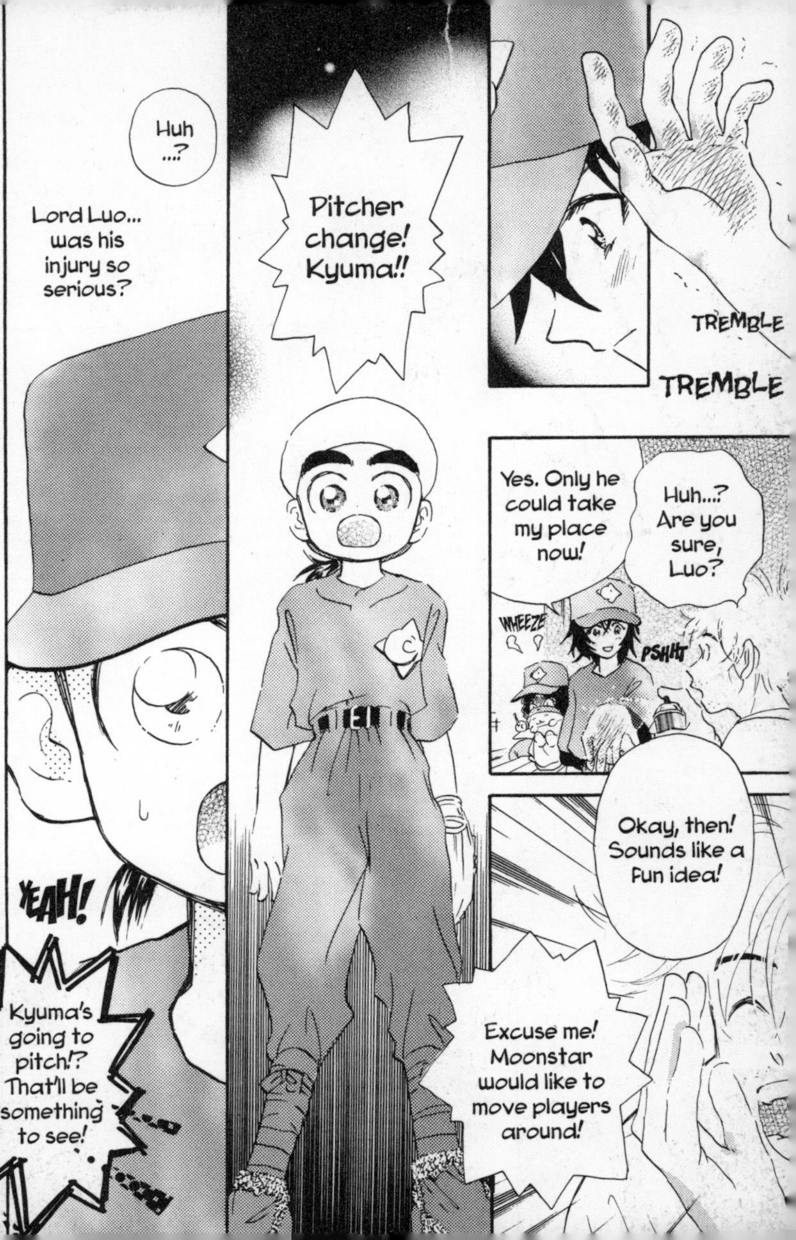
TREMBLE
TREMBLE
Huh...? Are you sure, Luo?
Yes. Only he could take my place now!
PSHHT
WHEEZE
Okay, then! Sounds like a fun idea!
Excuse me! Moonstar would like to move players around!
Pitcher change! Kyuma!!
Huh ...?
Lord Luo... was his injury so serious?
YEAH!
Kyuma's going to pitch!? That'll be something to see!

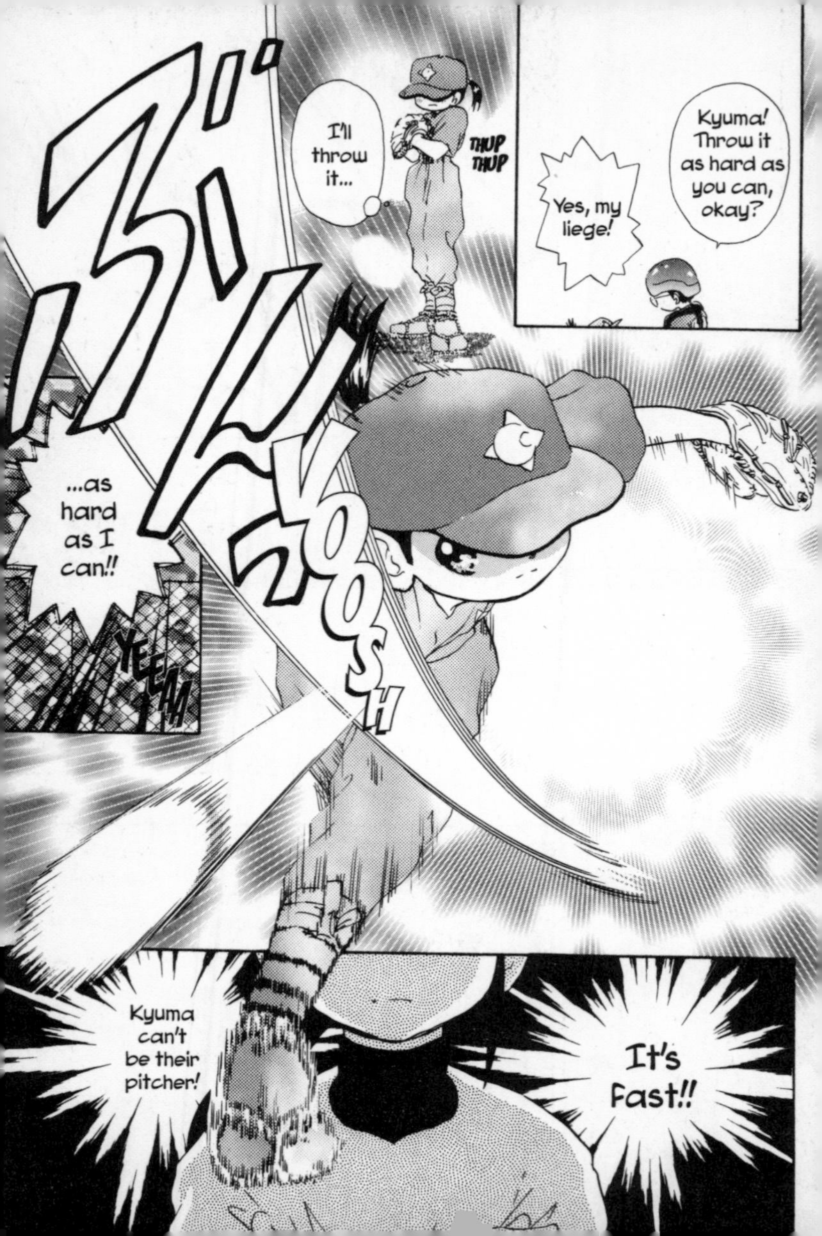
Kyuma! Throw it as hard as you can, okay?
Yes, my liege!
I'll throw it...
THUP THUP
...as hard as I can!!
YEEEAH
VOOOSH
It's Fast!!
Kyuma can't be their pitcher!

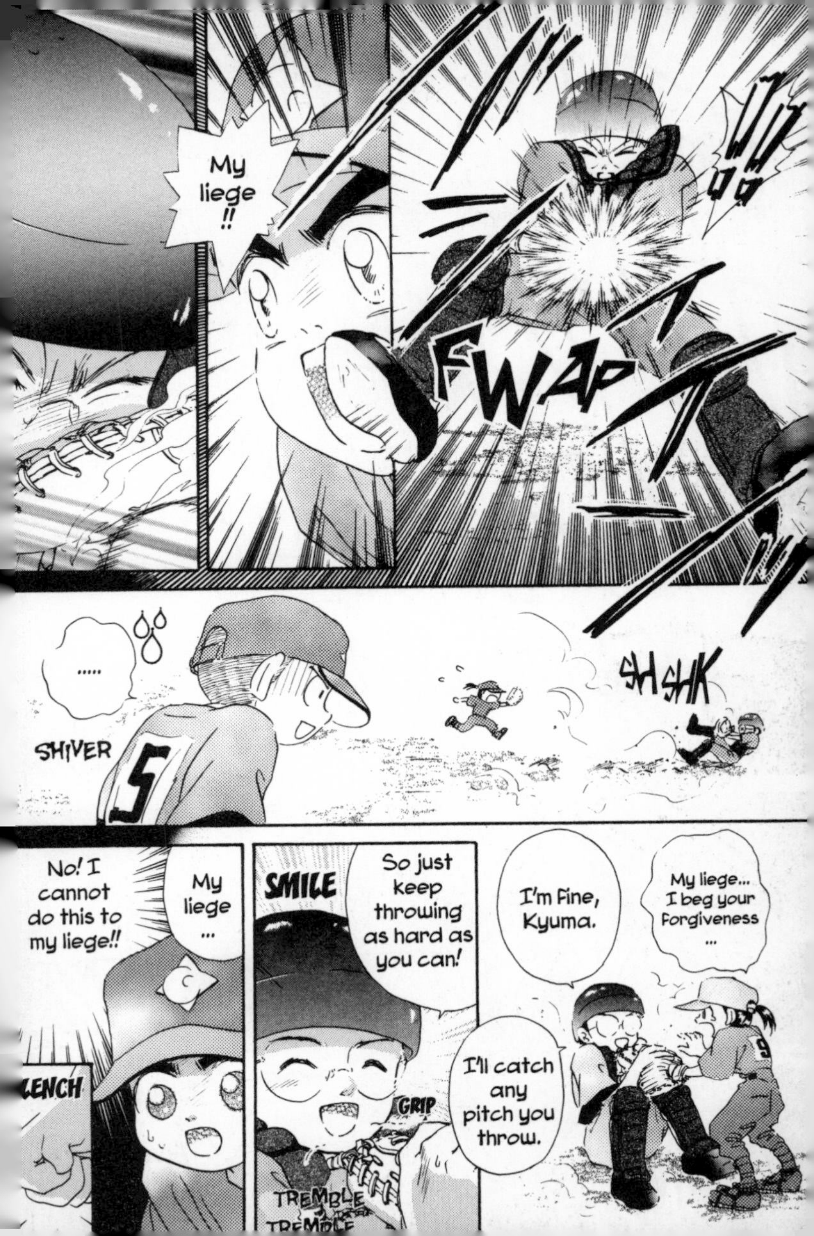
FWAP
My liege !!
SH SHK
.....
SHIVER
My liege... I beg your forgiveness ...
I'm fine, Kyuma.
I'll catch any pitch you throw.
So just keep throwing as hard as you can!
SMILE
GRIP
TREMBLE TREMBLE
My liege ...
No! I cannot do this to my liege!!
LENCH

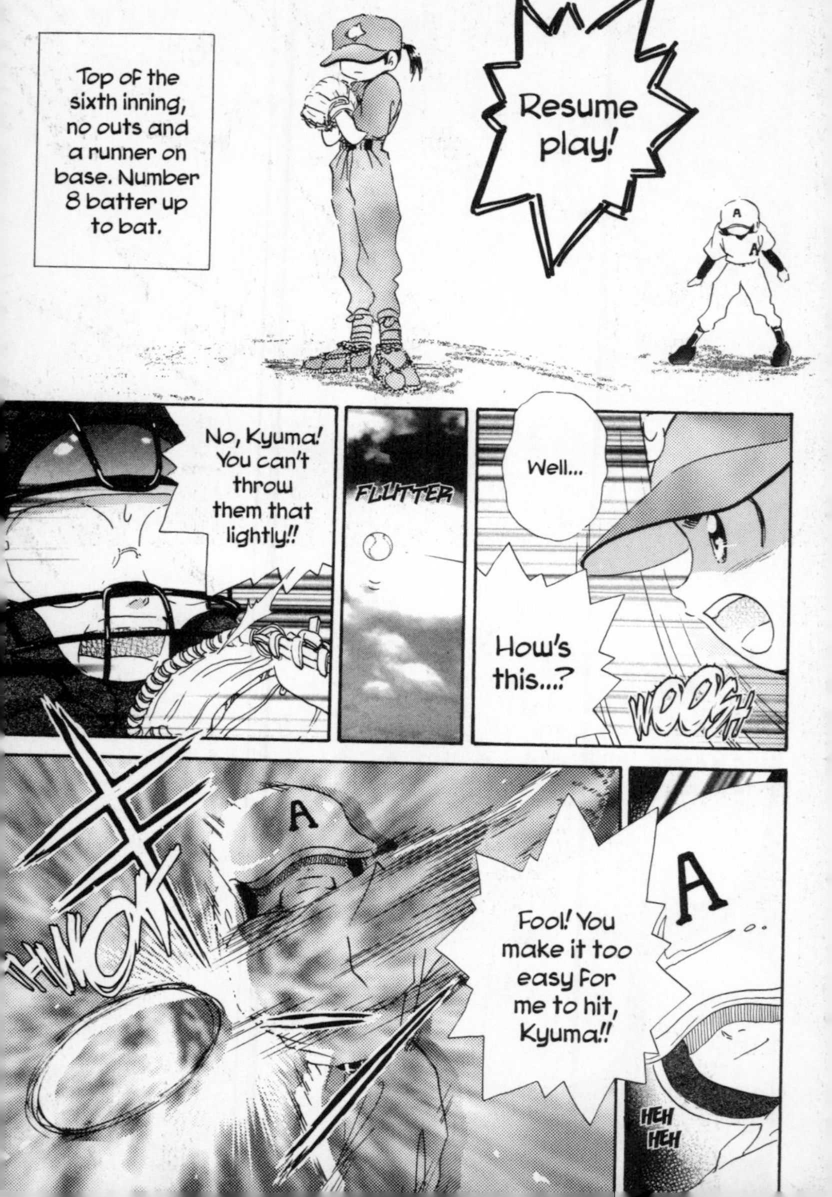
Resume play!
Top of the sixth inning, no outs and a runner on base. Number 8 batter up to bat.
Well...
How's this...?
WOOSH
FLUTTER
No, Kyuma! You can't throw them that lightly!!
Fool! You make it too easy for me to hit, Kyuma!!
HEH HEH
THWOK

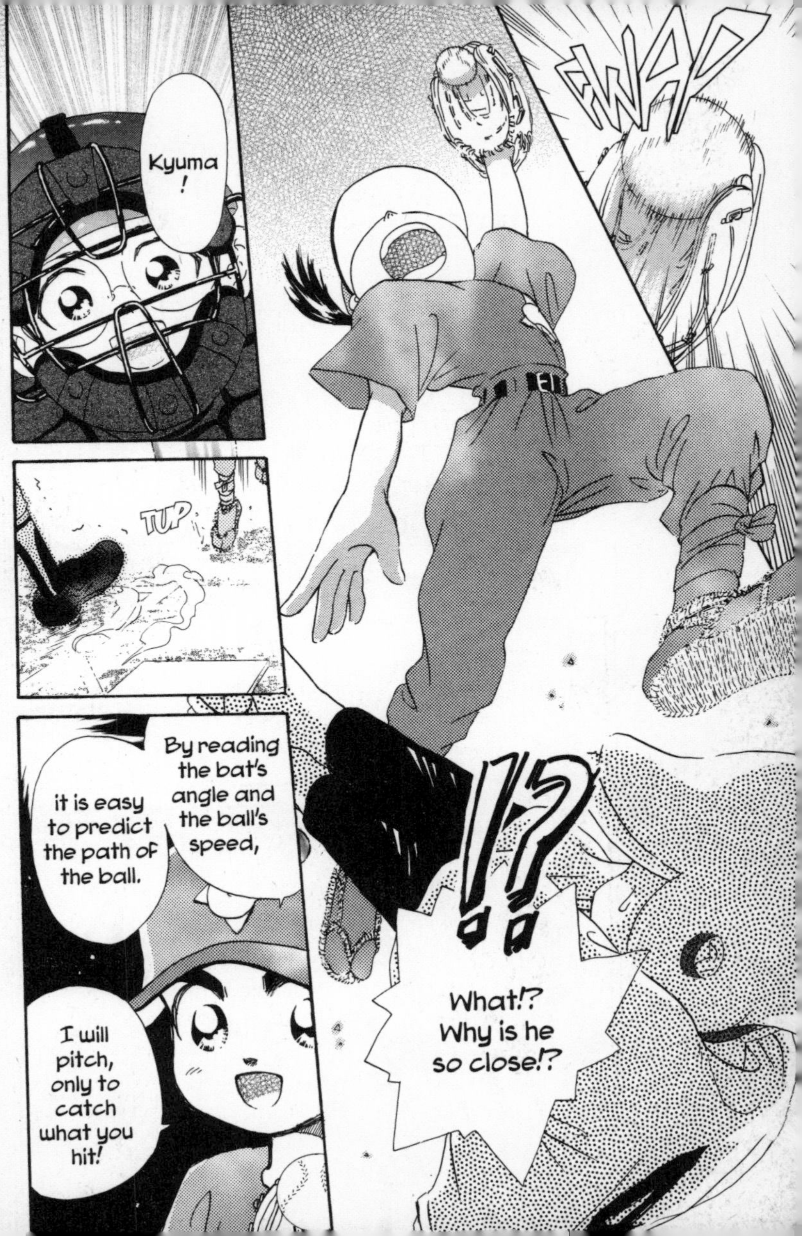
WHAP
!?
What!? Why is he so close!?
Kyuma!
TUP
By reading the bat's angle and the ball's speed,
it is easy to predict the path of the ball.
I will pitch, only to catch what you hit!

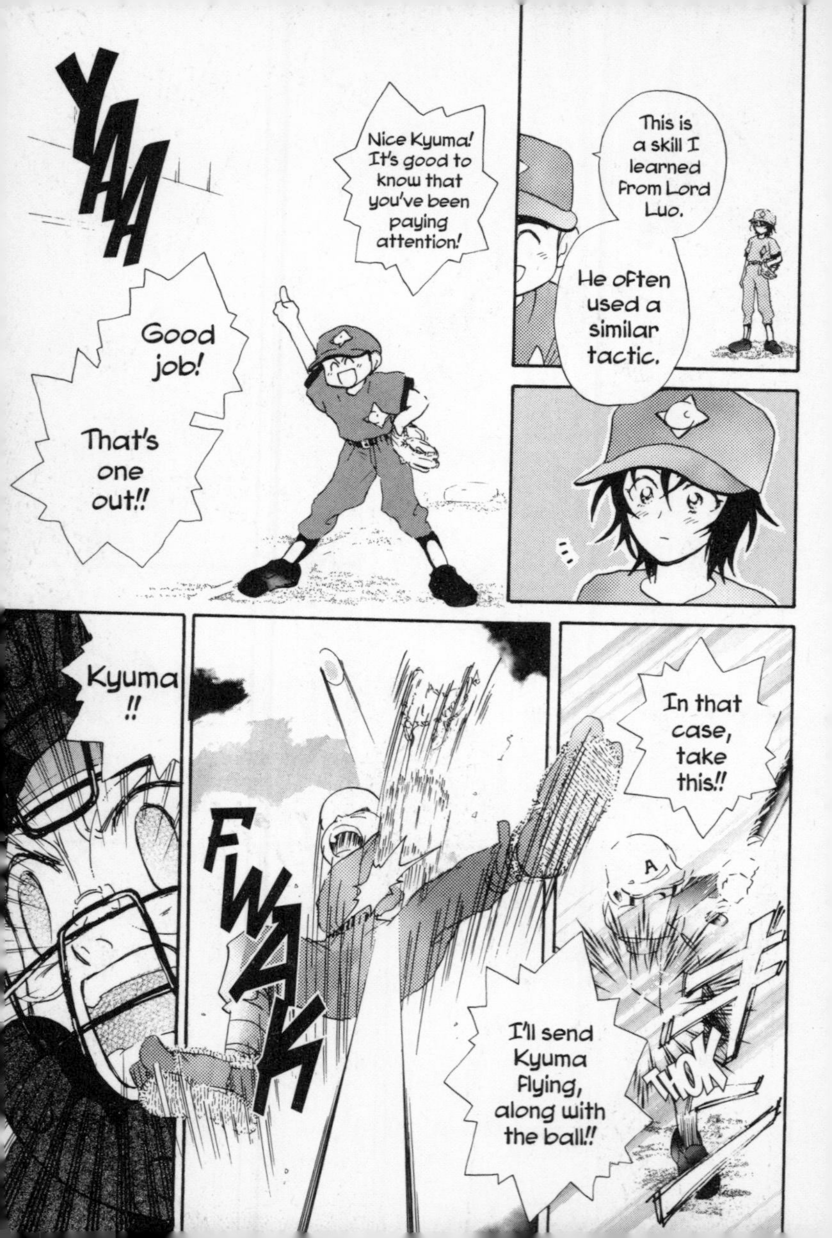

This is a skill I learned from Lord Luo.
He often used a similar tactic.
Nice Kyuma! It's good to know that you've been paying attention!
YAAA
Good job!
That's one out!!
In that case, take this!!
THOK
I'll send Kyuma flying, along with the ball!!
FWAK
Kyuma!!

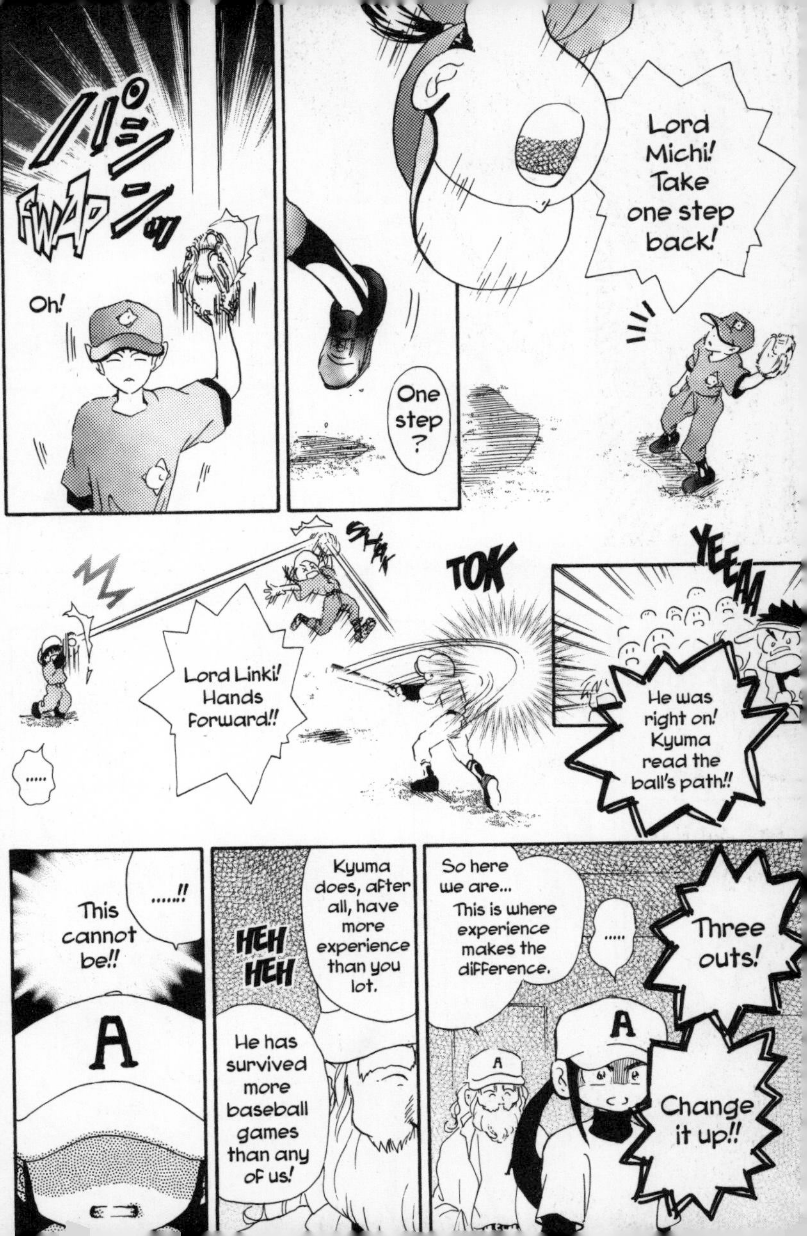
Lord Michi! Take one step back!
One step?
FWAP
Oh!
YEEAAA
He was right on! Kyuma read the ball's path!!
TOK
Lord Linki! Hands forward!!
......
Three outs!
So here we are... This is where experience makes the difference.
.....
Change it up!!
Kyuma does, after all, have more experience than you lot.
HEH HEH
He has survived more baseball games than any of us!
......!!
This cannot be!!

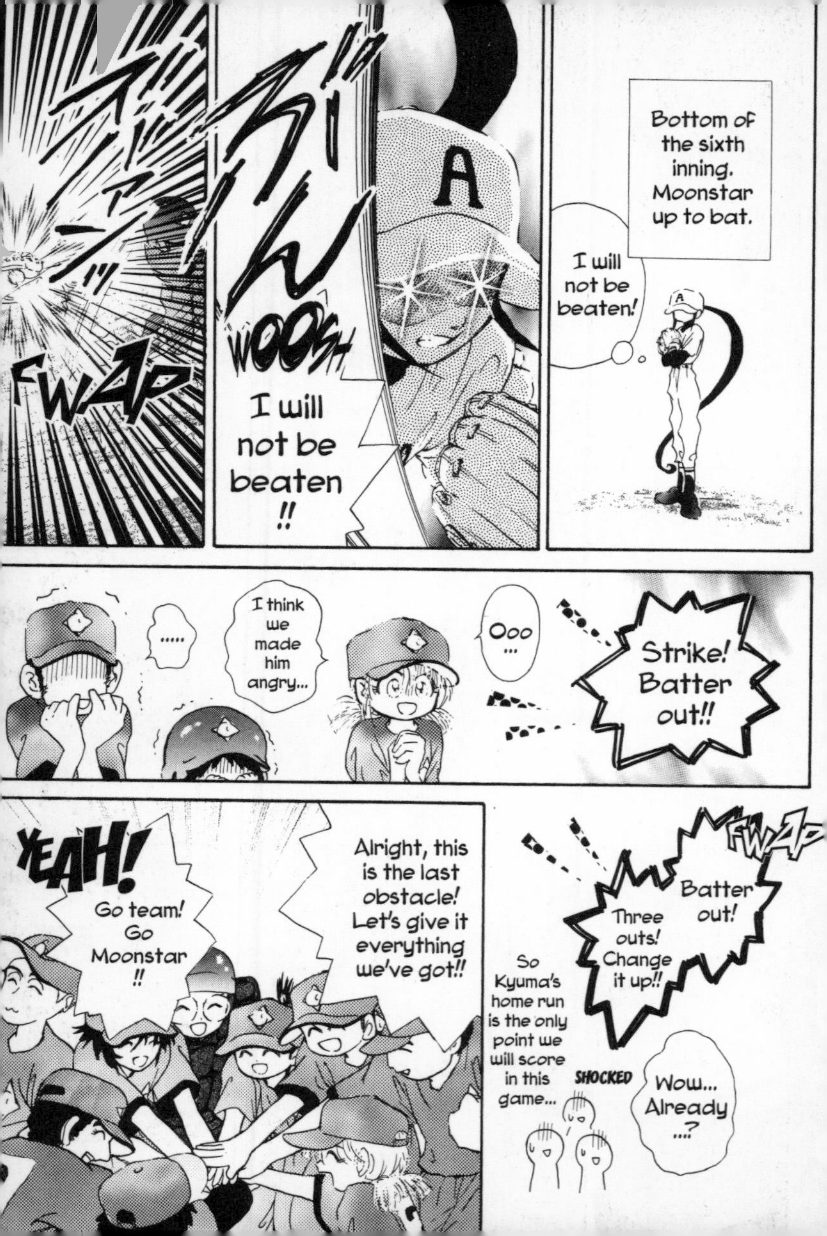
Bottom of the sixth inning. Moonstar up to bat.
I will not be beaten!
WOOSH
I will not be beaten !!
FWAP
Strike! Batter out!!
Ooo ...
I think we made him angry...
......
FWAP
Batter out!
Three outs! Change it up!!
So Kyuma's home run is the only point we will score in this game...
SHOCKED
Wow... Already ...?
Alright, this is the last obstacle! Let's give it everything we've got!!
Go team! Go Moonstar !!
YEAH!

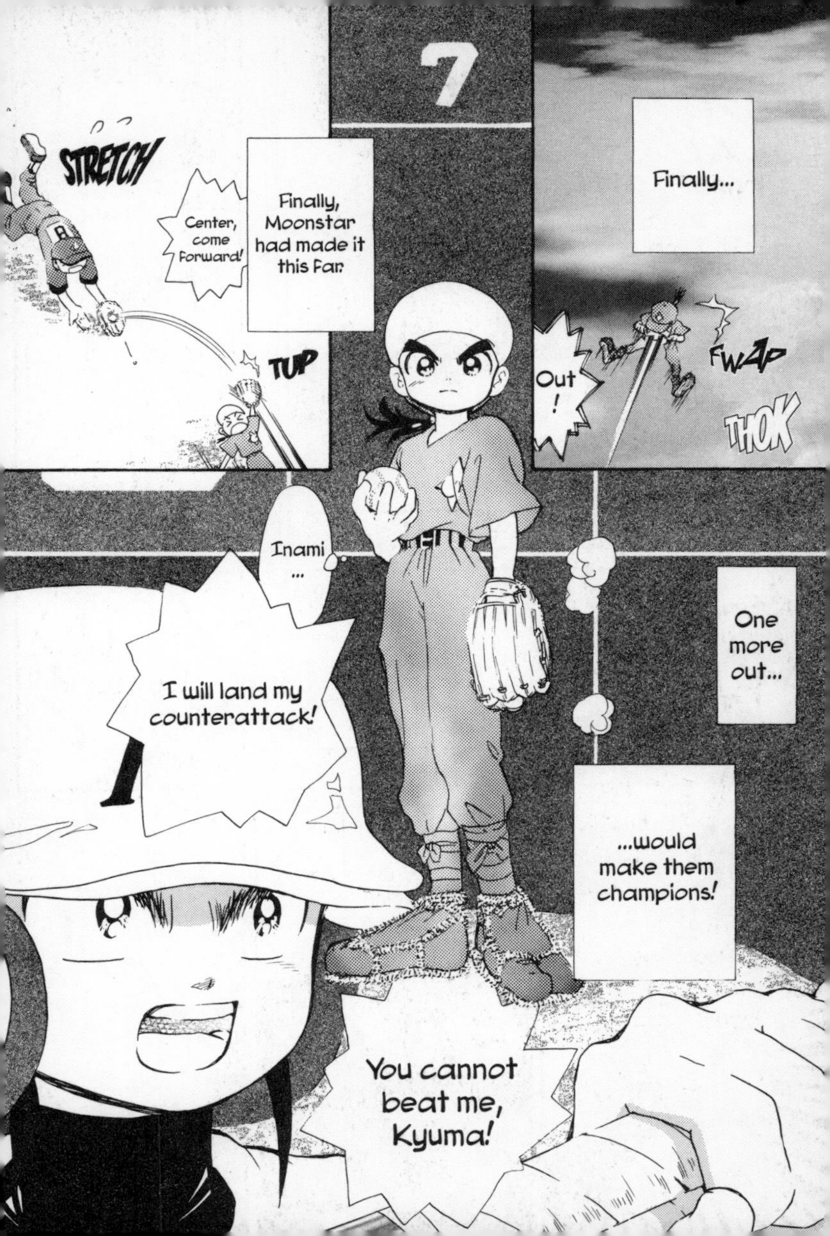

Finally...
Out!
FWAP
THOK
Finally, Moonstar had made it this far.
Center, come forward!
STRETCH
TUP
One more out...
...would make them champions!
Inami...
I will land my counterattack!
You cannot beat me, Kyuma!

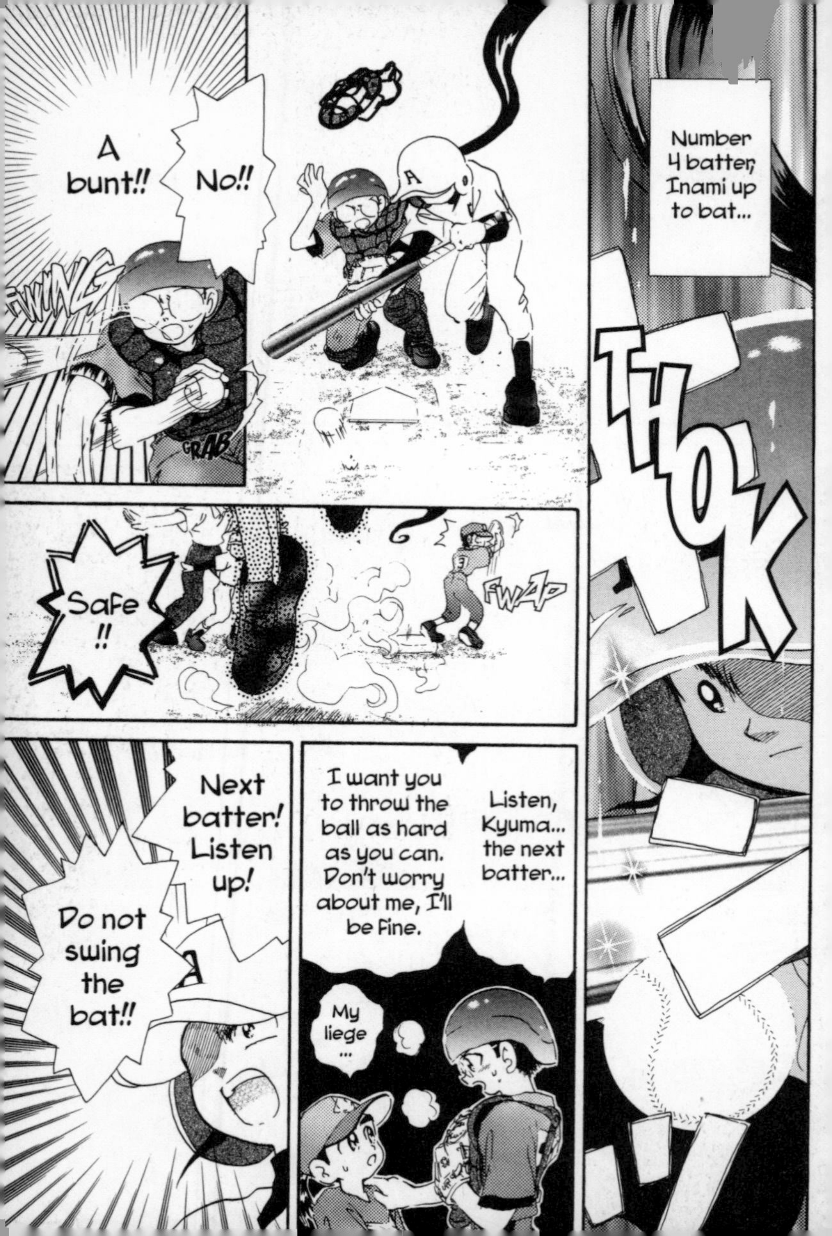
Number 4 batter, Inami up to bat...
THOK
No!!
A bunt!!
FWUNG
GRAB
FWAP
Safe!!
Listen, Kyuma... the next batter...
I want you to throw the ball as hard as you can. Don't worry about me, I'll be fine.
My liege ...
Next batter! Listen up!
Do not swing the bat!!

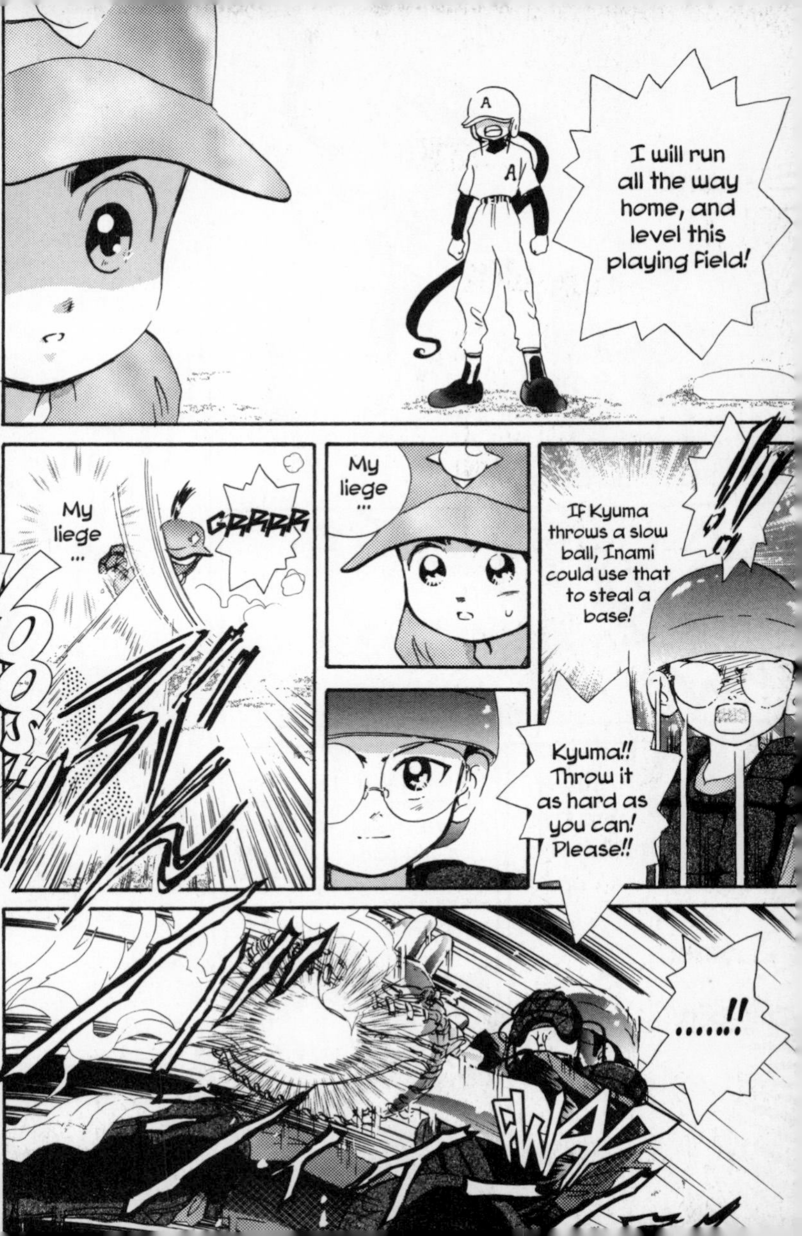
I will run all the way home, and level this playing field!
If Kyuma throws a slow ball, Inami could use that to steal a base!
My liege ...
Kyuma!! Throw it as hard as you can! Please!!
My liege ...
GRRRR
VOOSH
......!!

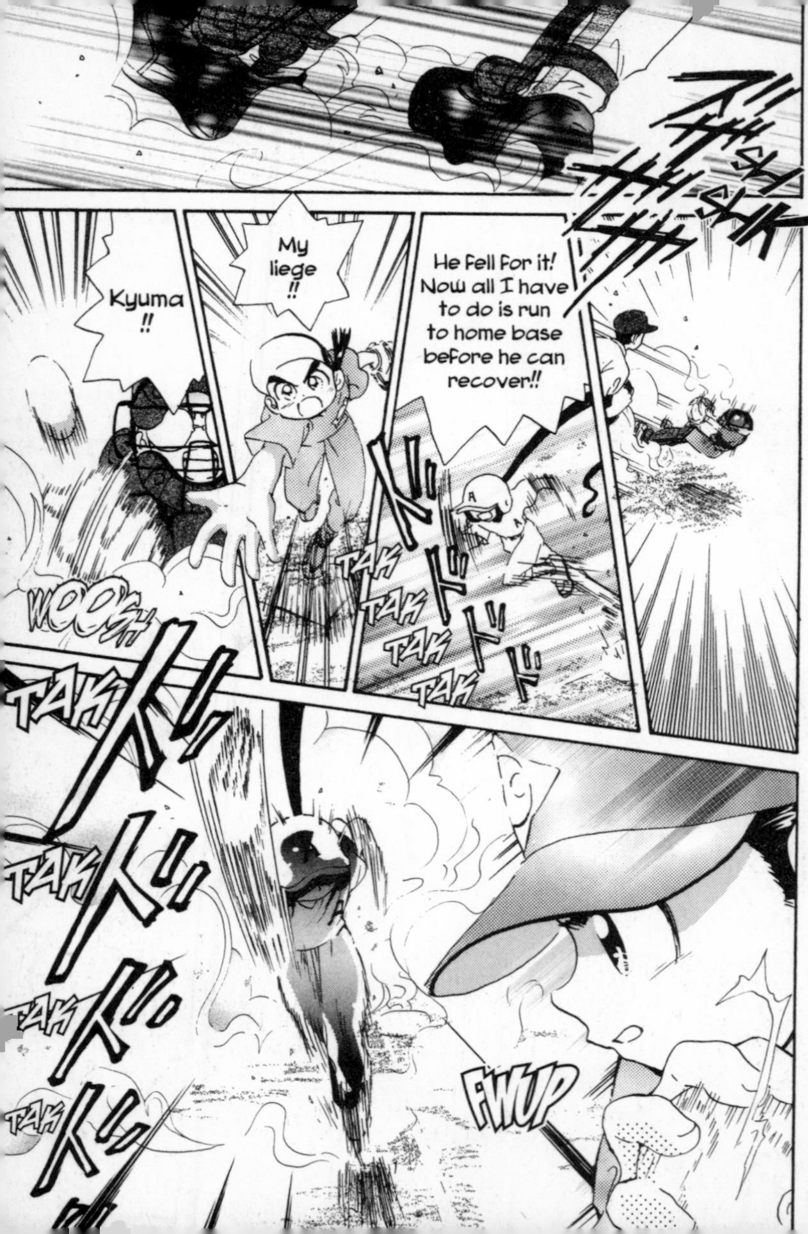

SHSHK
He fell for it! Now all I have to do is run to home base before he can recover!!
TAK
TAK
TAK
TAK
My liege !!
Kyuma !!
WOOSH
FWUP
TAK
TAK
TAK
TAK

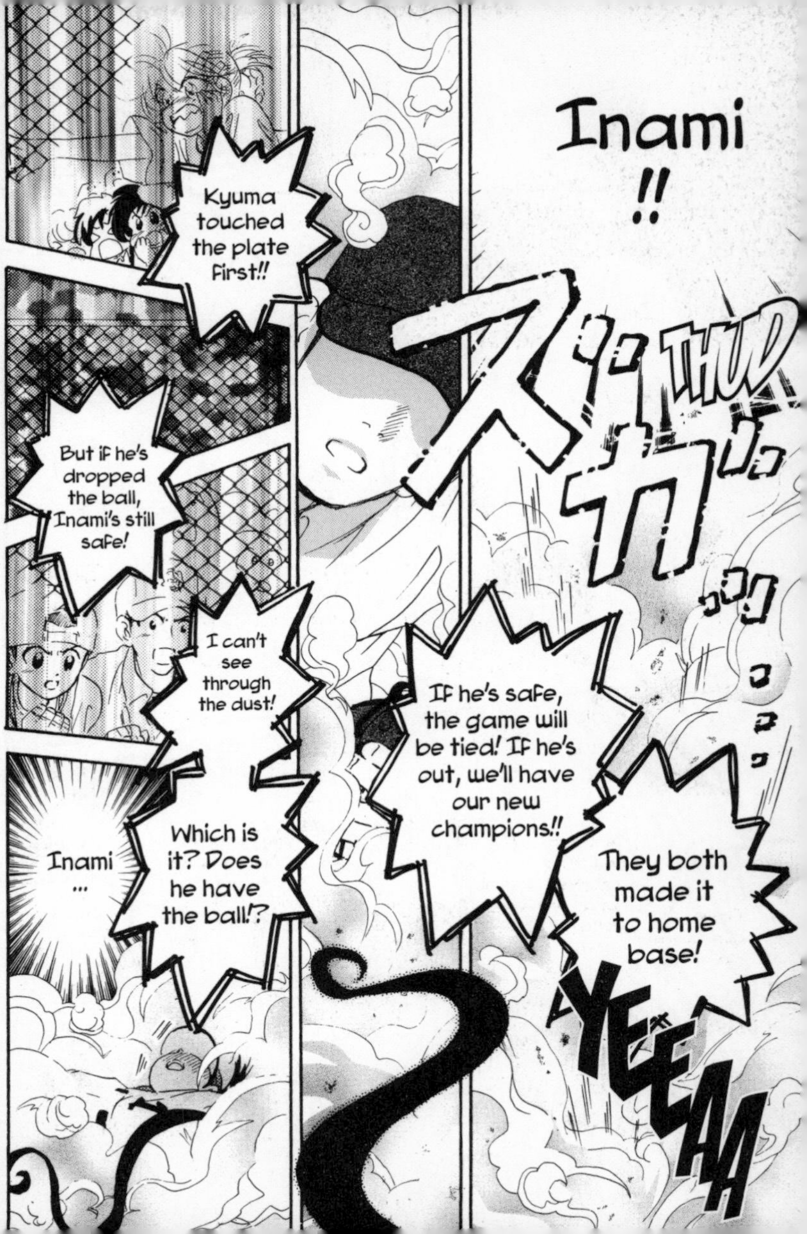
Inami !!
THUD
If he's safe, the game will be tied! If he's out, we'll have our new champions!!
They both made it to home base!
YEEAA
Kyuma touched the plate first!!
But if he's dropped the ball, Inami's still safe!
I can't see through the dust!
Which is it? Does he have the ball!?
Inami ...

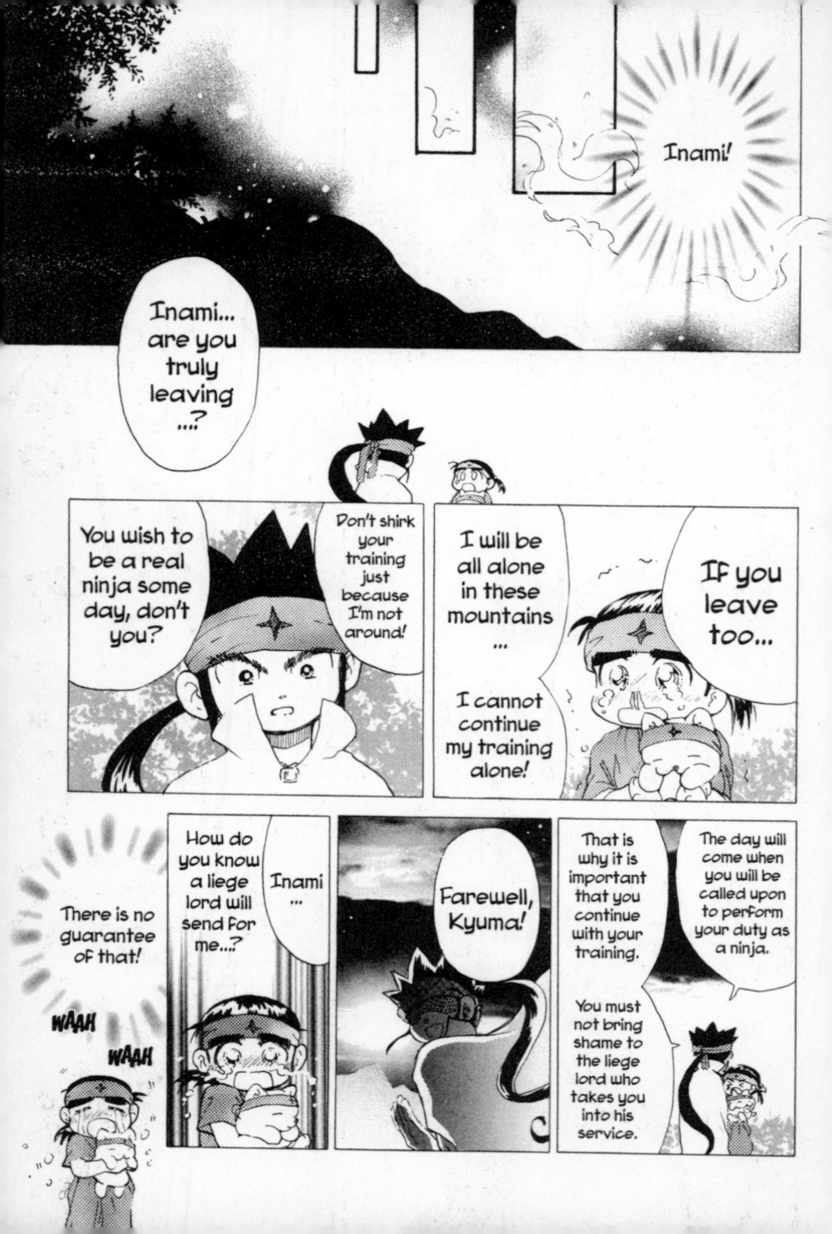
Inami!
Inami... are you truly leaving ...?
If you leave too...
I will be all alone in these mountains ...
I cannot continue my training alone!
Don't shirk your training just because I'm not around!
You wish to be a real ninja some day, don't you?
The day will come when you will be called upon to perform your duty as a ninja.
That is why it is important that you continue with your training.
You must not bring shame to the liege lord who takes you into his service.
Farewell, Kyuma!
Inami ...
How do you know a liege lord will send for me...?
There is no guarantee of that!
WAAH
WAAH

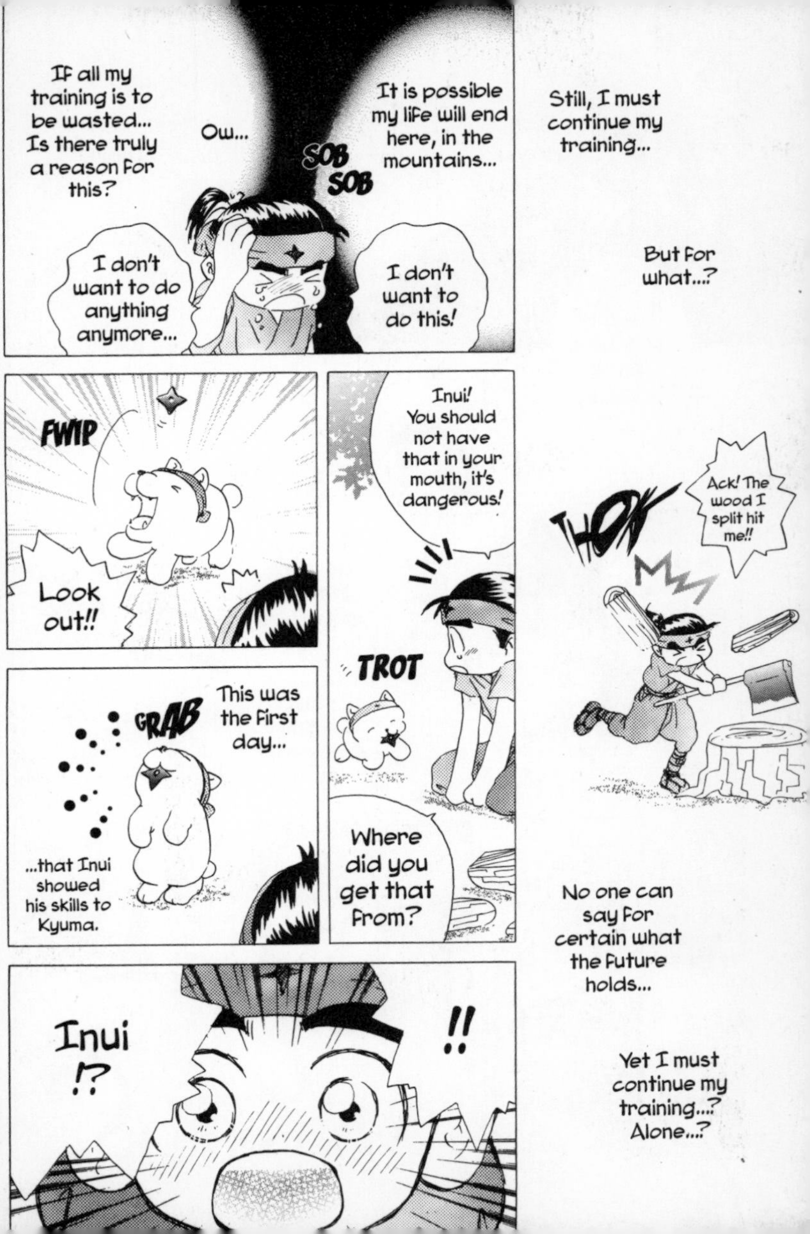
Still, I must continue my training...
But for what...?
Ack! The wood I split hit me!!
THOK
No one can say for certain what the future holds...
Yet I must continue my training...? Alone...?
It is possible my life will end here, in the mountains...
SOB SOB
Ow...
If all my training is to be wasted... Is there truly a reason for this?
I don't want to do this!
I don't want to do anything anymore...
Inui! You should not have that in your mouth, it's dangerous!
TROT
Where did you get that from?
FWIP
Look out!!
This was the first day...
GRAB
...that Inui showed his skills to Kyuma.
!!
Inui !?

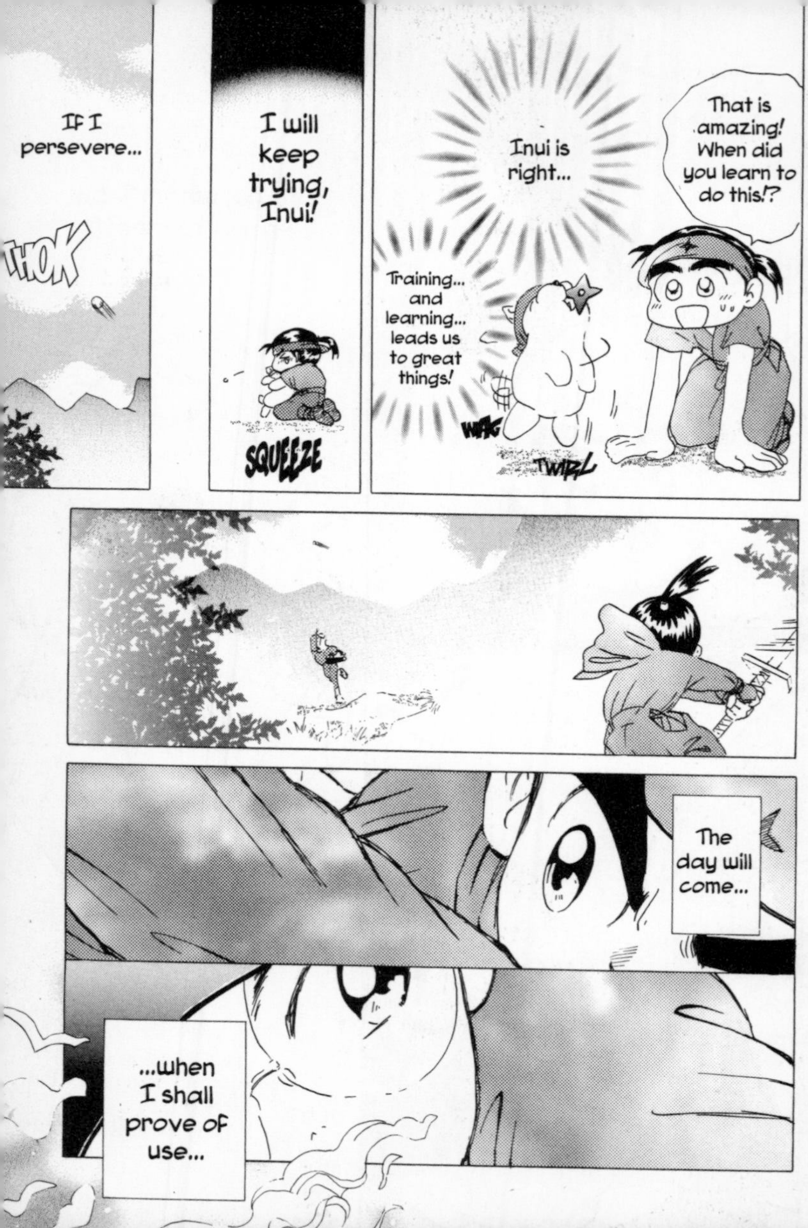
That is amazing! When did you learn to do this!?
Inui is right...
Training... and learning... leads us to great things!
WAG
TWIRL
I will keep trying, Inui!
SQUEEZE
If I persevere...
THOK
The day will come...
...when I shall prove of use...

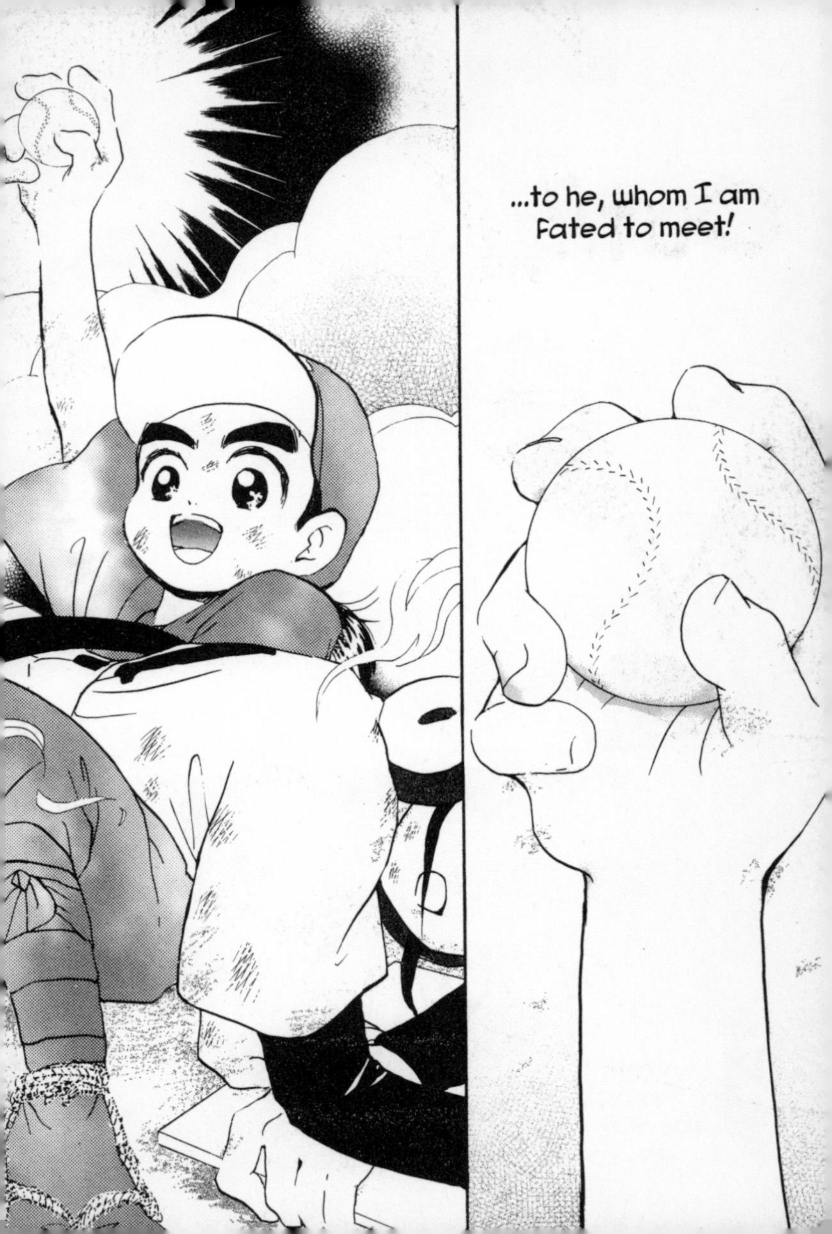
...to he, whom I am
fated to meet!

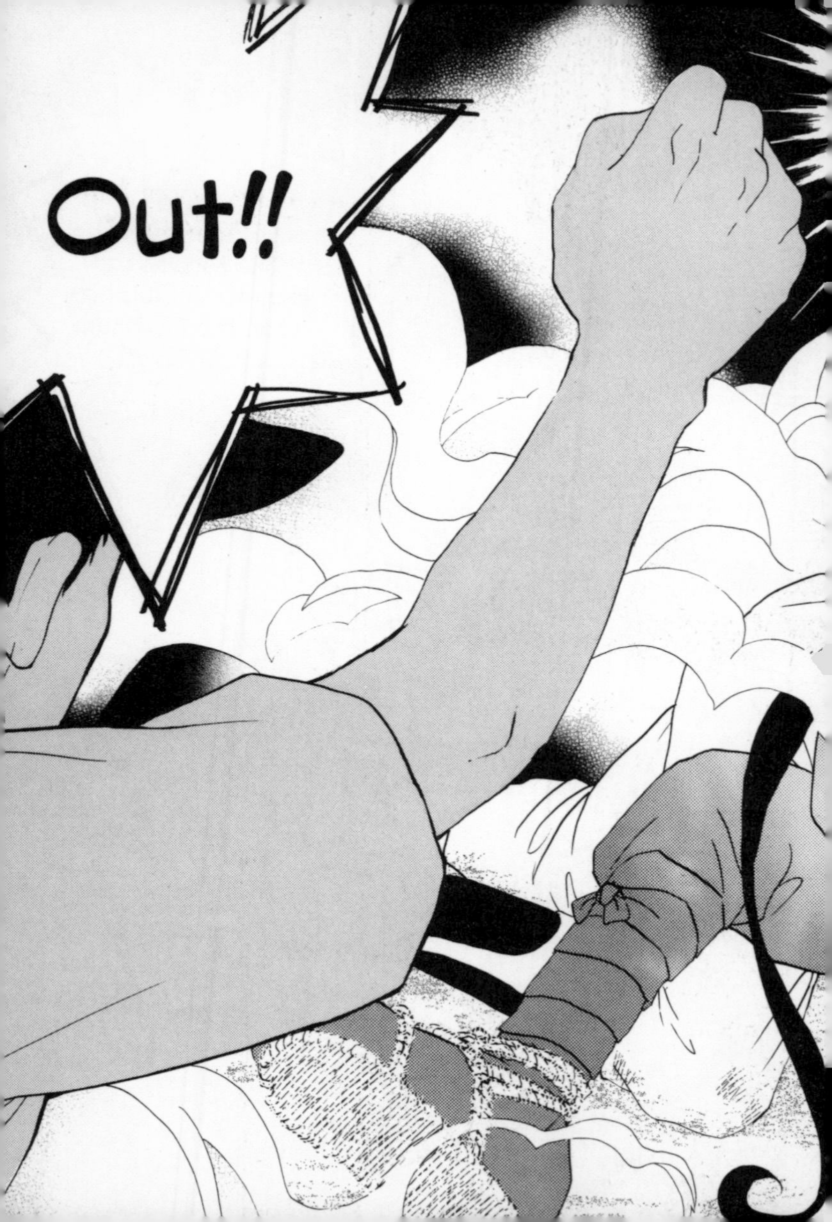
Out!!

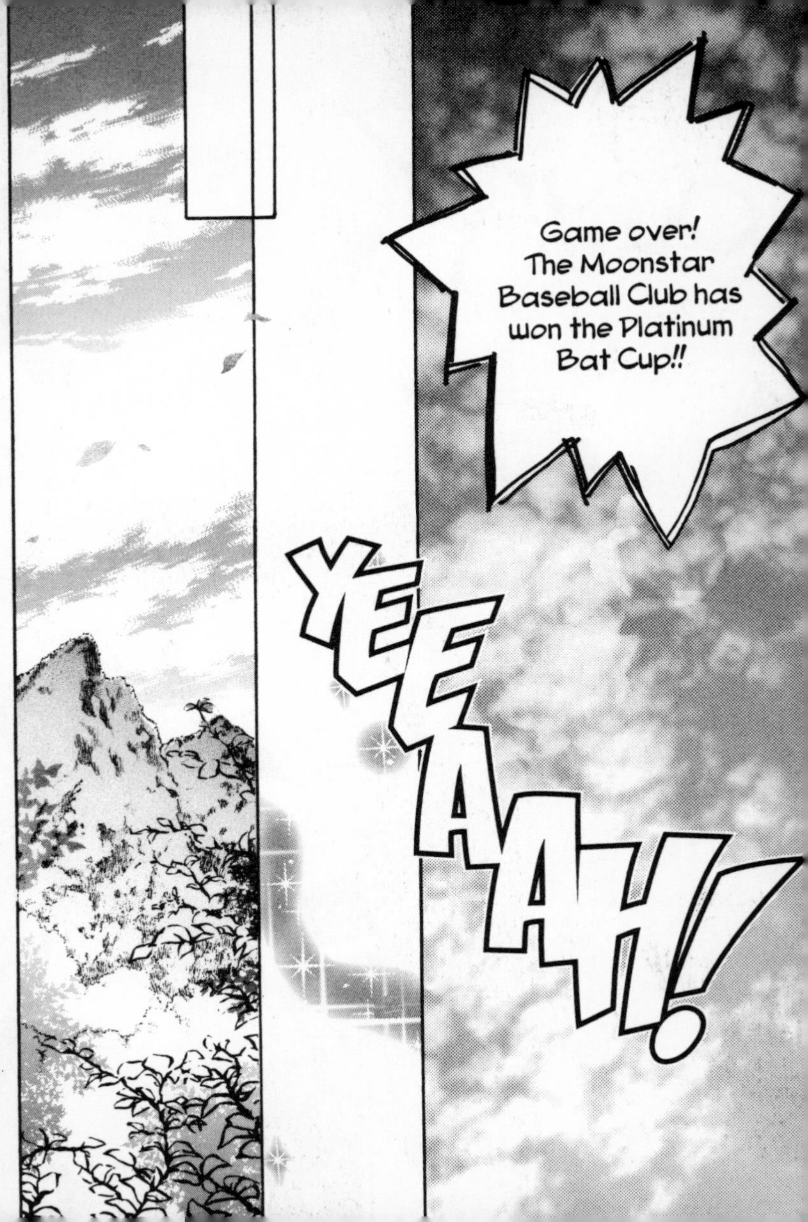
Game over! The Moonstar Baseball Club has won the Platinum Bat Cup!!
YEEAAH!

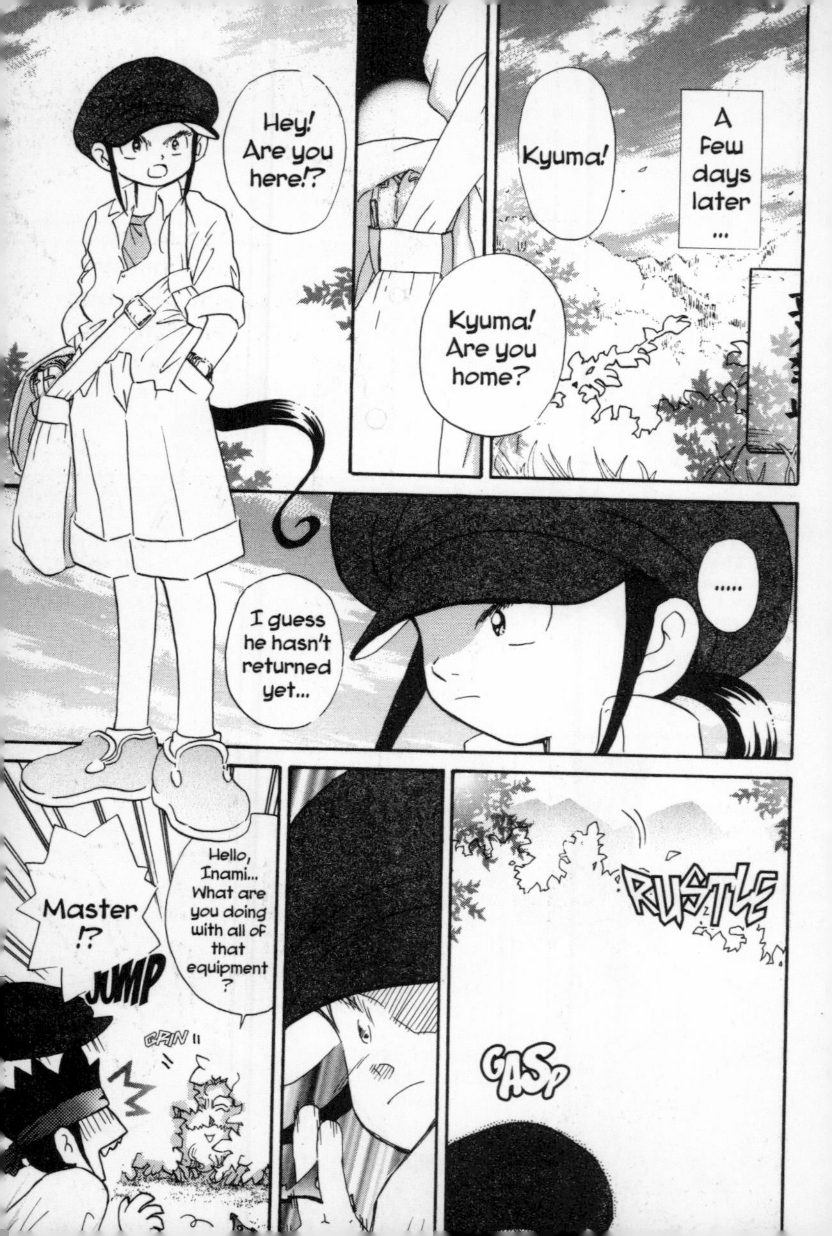
A few days later ...
Kyuma!
Kyuma! Are you home?
.....
I guess he hasn't returned yet...
Hey! Are you here!?
RUSTLE
GASP
Master !?
Hello, Inami... What are you doing with all of that equipment ?
JUMP
GRIN

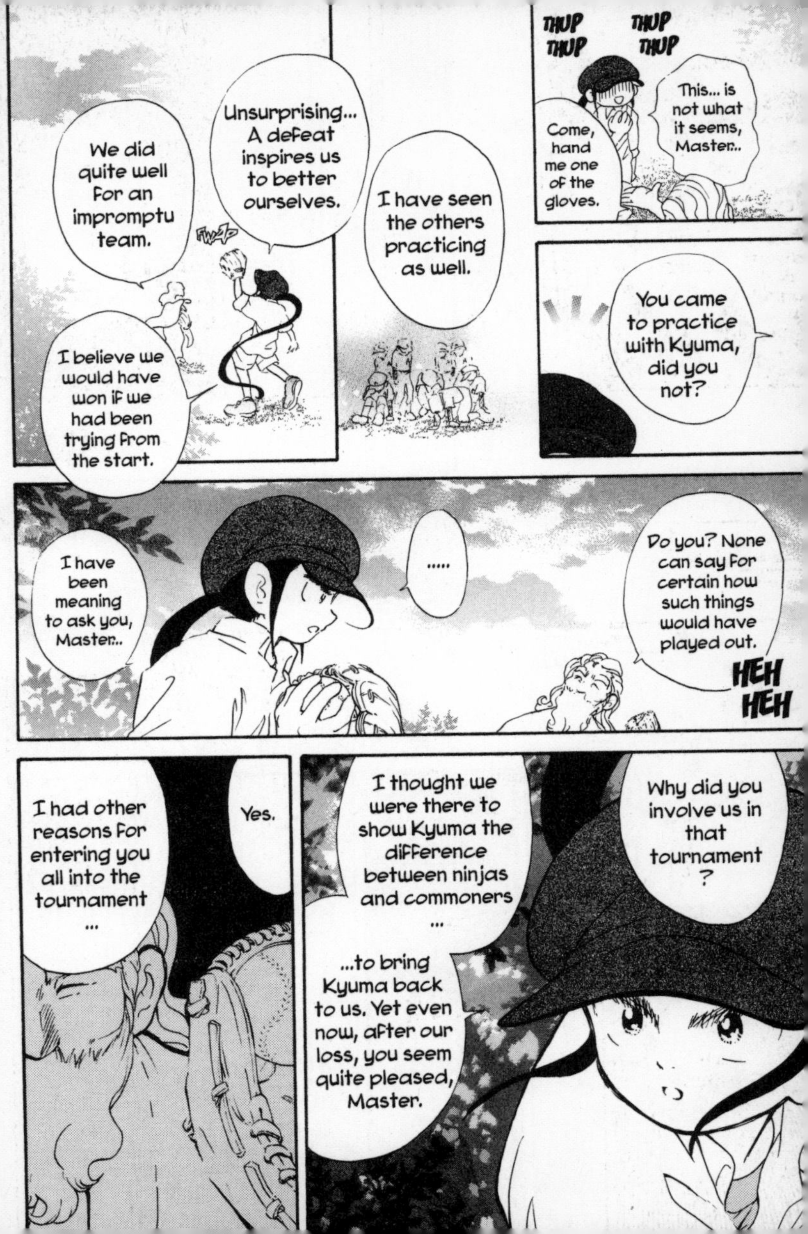
THUP THUP
THUP THUP
This... is not what it seems, Master..
Come, hand me one of the gloves.
You came to practice with Kyuma, did you not?
I have seen the others practicing as well.
Unsurprising... A defeat inspires us to better ourselves.
We did quite well for an impromptu team.
I believe we would have won if we had been trying from the start.
Do you? None can say for certain how such things would have played out.
HEH HEH
.....
I have been meaning to ask you, Master..
Why did you involve us in that tournament?
I thought we were there to show Kyuma the difference between ninjas and commoners...
...to bring Kyuma back to us. Yet even now, after our loss, you seem quite pleased, Master.
Yes.
I had other reasons for entering you all into the tournament...

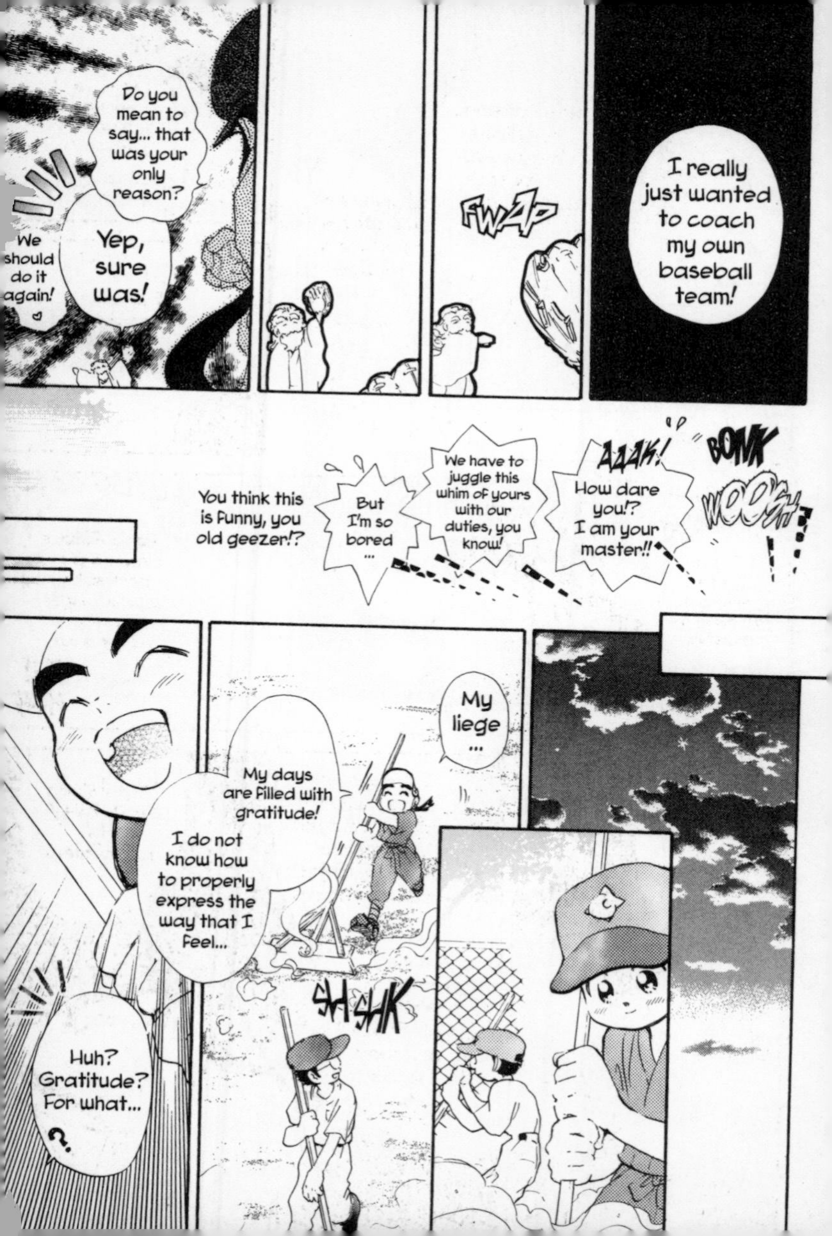
I really just wanted to coach my own baseball team!
FWAP
Do you mean to say... that was your only reason?
Yep, sure was!
We should do it again!
BONK
WOOSH
AAAK!
How dare you!? I am your master!!
We have to juggle this whim of yours with our duties, you know!
But I'm so bored ...
You think this is funny, you old geezer!?
My liege ...
My days are filled with gratitude!
I do not know how to properly express the way that I feel...
SHA SHK
Huh? Gratitude? For what...

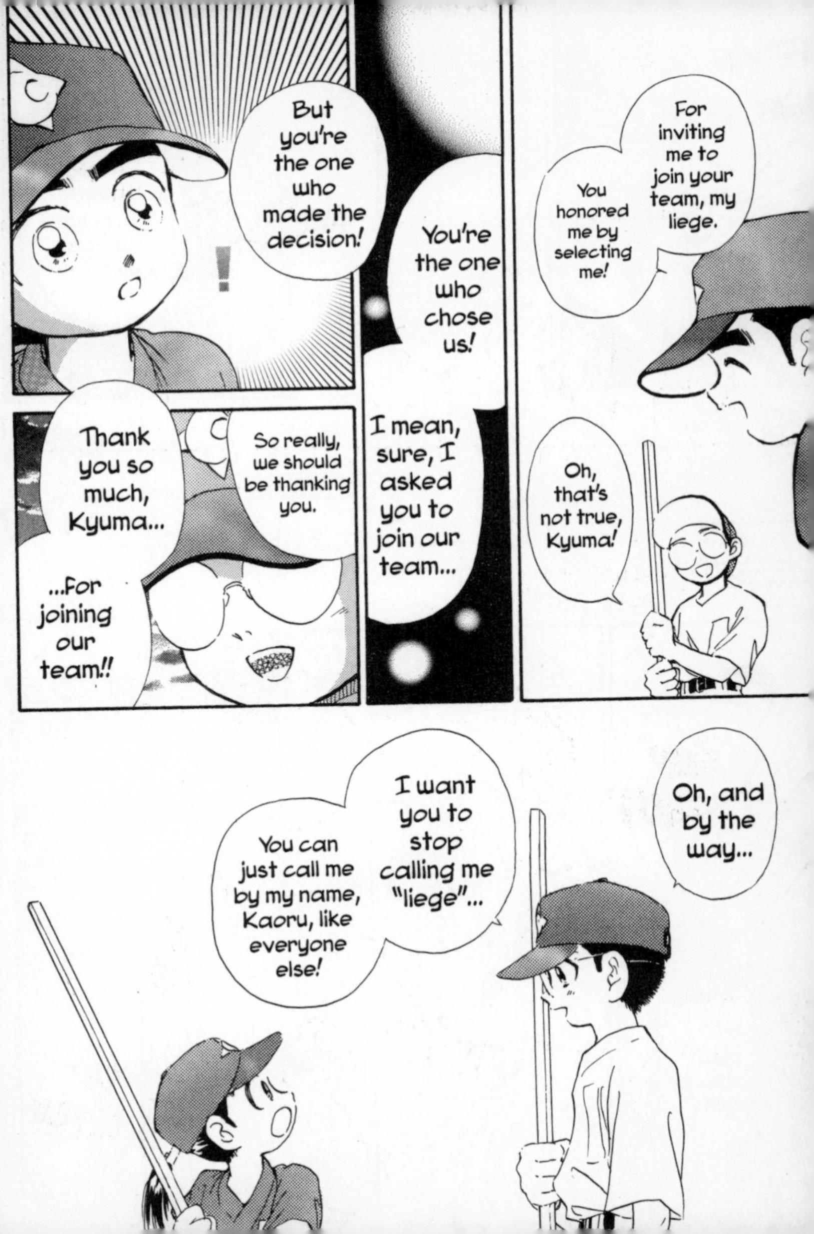
For inviting me to join your team, my liege.
You honored me by selecting me!
Oh, that's not true, Kyuma!
I mean, sure, I asked you to join our team...
But you're the one who made the decision!
You're the one who chose us!
So really, we should be thanking you.
Thank you so much, Kyuma...
...For joining our team!!
Oh, and by the way...
I want you to stop calling me "liege"...
You can just call me by my name, Kaoru, like everyone else!

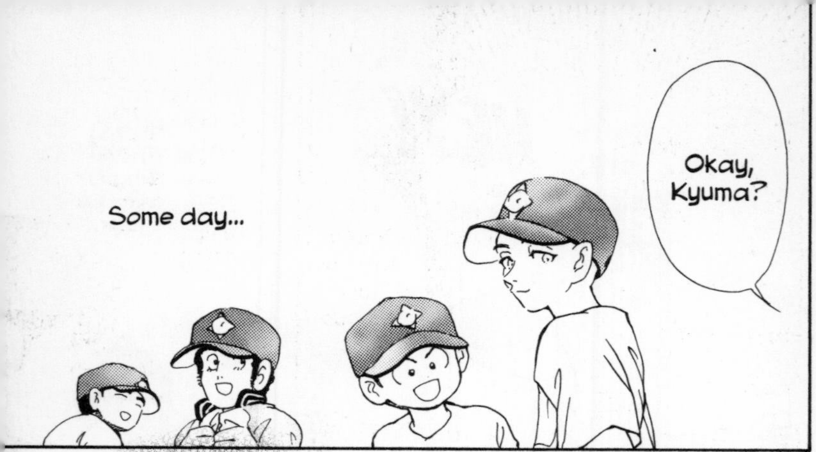
Okay, Kyuma?
Some day...

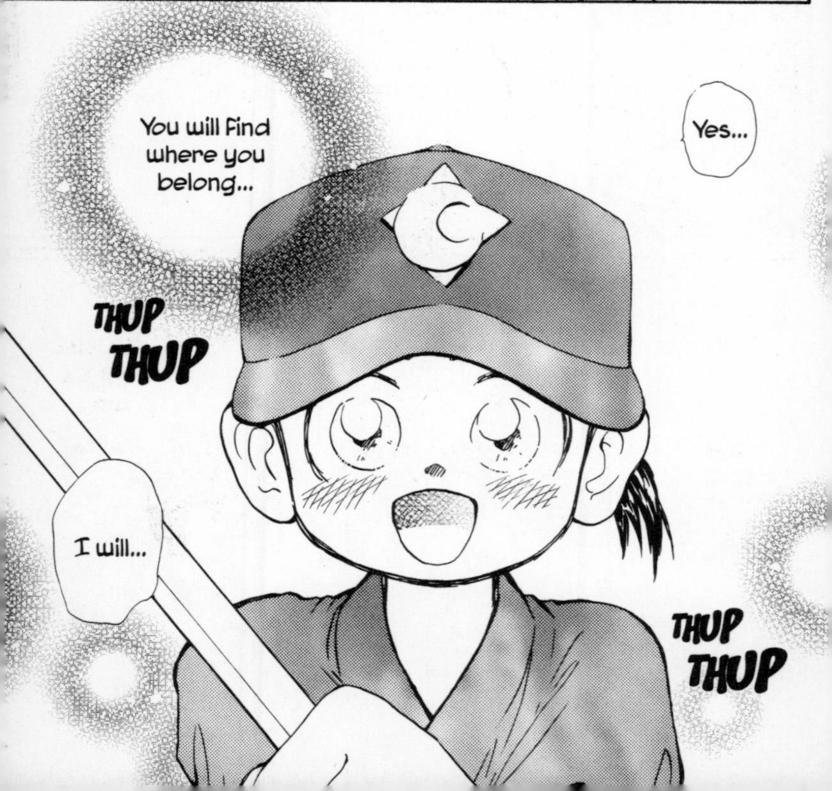
Yes...
You will find where you belong...
THUP THUP
I will...
THUP THUP

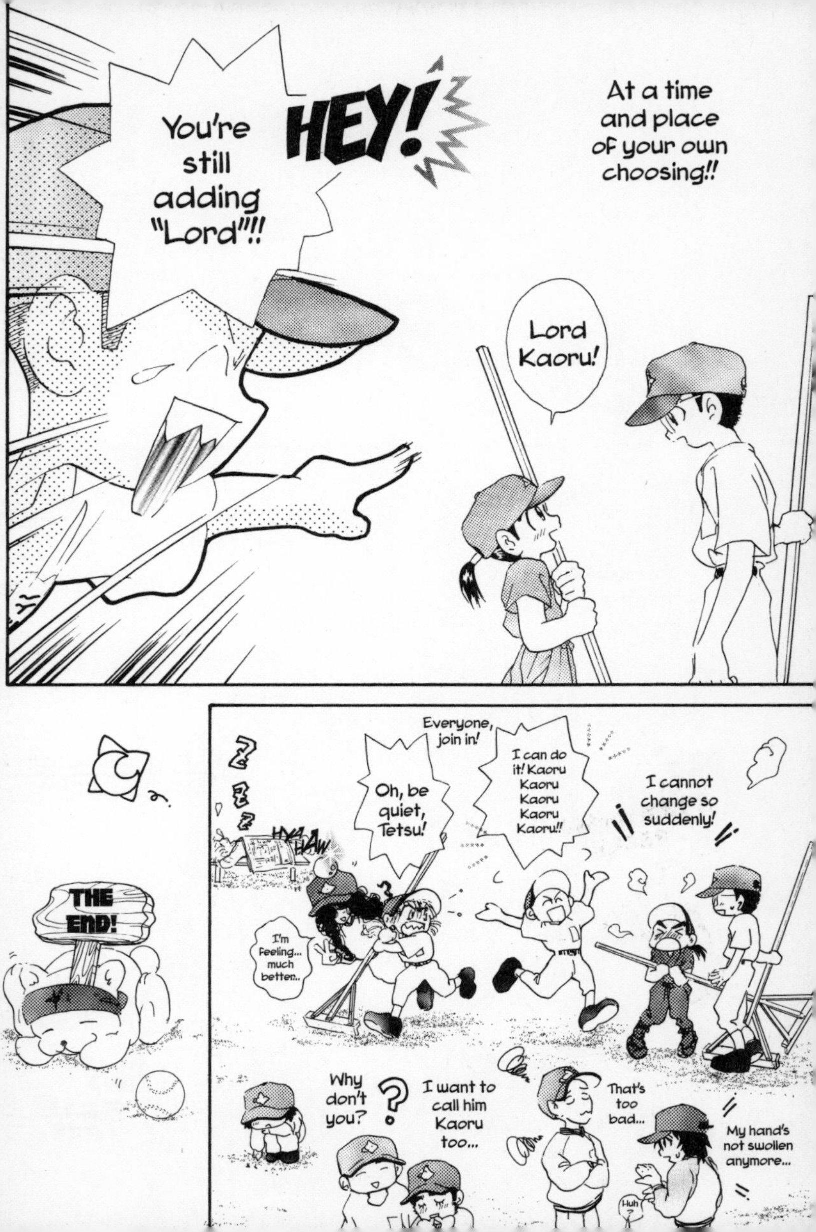
At a time and place of your own choosing!!
Lord Kaoru!
HEY!
You're still adding "Lord"!!
I cannot change so suddenly!
I can do it! Kaoru Kaoru Kaoru Kaoru Kaoru!!
Everyone, join in!
Oh, be quiet, Tetsu!
HYAHAW
I'm feeling... much better...
My hand's not swollen anymore...
Huh?
That's too bad...
I want to call him Kaoru too...
Why don't you?
THE END!

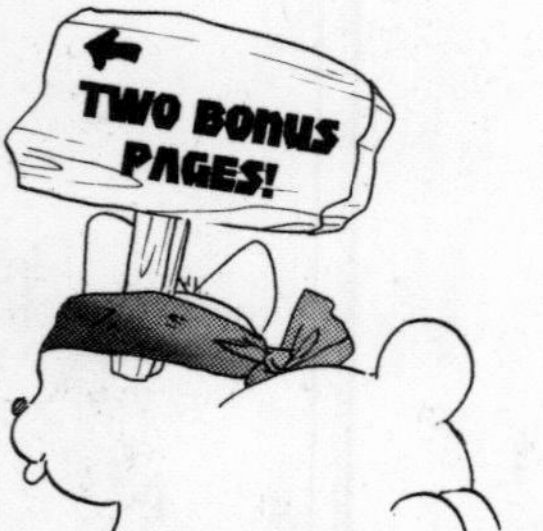

TWO BONUS PAGES!

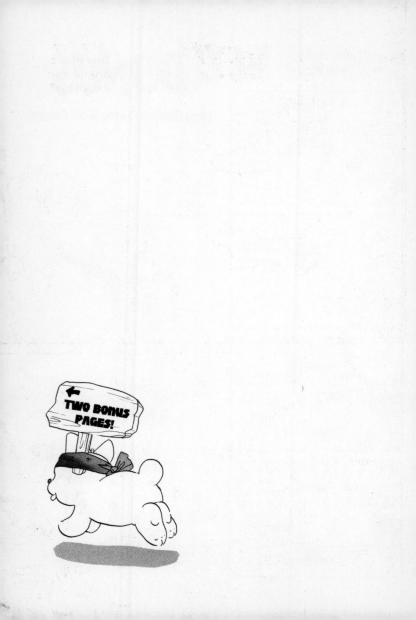

BONUS

Ninja Baseball Kyuma Short Comics

Find out what the Moonstar Club is like when they're not playing baseball!

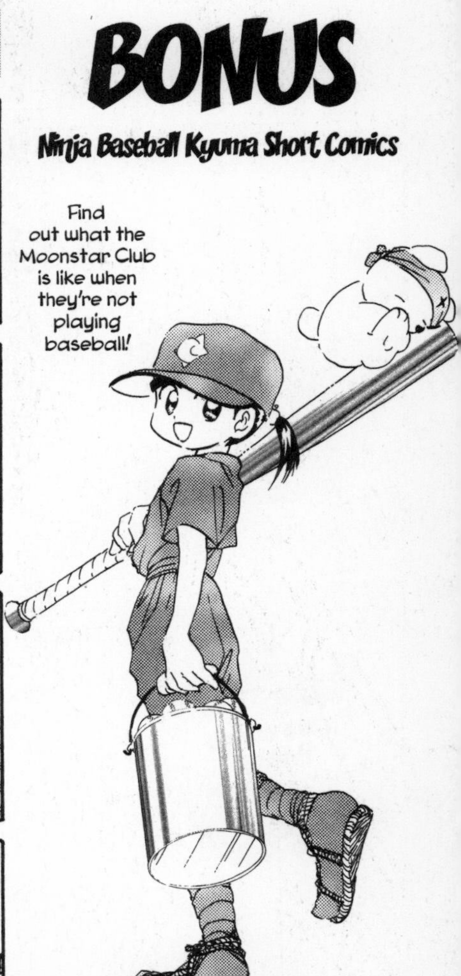

Kyuma and a Cell Phone

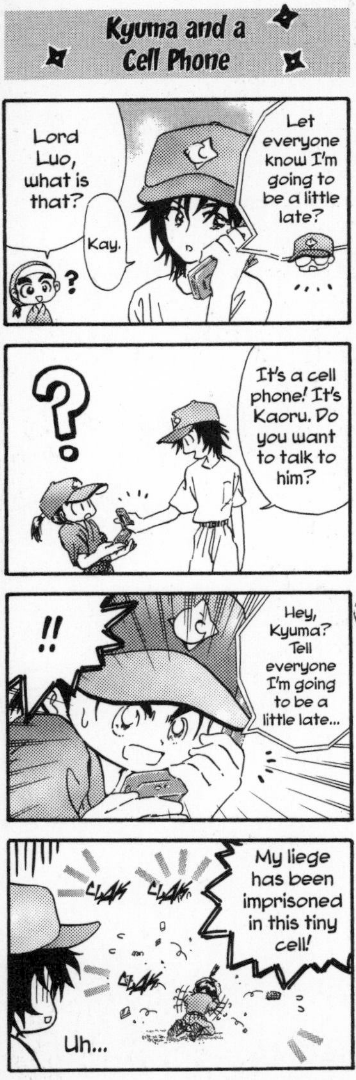

Let everyone know I'm going to be a little late?
Kay.
Lord Luo, what is that?
?
It's a cell phone! It's Kaoru. Do you want to talk to him?
?
Hey, Kyuma? Tell everyone I'm going to be a little late...
!!
My liege has been imprisoned in this tiny cell!
CLAK
CLAK
CLAK
Uh...

Ninja Training or Dog Training? Inui's Tricks!

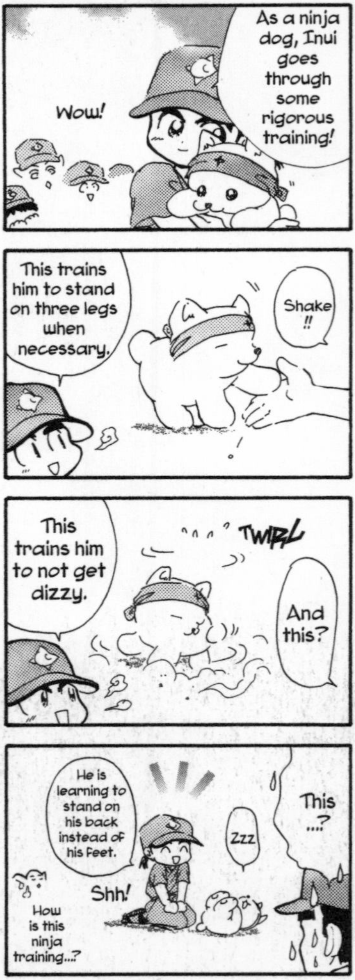
As a ninja dog, Inui goes through some rigorous training!
Wow!
Shake!!
This trains him to stand on three legs when necessary.
TWIRL
And this?
This trains him to not get dizzy.
This ...?
Zzz
He is learning to stand on his back instead of his feet.
Shh!
How is this ninja training...?

Don't give up, Coach!!

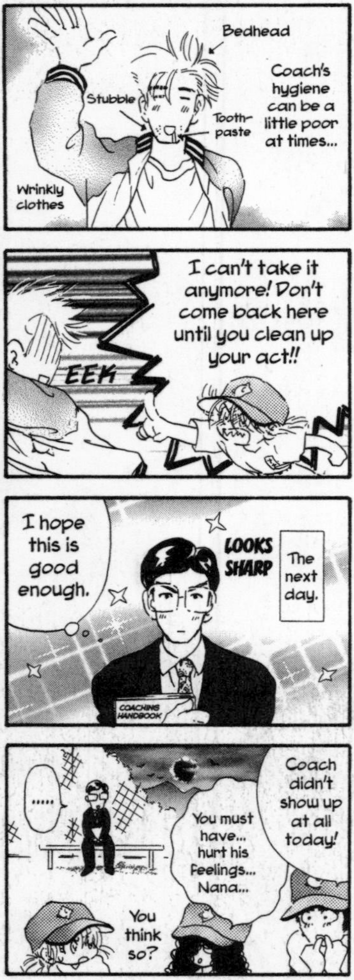
Coach's hygiene can be a little poor at times...
Bedhead
Stubble
Toothpaste
Wrinkly clothes
I can't take it anymore! Don't come back here until you clean up your act!!
EEK
The next day.
LOOKS SHARP
I hope this is good enough.
COACHING HANDBOOK
Coach didn't show up at all today!
You must have... hurt his feelings... Nana...
You think so?
......

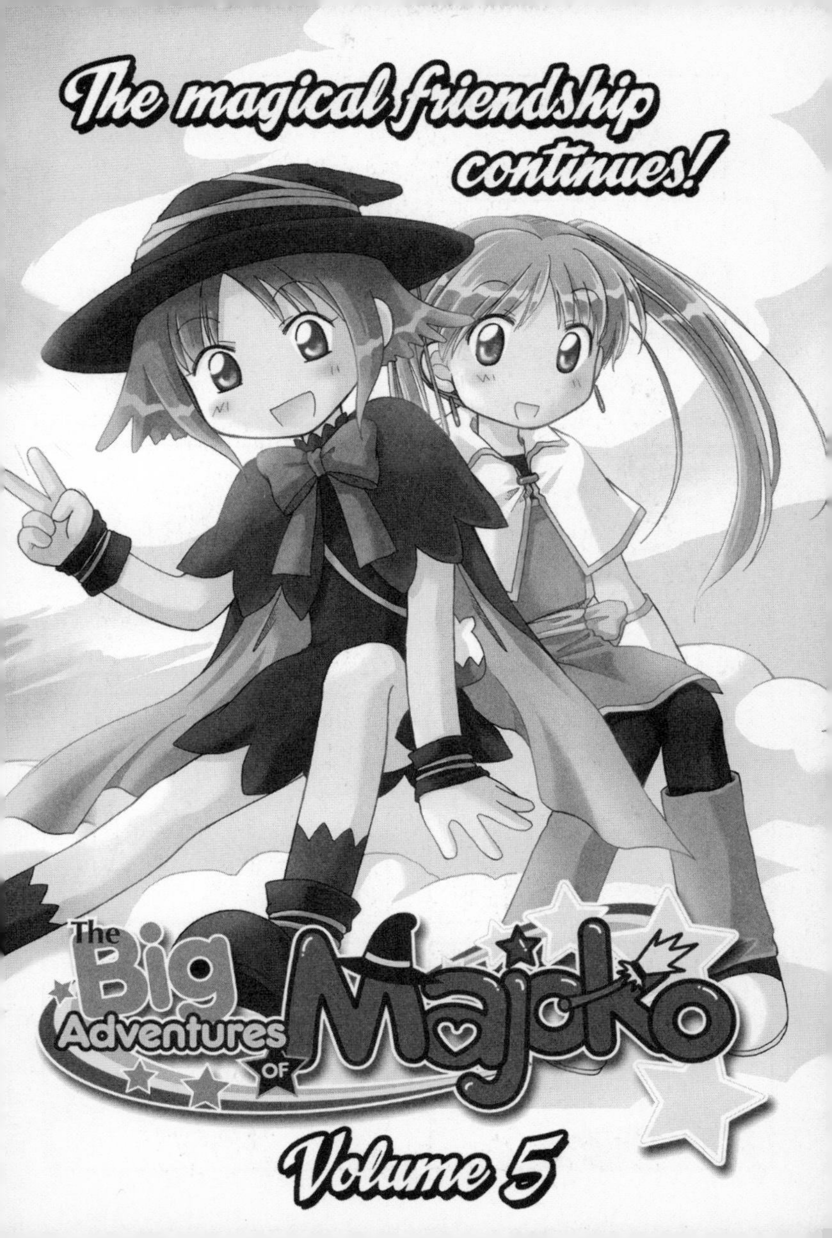

The magical friendship continues!
The Big Adventures of Majoko
Volume 5

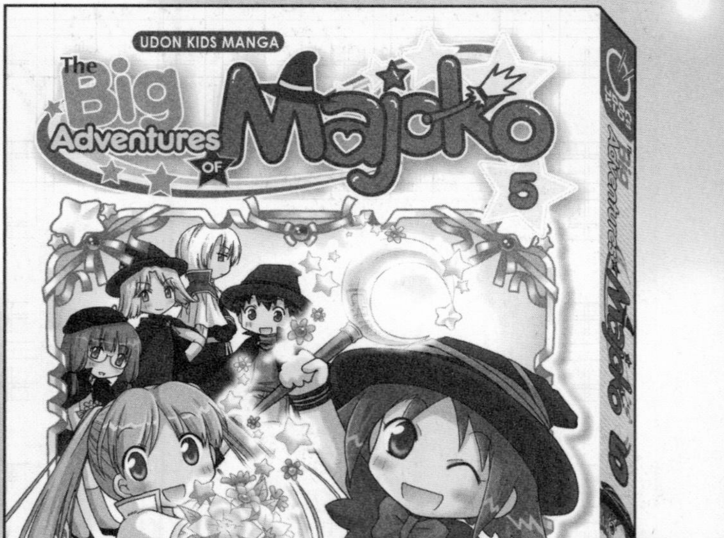
UDON KIDS MANGA
The Big Adventures OF Majoko
5
Original Work / Supervision
MACHIKO FUJI
Manga by
TOMOMI MIZUNA
FUJI / MIZUNA

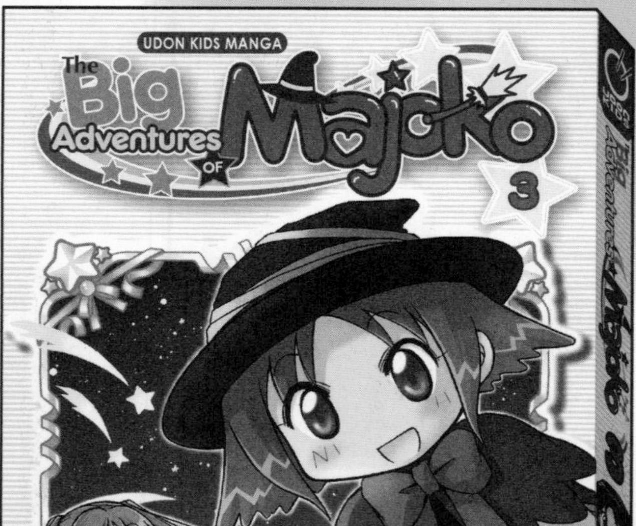
UDON KIDS MANGA
The Big Adventures of Majoko
3
Original Work / Supervision
MACHIKO FUJI
Manga by
TOMOMI MIZUNA
Big Adventures of Majoko 3
FUJI / MIZUNA
POPLAR

THE GALAXY HAS SOME NEW BEST FRIENDS!

SWANS in SPACE

SCI-FI ADVENTURES FOR GIRLS!

SWANS IN SPACE Vol.1
ISBN: 978-1-897376-93-5

VOLUME 2

AVAILABLE NOW!

SWANS IN SPACE Vol.2
ISBN: 978-1-897376-94-2

COMING SOON:

SWANS in SPACE

VOLUME 3

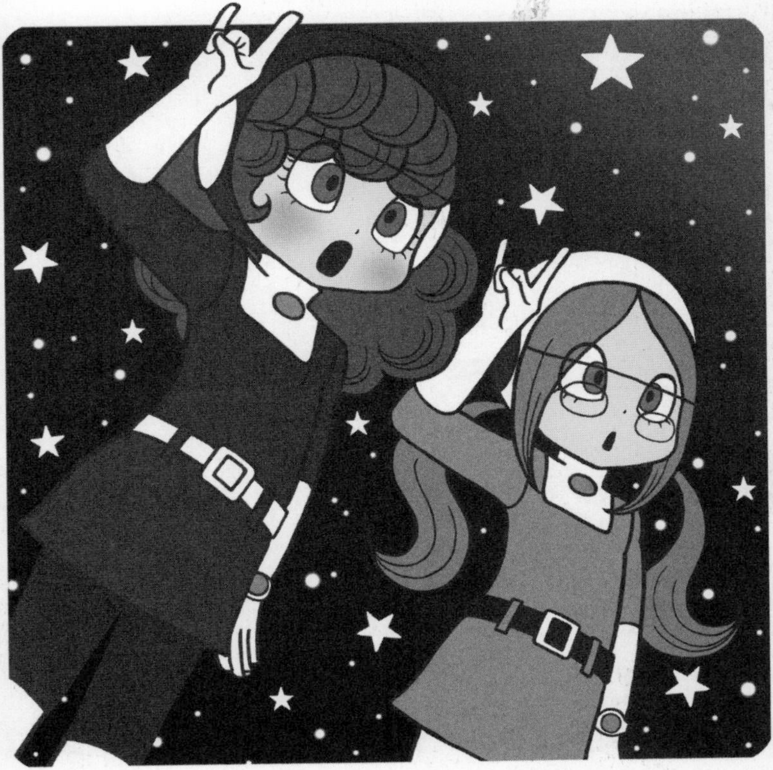

ARRIVING SEPTEMBER 2010

SWANS IN SPACE Vol.3
ISBN: 978-1-897376-95-9

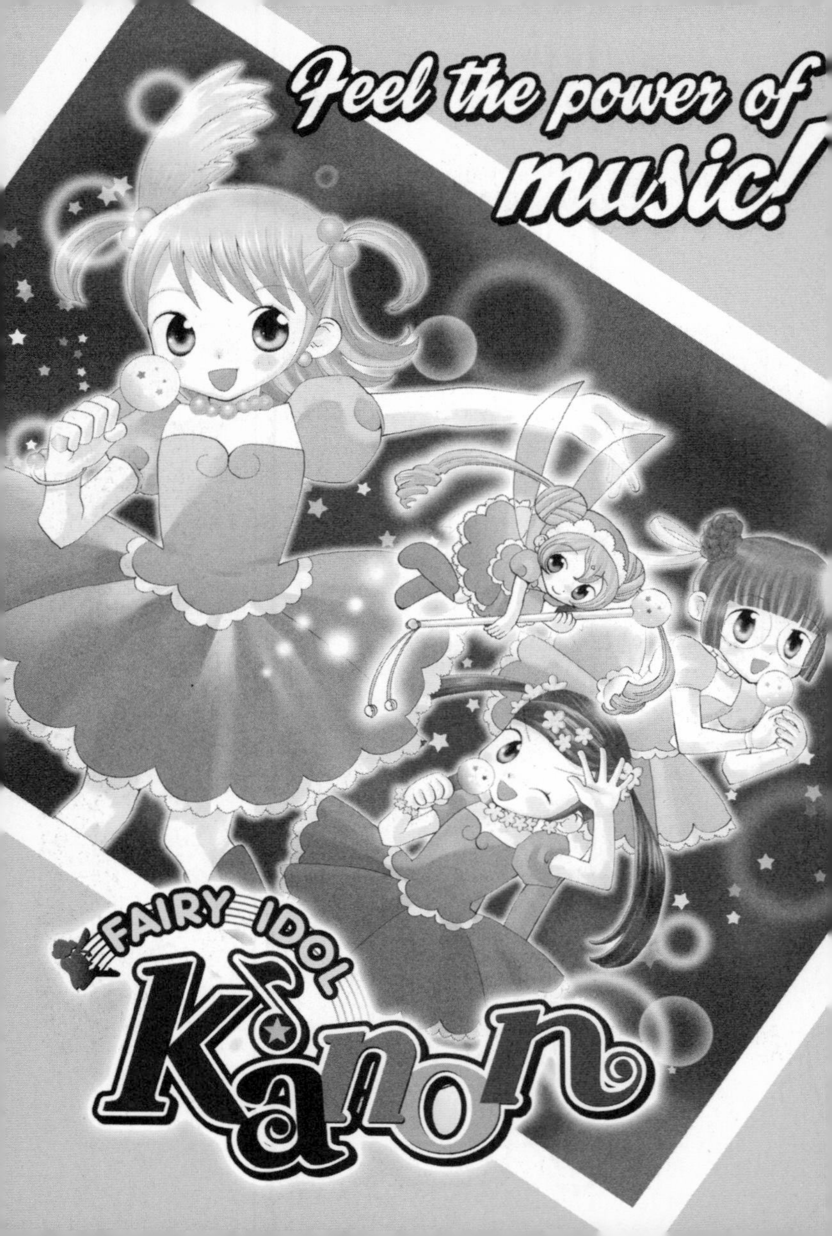

Feel the power of music!
FAIRY IDOL
Kanon

FAIRY IDOL KANON Vol.3
ISBN: 978-1-897376-91-1

On sale now!

FAIRY IDOL KANON Vol.2
ISBN: 978-1-897376-90-4

Available Now!

THE BIG ADVENTURES OF MAJOKO

Vol.1
ISBN: 978-1-897376-81-2

Vol.2
ISBN: 978-1-897376-82-9

Vol.3
ISBN: 978-1-897376-83-6

Vol.4
ISBN: 978-1-897376-84-3

Vol.5 *(June 2010)*
ISBN: 978-1-897376-85-0

NINJA BASEBALL KYUMA

Vol.1
ISBN: 978-1-897376-86-7

Vol.2
ISBN: 978-1-897376-87-4

Vol.3 *(May 2010)*
ISBN: 978-1-897376-88-1

NINJA BASEBALL Kyuma! VOLUME 3

Story & Art: Shunshin Maeda

Translation: M. Kirie Hayashi
Lettering: Ben Lee
Art Cleanups: Jennifer Skarupa
English Logo Design: Hanna Chan

UDON STAFF
Chief of Operations: Erik Ko
Managing Editor: Matt Moylan
Project Manager: Jim Zubkavich
Market Manager: Stacy King
Editor, Japanese Publications: M. Kirie Hayashi

Kyuma! Vol.3
©Shunshin Maeda 2005
All rights reserved.

Original Japanese edition published by POPLAR Publishing Co., Ltd. Tokyo
English translation rights arranged directly with POPLAR Publishing Co., Ltd.

English edition of NINJA BASEBALL KYUMA Vol. 3
©2010 UDON Entertainment Corp.

Any similarities to persons living or dead is purely coincidental.

English language version produced and published by UDON Entertainment Corp.
P.O. Box 5002, RPO MAJOR MACKENZIE
Richmond Hill, Ontario, L4S 0B7, Canada

www.udonentertainment.com

First Printing: July 2010
ISBN-13: 978-1-897376-88-1   ISBN-10 : 1-897376-88-X
Printed in the United States

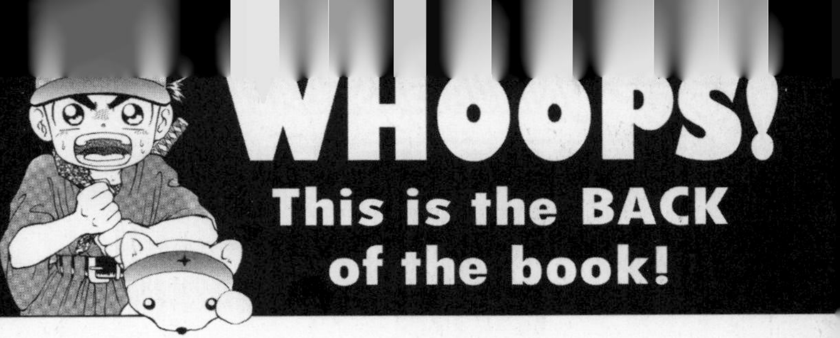

WHOOPS!

This is the BACK of the book!

Ninja Baseball Kyuma is a comic book created in Japan, where comics are called **manga.** Manga is read from right-to-left, which is backwards from the normal books you know. This means that you will find the first page where you expect to find the last page! It also means that each page begins in the top right corner.

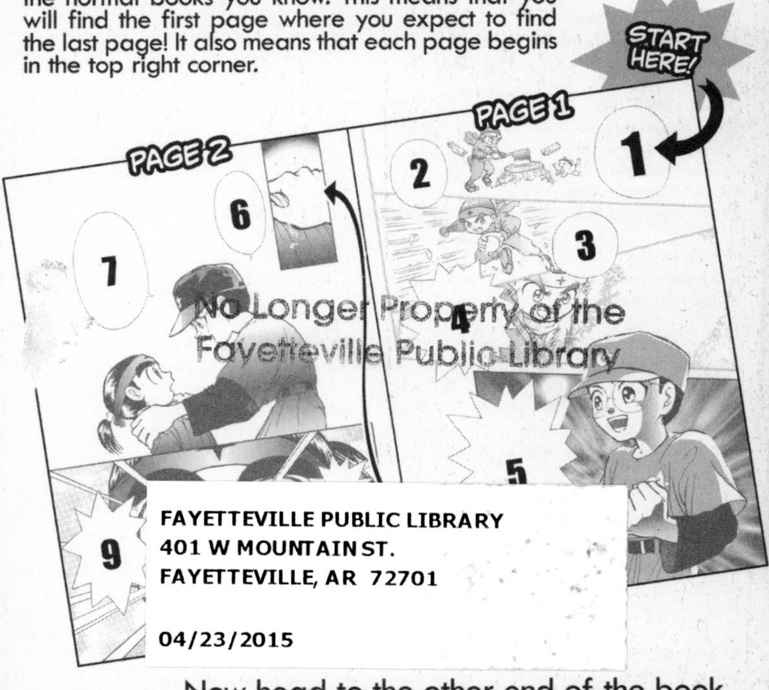
START HERE!
PAGE 1
1
2
3
4
5
PAGE 2
6
7
9

Now head to the other end of the book and enjoy **Ninja Baseball Kyuma!**

SWANS IN SPACE

Vol.1
ISBN: 978-1-897376-93-5

Vol.2
ISBN: 978-1-897376-94-2

Vol.3 *(July 2010)*
ISBN: 978-1-897376-95-9

FAIRY IDOL KANON

Vol.1
ISBN: 978-1-897376-89-8

Vol.2
ISBN: 978-1-897376-90-4

Vol.3
ISBN: 978-1-897376-91-1

Vol.4 *(June 2010)*
ISBN: 978-1-897376-92-8

NINJA BASEBALL
Kyuma!